The

PepperAsh

Locket

Franky Sayer

The PepperAsh Locket

Published by Sirob Press

Copyright © 2019 Franky Sayer

The right of Franky Sayer to be identified as author of this work has been asserted in accordance with the Copyright, Designs and Patents Act 1988.

British Library Cataloguing in Publication Data.

A CIP catalogue record for this book is available from the British Library.

ISBN: 978-1-9997108-2-8

Late Summer, 2007

Prologue

Sixteen-year-old Sarah Stickleback strode furiously away from the Old Police House in Pepper Hill. Although her cheek was not hurting quite so much now from her mother's slap, she still held her hand to her face. It wouldn't be long before her twin brother, Duncan, and her father, Henry, realised she was missing. She knew they wouldn't immediately worry about her disappearance: they – and her mother – would simply expect her to go to The Fighting Cock. But she was walking in the opposite direction to the pub, towards the old Second World War airfield at the top of Pepper Hill, which had been reopened and was now a thriving private airport. She was not planning to stow away on board an aeroplane to escape from her family, although any mode of transport would be preferable to – and obviously faster than – walking.

But the initial energy that accompanied her leaving quickly diminished and her shoulders ached from carrying her two over-loaded bags. She had a little money and, now that she was thinking more rationally, she wondered if she could reach the bus stop just beyond the airfield, catch a bus to Mattingburgh, the nearest city, and then … And then.

Sarah heard a vehicle approaching from behind. She turned and saw it was the postman; he was driving his own car rather than his usual red van with the crown insignia. Postman Jim the Second (so called because his name was Paul James and his predecessor, Jim, was known as Postman Jim) slowed his vehicle and wound down the passenger window.

'Are you all right there, young Sarah?' he enquired. He might not yet have a family of his own, but being a *postie*, he caught many glimpses into others' families. He knew, for instance, that this particular collection of related individuals – the Sticklebacks and the Tillingers – had many problems. And this young lady had recently received a large envelope bearing the Perrona Dawn logo, a holiday company from whom her maternal grandparents, Annie and Derek Tillinger, had hired a river boat and subsequently died of carbon monoxide poisoning during their first night on board. She was carrying two rather full, obviously hastily filled, shoulder bags – the epitome of the teenager running away from home. He could also see that she had recently been crying.

'I need to get to …' She had a sudden idea: if she travelled to Fenstone instead of Mattingburgh, maybe Perrona Dawn would let her stay there and she could start work immediately – after all, the forms held two signatures. She realised she would have to be careful how she worded any explanation so as not to say outright that her Mum and Dad had both signed.

Upstairs at home, before she'd left, she was glad she snatched the forms off the kitchen table without either Duncan or her Dad realising. She also had the foresight to use a different pen for each of their names – both blue, but of subtly different shades. She had been practising for weeks, knowing her mother would never agree to her choice of career, and that her father would support her mother's decision.

'Okay,' Jim said slowly. 'But it looks as if it's about to rain and you've forgotten to bring your coat.'

'I won't need a coat where I'm going! They'll give me a uniform.'

Jim paused before speaking again. 'You know, Sarah, sometimes, in the heat of the moment, tempers flare and things are said. Most of the time, though, the best thing to do is just … well, nothing. Now, I don't know what's just happened, but I bet that right at this minute, you just want to get away from home and make your parents worry – punish them in some way.'

Sarah stood up straight, away from the passenger window. She wanted to talk to someone, but the only other person she could confide in was her Uncle George, and he was working offshore at the moment. She definitely did not want to hear the kind of advice Postman Jim the Second was telling her.

'No, I want to go and start work so I can be independent,' she declared defiantly.

'And that will make you feel grown up?'

'Yes,' she replied, trying to lift the bag's strap off her right shoulder which had become painful.

'Well, the most grown-up thing you can do now is ring your Mum, or your Dad, or both – or even Duncan, because you wouldn't want him to think you'd just upped and left him behind, would you?'

'But I don't want to go back there.'

'Where?'

'Home, of course. Or to the pub. I don't want to see either of them – any of them.'

'No, well. I tell you what. Why don't I drive you to the

Rectory? I've just dropped Quinny off. He's been visiting Mr and Mrs Ervsgreaves. By now he'll have the kettle on and be ready to start on the cake Mrs E baked for him. And he can't eat it all on his own. We could help him. And you can use his phone – that is if you haven't got your mobile.'

'Haven't you got to work?' She ignored his inference but was, at the same time, trying to pat her pocket to check if her phone was in her jeans.

'Nope. I've finished for the day. I live just a bit beyond the airfield. Hop in and I'll turn round and take you to St Jude's rectory.'

Sarah hesitated for a moment before removing the two heavy bags from her shoulders. She opened the rear door and threw them in.

'Thanks,' she said as she sat down in the passenger seat. She tried to smile, but it made her cheek smart. She would never forgive her mother for slapping her, but she could, somewhat reluctantly, appreciate the frustration she'd caused that led to the incident. And, yes, if she was being honest, she had argued deliberately, hoping to bring about a confrontation.

There was a lot for her to think about. And she was hungry. Very hungry.

2015

Chapter 1

'But *why* can't you come home?' Tina demanded of George, her husband. The phone link was weak, but she tried to make her voice sound strong as she struggled to control her disappointment.

George Tillinger worked for MaCold (an acronym of Maintenance and Construction of Offshore to On-Land Direct), a company involved in the oil and gas extraction industry. He had been based at Aberdeen for the last four years and was, at the moment of talking to his wife, still offshore. He was due home the following day: Tina and George had been invited to her friend Mona's wedding at the weekend.

George did not like Mona. He claimed she was aptly named because she was always moaning. But he had, under protest, agreed to go. His leave was arranged and his seat on the helicopter flight from the platform booked. Tina was wrapping the gift to take with them when the telephone rang.

'I've given my seat to Paddy because his wife's gone into labour three weeks early,' George was explaining, the static on the line emphasising the vast expanse of rough sea between them.

Sitting in her lounge in Treemoore, Tina was devastated. George had been away for nine weeks and, naturally, she missed him. She definitely did not want to go to Mona's wedding alone.

'You promised,' she heard herself whine. But she knew it was useless. The more she niggled, the less inclined he would be to change his mind.

George compartmentalised his life: when at home, he never mentioned work; equally, when absorbed by

MaCold, he totally forgot about family life. Tina thought she might as well not exist.

Tina met George seven years ago when she was serving behind the post office counter in Cliffend, a seaside town on the east coast. It had been a quiet day, and they chatted as she dealt with his transaction. She called him Mr Tillinger, the name printed as being the sender on the parcel he was posting. He corrected this to George and addressed her as Miss Guthrie; her identity badge gave her initial as 'B' for Bettina, but she never used her full name.

She noticed he was tall and had straw-coloured hair which was beginning to recede. He looked strong and his hands were slightly calloused, as if he were used to manual work. She later discovered that he was eleven years older than her and although her grandmother, Hilda, thought this was too much, Tina herself did not mind.

Initially, George was impressed by Tina's politeness. She was pretty, delightfully more so when she smiled and, during that first encounter, he tried to cheer her in order to make this happen. As his business concluded, George asked Tina if she would meet him later for a drink. She courteously declined.

George, determined to get to know Tina more, returned several times to the Cliffend post office. She had not been working on Saturday morning, but had gone into town anyway and sat in the café opposite to watch from the table by the window. True to recent form, George walked into the post office. Only a few moments later came out again and marched across the road to the café. She finally agreed to see him.

Tina and George spent the entire weekend, which happened to be a Bank Holiday, together. They hired a river cruiser from the same company as Annie and Derek Tillinger, George's parents, who'd subsequently died on board.

The young couple enjoyed their time just getting to know each other, talking, relaxing, exploring. And then, on the Bank Holiday Monday, Tina met George's family. The Sticklebacks. Most importantly was George's older sister, Rosalie, estranged wife of Henry and mother of twins Sarah and Duncan who were fourteen at the time.

Tina found it quite an ordeal, with only two glasses of wine to smooth the experience. She mused that the only redeeming feature, apart from the fact that they were in a pub, was the family's little chocolate Labrador puppy, Ben.

Six months later, Tina rented a flat near the park in Cliffend, George joined her there when he was not offshore. At that time he was working as an engineer for MaCold, who were one of the largest employers in Cliffend. Their fabrication yard and dock occupied a prime quay-side site near the mouth of the River Potch, but the company had branches all over the country.

Tina and George were married in a quiet ceremony at the register office in Cliffend Town Hall. Tina's grandmother, Hilda Guthrie – her only known relative, who passed away soon afterwards – and George's brother-in-law, Henry Stickleback, were witnesses. The reception at Cliffend's grandest hotel, The Thrimbale, catered for less than a dozen guests.

Neither Tina nor George talked much about their childhoods. Tina had been abandoned into her grandmother's care immediately after she was born.

Although Tina was happy with her grandmother, she harboured the ideal that, when she had children of her own, she would love, cherish and nurture them in the way she wished her parents had her. But she was not completely naïve: she knew no one's life was perfect.

The first eighteen months of Tina and George's marriage had been happy and hopeful, but then George applied for the position of contract engineer for a new project MaCold had won. The only problem being that the job was based at the company's fabrication yard in Treemoore, a couple of hundred miles away from Cliffend.

George and Tina bought a house in Treemoore, Tina transferred to the town's post office and they settled. They even discussed having children. But then George indulged himself and bought an expensive sports car. It was bright yellow; he called it *Hercules*, which Tina thought was a little boyish and immature. When she pointed out that it would be too small for a family, George simply said he would upgrade their other car later, when and if they needed to.

However, within twelve months of moving, George was asked to take over as manager of a project in Aberdeen. Tina had no desire to move again, so they agreed that she would remain in Treemoore whilst George used bed and breakfast accommodation when he was needed onshore at the Scottish base.

This particular evening, though, as Tina listened to George's voice, she grew more and more upset. And angry. If he were standing next to her, she thought she might even have thumped him.

'You can drive *Hercules* to the wedding, if you wish, Tina.' George hoped this would prevent her drinking too much at the reception afterwards.

At this point in the conversation, Tina realised

George's motive for not coming home wasn't about attending Moaning Mona's nuptials: he simply did not want to be with her. Their marriage was over. She clicked off her phone.

There was a bottle of white wine chilling in the fridge. She poured herself a glass.

She knew she shouldn't drink on her own like this, but nothing else mattered now, beyond reaching oblivion in order to avoid the hurt George was inflicting upon her.

Chapter 2

Tina poured herself a second glass. She did not drink because she liked the taste; she just wanted to do something to make herself feel better. But this was not working.

She walked unsteadily through the integral door from the kitchen into the darkened garage. The light from the room behind her revealed the gleaming yellow sports' car tucked inside – *Hercules.*

Bloody Hercules! She laughed to herself. *But for it to be bloody, it would have to be red,* she thought.

The car was not red. It was bright yellow! Tina flicked on the light switch; it caused her to sway as it shuddered and snapped into life. She held onto George's work bench to steady herself.

There were many reasons why Tina resented *Hercules* so much – not least because it occupied the garage all the time while her own car had to be left out on the road. George had installed a CCTV camera on the corner of the house covering the front and garage doors. He could monitor the images on his laptop when he was working away.

Tina smirked: even if he were watching right at this minute, George would not have seen her coming into the garage through the door from the kitchen. But, if the car came to harm and no one had entered from the front, she would automatically be the prime suspect. Asking herself if she cared, she shrugged her shoulders and shook her head, causing a hic-cup to bring the taste of wine back to her tongue.

'Pardon me,' she slurred as she let go of the bench and looked around.

George had been storing a few bricks under the work bench; the corner of one now caught her attention. She was not exactly sure what she meant to do as she bent down unsteadily and picked it up. It was a dull red – almost the colour of dried blood – and heavy. It was an engineering brick, George had told her proudly, assuming she would not know the difference between this and an ordinary house brick.

'Smart arse!' she sneered. The brick's actual purpose did not matter; any old brick would suffice.

She crept carefully to the front of the car's gleaming yellow bonnet. She giggled, which caused her to lose concentration. She tripped and lunged forward, unwillingly hurling the brick away in order to use her hands to break her fall.

The crashing, smashing, splintering sounds resonated in her ears for seemingly an age, her mind being in that faraway place unknown to the temperate.

When all was silent again, she opened her eyes to find her head resting next to the driver's side front tyre. She tried to breathe evenly, but sneezed on the first inhalation, having taken in a nose-full of the dust covering the concrete floor. As she struggled to sit upright, she became aware of various injuries – a jarred wrist, grazed temple, scuffed knees and a cut elbow.

Eventually, she carefully stood up. Her grubby hands slipped off the polished surface of the car's smooth, perfectly rounded metal wing which she had tried to use for support. As she clutched onto a wall stanchion behind her, she saw that she'd left dirty and bloodied marks on the pristine yellow paintwork.

Tina finally focused on the windscreen. An old-fashioned star-cum-spider's web-shaped smash stared back at her, with a large jagged hole in the centre. The brick must have caught a weak spot. She was very surprised, being of the understanding that, in a car of this calibre, the glass should not actually break, no matter how dense the missile.

In all fairness, she silently defended claims against the manufacturer's guarantee; *a brick is somewhat larger than a chip kicked up off a newly re-surfaced road.*

The drunken giggling began again, accompanied by a rumble from Tina's empty stomach. *I'll tell George a chip went through the windscreen,* she mused whilst dusting down her clothes. She reached into her jeans pocket, found a few coins and made a decision.

Chips it was.

Chapter 3

Tina returned to the kitchen, switching off the garage light as she left. She continued through the house to the hall, unhooked her jacket from the pegs by the front door and went out.

There was a fish and chip shop about ten minutes' walk from her house. She wondered if other pedestrians could tell she was drunk. She realised she hadn't checked in the hall mirror before she left to see that her face was clean or if her hair needed brushing. Her hands were certainly grimy. She decided she didn't care. Her knees felt a little stiff to begin with, but they seemed to ease as she walked. She held her head up unnaturally high and ignored any strange looks she received.

The stance on her appearance was vindicated when she reached the shop: people in the queue included a young woman wearing paint-splattered dungarees with contrasting splodges in her bright purple hair, and a man sporting fluorescent green cycling shorts with the crotch stretched so tight that it was obscene – a toddler in a wheel chair buggy sat transfixed by the bulge.

Tina was not sure if it was the sight of the cyclist's lack of modesty that made her eyes water, or the greasy steam from the fryers behind the counter. Either way, she was glad when it was her turn to be served.

Back outside in the street lit by dismally inadequate energy-saving lamps, Tina opened the polystyrene box containing the chips. The smell of freshly fried starch drenched in salt and malt vinegar brought a wave of saliva gushing into her mouth. At the same time she experienced a volcanic grumble from her stomach, culminating in an acidic belch.

Pinching her finger and thumb onto the handle of the wooden fork provided, she stabbed the first chip. It was long, golden and sumptuous. And delicious. But just a little too hot, she discovered. She quickly under-chewed then swallowed it. She felt the bolus being pushed across her throat. It descended her gullet and finally disappeared in the melee of her stomach where, thankfully, she lost all awareness of it.

Tina's mind then quickly started to formulate her plan. She would place a single chip inside the car – a *French fry* as the rest of the world referred to them. She smiled a ridiculous grin as she followed the thought that her scheme would not work anywhere else, because only here did one word describe both a sliver of fried potato and a sharp fragment of stone – not that the latter included an engineering brick. Anyway, here was where George should be. But he wasn't! So this would have to do.

A chip went through the windscreen, she rehearsed, as she looked for a suitable candidate. But they all looked too enticing to be sacrificed. She tried *a French fry pierced the windshield!* But this didn't quite seem right.

Tina had only finished half of her chips by the time she reached her house again. She licked her fingers before searching her pockets, but was quickly struck with horror: she could not find her front door key.

She desperately looked back along the road. It was too dark to see much, despite the street lights. She realised that, even if she retraced her steps, she would be unlikely to find anything as small as a key. Standing at the front door, holding the carton, she became fully aware that George's DIY CCTV would be watching her. She fumed at her stupidity.

Tentatively, she tried the door handle. It opened.

Her first reaction was that George was home. A cold sweat flushed over her skin, soaking her in guilt and foolishness as she realised the seriousness of her recent actions – the vandalism of George's car and leaving her house unlocked.

She called George's name. The word echoed through the empty house. There was no reply. Then she realised George could not be home: he'd just telephoned to say he had to stay offshore.

Almost sober by now, Tina disposed of the remaining chips in the kitchen waste bin. She then wiped the grease from her hands on the thighs of her jeans, collected the vacuum cleaner from the cupboard and made her way into the garage.

As she approached *Hercules*, she whispered, 'Bastard' to the unharmed red engineering brick. She opened the driver's door as gently as she could but, with a waterfall of crystal tinkling, the remains of the windscreen fell inwards.

Tina returned the undamaged brick to the pile under the workbench and spent the next hour or so meticulously cleaning up every fragment of glass.

Later that evening, contrite and humiliated, Tina emailed George to confess her actions. She added that she intended to contact her area manager, Mr Arthur Dentforth (*'You remember him don't you, George,'* she typed, *'with the really bad breath?'*), on Monday. A temporary job had recently been advertised internally for a post-mistress at a place called Cordnell, with an immediate start. Fortunately, a one-bedroom, semi-furnished flat was available to the successful applicant. Suddenly, Tina actually wanted to be on her own.

She did not attend Mona's wedding.

Summer, 2016

Chapter 4

On the first Saturday in June, above the shop and post office in Pepper Hill, the awakening dawn slowly alighted on the newly installed At Hand shop sign.

Poskett's alarm clock rang at four forty-five a.m. The bedroom was still in darkness. Poskett was now eighty years old; these early mornings were not easy for him.

Without looking, he switched off the alarm before its second ring. He rubbed his eyes, slowly sat up and carefully – as if to avoid disturbing someone – climbed out of bed. He needed to be up for the newspaper delivery, which arrived promptly at five o'clock every day, except Sunday, when they came an hour later.

He habitually showered and shaved in the evenings before retiring to avoid extra rigmarole in the mornings. Having quietly dressed, he crept downstairs to the back room – a large kitchen-cum-lounge extension to the main building. He made a pot of tea and let it brew before pouring a cup. He sat down in his favourite armchair, cleaned his glasses and listened to the morning silence as he drank. After the designated ten minutes, he poured another for himself and a second cup for the delivery man, Philip.

Poskett walked stiffly through to the hall and deactivated the security alarm. He wedged open the doors leading to the shop so he could hear the arrival of the papers. After this, he sat back down in the armchair and closed his eyes.

He half dreamt of that day years ago when he met a pretty young girl – her name meant 'of the sea'. He thought they would be together for ever. How foolish and romantic and old-fashioned that idea had been.

There were accountants to meet, appointments with the estate agents, the bank and … He couldn't remember them all now. Neither did he recall the reason Maris had given for not wanting to see him anymore. But he knew she was too ambitious – or too lazy – to be a shop keeper's wife.

Poskett's face relaxed and, although his eyes were closed, he smiled. The shop brought in a decent living – it was hard work, but then, what else would he do with his time? And, in the past couple of decades, his enterprise had thrived, especially as more and more rural shops and post offices in the surrounding area closed. He liked talking to people, helping them in any way he could. He had extended his opening hours to accommodate commuters on their way to and from Cliffend, and this proved both lucrative, as well as popular.

And then the national At Hand franchise company expressed an interest in the business. They recognised the contribution to society that small, independent shops made, and they wanted their name to be part of that. At Hand approved of the post office already in situ; they knew this helped to attract customers. Modifications were needed to the premises to make their corporate operation viable. These resulted in the back room, where Poskett now waited, being built as his previous accommodation was integrated into the shop floor.

Chapter 5

Phil arrived at three minutes past five. He was looking forward to his cup of tea. Old Poskett always served it in a china cup and matching saucer, which somehow made it taste better. Phil never called him 'Old Poskett' to his face; he always addressed him as Mr Poskett – he didn't even know his Christian name. As he climbed out of his van, Phil noticed there were no lights on in the shop, but this was not unusual.

He collected two bundles of newspapers and a small pile of assorted magazines from the rear of the vehicle and carried them to the double-door shop front entrance. He banged on the glass with his elbow and shouted, 'Mr Poskett? Papers!' After a moment's wait, he tried again, then again – this time augmenting his knock with a not so gentle rap to the bottom of the door frame with his foot. There was no reply.

With a mild curse, Phil heaped the bundles onto the ground outside the shop. He walked along the path between the building and the garage, knocked on the back door and waited. When again there was no response, he peered through the adjacent window.

Phil's curse was not so mild when he saw Poskett sitting in the easy chair, apparently asleep with two cups of tea already poured on the table beside him.

'Oi, come on, Mr Poskett, answer the door,' Phil shouted as he tapped the window. He then repeated his call a little louder. Poskett failed to stir.

After several more minutes of struggling with the door handle, calling and cajoling, Phil picked up a large stone from the path and threw it at the window. The glass flew everywhere. Phil swore as a shard ripped one of the knees of his trousers.

At last he forced his way into the room. He stumbled across towards Poskett and called his name. Still the man did not respond.

Phil could see Poskett's lips were blue. He felt for a pulse, but there was none. He then checked for a heartbeat and listened for breathing.

Nothing.

He loosened his tie and collar then repeated the routine. There was still nothing. The old man's skin was cold and, although trained in the rudiments of first aid, Phil did not attempt to resuscitate him. Instead he dialled 999. Even though the screen on his phone showed there was no signal for normal calls, he was able to reach the emergency services.

Phil asked for an ambulance when his call was answered. A different voice asked for details, which he supplied as well as he was able. He was assured help was on its way.

But Phil knew it was too late. Poskett was dead. The delivery driver began to tremble as shock set in. He had never seen a deceased person before, yet alone handled one.

Chapter 6

St Jude's rectory stood adjacent the flint Saxon church, midway between the two hamlets that comprised the village of PepperAsh – Pepper Hill in the west and Ashfield to the east. Early that Saturday morning, Reverend Quintin Boyce, the present incumbent, was listening to the news on the radio. The awful things that God let happen in the world thoroughly disheartened him.

He sighed and decided that maybe a few moments of fresh air might help cheer his mood. He stood up and slowly straightened his gammy knees – *gammy*, according to his doctor, was an official term for the infernal pain that haunted his limbs.

Quinny walked carefully to the rectory's front door and covered the short length of his miniscule, dew-laden lawn. He stood in his slippers by the open gate.

The sky was clear and bright with the early morning summer freshness. The sun swirled a fierce yellow as it saluted the good folks of Cliffend, the first of the nation's residents to be greeted each day.

Quinny, as he was known to his congregation and parishioners, smiled at this idea. As if arthritic knees were not enough, he suffered from depression. It had crept in so slowly and quietly during his childhood and youth that he almost didn't notice. Shortly after moving to PepperAsh, he'd heard a very interesting programme on the radio – he rarely watched television. The topic under discussion was obsessions and mild addictions. A knowledgeable presenter advised listeners to keep a rubber band on their wrist, and to ping the band when the depressing thoughts became acute.

Of course it all sounded too simple, but Quinny tried it and, over the years, had been surprised at its effectiveness.

He continued to watch the morning, thinking and wondering. He was past retirement age but, as he did not cause any problems to the parish or the diocese, he was left in situ. Bishop Clement, who himself was probably old enough to retire as well, lived in his palatial residence near Mattingburgh Cathedral. The bishop rarely visited the wilds of PepperAsh and most of the time Quinny thought he'd been forgotten about.

Quinny did not drive, having failed to learn when he was young. He had a bicycle, but he was too old now to survive amongst the crazy motorists who thought trying to knock a rector off his bike was good sport. Despite his age and frailties, Quinny enjoyed walking, but it felt like a long way from the rectory to either Pepper Hill or Ashfield. It was only just over a mile between the two communities, St Jude's Church being in the middle.

This morning, the weather promised to be fine again. Quinny thought he would stroll over to Ashfield later and cadge a pint off old Henry at The Fighting Cock – *old Henry* happened to be at least a generation younger than himself, perhaps considerably more.

Whilst still grinning at this, Quinny became aware of a siren in the far distance. An ambulance chased along the road from the Ashfield direction towards Pepper Hill. As it sped past Quinny, it seemed to physically pull him into its slipstream.

What in God's name is the world coming to, Quinny thought angrily, *when an ambulance tries to suck in extra victims?*

What indeed? a solitary seagull wheeling a wide circle

above him, squawked down.

There's no such thing as seagulls, he told it.

There's no such thing as people, it skirled back. *Doesn't stop them existing, though!*

Following this, Quinny could not recapture his former peace. Sighing, he walked a few paces down the road and peered in the wake of the ambulance's rear lights.

He stepped back quickly when he heard another siren. Looking in the opposite direction, towards Ashfield again, he saw flashes of blue lights echoing across the landscape long before the vehicle came into view.

The rector shivered. There was obviously an emergency nearby. Something might have happened within his parish. He may be able to help – although exactly how, he couldn't yet imagine: even he appreciated that the presence of an old man in a dog collar on the scene of an accident would probably not be welcome.

As the other siren approached, he could tell this vehicle was not travelling as fast as the previous one. It slowed and stopped just beyond him. He saw that one of the car's brake lights was not working.

'Oi, what d'you think you're doing? You'll have another emergency on your hands if you run me over!' Quinny warned PC Owen Yates. 'And you should have a look at the lights on that pansy car! Your near side brake bulb has fused.'

The police officer looked back at his patrol car in astonishment, not quite believing that the rector had called his state-of-the-art vehicle a 'pansy car'. Then he thought he'd probably said 'panda car': he was of that era.

'Oh, er, right,' he stammered. 'I'll get the lads at the garage to have a look later. And, never mind what I'm doing. Why are you out at this time of the morning, anyway?'

'If it's any business of yours, which I imagine it isn't, I'm no doubt off to the same place as you are!'

'What, in your slippers?'

'Yes,' Quinny replied defiantly, without looking down at his feet. 'And if you're now driving up there, you can give me a lift.'

'And why would I do that?' PC Yates asked, knowing full well he was going to lose this argument even before it started. But he felt he had to have his say. 'If there has been an accident, I expect the sight of the vicar …'

'Rector, son. Get your facts straight.'

'Rector. Whatever. The sight of you would make anyone involved think the worst.'

'What, that they'd died and gone to heaven? No chance if they saw you there too!'

'Even less reason for me to take you with me,' Yates snapped. Then he hesitated. The chief constable was forever sending emails to encourage interaction with the public in order to maintain 'good working relationships'. The emergency call had stated possible sudden death, and anything to do with this (dare he say?) God-forsaken village would probably need a referee; a man of the cloth could possibly just about qualify.

He still felt the need to query this though. 'Is there any reason you feel you should attend, other than just to have a look?'

'I may be able to help,' Quinny responded. 'And, of course, if you do give me a lift, I'll bless your every waking hour henceforth.'

'And if I don't?'

'I'll put in a special word to ensure your eternal damnation!' he laughed.

'Aren't you clergy supposed to be nice people?' Yates asked, somewhat shocked.

'Not necessarily,' Quinny replied thoughtfully. 'At least, I can't remember reading it in the job description.'

'Okay, then. Get in. I'm not supposed to carry unofficial passengers …'

'It's funny, but that's exactly what the postman says.'

'…but I suppose I could stretch the point with you. You possibly just about qualify as an *official person,* anyway.'

'Bless you, my son. I certainly do. After all, I might be able to save a couple of souls when we get there.'

'The only *soles* you're ever likely to save are those on the bottoms of your slippers!' Yates responded acerbically.

Chapter 7

As soon as they arrived at Poskett's shop and post office, the two paramedics in green uniforms quietly moved Phil aside and began to work on the old man.

'What's the patient's name?' they asked whilst unbuttoning his shirt and attaching round pads with wires to his chest.

'Poskett, Mr Poskett,' a bewildered Phil replied.

'First name?' the older, obviously more experienced of the paramedics enquired.

Phil shook his head and shrugged his shoulders.

'I don't know. We all just call him Poskett.'

After a united look of disbelief, the paramedics continued to call his name, but there was no response.

'How long has the patient been unconscious?'

'I don't know. I'd only been here a few minutes when I called you. I couldn't get any reply from the front door so I came round the back. He always has a cup of tea for me.' He indicated to the crockery on the table.

One of the men touched the nearest vessel.

'It's still quite warm, so it can't have been too long.'

Phil glanced at the tea and nausea began to rise into his throat.

'Was he sitting here like this when you found him?'
'Yeah.'

'You didn't see him walking around, or stumble into the chair, or anything?'

'No, I found him exactly like that.'

'Does he have any medical conditions that you know of?'

'No, no. I told you I just found him sitting there.' Phil looked desperately around the room before continuing.

'Look, I only deliver the newspapers to the shop here every morning, and he makes me a cup of tea. We chat about the weather, or the state of the world, the football results – you know, general stuff. He's never said anything about being ill, as far as I can remember.'

The local policeman then appeared, together with the rector – the latter still wearing slippers. This seemed to be the switch that altered the paramedics focus. They conferred and one began to write something down in an official carbon-duplicated pad of documents whilst the other packed their equipment away.

The policeman spoke to Phil, who felt he was hearing the voice from a great distance; he could not understand what was being said. PC Yates touched his upper arm reassuringly and told him he would talk to him again later.

Quinny stood in front of Poskett with his head bowed. It was only then that Phil dashed from the overcrowded kitchen into the garden and vomited against the nearest bush.

Chapter 8

After breakfast on Wednesday, Quinny walked the short distance from the rectory to St Jude's Church. It was a bright summer's morning. He felt cheerful and optimistic, despite the fact that the church needed to be locked overnight and the key was large and too heavy to carry far. He pinged the rubber band on his wrist. It stung. Yes, he was alive.

He began to mentally list the prayers he could offer: gratitude for the goodness of the day, a petition for all those with troubles in their lives and clemency for the soul of the recently departed Mr Poskett. (He reminded himself that he was still waiting to hear from the police, the coroner, the funeral director – anyone, as to the details of Poskett's family.) And so on. Plus, at the end, a quick petition for a cure for his arthritis!

When there was no immediate reply to this last request, he sighed and looked up at the church. The sunlight reflected off the stone, turning the flint-grey into almost lime white. The tower was tall and round, being listed as one of a rare number built to that design.

For health and safety reasons, few people nowadays were allowed to climb to the top. Access was via a stone spiral staircase built into the hollow wall inside the tower. This reached as far as the bell cradle, about two-thirds of the way up. A wooden ladder stretched from the base of the cradle to a hatch door in the ceiling, which was protected from the elements by a stone arch that formed part of the decorative crenellations around the edges.

Quinny had been to the top a long, long time ago, when his knees hadn't hurt all the time. Even then it was an exhausting climb. When he had finally stepped out through the covered hatch at the top and into the massive blue sky around him, the freedom was exhilarating. Several minutes passed before he reminded himself that he was there to inspect the metal flag-pole planted in the middle of the tower roof, not to admire the view.

When Quinny first arrived in PepperAsh, the St George's Cross was raised on 23rd April and other festive days, including 19th June and 28th October – both of which were dedicated to their patron saint, St Jude. The then churchwarden, a relative of Mrs Delilah Ervsgreaves, had climbed the tower regularly since being a lad, and doggedly continued to do so long after those in authority forbade it. But he died many years ago, of septicaemia caused by an untreated boil on his neck – nothing whatsoever to do with defying regulations.

Now, the flagpole's only purpose was to act as a lightning conductor. It was waiting, Quinny suspected, for the day it could channel God's wrath downwards and wreak even more havoc on PepperAsh than the residents managed themselves. Quinny raised his eyes heavenward and chuckled. The *Old Man Upstairs* had missed a good opportunity during a cracking thunderstorm after Henry and Rosalie Stickleback's wedding some twenty-six years ago.

The legendary division of the graveyard was clearly visible from the top of the tower: Pepper Hill's half snuggled on the north side, the larger of the two areas; whilst Ashfield's portion crouched in front and led down to the gates by the road.

As Quinny approached the church's porch the atmosphere changed from pleasantly warm and sunny to slightly chilled and subdued. He unlocked and opened the large and heavy dark oak door. But he forgot to concentrate and misplaced his foot as he stepped down, twisting his ankle in the process.

'Bugger,' he muttered.

Then he thought he heard a voice from above laughing at him, reminding him that he was in the Lord's house and really ought not to swear.

Although the church's interior was painted white and light flowed colourfully through the stained glass windows, Quinny's eyes took a moment to adjust.

When he could see clearly, a quick glance to the wall at the side of the door reassured him the alms box was still intact; the postcards, diaries, leaflets and souvenirs on the table also seemed in order. It was his fear that someone would break in and steal from the church. He didn't think he could face the commotion, trauma and defilement this would cause, never mind coping with visits from PC Yates and filling out all the paperwork.

He walked slowly down the aisle of the nave towards the chancel, the sound of his shoes' soft soles were absorbed by the stone floor. He stopped at his favourite pew, paid lip service to genuflection and shuffled in. He was unable to prevent a groan escaping as he knelt stiffly down onto the garishly embroidered hassock to start his prayers.

Chapter 9

Rosalie Stickleback lived in the Old Police House in Pepper Hill, nearly opposite the post office and shop. It was Thursday, mid-afternoon and she was tidying her front garden – a job she did not particularly enjoy. Her elderly chocolate Labrador, Ben, was lying on the grass close by, chewing a cow-hide bone. His coat was moulting and he was going grey around his muzzle; his eyes seemed to be struggling to stay open in the sunshine.

Rosalie was short, in her mid-forties, with wiry blonde hair, a clear complexion and soft blue eyes. As she worked, she tried not to wrinkle her nose at the unpleasant smell around her.

Unfortunately, her household septic tank was located under her front lawn. This was convenient for the process of emptying, but less pleasant for passers-by when the weather was hot and, as at present, the tank was full. It needed emptying urgently.

Neither Pepper Hill nor Ashfield were connected to a sewerage system; every property relied on cesspits and septic tanks. Rosalie's son, Duncan Stickleback, ran a domestic effluent disposal business. He lived with his wife, Lily, and their three-year-old son, Jack, in a cottage on a small farm called Tidal Reach at Ashfield. This was directly opposite The Fighting Cock public house, where his father, Henry, was landlord.

Duncan helped out in the pub but Rosalie felt Henry tended to impose on his good nature. She'd left a message on Duncan's answerphone three days ago asking if he could empty her septic tank, but had not yet heard back from him.

The insidious stench reinforced Rosalie's paranoia: even after twenty-six years of separation, she was convinced Henry was obstructing her every move. She imagined he must have heard the telephone message, or maybe Duncan had innocently mentioned something during the course of conversation.

Her patience and endurance both suddenly snapped. She called Ben indoors then stomped towards her car. She climbed in and set off with determination and purpose in the direction of Ashfield.

Half-way along her journey, she passed the rectory and St Jude's Church standing on the left. Soon, the first dwellings of Ashfield came into sight. Immediately beyond were The Fighting Cock on the left and Tidal Reach on the right.

A cloud of dust rose as she drove around the cottage and into the back yard of her son's smallholding – the property that had originally been bought for her and Henry as a wedding present from Henry's mother, Nora. Duncan had taken it over before he and Lily married.

Rosalie parked on an area in the centre of the outbuildings, which included a tall barn and a cart shed in which Duncan housed his machinery and equipment. Two large fields surrounded these, and pasture land sloped downwards behind the buildings towards the marshes before eventually reaching the banks of the River Potch.

Duncan's plant was unmistakeable: his livery was bright yellow with purple lettering. He owned two slurry tankers – one being ready to use at any given time, whilst the other was emptying into the ground of the lower meadows, the area where he was licensed to dispose of domestic effluent. The process involved filtering off the liquid, then drying and purifying the solids, which he then sold to local farmers as fertiliser.

Of his three tractors, one was barely roadworthy and only used to ferry the tankers between the lower meadows and the yard, its engine also being useful to pump out the effluent. The other two tractors were available to tow the remaining tanker or to transport the fertiliser, or anything else that was required.

However, Duncan's second best tractor had recently been causing problems. The mechanism operating the front loading arm, with the prong for carrying the enormous round bales, was faulty: it would not lock in the *carry* position. Duncan tried, but he couldn't fix it himself. The tractor had been parked in the corner of the yard for several days, waiting for Duncan to ring the mechanic to come and repair it. His father was aware of the defect but his mother knew nothing about it.

As Rosalie climbed out of her car, she could see Duncan's green truck inside the barn with the bonnet propped open.

The other tractor, the one in working order, was standing just outside the building, gleaming bright yellow in the sunlight. An equally vivid tanker was hitched to it. Rosalie stepped tentatively towards the latter, reached up her hand and knocked on the rounded belly, feeling the burning heat of the metal with her knuckles. It sounded hollow. She wondered if this meant Duncan intended to empty her septic tank as soon as he could.

She called her son's name. There was no reply. She looked at her watch; it was mid-afternoon which probably meant Duncan would be working at the pub until the evening shift started. Although thinking it was futile, Rosalie walked to the back door of the cottage, grasped the handle and tried to open it. The door was locked.

Looking around, she could not see her daughter-in-law's car. Lily usually took Jack to Cliffend to see her own mum and dad, Vince and Irene Hallett, a couple of times a week. Lily called them the *sensible grandparents*, as opposed to herself and Henry, whom she had labelled the *idiot grandparents*.

Rosalie did not particularly care what Lily thought of her. She walked around to the back of the farm buildings where her son's pastureland sloped down to the marshes. She could see the second tanker and the oldest tractor in the distance, glinting in the sunshine as they discharged the effluent.

Returning to the buildings, she called Duncan's name again. She then approached the tanker and climbed up onto the tractor. The smell of engine oil and the feel of the footplate mouldings through her soles gave Rosalie a thrill of daring and excitement. Checking inside the cab, she saw the key was in the ignition.

Stepping down again, she retrieved a pen and note pad from her car and wrote a quick explanation to Duncan. She walked around to the front door of the cottage and pushed the note through the letter box. But, as she did so, she heard a roar of men's laughter from the open pub door on the opposite side of the road. She recognised one of the voices as belonging to Henry – her estranged husband. This reignited the ever-smouldering rage inside her. She took a deep breath and strode back.

Hitching up her skirt, Rosalie climbed up again and settled herself onto the seat in the tractor cab. She turned the key and smiled as the engine pounded into life, vibrating the entire vehicle with energy as it did so, causing a stream of blue smoke to erupt from the exhaust pipe attached vertically to the bonnet in front of her. She eased the tractor and tanker into motion and carefully negotiated the driveway from behind the buildings. She swung wide around the cottage, ensuring there was enough room for the length of her vehicle to pass without damaging the corner of the building, and headed towards the road. There was no traffic in sight, so she pulled out and set off triumphantly towards her home in Pepper Hill.

Chapter 10

Henry Stickleback had been in the bar of his pub, The Fighting Cock, joking with a group of his regular customers. He was a big man; his dark hair was flecked with silver and his beard still held a hint of red mixed in with the grey. He stopped for a moment when he thought he heard a tractor leave his son's property across the road.

Duncan was working down in the cellar, rotating the stock of barrels and moving the empties near to the hatch ready for collection the following day. For this reason, Henry knew it was not Duncan driving the tractor; Lily, in Henry's opinion, would never willingly have anything to do with equipment that emptied septic tanks, despite it being her husband's livelihood and their main source of income.

Lily was a very good wife and mother, and she and Duncan had been together since their mid-teens. But she was not exactly enamoured with the Stickleback family and their way of life. Her own father, Vince Hallett, was a pilot who owned a small airfield the other side of Pepper Hill. It was part of an aerodrome that had been constructed during the Second World War. Although officially retired, he was still involved in running the business. Vince and his wife, Irene, lived on the outskirts of Cliffend; he sometimes stopped off at the pub on his way home. Henry shook his head as he finished preparing a round of drinks, thinking that he hadn't seen his son's father-in-law for a while. Then he thought he ought to check on Duncan.

'Everything all right?' Duncan asked when he saw his father's shadowed bulk descending the steps.

Duncan had inherited his father's nearly black hair and the stubble on his face showed shadows of the same red. He was as tall as Henry but not so rounded. His temperament was lighter, more jovial, but he had a slightly nervous edge to his personality which Lily attributed to his parents constantly being at war with each other.

'I thought I just heard a tractor leaving yours. Must've been mistaken,' Henry said as he surveyed the neatness of the storage area. Duncan was a tidy person – a trait inherited from neither Henry nor Rosalie.

The younger man frowned as he looked up, then suddenly realised what was probably happening.

'Oh no!' he shouted as he pushed past Henry and dashed up the steps.

Duncan only just remembered to look both ways before he ran across the road from The Fighting Cock to Tidal Reach. He found his mother's car behind the cottage. He tried to open his back door because he thought – hoped – perhaps she was inside. It was locked. Then he realised Lily's car was not in the yard, which meant she had possibly taken Jack to visit her parents.

'Mum?' he shouted several times as he walked quickly around the farm buildings. He then stood in horror when he noticed the tractor hitched to the empty tanker had gone: he'd left it in the yard ready to use as soon as he finished at the pub.

Henry arrived alongside Duncan, breathing hard with sweat glistening on the top half of his flushed face. Polly had not yet arrived and he managed to bribe a regular customer, Max, to look after the bar for a few moments before following Duncan.

'What's wrong, son?' he asked.

'Mum's taken the tanker – or, at least I think she has. I told you she needed her septic tank emptying.'

Henry chuckled to himself, but this made Duncan angry.

'I wish you two would start behaving like adults instead of always niggling and fighting,' he shouted. 'No wonder Lily doesn't like Jack spending time with either of you.'

Henry's face clouded.

'Don't blame me if you have to do two jobs to provide for what Lily wants,' he retorted. 'Maybe you shouldn't've married the likes of that madam ...'

'Save it, Dad. I've had enough! I'd better try and catch Mum before she crashes the tractor. Or spills the sludge out over the road if she tries to do the job herself.'

'Well, it's hardly my fault if she's gone off ...'

'Oh, yes it is!' Duncan interrupted his father again, which was unheard of once in a conversation, never mind twice. He left Henry stunned to silence standing outside the barn while he hurried inside to his green truck. He stopped when he saw the bonnet was up and remembered he had been interrupted yesterday before he could finish changing the oil.

'I'll have to take the other tractor,' he said, motioning towards the vehicle beyond his truck. 'I just hope the loading arm doesn't drop while I'm driving!'

'Use my car, son, you can probably still catch up with her,' Henry offered as he threw the keys to Duncan. 'I'll get this old jalopy going and follow on.'

Duncan thought for a minute then agreed. But he warned, 'Dad, don't do anything to make the situation worse!' He paused before adding, 'please.'

'I won't. I promise I won't,' Henry said, smiling and

raising his hands to indicate resignation. 'Now just go.'

During the drive to Pepper Hill, Duncan wished he could do something to change his parents' behaviour. But he knew it was useless to try – they'd been at war with each other since before he was born. He only wished he'd had the courage to leave home when he was sixteen as Sarah, his twin, had.

Duncan arrived at the Old Police House in Pepper Hill just in time to see his mother very capably feeding the pipe down into the pit in her front garden, having somehow first removed the heavy metal cover. He parked Henry's car on her front driveway and hurried across to her.

'Here, let me do that,' Duncan shouted above the throb of the tractor engine.

'I can manage myself, thank you!' Rosalie replied defiantly. 'You've had three days to help me and didn't, so don't think I need you now!'

'That's not the point, Mum, and you know it. You can't just take my equipment. You're not insured to start with …'

But Rosalie switched on the pump, the noise smothering Duncan's voice however loud he shouted. He quickly gave up trying to reason with her. Instead, he turned and watched the hose snaking as it sucked out the contents of the pit.

Luckily, they were both several feet away from the tanker when they heard an excruciating crunch and splintering of metal from behind them. The whole contraption jolted forward a couple of feet. Then the smell, which was already pungent, flooded their nostrils.

Rosalie screamed as effluent showered out of the back of the tanker, just missing her and her son. They both spun around to see the bale spike on the front loader of the other yellow tractor, which Henry had been driving, embedded into the rear terminal of the tanker, straight through the figures of Duncan's telephone number. The slurry going in from the hose was immediately being forced out again through the penetration hole around the metal spike and causing a brown fountain to spray backwards.

First one car then another approached the rear of the farm vehicles locked in what looked like a prehistoric mating ritual. As well as the spray, blue exhaust fumes belched from both tractors' exhaust pipes. As the slurry quickly covered the cars, the drivers pulled back to a safe distance. None of the occupants were particularly keen to climb out and help, although one started to make a call on his mobile phone. He gave up when he discovered there wasn't a signal, not even for emergency services.

Henry was shaking quite badly as he slowly descended from the tractor cab. Avoiding the spray, he started to walk towards Rosalie and Duncan.

'What on earth were you doing?' Duncan yelled at him. 'You could see she was stopped! Why didn't you brake?'

These questions were repeated several times with various expletives. Henry bet to himself his son did not dare speak like that when Lily was within earshot!

At last, somebody had the presence of mind to switch off the tractor engine and tanker pump. The noise and effluent spurts abated. But the stench did not. Then a third car arrived. *Oh God,* thought Henry. *You can go for weeks without seeing a policeman, then one has to turn up now!*

Chapter 11

PC Owen Yates regularly cursed his luck at being the area beat officer for PepperAsh. He was warned by his sergeant at Cliffend police station on his first day, over twenty-five years ago now, that most of the trouble in the village emanated from the conflict between Henry Stickleback of Ashfield and his estranged wife, Rosalie from Pepper Hill.

Yates tried not to breathe in too deeply as he walked towards the obvious perpetrators of the fracas. He snorted with derision as he read the words *Non-hazardous Waste* painted on the pierced tanker. The two other drivers remained in their cars; he acknowledged they were right to do so.

Vince Hallett sat on the sofa with his grandson, Jack, on his lap. They had been reading and playing, and generally enjoying each other's company. Vince and his wife, Irene, had wanted more children, but only one – Lily – had come along. So they made the best of her, and now also Jack, cherishing the hours spent with them.

Lily and Irene were in the kitchen. The telephone rang and Vince let one of them answer it. He and Jack were deciding what they would like for tea, while Vince tried to ignore the anxious tone in which Irene called Lily to the phone.

'They've done what?' his daughter almost screamed.

Vince looked at Jack then lifted him off his knee and started to walk through to the kitchen.

'Come on, young man. We'd better go and see what's happened now. Shall we bet your Grandad

Henry and Grandma Rosalie have got themselves into trouble again?'

Jack nodded enthusiastically. Vince instantly regretted planting the seed of disrespect into his grandson's mind.

Chapter 12

The following morning, Friday, Duncan woke early with a pounding headache. It was not the first time this had happened recently. The pain centred in his right eye, his sinus was blocked and he felt as if an axe had embedded itself in the top of his head. He found himself gritting his teeth against the discomfort.

Lily was still asleep next to him; he could feel rather than hear her breathing. She often told him that his parents' antagonistic behaviour towards each other was making him ill. Although Duncan agreed, he felt he couldn't do anything about it. Maybe now he would have to, but he was not looking forward to trying.

The morning sun shone through the landing window and entered their bedroom via the open door which was never closed in case Jack woke up during the night. Duncan guessed the time was about five o'clock. As he moved, a wave of nausea flooded him. He closed his eyes and waited for it to pass. Then the memories of yesterday's disaster coursed through his mind.

PC Owen Yates had been in an extremely ugly mood, but Duncan thought it understandable in the circumstances. His first command was for Henry and Rosalie to get in the back of the police car. He regretted this as soon as he realised how badly they stank. Having issued dire threats of what would happen to them both if they caused any more trouble, he left them there.

He noted the details of the two cars onto which some of the sludge had sprayed and said he would contact the drivers later for statements. He then forcefully encouraged the spectators and traffic blocking the highway to disperse. He told Duncan to sort the tangled machinery and wash the mess off the road before following on. Finally, he drove Henry and Rosalie to Cliffend's police station.

When everyone had gone, Duncan climbed wearily onto the faulty tractor and tried to reverse the spike out of the tanker. The sound of scraping metal was as sickening as the stench from the effluent. The tractor bucked and protested, the effort lifting the tanker's wheels off the ground and ripping the hole wider. When the spike was finally freed, the front loading arm crashed against the road surface and stubbornly refused to lift again.

Duncan had switched off the engine, climbed down from the tractor and went to survey the damage. Lying in bed now, he winced as he remembered.

He managed to plug the gap in the tanker with old hessian sacking he'd found in his mother's shed, hoping any residual sludge would not slop out of the bung on the journey back to Tidal Reach. He connected his mother's garden hose to the outdoor tap by the back door, dragged most of its length around to the road at the front and, with a yard broom he'd also borrowed, he gave the road a good sluice and sweep down.

Duncan then moved his father's car, which he'd driven over from Ashfield, and parked it a little way from the scene, leaving the area clear to sort out the tractors and tanker. On restarting the faulty tractor's engine, he finally cajoled and persuaded the loading arm to lift, eventually locking it into position. He prayed it would stay up while he reversed the vehicle onto the driveway of the Old Police House, squeezing it as far back as possible in order to leave enough room to park the damaged tanker there as well.

When it was in place, he lowered the arm to the ground, trudged to the other tractor with its stricken tanker, started up the engine and backed the unit onto the driveway also. He unhitched the tanker, now safely off the road, and parked the good tractor across the entrance, half on and half off the carriageway.

Finally, he climbed into his father's car and set off to join his parents at Cliffend police station. He thought he ought to stop off at Tidal Reach on the way, have a shower and change first, but he dared not delay.

Luckily PC Yates did not comment on Duncan's unfortunate odour; he'd probably lost his sense of smell after dealing with Henry and Rosalie.

Duncan was charged with allowing a vehicle with a known mechanical fault to be driven on the highway. Luckily, both tractors were taxed and insured, and everything else was in order.

But he did not feel very lucky when this was pointed out to him.

His mother's crime was stated as taking a vehicle without the owner's consent. Duncan had been forced to admit in his statement that he had not said she could drive the tractor and tanker on that particular occasion – and, no, she was not included on the business's insurance, even if she had permission.

Henry's misdemeanours amounted to driving an unroadworthy vehicle and dangerous driving. PC Yates explained to him that, even if he were not aware of the fault with the tractor's front loading arm, it was always the driver's responsibility to ensure any vehicle was safe to drive. And, yes, luckily he was included on Duncan's insurance.

Unlike Rosalie, Henry had obtained Duncan's permission to drive the tractor although the younger man's memory of the conversation was more his father telling him he would take it rather than asking.

When questioned as to why he had not braked and stopped at a safe distance behind the stationary tanker, Henry claimed he had been distracted when the front loading arm started to descend. The policeman did not seem particularly satisfied with this explanation.

Although still light outside, it was after nine in the evening when the three of them were released. They were each told to expect a summons to the magistrates' court soon. Henry had driven them in his car to Duncan's cottage in Ashfield where Rosalie's vehicle was waiting. She then drove Henry and Duncan to her house in Pepper Hill.

Repeating her apology to her son in a quiet, contrite voice, Rosalie retreated indoors. Ben greeted her as though their separation had been months rather than hours.

Duncan knew his mother was truly sorry for the trouble she'd caused, but the fact remained that his livelihood would suffer as a result of her foolishness. Henry was also unusually quiet as they turned around the good tractor and hitched up the tanker again. The smell did not seem to have dissipated much during their absence and, as Duncan towed home his broken plant, he wondered when his parents' fighting would end.

Henry had offered to drive the faulty tractor, agreeing to face any consequences of possibly breaking the law again in an effort to appease his son. By that time, Duncan was too exhausted to argue; it had to be moved anyway, and he was desperate to get home to Lily and Jack.

Duncan was worried sick that his business could fail

as a result of all this. He would now be without the use of one tanker and one tractor, plus he would have repair costs to meet because he was certain his insurance would not cover this type of accident. It had been too dark for Duncan to survey the damage properly when he'd arrived back at Tidal Reach last night; he'd only just mustered the energy to drive the tanker down to the pasture and set it off to drain out.

His stomach knotted inside him now as he remembered the feelings of helplessness and futility that accompanied his explanations to Lily. He felt humiliated that he had to supplement his income to support his family by working at Henry's pub.

Lying in bed next to Lily, letting these worries take hold of him again, Duncan suddenly felt very sick.

He only just reached the bathroom but did not manage to close the door. His hasty exit from their bed and the sound of his subsequent retching disturbed Lily. He heard her call through, asking if he was all right. No, he wasn't. The last thing Duncan remembered was watching the floor float up to meet him.

Duncan was not unconscious for long, but Lily rang for an ambulance. She cleaned his mouth as best she could and rolled him onto his side – the bathroom was not a very big area to manoeuvre in. He'd hit his head against the corner of the bath when he fell; blood was oozing from a nasty gash on his temple. Lily held a towel to the cut and Duncan was trying to tell her that he felt sick again when the doorbell rang.

Jack was waiting downstairs. He could just about reach the door handle, if he stood on tip-toes. He stretched up with all his might, opened the door and, bless him, led the paramedics up the stairs. He was very sensible, *unlike his Stickleback grandparents,* Lily thought.

Lily explained to the paramedics what had happened. She was crying by the time she'd finished. The ambulance man told her to try not to worry, they would help Duncan. She took Jack out of the bathroom as the second man, having pulled on latex gloves, gently drew the blood-soaked towel away from Duncan's head to examine the wound.

Lily looked down and saw she had wiped blood onto her dressing gown. She went to her bedroom and cleaned her hands with cleansing wipes before quickly dressing. Jack was still in his pyjamas, but it was a warm day and he looked as if he was wearing a playsuit. She gently cuddled him and gave him one of his dinosaurs to hold.

When she carried her son back to the bathroom, her home suddenly seemed very small with the two extra people and all their equipment.

'I don't think it's anything serious,' the first paramedic told her. 'But we'll take him to hospital anyway. He's still nauseous, and the cut to his head is quite deep. I think it needs proper attention.'

Lily looked at Duncan. His face was a pasty-white colour, his eyes were closed and he was wearing an oxygen mask. They asked him if he could sit up. He tried but seemed to faint again.

The man drew Lily away for a moment.

'Do you want to come in the ambulance, or will you follow?' he asked. Lily was not sure she would be able to concentrate enough to drive.

'I'll stay with Duncan, if that's okay,' she replied.

'What about your little boy? Can someone come and look after him?'

'No.' Lily shook her head vehemently. 'I'll ring my

parents when we get to the hospital. And Duncan's. But I want Jack with me.'

Chapter 13

Henry Stickleback did not drink, mainly because his father, Woodrow – Woody – landlord of The Fighting Cock before him, had been an alcoholic. Henry's first memories were of his dad being 'merry'. He also distinctly recalled trying some of his father's whisky when he was about nine years old. He'd been bored one day after school and had found a bottle hidden under the bar by the cash register. But he had hated the taste and spilt quite a lot on the floor. He was trying to clean this when his Dad found him, closely followed by his Mum. Luckily, Henry believed she thought he was helping Woody clear up the spillage, but then he saw the disappointment on her face. He never drank again, although when he was younger, sometimes at parties, weddings or such like, out of politeness, he would pretend to have a sip of wine or champagne to join in a toast. But he never swallowed any. His father, Woody's, problems were not a secret and everyone accepted this was the reason Henry did not drink.

Henry's main choice of beverage, however, did cause a great deal of comment. And, on Friday morning at the pub, with visions of the previous day's shenanigans still clear in his mind, he went to the kitchen to make his first brew of the day.

He took from the cupboard an old cream-coloured ceramic pint mug with a handsome cockerel painted on the outside. Into this he placed a tea-bag, followed by three heaped teaspoons of instant coffee. After pouring in the boiling water, he added milk and two dessert-spoons of sugar. He always left the tea-bag in the mug and stirred the concoction constantly with the dessert-spoon – teaspoons were not long enough and sundae spoons too effeminate. By the time he had nearly finished drinking, the liquid left in the bottom was very strong and stagnant. Yes, the taste was shocking, and disgusting. But it wasn't inebriating.

The door from the bar to the kitchen was open and Henry heard the telephone ring. He decided to let the call go to the answer machine as he'd only half finished his drink. When he recognised Lily's voice, however, he changed his mind and walked through to pick up the receiver. She had finished speaking by the time he reached the phone. He played back the message.

'Henry? It's Lily. I'm at Cliffend Hospital. Duncan has just been brought in. He passed out in the bathroom this morning and I'm not sure what's wrong. The doctor is with him now.'

Lily gave an exasperated, annoyed sigh then continued, 'I thought perhaps you might've noticed the ambulance outside ours this morning? It was there for over half an hour!'

Ouch, thought Henry. His daughter-in-law could be a bit sharp at times. No, he hadn't noticed anything, but he had only been up for about twenty minutes. He hadn't finished clearing up in the bar until gone midnight.

'I'll ring later and let you know what's wrong with Duncan. I expect it has something to do with you and Rosalie …' There was a brief, angry pause. 'I just hope you two are pleased with yourselves!'

The same click sounds on answer machines whether the caller finishes calmly or in anger. Pressing a button to terminate the connection does not have the same dramatic effect as slamming down the receiver, Henry thought. But he could imagine Lily's venom as she ended that particular call.

Henry wanted to help Duncan, give him a good start in life; that was why he allocated him as many shifts at the pub as he needed. Polly Merton was Henry's only permanent member of staff, although various other people helped out from time to time. He would have employed Lily as well, if she was interested. She almost accepted his offer of a few shifts now and then when the smoking ban came into force. She could not stand the smell of cigarette smoke, and woe betide anyone who even now dared to light up near Jack! But Henry and Rosalie had had another argument – he could not remember what it was about - and Lily said she did not want to be involved with them any more than she had to. Henry couldn't really blame her.

On the whole, Henry liked Lily as a person, daughter-in-law and the mother of his grandchild. She was pretty and petite, but a bit spoilt. He thought Lily had some strange ideas about how to bring up Jack, but wisely kept this to himself as he realised he and Rosalie had not set a very good parenting example.

Henry erased Lily's message and stood up straight. He and Rosalie had been at odds with each other since the morning after their wedding day. It was their business – no one else's!

Chapter 14

Rosalie's dog, Ben, was eleven years old, but he still liked to go for a walk. His tail wagged and his pink tongue panted enthusiastically whenever she picked up his lead. Sometimes on their way home, they used to stop at the shop to buy a newspaper – Poskett didn't mind Ben just coming inside for a few minutes if it meant a sale, despite At Hand's policy that no dogs, except guide dogs of course, should be allowed on the premises. But everything had been closed up since the old man's death.

As she walked with Ben down the drive and onto the road that Friday morning, Rosalie smelt the lingering stench of sewage, despite Duncan having cleaned and swept the area. Although she did not worry about other people's opinions of her, she realised this latest incident was going to be the topic of local gossip for many months. She felt a little ashamed of the effect it could possibly have on Duncan.

When she thought Ben had walked far enough along the road, she turned around. Upon her return home, she saw the light was flashing on her telephone. She dialled to receive her message. It was from Lily. Her heart froze when she heard the barely controlled anger in her daughter-in-law's voice.

Rosalie unclipped Ben's lead from his collar, ruffled his ears and took a biscuit out of the cupboard for him. She snatched her handbag from the chair at the kitchen table, found her car keys and checked to make sure the back door was locked.

Ben released a noisy groan and made himself comfortable in his basket by the stove which, although not lit during the summer, was nevertheless comforting. He licked his greying muzzle as his red-rimmed and somewhat sad brown eyes watched Rosalie leave. Anticipating a nap, he placed his chin on his forepaws and gave another satisfied moan. He licked his lips again, closed his eyes and went to sleep – only opening one eye when his mistress barged back into the house to collect something she'd obviously forgotten.

Rosalie pulled in and parked at Cliffend hospital. Whilst hurriedly climbing out, she caught her skirt in the driver's door as she slammed it shut. Having released herself, she found the electronic key would not work when she clicked it towards the car: she had to lock it manually. As she withdrew the key, however, she saw she'd left her handbag on the passenger seat.

When she finally arrived at the enquiries desk just inside the main door, there was no one on duty. She looked at her watch; it was only a quarter to eight. The clock above the doors beyond the desk showed 7:45 a.m. in large, bold figures.

Rosalie hated digital clocks, she liked sunny, round faces with hands and numbers. She remembered when she had bought the twins each a watch for their eighth birthdays and taught them to tell the time on both kinds. Her smile faded now as she glanced around, trying to decide what to do. After a few moments' hesitation, she marched resolutely down a corridor following the directions for the accident and emergency department.

Chapter 15

Henry arrived at Cliffend hospital shortly after Rosalie. They, plus Lily and Jack, now sat on unyielding blue plastic seats in a waiting zone outside the accident and emergency treatment area.

Duncan had been seen by one doctor, who wanted a specialist to carry out a second assessment before speaking to the family.

An uncomfortable atmosphere had settled over the three adults. Jack, whom Rosalie noticed was still wearing his pyjamas, had fallen asleep on the seat between Lily and Henry. Lily's in-laws instinctively knew better than to do anything to disturb their grandson. Lily had said little to them since they arrived. They realised she was very angry, obviously blaming them for Duncan's present predicament.

The door from the treatment area into the waiting zone opened and they all looked up as a doctor entered. He was tall, tired-looking, young and dark-haired. He wore a creased white coat with a badge pinned onto the lapel bearing his photograph and name, Dr Oliver Kittson.

'Mrs Stickleback?' he enquired of the group.

Rosalie stood up quickly and started walking towards him. She was suddenly halted by Lily's voice.

'He means me!'

'Yes, of course,' Rosalie replied as she turned around, blushing at her mistake. 'We'll look after Jack, you go through.'

Lily was seething at Rosalie's audacity, but she did not say anything. She gently touched Jack's arm as he slept, glared at Henry and Rosalie in turn then followed

Dr Kittson. Rosalie sat down on the seat Lily had vacated and also stroked Jack's arm. The child stirred but quickly settled again.

Henry and Rosalie waited in silence with only the sound of their grandson's breathing audible. After only a few minutes, which seemed much longer, Lily returned. They both looked towards her, neither dared to speak.

'Dr Kittson says they're going to keep Duncan in hospital for observation, just for a day or two. They're trying to find a bed on one of the wards for him now. The only thing they can actually find wrong at the moment is that his blood pressure is very low. He also needed a couple of stitches in his head where he hit the bath when he fainted.'

Suddenly, Lily faltered. She cast her eyes downwards as she continued. 'Only they don't use stitches as such now, do they? Just very thin strips of plaster, but they have to be put on properly.' Her voice was fading; there were tears in her eyes as she stopped speaking.

When she felt able to, she added, 'I just want to ring Mum and Dad to ask them to fetch me.' She looked up again and sniffed. 'Could you mind Jack again for a couple of minutes, please?'

Lily knew Henry and Rosalie were just as anxious about Duncan as she was, but she was still furious with them.

'One of us will run you to your parents', we've both got our cars here,' Rosalie offered.

'No,' Lily almost shouted. The sound disturbed Jack. She went to him, picked up his sleepy body, held him tightly to her then turned to face them again.

'No,' she repeated quietly. 'You two have done

enough, thank you. Duncan is exhausted and needs to rest. He'll only be allowed to see Jack and me today, so just go home. I'll hang on to Jack now he's waking up, and go ring Mum and Dad.'

Both Rosalie and Henry looked as if they were about to protest, but Lily interrupted them, sternly. 'I'll telephone you if there is any change. Please, go.'

Rosalie and Henry exchanged defiant glances. No one ever told either of them what to do. But Lily and Jack left the waiting area before they rallied enough to contradict.

'Well, I'd better be getting back to the pub,' Henry said, looking at his watch. It was half past ten. Polly's shift did not start until noon and, although trade had recently slackened off a little during the day, he could bet there would be a queue if he were late opening.

He left the hospital with a cursory farewell to his estranged wife in the car park. And, yes, as predicted, a group of thirsty customers – in this case, four serious ramblers complete with sun hats, shorts, sticks and red socks in sturdy walking boots – were waiting outside for The Fighting Cock to open.

Chapter 16

Vince Hallett responded immediately to his daughter's call. He collected her and Jack from Cliffend Hospital and drove them back out to Tidal Reach at Ashfield. Lily quickly dressed Jack in summer play clothes whilst Vince made a pot of tea. As soon as Jack was settled with orange juice and a bowl of cereal for his proper breakfast – he'd had a snack earlier at the hospital – Vince assured her he could look after his grandson for a while.

Lily first tackled the mess in the bathroom. There was blood on the floor and corner of the bath, along with vomit around the toilet. With the cleaning completed, Lily turned her attention to herself.

Although she could not be described as vain, she was always careful with her appearance. She was naturally neat, but had dressed in a hurry this morning whilst the paramedics helped Duncan. She could have a shower and take her time now – not too long, though, because she had been told she could return to see Duncan after lunch, which she presumed meant about two o'clock.

When Lily was ready, she took a small hold-all bag from the top shelf of the wardrobe and packed a few things for Duncan's stay in hospital: sleeping shorts and a light dressing gown.

She went through to the bathroom again to collect his toiletries. She accidentally dropped the razor on the floor and, whilst picking this up, she saw there was still a blood mark under the corner of the bath.

It was just too much. Lily started to cry, suddenly unable to contain her fear and frustration. She felt guilty too. She wanted to create a nice home for her husband

and son. But she did not work at the moment and therefore did not contribute to the family income. She intended to look for a part-time job when Jack started nursery school next year, but that would depend upon her circumstances: she was hoping there soon might be a little brother or sister for Jack. Anyway, she did not see the point of paying for a child-minder just so she could earn the money to cover their fees. Besides which, she felt she already had an important job – looking after Duncan and Jack.

Duncan agreed with her on this matter and so did her parents. But she always felt Henry and Rosalie thought she was lazy.

'Lily?' she heard her father call as he walked quietly up the stairs.

'I'm okay, Dad,' she replied from the bathroom as she dabbed at her eyes with a tissue, realising she would have to re-apply her make-up. 'I was just collecting Duncan's shaving gear when I saw that I hadn't cleaned up properly.' Then she cried again.

Vince was quickly at his daughter's side. He encouraged her into his embrace and held her while she wept. He remembered all the times through the long years of her short life when he had comforted her.

Irene and Vince both loved Duncan and had supported the couple during their friendship from a young age. They knew Duncan treated Lily very well. But he knew the in-laws – the legendary Sticklebacks – caused them nightmares. When Henry and Rosalie went on the rampage, someone always ended up hurt. And it was usually Duncan, Sarah having wisely – in their opinion – escaped years ago.

Eventually, his daughter said, 'I'm fine really, Dad. It was just seeing Duncan so ill and … when he collapsed in here ...' She pressed her face into her father's chest again.

'Don't worry, love. It'll be okay, honestly. I do understand, you know I do. I sobbed like a baby when your mother had her hysterectomy – I felt so helpless.'

Lily smiled at the memory. It happened only a few weeks before Jack was born and, yes, he had wept. His tears flowed again when he held his grandson for the first time.

'Where's Jack?' Lily suddenly asked.

'He's okay. I put the television on for him when he finished eating. Listen.' They both remained very still and, drifting up from the lounge, they could hear Jack singing along to one of his favourite cartoons.

'I'd better go and see what he's up to,' Vince said as he gave his daughter a light squeeze. Walking back downstairs, Vince had to admit to himself that he still found it hard to realise Lily was a grown-up, married woman with a baby of her own. Even so, he knew she still needed him, her Dad. Trying not to interfere was the hardest thing he had to do.

Chapter 17

Three different doctors, including Dr Kittson, had seen Duncan since his admission on Friday morning. They all agreed with the initial diagnosis: in layman's terms, Duncan was suffering from a form of nervous exhaustion. They were also worried by his continuing low blood pressure.

Duncan was moved on Friday afternoon to a side room just off one of the main wards. It was thought he could be monitored more easily there without disturbing other patients. He was anxious when Lily and Jack arrived but told her he just felt tired.

'I'm sure I'll feel better tomorrow after I've had a good rest,' he assured her.

However, Duncan could not sleep that night. The cut to his head hurt, although he did not mention this to anyone. He also missed Lily and Jack; he wanted to go home – the hospital felt stark and alien.

During Saturday morning, Duncan was wheeled into a bay of six beds in a main ward. Mr Millston, his neighbour on his right, introduced himself as soon as the porter had applied the safety brake and left. The bed on his other side, nearest the window, was empty and only one of the three opposite was occupied.

After a quick chat with Mr Millston, Duncan began to take an interest in the comings and goings on the ward. He was feeling a lot brighter by lunchtime, even though everyone he spoke to commented on his colourful bruising.

When the senior nurse, Beverley, made her rounds just before visiting time after lunch, she suggested that Duncan might like to get up. He had been sitting in the chair by the bed in his dressing gown for half an hour or so when Lily and Jack arrived.

Jack sat on Duncan's lap and was very interested in his Dad's wound, demanding several times if it hurt when he prodded it with his finger. Duncan quickly distracted him by asking him to describe the game he had been playing on Grandpa Vince's computer.

After a while, Lily noticed that Duncan looked very tired. She lifted Jack from his lap and held him firmly on her own. But Jack soon began to wriggle; he wanted to explore.

'You can't just run around in here like you do at home,' she tried to reason with him. 'People are not well, they want peace and quiet.'

'We could go down to the restaurant and have a cup of tea,' Duncan suggested.

'Is that okay?' Lily asked.

'I think so. The chap in the corner bed opposite went out with his wife a little while ago and I think that's where they said they were going. Just check with the nurse, but I'm sure it'll be okay.'

Lily set Jack on his feet, took his hand and walked with him across to the nurses' station just outside the bay. She returned a few minutes later, smiling.

'She said yes, as long as we're not gone more than half an hour. Apparently they want to do their checks again soon, but they'll wait until you're settled after you get back.'

Duncan stood up carefully and, when he was steady, he reached down for Jack's other hand. He felt a little dizzy but tried to ignore it. He remembered walking towards the nurses' station, then someone – no, several people – were calling his name.

He was back in bed when he came round again.

'What happened?' he asked Lily, who was sitting in the chair he had recently occupied.

'You passed out again, so the nurses brought you back here. They've put out a call for your doctor,' she explained.

'Where's Jack?' He couldn't see his son and panicked for a moment.

'He's just persuaded a nice hospital volunteer to take him to the swings in the kiddies' garden outside.' Lily held Duncan's hand. 'They said I could stay until the doctor sees you, then you'll need to rest.'

She leant forward and touched his forehead with the back of her fingers, carefully avoiding the cut and bruising. 'Oh Duncan, I'm so worried about you.'

'It's okay, love. I'm sure it's just exhaustion. Maybe I'm sick of Mum and Dad!' He smiled at his attempt at a joke. But Lily's face remained serious.

'Something's got to change, you know that, don't you?' she said. She realised it was not fair to talk about this now, but she thought Duncan would find it easier to start severing ties when he came home from hospital if he slowly grew used to the idea. He was hardworking, clever and honest; she was confident he would find another part-time job to supplement the septic tank emptying business if he needed to. Maybe they could even move away – not too far, possibly just to Cliffend, nearer her parents. He could train for a completely different career.

Duncan nodded a silent acknowledgement. His eyelids began to close and he drifted into sleep.

He was still dozing when Dr Kittson arrived at his bedside. The doctor greeted Lily quietly then consulted Duncan's notes at the end of the bed before moving to the patient's side.

'Mr Stickleback? Duncan? How are you feeling now?' Dr Kittson examined the wound on Duncan's temple. His touch more than the questions caused Duncan to open his eyes.

He looked at Dr Kittson and slowly replied,

'Sleepy. Light-headed.'

'Okay, let me just listen to your heart for a moment,' the doctor said as he bent over the bed and positioned the stethoscope ear-pieces. He pressed the cold metal disc onto Duncan's chest and frowned as he listened.

'There seems to be a bit of an irregularity,' he eventually said. 'We'll keep an eye on it for a while. Maybe I'll arrange for some tests to be done on Monday. Meanwhile, just rest and stay as calm as you can. I'll check on you later.'

'Will it be okay to visit again this evening?' Lily asked. 'I think his mother was hoping to come as well.'

Dr Kittson noticed Duncan's look of alarm.

'No, just you today, Mrs Stickleback. It might even be best to find a babysitter for your son. Duncan needs complete rest. Maybe other members of your family could pop in tomorrow, but they mustn't stay for too long at a time.' Dr Kittson then left.

'I'm so sorry about this,' said Duncan.

'Why? It isn't your fault. You can't help being ill,' Lily replied glumly.

Chapter 18

Tina Tillinger's six months at Cordnell Post Office was at an end. The audit had been arranged to take place on the Friday evening after close of business. The new manager, who lived in the town, was due to start on Monday. Tina was living in a flat near the post office and had given notice to the landlord that she would vacate after the weekend.

Although she hadn't made any close friends in Cordnell, she had become acquainted with many people, mainly through work. She was a little sad to leave.

Mr Arthur Dentforth, Tina's area manager, visited Cordnell's post office a couple of weeks before her contract terminated. He stated that they did not have another placement for her immediately. She delayed searching for somewhere to move to because she thought she might contact George and go to see him for a while – wherever he was at the moment. However, two days ago, Dentforth called in again and asked if she would be willing to re-locate further afield. Tina nodded, leaning away to avoid inhaling his halitosis.

'A vacancy has just arisen,' he explained. 'The postmaster died!' Dentforth seemed to think this was amazing news instead of appreciating the devastation it would mean for the family involved. 'And the post office there is integrated with an At Hand shop – you know the ones, don't you? All glitz, no knickers, but keen as hell on saving the pennies.'

'Yes, I know them,' Tina replied, thinking she was not so much of a snob that she didn't have to use discount outlets. She also wondered why he'd made reference to underwear: the occasion did not warrant it.

Tina first met Dentforth several years ago. Her immediate instinct then had been not to trust him. Along with his very bad breath, he was middle-aged, overweight and red-faced with a permanent damp sheen to his skin. His close proximity made her uncomfortable. Whenever he talked to her, his eyes strayed from her face to her bust and then to her lower body and legs. She did not like that and, if she knew they were to meet, she wore clothes that showed as little of her flesh and shape as possible.

'Well, in order to reopen the shop and comply with the contract, Poskett's solicitor – er, a Mr Andrew Brideman of Banthrop, Brideman and Birch in Cliffend – had to go to court for legal powers to handle the old boy's business affairs.' When Mr Dentforth saw Tina frown, he placed a friendly hand on her forearm.

'I'm dealing with all the red tape,' he reassured her.

Tina tried not to wince as felt his clammy palms through her sleeve. Surreptitiously, she stepped backwards. But he leant towards her, almost closing the gap she'd made between them.

'All you have to do is reopen the shop and post office as soon as possible – the regional At Hand franchise manager is keen for it to be up and running again as soon as possible – so much so that he's ordered a complete refurbishment and re-stock. There's accommodation available.'

Tina's frown deepened; she was desperate to move further away from Dentforth.

'If you make your way over on the Monday when my new man takes over here,' he continued. 'Someone will meet you, show you around and sort out what's what with Poskett's place. Of course, if I can get there,

I'll do it myself. As I said, the solicitor is involved, so we are perfectly legal and entitled to reopen, if we can find the right person to do so. And that's why I thought of you.'

Tina extricated her arm from his hand before replying, 'I don't think you said where I had to go, did you?'

'Oh, didn't I? I thought I did. It's PepperAsh – funny place over on the east coast near Cliffend. There's two small villages really, Pepper Hill and Ashfield with about a mile of road through farmland and the like between them. The post office is in the first village. Do you know it?'

Tina closed her eyes and looked downwards in despair. The question sounded casual but she knew Dentforth would be aware she hailed from that area.

'Yes, oh yes.' She looked up, trying to smile as she replied. 'I know it very well. In fact ...' But she decided against further explanation. 'Yes, that will be okay.' Yet the voice in her head screamed, *No, it will NOT be okay.*

It was a trap, a game. But Tina did not know why Dentforth was playing with her.

Thinking about this on the Saturday unsettled her and, despite a brisk wind blowing, she went out for a final walk around Cordnell.

Although not really in the mood to be sociable, Tina found herself drawn to a fête being held on the sports' field behind the High Street. She paid her entrance fee and chatted to the ladies on the gate – former customers of the post office to whom she had bade farewell during the week, but again they wished her good luck for her next assignment.

Mrs Moddson, the epitome of using one's energy and spare time for the good of the community, was manning one of the stalls. She was a busy, bustling lady, a member of Cordnell's various local social groups and chair of the committee that organised the fête. She had even asked Tina last week to display a notice in the post office advertising this event.

Now, Mrs Moddson was rallying interest in naming an enormous, but unfortunately rather ugly, brown velveteen teddy bear. When she saw Tina approaching, she held her flamboyant hat on her head with one hand and thrust forward a clipboard with the other. Clamped to this was a piece of paper ruled into a grid. Each box on the page held a name, some male and some female, plus a few that could be either: Hilary, Taylor, Jude, Sheridan, Bobby and Kim.

'The vicar is keeping a note of the chosen name until the draw at the end of the afternoon,' Mrs Moddson explained, shouting against the breeze as it whipped the nearby canvas awnings and gazebos.

Tina took the clipboard and scanned the suggestions. Nothing seemed to stand out. However, when she re-read the names, her eyes rested on 'Bertha' in a square half way down the piece of paper.

She paused for a few minutes then looked up at the hapless teddy bear sitting dejectedly on the stall's bench with a ragged orangey-coloured ribbon fastened around its neck. She glanced through the remaining names. Eventually, she returned to Bertha.

Tina was in a rather belligerent mood, standing with the wind buffeting her face. She held the pen over 'Bertha' and, on impulse, scribbled underneath the surname 'Bunfighter'. She then wrote her details in the square.

'But I'm leaving Cordnell on Monday,' she reminded Mrs Moddson.

After a short while a summer shower fell and Tina walked swiftly off the sports' field, along the High Street and into a small café she had recently enjoyed frequenting. She treated herself to a latte and a large slice of lemon cheesecake before returning to her flat. Despite the furniture and fittings still being in place, it echoed with the sad emptiness of a departing tenant.

Tina felt very much alone. She missed George, and now the opportunity for her to visit him had escaped her. She brightened a little, however, when she realised she would have to contact him to let him know her new address; she even hoped her proximity to his family might entice a reply, maybe a meeting.

Chapter 19

The following day, Sunday, Tina packed most of her belongings then cleaned and tidied the flat. Her meals consisted of whatever cans and packets were left over in the cupboards. She sluiced these down with the remains of a carton of orange juice, which just needed the dregs of the vodka bottle to make the entire vitamin-enriched experience more palatable.

In the evening, with only her overnight essentials left to cram into her luggage, she opened her laptop and read the information Mr Dentforth had emailed to her about her new place of work.

The unique circumstances at PepperAsh's post office, *i.e.* Mr Dentforth had elucidated unnecessarily, *Poskett's untimely death*, meant that the accounts could not be authenticated, but Tina would commence trading with a temporary licence. However, because new rules had recently been imposed regarding cash security, she would need to have additional training. As it happened, a course had been organised to take place in September at the Perrona Dawn leisure complex in Fenstone, just up the coast from Cliffend. 'It is a regular venue,' he assured her.

Tina was unimpressed. This was all fairly standard work practice. She had undertaken the process twice recently anyway, with the exception of the training course. At the end of the email, her smarmy area manager suggested a few websites with information about the district which included PepperAsh, the two coastal towns of Fenstone and Cliffend, and the city of Mattingburgh, along with many more places of interest. 'In case you need to refresh your memory,' he concluded sarcastically.

Tina snorted. Despite this, she opened each recommended website in turn but learnt little she didn't already know. At least the final article gave a good description of PepperAsh:

Present day facilities include a public house in Ashfield called The Fighting Cock, a post office and shop in Pepper Hill, with the church, dedicated to St Jude, situated midway between the two communities.

It concluded with wistful nostalgia of the time when the hamlets boasted their own school and police house (Tina wasn't sure whether it was favourable for people to read that such small communities needed the law to be enforced quite so locally. But then she remembered the warring Stickleback family, of which she was actually a part!). And, at times, there had been an off-licence and dairy, as well as a cobblers and bakers. The remainder of the text described the nearby coastal town of Cliffend.

Switching off her computer, Tina's mind swirled with a mixture of dread and anticipation. She reached for an unopened bottle of white wine.

Chapter 20

Tina woke on Monday, predictably, with a headache. She refused to believe it was a hangover, though. She had only drunk one bottle of wine the previous evening. But, she eventually reminded herself, there was also the vodka earlier to finish up the orange juice.

When Tina bent down in the hallway, the pounding in her head increased, matching her heart beat for beat. She snapped shut the padlock that fastened the two main zip rings on the second of her fully expanded suitcases.

A knock on the door made her groan as she struggled to manoeuvre the case up and wheel it aside. She did not feel like receiving visitors, not even well-wishers: she had already said all her goodbyes. And there were only twenty minutes or so – half an hour at most – before she planned to leave. It was a long drive from Cordnell to PepperAsh; she needed to be in Pepper Hill by two o'clock.

Tina reluctantly opened the front door and was greeted by a large yellow plastic bag advertising a local department store. The bag was held aloft by the exuberant Mrs Moddson.

'Good morning, Tina. I'm glad I caught you.' Mrs Moddson pronounced each word precisely and sharply. Tina winced at the volume, being reminded of bagpipes in that they were designed to carry far across the vast outside but, in her opinion, were too loud for use indoors.

'Hello, Mrs Moddson,' Tina greeted the carrier bag as it was jiffled through the door. Despite being forced to step backwards, she added, 'I'm sorry, but I can't ask you in. I'm about to leave.'

'Oh yes,' Mrs Moddson said as she revealed her face. Her disappointment at not being invited over the threshold was evident in her voice. 'You're moving on, aren't you? Er, where did you say you were off to?'

Tina had deliberately not told anyone; she just wanted to start anew elsewhere. Not that she would particularly be able to do this with all the history awaiting her in PepperAsh.

'It's somewhere over on the east coast. I'll know exactly where at the other end of the journey,' she lied, blatantly. 'I've got the co-ordinates to feed into the satnav!' Before her indomitable visitor could question this, Tina at last asked, 'what on earth is in that bag?'

'It's the teddy bear from my stall at Saturday's fête. You won! The bear's name is 'Bertha'. Well done, Tina, well done indeed! Unfortunately you'd gone by the time all the prizes were given out. So many people disappeared when the rain started. Anyway, as I knew where you lived, I told the vicar I'd drop it in. Obviously I didn't have time yesterday, it being Sunday. So I came this morning. What a wonderful second name to come up with too. 'Bunfighter!' Such a fertile imagination you have. You should write a book!'

'Thank you, Mrs Moddson. I'll give your suggestion some thought,' Tina said with barely disguised sarcasm. 'And thank you for the bear. I'm sure I'll treasure it and, hopefully, find a use for it!'

These were the words Tina's mouth spoke; her brain, however, was less polite. *'Well, thank you, you condescending old battle-axe! D'you think that, at a time like this, I need someone to tell me what I should be doing? And what the …'* Tina stopped her thoughts swearing again *'… am I supposed to do with an over-sized, moth-eaten, ugly*

… ?

As if it could hear Tina's unkind rantings, the large brown teddy bear fell out of the carrier bag. Tina bent down and shook her head as she picked it up. She examined its face, admitting to herself that she did not remember it looking so sad at the fête. Perhaps the bear – good old Bertha Bunfighter – was as happy with her new owner as Tina was to be that person. Feeling chastised, Tina spoke more courteously when she continued.

'Thank you, Mrs Moddson. I'm glad to have won it and I promise I'll look after it. Thank you. But I must be going now. I have a long journey.'

Mrs Moddson backed away, turned and walked down the path. Tina quickly closed the door. She then consulted her wrist watch and found she only had fifteen minutes before she needed to leave.

She loaded her suitcases (two), carry-all linen bags (three), assorted boxes of various sizes (five), plus her shoulder bag and handbag (one each) into the car. The cases and most of the boxes fitted into the boot, the remainder was squeezed onto the back seat, with the shoulder bag – containing, amongst other things, snacks for the journey – placed in the passenger side footwell. There was just the bear left.

Tina gave Bertha a hug, vaguely registering that there seemed to be a lump inside. A closer inspection revealed a short length of repair, roughly stitched and using a brown thread slightly lighter than the body fabric.

Tina wondered if the bear was originally a *growler* but the mechanism broke and mending was unsuccessful. However, as she tried to find a space in her fully loaded vehicle, she decided it must just be where the stuffing had bunched together. Maybe someone had given the bear a swirl in a washing machine before consigning it to the fête – or, as it had ended up with her, to its fate.

Tina finally perched the bear on the front seat: it was too big to fit in anywhere else. She then returned for a final look around the puny one-bedroomed flat which had recently been her home.

With the exception of the box in the kitchen containing empty wine and spirit bottles and a marmalade jar – Tina could not be bothered to visit the recycling centre – plus the large, garishly-yellow plastic bag in which Bertha had arrived earlier, there was nothing left behind. She hoped the landlord would be satisfied that everything was in the same condition as when she signed the lease – ignoring the empties, of course. She finally locked the front door from the outside and pushed the keys through the letter box.

'If I've forgotten anything, it's too late now,' she voiced quietly.

Tina climbed into the driver's seat, made herself comfortable and strapped herself in then slipped her key into the ignition. However, as soon as the electrics engaged, her attention was drawn to the seat belt warning light flashing on the dashboard. She looked over to the passenger seat where Bertha slumped on what seemed an enormous bottom. Her face was still sad.

Tina suddenly wondered how many times Bertha had been a raffle prize or a gift to an ungrateful recipient, or simply just outgrown and discarded; she certainly wasn't new and had probably been passed from pillar to post, as Tina felt she herself had. A peripatetic or temporary post mistress, assigned here and there. But at least she would live onsite in Pepper Hill, which would be much more convenient than the arrangements here in Cordnell. Yes, she and Bertha should be quite happy together.

But it seemed poor old Bertha was so obese that she engaged the seatbelt warning light. Tina frowned and lifted the toy. She thought maybe it was a bit heavy but could not really believe it would cause the car to think (*wait a minute,* Tina's brain raged, *cars don't think!*) that a person was sitting there and needed to wear a seat belt.

Then she saw her handbag underneath. She decided to leave it hidden and, with amusement, strapped Bertha in on top. At least this cancelled the light on the dashboard.

Tina didn't like driving long distances, but today it was an evil necessity. Most of her journey from Cordnell to PepperAsh was due north-east. Luckily, the June sun was high in the sky and too far round to the south to shine straight into the windscreen. However, for some of the way, the sunlight flickered through the heavily-leaved trees in the hedgerows and made Tina's headache worse.

Two hours later, just before two o'clock, she arrived at her destination: the At Hand shop and post office, in the hamlet of Pepper Hill.

'Well, here we are!' Tina proclaimed to Bertha Bunfighter, who had been sitting silently, watching the road in front being swallowed by the car bonnet. The bear remained staring ahead even when they stopped.

'Huh! You're no help,' muttered Tina, feeling hungry but slightly sick and very grumpy. Mr Dentforth said someone – and she hoped it wasn't him – would be here to meet her.

There was nobody in sight.

Chapter 21

As a result of an early morning dental appointment, Paul James, known as Postman Jim the Second, had re-arranged his route. Today, Monday, residents of Pepper Hill and Ashfield would not receive their mail until after lunch. Just before one o'clock, Henry Stickleback was in the bar of The Fighting Cock public house in Ashfield, serving Reverend Quintin Boyce.

Quinny liked a pint of beer. He could relax in the pub and forget about the elastic bands he habitually wore around his wrist; the reasons he needed to ping them against his skin usually retreated in the noisy, company-filled lounge-bar. He tried not to stay too long, always stating that he had somewhere to go or someone to see, which was outwardly believable because, after all, he was the rector. But, as he didn't have a vehicle – and indeed, couldn't drive – he was dependent on lifts and therefore needed to be sociable.

He liked talking to Henry, mainly because he enjoyed gossip – well, hearing it anyway: as rector of the parish, he could not possibly pass on any information!

Today, however, he was on official pastoral business: Quinny had called in to enquire after Duncan and to ask whether a visit, either in hospital or at home, would be appropriate. So far, however, he hadn't received a reply: Henry seemed distracted.

The pub's front door was open and Henry was watching for activities at Tidal Reach opposite. He eventually told Quinny that, although Duncan had had some kind of a *turn* on Saturday, he seemed much better when he'd seen him on Sunday.

There was a short silence before Quinny spied the Royal Mail van drawing up outside. 'Here comes your post, Henry,' he announced brightly.

Postman Jim the Second walked into the bar, wearing grey shorts, a red T-shirt and a fluorescent yellow high-visibility waistcoat. The outfit looked too casual to be a uniform, but the vest bore the red Royal Mail logo. The postman, in his early thirties, wore an official name badge on his vest, and underneath he'd added a home printed label proudly stating *Postman Jim the Second*.

Jim greeted the two gentlemen before looking seriously at Henry, who was standing behind the bar. His demeanour changed as he read the name printed on the envelope in his hand. He looked up.

'Are you Mr Henry Stickleback? I know you are, but I have to ask.'

'Yes, I am,' Henry confirmed. 'Why?'

'There's a letter here you need to sign for,' Jim replied as he handed Henry an electronic gadget with the plastic pen-shaped stylus attached. He then indicated to the line on a small rectangular screen for Henry's signature. 'Just where it's marked with a cross – er, no disrespect meant, vicar.'

'Rector,' Quinny corrected him.

'Rector,' the postman repeated. Then he asked, 'What's the difference?'

Quinny sighed. He took a long drink from his glass before reciting, 'rectors used to receive rents from land and property owned by the church within their parishes, but poor old vicars didn't. Now though, no one gets any money because there's no land and no property since the church went and sold it all, and then squandered all the dosh on goodness knows what. Now we all have to live off the generosity of our parishioners – supposedly!'

Whilst Quinny was explaining this, Henry signed the device with a bewildered frown.

Quinny looked over and commented with a smile, 'I reckon they've just about caught up with you after your prang with Rosalie last week.' Turning to the young postman, he added, 'you heard 'bout what him and his ex-missus been up to now?'

Jim sighed and said, 'Yes, vic ... rector – the whole of the Cliffend and Fenstone areas and out as far as Mattingburgh must've heard by now.'

Henry glared thunderously.

'Sorry, sir. None of my business,' he mumbled before turning to Quinny. 'Gotta go.'

Reverend Boyce muttered humorously to himself as the postman retreated. Through the open pub door, he watched him climb into his van, start the engine, drive across the road and park outside Tidal Reach.

'Duncan not back yet?' Quinny asked, indicating to Duncan's cottage. Henry's explanation had been interrupted by the postman. He was now studying the envelope with a scowl – it was white and bore an official frank mark. When Quinny's question registered he looked up.

'No, not yet' he replied. 'Depends on what his doctor has to say. If his blood pressure goes back to normal – even at the lower range of normal – he could come out today.'

He raised his eyes from the envelope and looked straight at Quinny before continuing. 'But, you know how doctors talk. They use a lot of words and phrases they think the likes of us don't understand, probably to make sure we won't ask too many questions that make us look even more stupid than they already think we are!'

Quinny returned Henry's stare. Keeping his eyes on the publican, he picked up his pint and took a long drink. He wasn't actually sure he completely understood Henry's explanation, but it didn't seem worth challenging. For a man of the cloth, Quinny could appear quite slow, but he wasn't stupid, although he didn't like to let too many people in on that secret. He replaced his nearly empty glass on the bar and indicated to the envelope still in Henry's hand.

'Aren't you going to open that?' he enquired.

'Not in front of you,' Henry bellowed indignantly. He walked out of the bar area into his kitchen.

Quinny shrugged and reluctantly admitted that not everyone wanted to share their troubles with the rector. Shame, though!

He finished his drink, struggled off the stool he had been sitting on at the bar and reached over to where the crisp packets were stacked near the till. As he turned to walk out of the pub, he opened the bag and blanched as the aroma of smoky bacon and barbecue sauce hit him. It was one of King's Krisps innovative flavours. Not his favourite, he concluded, but opportunists couldn't always be choosers.

'I saw that!' Henry shouted through.

'You'll be rewarded for your generosity in a future life, my son,' Quinny yelled back, waving the crisp packet. 'In other words, deduct these from your contribution to next Sunday's collection!'

'Anyone would think I was running a bloody charity here,' Henry muttered to himself as he placed the envelope on the kitchen table. He switched on the kettle, made himself a mug of his tea/coffee concoction then sat down. Still listening for customers entering the bar, he picked up the envelope and carefully opened it.

It was an official summons to attend Cliffend Magistrates' Court on Wednesday morning at 10:30 a.m. to answer the charges of (a) driving an unroadworthy vehicle and (b) dangerous driving, both on the occasion quoted.

Upon receipt of this summons, he was advised to enter his plea on the attached portion, complete all the necessary details and confirm that he would attend court on the specified date and time. He then needed to return the slip as soon as possible. He was further advised that he could engage a solicitor if he wished, or he could represent himself.

Henry felt a sudden flood of perspiration flow over him; his hands started to shake. He had never been in trouble with the police before – well, except when he and Rosalie were both rebuked for a public disorder offence. But that was over sixteen years ago, and it hadn't gone on record. If it had, it would have affected his pub licence status. Anyway, the incident hadn't been his fault; it was entirely instigated by Rosalie.

It happened at the PepperAsh Bonfire Night party held at the village hall in Pepper Hill when the twins were nine years old. Henry was in charge of the barbecue. Rosalie bought a baked potatoes and sausages for the three of them. However, a few minutes later she returned. She pushed to the front of the queue and complained that her potato was still hard in the middle, swearing in the process and offending a young mother with her two children awaiting their turn. Henry was surprised as no one else had found fault; he offered to replace it anyway.

He was asking if she would like sausages and onions

with it this time when, without warning, Rosalie threw the spud at him. It hit him squarely on the cheek. The butter (actually, it was cheap supermarket margarine) had melted, smoothing the way for pieces of potato to ooze down his face into his beard, down his chest and onto the ground.

Duncan and Sarah were sitting a short distance away on plastic seating near the village hall. After their mother left them to confront their father, they both decided they needed the toilet and quietly slipped into the hall. When Rosalie glanced over to the chairs, she noticed the twins were missing. A short but nevertheless frantic search came to an abrupt end when Duncan and Sarah re-appeared, but this did not prevent Rosalie and Henry receiving a reprimand from PC Yates about their behaviour.

The incident ruined the evening. That was the first Bonfire Night party organised by Pepper Hill Village Hall Committee, and the last.

Chapter 22

The postman approached the Old Police House. The smell from last Thursday's sludge wagon prang still pervaded the air; he parked a little way along the road to avoid stepping in anything unpleasant. He gathered up the last of the three envelopes from the court, together with the gadget for the signature, walked up to the front door and knocked.

Rosalie answered and signed for her letter, only muttering 'thanks,' as she closed the door. Although she guessed the envelope's contents, she felt dizzy as she opened it. A summons. She was ashamed that her private business had now become so public.

And, of course, it was all Henry's fault! The anger grew inside her again. Why should she and Duncan have to go to court because of Henry's actions? If he'd been in control of the tractor and braked properly, he would not have hit the tanker. If he hadn't kept Duncan so busy at the pub that he was unable to do a simple job for her, none of this would ever have happened.

Rosalie sat down heavily on the chair drawn out from the kitchen table. Her mind instantly flicked from Henry to her son. She hadn't heard from Duncan today and was extremely worried, but she dared not contact Lily in case she was deemed to be interfering. The telephone rang, harshly interrupting her despair.

'Hello, Rosalie here,' she said.

'It's Henry,' came the terse reply.

'What do you want?' she asked brusquely, knowing full well why he was ringing.

'Have you got your summons?'

'Yes, it's just arrived.' She picked up the letter and

read out the details.

'Same here,' he confirmed. 'Except mine is for dangerous driving and for driving an unroadworthy vehicle.'

Ben, Rosalie's elderly chocolate Labrador, suddenly started to cough. He struggled out of his basket by the stove and limped towards the back door.

'Got to go,' Rosalie stated abruptly, seizing the opportunity to end the call. 'Something's wrong with Ben. I'll see you Wednesday.' She replaced the receiver.

'What's the matter, old boy?' she asked Ben as she gently urged him outside.

In the back garden, Ben stood with his head hanging down. His normally ever-wagging tail was tucked under his tum and he struggled to gulp back the rising bile. Eventually, he flopped down and lay in the shade on the lawn.

'What's wrong?' Rosalie asked as she crouched in front of him, holding his face in her hands and taking comfort from his familiar feel and smell.

Ben looked at her with glazed pupils. Rosalie knew he had cataracts, but he was too old for an operation. His tongue lolled out of the side of his mouth and his breathing was laboured.

She knelt and gently coaxed him for a while. Feeling the damp grass through her knees she realised that, although it was June, the cold ground was probably not doing Ben any good.

'Come on, let's get you back indoors,' she said as she tried to encourage him up.

Eventually he managed to sit. He rested for a moment, looking at her with a helpless expression.

'Stay there,' she commanded softly. She rushed indoors and quickly returned with a handful of his favourite biscuits.

'Come on, Ben. Have a treat.' She held out a whole digestive to him (human food was always more appealing than canine). But he could not get up to reach it. She gave it to him anyway. He dropped it on the grass in front of him and just looked unseeingly at her.

Sadly, Rosalie acknowledged that he must indeed be ill if he was not interested in food. Tears trickled from her eyes. Although she knew Ben was old for his breed, she dreaded losing him. Aided and abetted by Henry, Duncan and Sarah had bought him for her as a birthday present. They really wanted a puppy for themselves; being in their early teens at the time, they considered they were responsible enough to care for a pet.

This had been a very clever ruse, one which Rosalie had colluded with. She had said 'no' for so long to their request for a dog that eventually she could not work out how to say 'yes'.

Rosalie returned indoors and went to the cupboard in the hall. She retrieved a plastic-backed picnic blanket, which had not been used for many years. The backing was cracked but she thought it might stop Ben feeling the damp from the earth.

She took this outside and spread it on the grass next to him. He was lying down on his front with his grey chin resting between his paws. The biscuit had vanished and he looked a little better.

Rosalie encouraged Ben onto the blanket next to her and they sat there until the sun moved the shadow of the Old Police House around and shone warmly down on them. She then stood up.

Ben watched her but did not try to move. She brought out a bowl of fresh water, but he would not drink. Satisfied that he was as comfortable as she could

make him, and it was not too hot for him, she left him
to rest.

Around mid-afternoon, Rosalie was in the house
when the telephone rang again. As she stood up, she
looked through the kitchen window out onto the lawn
where Ben was still lying.

'Hello, Rosalie here,' she said absent-mindedly into
the phone.

'Hi, Mum.' It was Duncan.

Rosalie felt her mood immediately lighten and a
smile came to her face.

'Duncan, lovely to hear you. How are you? I was
coming to see you later. Will you be at home or still in
hospital?' The worry about Ben had pushed aside her
concern for her son, and now she felt guilty. She had, in
the past, often accused her brother, George, of
compartmentalising his life – totally forgetting one
aspect whilst he dealt with another. Maybe she did a
little of that herself.

'I'm staying in for another couple of days. The only
thing that seems to be wrong is my blood pressure,
which is still low and they can't find the reason.
Tomorrow I have to go for some tests on my heart.'

'Oh, my goodness. That's sounds ...'

'Don't worry, Mum. I'm okay, or I will be. I just
thought I'd better let you know.'

'Thanks,' Rosalie said. 'Have you told your father
yet?'

'Lily said she'd call in to see him when she goes back
home to collect a few things. She and Jack are still at her
Mum and Dad's – it's closer to the hospital. Anyway,
has anything been happening since I've been away?'

Rosalie suddenly remembered the summons.

'Well, yes, as a matter of fact there is some news, but

it isn't good.' She thought she wouldn't mention Ben's deterioration.

'Oh, well you'd better tell me anyway.' Although he was pretending to be cheerful, he was really very worried.

'Your father and I have both received a summons to appear at Cliffend Magistrates' Court on Wednesday morning.'

'Oh no! Do I have to go?' Duncan asked anxiously.

'Yes, I think you probably do. I had to sign for my summons but, if there was nobody in at Tidal Reach when the postman called, he wouldn't've been able to deliver yours. I'll contact the court and explain the situation. You obviously can't be there if you're not well.'

'They might let me out of hospital tomorrow.'

'Even so, that would be too soon for you to be in court. No one would expect you to go if you're ill,' Rosalie said, hoping this was true. 'There's a telephone number here on the letter to ring if there are any queries. I'll get in touch then let you know. I'm sure they'll postpone the hearing if you're still in hospital. None of it was your fault anyway. Henry and I are to blame – well, your Dad is ...'

'Please don't argue with him again. I don't think I can stand any more. You just make things worse all the time,' Duncan pleaded.

Rosalie heard the desperation in his voice.

'No, son. I promise we won't argue,' she said quietly. 'Now get some rest and I'll try to sort things out. I'll be in to see you this evening.'

'Okay. Thanks, Mum.'

When the call ended, Rosalie heard the familiar sound of Ben's paws at the back door.

'Ben, come on in,' she said as she bent down towards him, pleased that he was up again. His back legs were obviously painful to move and he was panting hard. But he walked to her and received a biscuit in reward. She played with him for a few moments, stroking his head and rubbing his poor back. He then turned and plodded over to his basket. He groaned loudly as he lay down. He rested his chin on the edge and watched Rosalie bring in the blanket and water bowl from outside. He drifted off to sleep as she made the telephone call to the magistrates' court.

Chapter 23

Lily arrived at The Fighting Cock public house in Ashfield immediately after Rosalie had spoken to the court officer then relayed the information to Henry. She sat on a stool on the other side of the bar as Henry updated her. There were no customers as yet and Polly was busy polishing the tables.

'They told Rosalie that they'll accept a written plea from Duncan, but she and I will have to appear as summonsed. I'll sort out a solicitor then I'll go and see Duncan as soon as I can. Would you like a drink, Lily, a fruit juice or a coffee or tea?'

'I wouldn't mind a vodka and tonic, but I'd better settle for a coffee,' Lily replied. She smiled at her father-in-law, although she wasn't really feeling benevolent towards him. He caused so much chaos but she couldn't help liking him.

'Coffee it is then. Come on into the kitchen.' He indicated to the open door before calling across the bar, 'I'll just be through the back, Polly.'

'Right you are,' Polly replied.

'Sit yourself down. Where's young Jack, by the way?'

'He's with Dad – he asked if he could go to the airfield and have a look at the planes. Then he whispered, thinking I couldn't hear him, asking if he could go for a flight – well, he said ride but, there you are, I knew what he meant. Can you believe him? I keep saying he's too young to go up in a plane, but I wouldn't be surprised if Dad does take him one day.' She shook her head then held her brow. 'But I don't even want to think about that. I've got enough on my mind. I feel I've been chasing back and forth to the hospital, over to here and home to my parents ...' She stopped when she realised what she'd said.

'I know, love,' Henry said. 'Don't worry, I realise Tidal Reach doesn't feel much like home for you. When Duncan was taken into hospital last Friday, I thought it was just while he was away. But it isn't; it's because you're too near the quarrelling here, isn't it?'

Lily hung her head. 'Yes,' she replied.

'Listen, I'm so sorry about the effect his mother and I have on you and Duncan. We just can't seem to stop ourselves. It's even at the point where I'll stay away from the hospital this evening because Rosalie is visiting!'

Henry filled the kettle, switched it on and reached into the cupboard above for a bone china cup and saucer. He spooned in the normal amount of coffee for Lily and measured out his own into his large cockerel-decorated mug. He then added the tea bag and sugar. Lily watched, fascinated.

'What brought about all this fighting?' she enquired casually. It was a question she had been longing to ask for years; after all, she and Duncan began their friendship when they were both still at school. Gossip and rumours abounded even then.

The kettle boiled, the drinks were made and Henry poured a tot of milk from the carton in the fridge into a white jug. He placed it and Lily's coffee on the table in front of her, poured his own milk straight from the carton into his mug and stirred it with a dessert spoon. He then sat down opposite Lily.

'Rosalie and I went to the same school, but I was a few years ahead of her – a bit like you and Duncan,' he explained. 'I'd left and was working here when it all happened. We were having the pub renovated; Mum had just bought it from the brewery. Dad was an alcoholic, I expect you've heard the rumours. Annie and Derek, that's Rosalie and George's Mum and Dad, had taken a short holiday.'

'Yes, Duncan told me. Well, gave me a brief outline. They'd hired a boat for a week's holiday from Perrona Dawn. Isn't that the same company Sarah works for?'

'Yes. Well, it's a different branch. Sarah works in Fenstone, has done for nearly ten years now. Anyway, it looked like Derek and Annie settled down for the evening at Ashfield Staithe. It was chilly and the coroner thought they must've switched on the gas heating without checking the flue was clear. They were found dead the following afternoon – someone noticed there hadn't been any movement from their boat all day and took a look.'

'Carbon monoxide poisoning, wasn't it?' Lily enquired.

Henry nodded.

'Yes. Rosalie was sixteen and about to start her exams at school. George, her brother, was a couple of years younger. My mother was staying overnight at the Old Police House while Derek and Annie were away, and I was here at the pub with Dad. But he broke into the stock room and, well, drank himself to death. Mum was dealing with all that when news came through that Rosalie's parents were dead as well.'

'Gosh. When you explain it like that – all happening on the same day – it sounds incredible.'

'I think we were in shock, we just couldn't believe it. It was so sudden – well, maybe not with my Dad. He'd been warned by the doctors that another binge could be fatal, but he didn't seem to care. Anyway, we got through. Mum helped to look after Rosalie and George.

They spent most of their time living here so that's really how Rosalie and I got together.' Henry stopped speaking and sipped from his mug.

'Yes, but what made you and Rosalie break up? Duncan doesn't like to talk about it, even when I ask.'

'I don't think Duncan actually knows – or Sarah, come to that. Rosalie won't discuss it, although I believe she told George – and well, he keeps himself to himself. Have you met George?' Henry was deliberately avoiding the question: to say out loud the reason why he and Rosalie split up would make it sound ridiculous.

'No. Him and Tina, isn't it? They couldn't get to our wedding.' Lily seemed to forget her question.

'They're a strange couple,' Henry stated, shaking his head. 'Even when they lived around here, we didn't see much of them. They moved to a place called Treemoore, then George's job took him to Aberdeen but Tina stayed where she was – worked for the post office then. I presume she still does, but I think she's moved on as well now.'

Silence descended as each pursued their own thoughts.

'Duncan shouldn't have to go to court,' Lily said suddenly.

'No, I know. It should only be his mother and me in the dock.'

Lily paused to drink some of her coffee.

'Do they have a dock at the magistrates'?' she asked with a faint smile.

Henry furrowed his forehead. 'Not as such,' he said. 'At least not when I've been in for a licence extension or renewal. But I'll tell you Wednesday afternoon what the set-up is now – if I'm allowed to come home afterwards, that is.'

Chapter 24

Tina waited in a lay-by in front of the post office and shop, a pull-in that had been purpose-built for customers' cars. There was also a driveway space adjacent the actual building which led to a garage. A path squeezed between them through to the rear.

In order to stretch some of the journey's stiffness from her limbs, Tina got out of her car to have a look around. It was not an inviting sight; the large front windows were shuttered and the double entrance doors locked. She read a hand-written sign stating that the shop and post office were closed until further notice. She reached for the door handle anyway, but it would not open.

As Tina explored a little further, she became aware of a strange and unpleasant odour. It seemed to emanate from across the road – near the Old Police House, a place she was not keen to visit, it being the home of her erstwhile sister-in-law, Rosalie Stickleback.

That property, Tina understood, was sold off by the county constabulary in the late 1970s, when the village bobby retired and was not replaced. It was purchased by Derek and Annie Tillinger, her late mother- and father-in-law, and was the childhood home of her husband, George, and his older sister.

Rosalie moved back there immediately after her wedding day. George never divulged the reason Rosalie and Henry parted after just one night of married life, but it was obvious to Tina that he knew.

When Tina became involved with and then married George, she never felt welcomed into his family. They seemed to argue and disagree between themselves but, if anyone else became embroiled, they immediately banded together against them. George accused her of not trying to get along. In truth, she had been quite glad to move away to Treemoore to be free of them.

As she stood in the open air, she was suddenly unsure if taking on this assignment had been a good idea. She did not want to be drawn into George's family arguments; she had enough problems of her own.

Tina walked back to the post office and tried the door again. Still it would not open. She returned to her car to update Bertha.

As she sat there, several vehicles travelled along the road through Pepper Hill in quick succession. There was a lengthy lull before another car appeared, others then followed leisurely. A lorry thundered across her vision, pursued by a pair of cyclists, clad in tight black and orange Lycra. Tina was reminded of the chap in the queue at the Treemoore's chip shop the evening she'd damaged George's car windscreen. Finally, a tractor pulling a trailer fully loaded with big round hay bales puffed its way past.

She sighed at the excitement of country life. Then, deciding she was hungry, she retrieved from her shoulder bag the plastic carton containing the cheese and pickle sandwiches purchased from the garage where she'd stopped to buy petrol earlier. She found herself offering the open packet to Bertha, who was still strapped into the front seat. Tina blushed as she realised how foolishly she was behaving.

Suddenly, she felt very lonely and wondered if she should ignore her pride and go across to the Old Police House. But she did not know Rosalie's stance on her and George's separation.

George. She wished George were here with her now.

She missed him dreadfully.

Tina believed George was in another relationship – why else would he not have contacted her more regularly since she left Treemoore? Maybe he didn't want to make an effort to save their marriage. She was convinced he might not have sought solace elsewhere if she hadn't been so bitter towards him when he was at home. Or maybe he simply disliked her drinking as much as she did.

Tina never enquired too deeply about George's job as an engineer; he had always been a little vague about the details, inferring she would not understand even if he explained. Tina was reminded of his attitude concerning the bricks in the garage.

She placed the empty sandwich packaging on the passenger's side floor, vowing she would clear it up later after unloading the car. As she continued to wait, Tina realised she was thirsty. She drank deeply from the bottle of water she'd also bought earlier.

Soon she needed the loo!

Tina told Bertha to wait there, wagging her index finger to emphasise the order. Leaving her handbag still wedged under the giant bear, she tentatively climbed out again and locked the door. *Can't be too careful,* she thought. *Bertha may be called* Bunfighter, *but that doesn't necessarily mean she has combat skills.*

Tina approached the front of the shop and post office again and wondered if Mr Dentforth had purposely forgotten about the arrangement for her to be met. It was ten minutes to three.

Despite her relief that Arthur Dentforth was not there in person – she did not relish the thought of him showing her around with no one else present – she knew someone should be here. Now wondering if they might already be inside, she tried to peer into the building through tiny cracks in the shutters. She could see nothing.

She walked along the path to the rear door and tapped gently, almost fearing to disturb anyone. There was no reply to her knock. She tried again, a little louder this time. After the echo inside died, silence returned.

The window next to the door looked as if the lower pane had recently been replaced; it was brighter and cleaner than the other. Tina looked through it. Directly opposite she saw an armchair and a table to one side with dining chairs tucked underneath. Further along were the cooker, worktops and cupboards, and all the other kitchen paraphernalia, with the sink and drainer directly under the window. The rest was not clearly visible to her, but she could just make out a sofa suite at the far end of the room.

Tina cautiously returned to the front, aware suddenly of how loud her heels clattered, even above the background noises of birdsong and traffic. She rattled each of the double front doors, but it was futile.

The sound of a vehicle slowing down on the road as it approached made Tina turn around. A bright red van bearing the Royal Mail insignia stopped in the lay-by in front of the shop, near her own car. The hand-brake was noisily anchored on but the engine continued to run as the young man climbed out of the driver's door.

'Hi,' he called over to Tina. 'The post office's shut. The old boy died a week or so ago and we're waiting for someone to come and take over.'

He was obviously the local postman, in his fluorescent vest and regulation shorts. He produced a set of keys and proceeded to empty the faded red post-box mounted into the wall alongside the building.

'I'm Paul James, by the way, but round here they all call me Jim the Second. Apparently my predecessor was Jim. Not very imaginative, I'm afraid.'

As Tina approached, she could see an ID badge pinned to his fluorescent vest. And, as if to confirm his statement, underneath sat an unofficial card printed with 'Postman Jim the Second'.

'Are you passing through?' he enquired as he retrieved just two envelopes from the box. He checked the addresses, substituted the day tag on the front of the door for tomorrow's from a pile inside the box then re-locked it.

'Tina Tillinger, the temporary post mistress. I've been sent to reopen the place – shop as well as post office,' she explained. 'There was supposed to be someone here to meet me, but no one has shown up yet. I'm not sure what to do.' She looked around and rubbed her hands together.

'Well, I can let you in,' Jim offered. 'I was given a key when Poskett died. It's only supposed to be used in emergencies. There's no money in there so the security alarm is off …'

'It's officially an emergency,' Tina interrupted. 'I want to go to the toilet – desperately!'

'Oh. Okay, I guess that qualifies,' he said, smiling. 'Hang on, I'll just get the key.'

But Tina thought he did not seem to appreciate the urgency as he sauntered over to his van and thrust the letters in the back before walking to the front, opening the passenger door and rummaging in the equivalent of the glove compartment.

'I suppose I should really ask for some kind of proof of identity before I let you in here, just to make sure you are who you say you are,' he added when he returned.

'Oh, I am who I say I am, all right! Why else d'you think I'd be waiting here, like an idiot, outside a closed shop and post office?' Tina snapped. 'Sorry, I'm just a bit fed up. Can you hurry, please?'

'Okay.' Jim laughed, not taking offence. 'Er, I don't know what it's like in there, probably a bit smelly. Nothing's been touched since the place was closed, possibly when Poskett shut up shop the evening before he died,' Jim explained whilst taking an age to select the correct key and undo the first lock. Another key was found and one of the double entrance doors was finally opened.

Tina hurried into the darkened premises, the shutters effectively keeping out the sunshine and rendering the interior dark and impenetrable. She suddenly stopped, holding her nose against the stench. It was different from the pong outside, and it was much worse.

'Right, there's a toilet just through there,' Jim pointed inside, speaking with his nostrils clenched. 'Through the door and under the stairs in the hall.'

Tina followed his directions, suddenly not in such a rush as she thought she was.

Despite the smell, the gloom and dusty neglect, she found the loo, purposely not inspecting it too closely for either cleanliness or home comforts. It was useable, that was all that mattered. When she returned to the shop area, Jim was standing just outside openly breathing the fresh air.

'Not too good, eh? I guess whoever should've met you here will sort it all out, eventually. And you'll definitely have to wait for your area manager to unlock all the post office bits for you.' He indicated behind her.

Tina turned around. In the dim light, she saw the

post office computerised-till installed in a kiosk-like structure next to the shop counter and cash register. The entire unit looked as if it had been lifted into place and bolted down.

'They'll have to feed your password and security code into the system and all that palaver,' Jim continued. 'Sorry to give you bad news.'

Tina was about to reply that she didn't mind, when a mouse ran over her foot.

Chapter 25

Postman Jim offered to take Tina to lunch the following day, saying he would collect her around noon.

'And I'd better leave you the key, hadn't I,' he laughed. 'Just hope I'm not in breach of some regulation or other.'

When he left to continue his rounds, Tina felt a little deflated. She tried to contact Mr Dentforth, but there was no phone signal.

Stepping back into the darkened and putrid atmosphere of the shop, she made her way to the stock room. In one corner was an office area with a computer and telephone extension on a desk. The monitor screen was blank and the telephone handset had been left off its cradle, which would undoubtedly mean it was out of charge. She docked the phone, noting at the same time that the messaging facility had reached capacity. Then she tried to switch on the computer. Nothing happened. After checking all the plugs and leads, she found that the modem was missing.

Tina was furious: without a signal for her mobile phone, she had no connection with the outside world. She wondered how she had allowed herself to be manipulated into this situation. She tried her mobile again. Nothing.

Filching a bottle of energy drink from a nearby shelf, Tina decided to explore. She walked out of the shop and through the internal door into the hall. She ventured up the brown-carpeted staircase where three doors led off a galleried landing. The first opened into a large airing cupboard. The second led to the bathroom – the downstairs toilet was presumably installed to save this Poskett bloke having to climb the stairs every time nature called. The third door was firmly locked and Tina presumed this led to the bedrooms.

Back downstairs again, Tina tried the remaining door in the hall. It was unlocked. She entered cautiously, as if trespassing.

She was in the room she had earlier spied through the repaired window. Her eyes rested on comfortable armchairs and a side table on which sat another telephone unit. She picked this up and held it to her ear, but it wasn't working either.

Looking around, she saw the sofa against the far wall converted into a bed. At least she would have somewhere to sleep tonight, although she did have to swallow down her revulsion at the thought of staying in the same room where someone had recently passed away.

Concluding that she may as well make herself at home, she filled the kettle with water, searched the cupboards and drawers for the necessary ingredients and made herself a cup of coffee.

She could only find powdered milk, although she did discover a blue-coloured bottle of sherry. Taking a deep breath, Tina convinced herself to ignore it.

However, she forgot powdered milk would not cool the drink as fresh milk did and almost scalded herself taking a sip. She pulled out a chair and sat at the table, deciding to unload her car when she had finished her coffee.

The first thing to be installed was her new mate, Bertha Bunfighter. Tina placed the big teddy bear on one of the dining chairs, told her not to wander off and get into any mischief, and then asked her – whilst she sat there not helping in any other way – if she could come up with any ideas how to make this ludicrous situation work.

I'm talking to the bear again, Tina chastised herself. *Give me strength!*

Chapter 26

It was late Monday afternoon when Tina heard a vehicle park in the layby. She walked around the outside of the premises to see a medium-sized plain white van from which emerged three men in green boiler suits with the At Hand shop logos printed across their shoulders.

'Hey, love, are you, er …?' The first of the men consulted an electronic tablet, which he could not seem to make work despite jabbing at it with his finger. His two colleagues came to stand with him, one being considerably taller than the others.

''Ow do,' they greeted Tina.

'What's happening?' Tina enquired askance, looking past them to the van.

'Well, love, you'll probably be delighted to know that we're the At Hand team,' the tallest of the three men explained, pausing for a moment for them all to adopt a position of corporate recognition, with heads tilted and fake smiles displaying almost sparkling teeth.

'My name's Bernie, this 'ere is Fred.' He pointed to the man standing next to him. 'And that's Fido,' he said as he turned towards the chap prodding the tablet.

Tina said a collective, 'hello,' and waited for an explanation.

'We've been assigned to clean out and re-fit the PepperAsh outlet,' Bernie stated, gesturing towards the shuttered shop. 'That's it, isn't it? We're in The Street, Pepper Hill, aren't we?' Tina nodded. 'Well, you'll be pleased to learn that you'll have the pleasure of our company for the next couple of days or so.'

'Stinks a bit round 'ere, don't it?' Fido stated as he

shuffled his feet, sniffing loudly. The first man ignored him.

'Er, you don't seem pleased to see us. Weren't you told? It's Mrs Poskett, isn't it?' he continued, his enthusiasm suddenly waning.

'No.' Tina then explained as much of the story as she was able. Having digested the main facts, the three men decided they had better check with head office. Bernie tried his mobile phone but there was no signal.

'Best just get on with it anyway,' he said decisively.

They made a noisy start on the shop clearance, firstly moving as much of the stock as they could into the store room. Then they started stripping the fittings, piling the debris outside the door and assuring Tina that a skip would arrive in the morning for it all to be loaded into and taken away.

Gentle hints were made as to the possibility of tea. Tina warned them she only had powdered milk. As compensation, however, on her way back with a loaded tray, she took a packet of chocolate digestive biscuits off one of the remaining shelves.

As she returned later to the back room, she confiscated a ready meal from the freezer – luckily all the chiller units were still working. After she'd eaten, Tina sat outside happily chatting, even flirting to some degree, with the workmen until about nine o'clock when the evening clouds finally pushed the daylight out of the sky. The men promised Tina they would return early in the morning and gave orders for tea upon their arrival. She noted that all the biscuits had been eaten.

When they left, Tina secured the entrance to the shop and post office and locked the door through to the hall. She tried to settle in the back room, but there wasn't much homeliness about it.

Tina needed to contact Dentforth to convey her dissatisfaction at the arrangements. She thought perhaps she also ought to let George know where she was. As there was no internet connection for her laptop, the business phone was still not charged and her mobile wouldn't work, she took a pen and notebook from one of her bags and began to list the things she needed to do in the morning – the first being to drive along the road until she found a phone signal.

Later, Tina had a good rummage in the airing cupboard upstairs where she found a duvet and pillow complete with cover sets, all still in their wrappers. Tina was sure Poskett wouldn't mind her using these.

She had a shower then pulled out the sofa bed and made it up. She was surprised to discover it was very comfortable.

As she settled down for the night, Tina could see Bertha Bunfighter sitting sadly on top of one of her boxes in the corner. She relented, crept over and drew the big brown velveteen bear to her. She returned to her bed and snuggled up to Bertha. Before drifting off, she vaguely registered the lump in one of its shoulders and wondered whether the bear would growl if she squeezed it.

Chapter 27

Duncan was left to rest on Sunday. But, from the moment activities started on Monday morning, he was disturbed every hour for his blood pressure to be taken. The lady who brought his breakfast helped him to sit up but this made him extremely dizzy. When he'd finished eating, he managed to slide back down the bed again.

Senior nurse Beverley arrived later. As well as checking his blood pressure, she removed the plaster strips from the wound on his temple.

'That's healing nicely,' she commented as she peeled off her latex gloves. 'The bruising looks very impressive now – all purple and yellow with a tasteful hint of blue.' She smiled before adding, 'anyway, young man, we've got to get you sitting up.'

Duncan tried to explain that his head began to spin if he did not stay flat. In the end he allowed himself to be propped up, more because he was too tired to argue than agreeing with the idea. But he did not last long: within a few minutes, he was lolling over to the side and ringing the bell because he was about to be sick.

The nurse did not arrive in time; his bed had to be completely re-made. Duncan was reluctantly moved onto the chair, his head turning crazy circles as he held grey cardboard bowls in front of him. He filled two. So much for breakfast.

Duncan was mortified when the nurses cleaned him up; luckily, Beverley was not one of them. They changed his shorts and manhandled him back into bed. This time they left him flat, with just one pillow under his head.

He closed his eyes and hoped the feeling of indignation and helplessness would wear off with the sickness. He longed to be at home where Lily could look after him. He knew how tenderly she treated their son; he wanted her to nurture him like that.

Duncan dozed, despite the noise and commotion all around him. Slowly, however, he became aware of movement in the bed next to him.

'Not feeling so good again, son?' his neighbouring patient, Mr Millston, asked. Duncan replied with a slight shake of his head, which he immediately regretted. 'Never mind, here comes our lovely Beverley and her magic machine. She's going to make us all better. Isn't that right, love?' Mr Millston seemed in annoyingly good humour. Yesterday, he told Duncan that he had been admitted last Thursday (*the day of the fateful prang,* Duncan thought) for a routine hernia repair, but there were complications and he was still awaiting the operation.

'It isn't a magic machine, Mr Millston, it only measures blood pressure,' Beverley explained in her *have patience with the patients* voice. 'Right, Duncan, let's take your blood pressure again.'

Duncan lifted his left arm a little way above the sheet covering him. He heard the electronic buzz as he felt the band squeezing tighter and tighter. When he thought he would have to say something to stop it, the pressure was suddenly released.

'It's still a little low,' she stated thoughtfully. 'We'll see how it is again in an hour or so. If it isn't any better, I'll have to speak to Dr Kittson.'

Duncan dosed for a while then, from a seemingly foggy distance, he heard a strange clanging noise as the lunch trolley was wheeled close by. Mr Millston exchanged cheery comments with the ladies delivering the meals.

A tray was placed on Duncan's table, which was then drawn up to his bed. He was still lying down and did not want to move in case the dizziness started again. And he did not trust his stomach to keep down any food, especially after the disaster following breakfast. As he carefully opened his eyes to see the lady retreating, various aromas slowly began to reach him: chicken, gravy and mashed potatoes.

Personally, Duncan thought when he had managed to hide his mind in a place where the smells from outside and the nausea within could not harm him, *I'd rather have chips*. But he had been told, although he could not remember by whom, that chips did not survive the journey from the kitchen to the ward without becoming soggy and unpalatable. Anyway, they were probably not considered a *healthy option* for a hospital menu, he concluded.

Duncan agreed that chips were definitely not good for one's health. He promptly started thinking about them in earnest, his mouth salivating in response. This in turn made him even queasier.

On one occasion, when Duncan and Sarah were young, Rosalie needed to go out but Henry was too busy to help. She reluctantly left them on their own – they were around twelve at the time. Thirteen was the legal age above which youngsters were deemed mature enough to look after themselves. Duncan remembered it was only about six months after Sarah had been rushed into hospital – in fact, this hospital – with suspected appendicitis.

During that particular evening, Sarah decided to cook chips. She switched on the cooker ring under the chip pan to melt the fat, peeled the potatoes, cut them up and placed them into the wire strainer. Something distracted her and she left the kitchen. When she returned, she lowered the chips into the pan. But, because the fat was very hot by then, it spat and flared then flooded down the pan sides and onto the glowing ring.

Sudden screams from the kitchen brought Duncan running through to see Sarah attempting to move the chip pan, which was on fire by then.

Everything happened so quickly. He pushed her aside, dropped the flaming pan back onto the cooker and then flicked off the ring switch. Boiling fat seared the air with acrid smoke and Duncan registered a burning sensation on the top of his wrist. They soaked towels under the taps in the sink and spread them over the top of the flaming chip pan – Sarah fetched more from the airing cupboard when those in the kitchen were used up. Eventually, the hissing flames died, but a trail of black greasy soot covered the wall behind and the ceiling above the cooker. Several towels and cloths were scorched and the stench was overpowering. The air was thick with oily grease and dark swirling smoke.

When Rosalie walked in through the front door, she was met by the smell of burning. Sarah was crying, her face covered with black marks and her clothes soaked with water and grease.

Duncan remembered quickly standing between Sarah and his mother, saying it was his fault because he wanted chips and he'd asked Sarah to make them. He knew his mother didn't believe him, but she didn't contradict him, nor did she argue when they asked to stay with their father at The Fighting Cock for a while.

Although it was a relatively small fire, the Old Police

House needed to be completely re-decorated. All the rooms, both upstairs and down were affected by the smoke. It seeped into all the soft furnishings and other fabrics as well as their clothes. Everything had to be replaced, which considerably increased Rosalie's house insurance premiums for the next few years.

Occasionally even now, Duncan felt an itch from the scar on his wrist caused by the burning fat. But he smiled sometimes, because it reminded him of how happy Sarah had been with all her new outfits, her shoes and bags, trinkets and make-up – everything a young lady needed to impress her school friends.

But even the seriousness of this incident could not stop their parents fighting.

And Duncan still liked chips.

'Didn't you want anything to eat?' Lily's voice startled him.

He struggled to open his eyes.

'Hello, love,' he said as he lifted his head a little way off the pillow and propped himself with his elbows.

Lily was standing by the bed-table, looking at the meal which was now cold, and soggy from condensation under the plastic cover.

'No, I was a bit sick this morning, so I thought I'd better let my stomach settle for a while. Maybe I'll feel like something later.'

'The bruise on your head is showing nicely now,' Lily commented lightly as she bent over to kiss him.

'Is it? The nurse said it looked impressive,' Duncan said. 'I haven't actually seen it, although it does feel sore if I touch it.' He winced a little. 'Where's Jack?' he suddenly asked as he slowly laid back on the pillows, swallowing hard several times as the curtain rail around the top of his bed began to weave and rock in and out of the lines on the ceiling.

'He's with Mum,' she replied. 'She spoils him, so does Dad. They're being so kind at the moment.'

'They're always kind,' Duncan agreed.

Lily sat down and took his hand. She sighed. 'So, what's happening? Has anyone told you when you can come home?'

'No. The nurse said she would speak to Dr Kittson. I suppose I'm just waiting until he comes to see me.'

Dr Kittson, together with the nurse, arrived a few minutes before the end of afternoon visiting.

'How are you now?' the doctor asked as he took the clipboard off the end of Duncan's bed and quickly read the details.

'Dizzy. I keep feeling as if I'm falling, even when I'm lying down,' Duncan answered.

Lily remained sitting in the chair on the opposite side of the bed to where the nurse and doctor were standing. She took Duncan's hand again.

'What's the matter with him?' she asked. She was very worried.

'We're not sure yet, Mrs Stickleback. That's why I want to run a few more tests, starting with your heart, Duncan. I'll just have a listen now.' He stooped, lowered the sheet and placed the stethoscope on Duncan's chest.

After a few moments, he took out the ear-pieces and turned to the nurse. 'Could you arrange for a cardiograph this afternoon, please? And a full blood test.' Then he turned to Duncan. 'No need to worry, I just want a reading of your heartbeat. The blood test should tell me if you're deficient in something that could be causing the dizziness. Is there anything you wish to ask me?'

'He hasn't eaten his lunch,' Lily responded. 'And I don't think he's had a drink for a long while either, definitely not since I've been here.'

'Mr Stickleback was very sick during the morning, Doctor,' the nurse stated. 'Haven't you had anything since then?' she asked Duncan.

'No,' he replied. He felt that they were ganging up against him now. So much for Lily's loyal support!

Dr Kittson looked at his watch then lifted the lid off the lunch plate. A cold, cloudy fug took its time to reach their nostrils but when it did it, made them all turn their heads away.

The doctor smiled. 'Best wait for tea now, I think.' He lowered the plastic cover and stood up. 'But, please do try and drink some water,' he added. 'And have another go at sitting up. Mrs Stickleback, if you would like to stay, I'm sure Duncan would appreciate your company. And, of course, you could see that he eats something later. Is that all right?'

Lily looked at her husband, who suddenly reminded her very much of their precious son, Jack. She replied, 'Yes, if it's okay, I'll stay. But I'll have to just ring my Mum, she's looking after our little boy.'

'Good, that's settled.' Dr Kittson then indicated for nurse Beverley to accompany him, and they walked away from Duncan's bedside.

Lily leant forward and kissed Duncan's cheek.

Duncan was aware that he needed a shave and, despite being washed earlier, he wanted a shower.

Lily felt his skin was cold. His face was pale in contrast to the bright scab and livid bruising.

Duncan smiled as he whispered, 'If you go and ring your Mum now, I think I might need taking to the bathroom when you get back.'

'Now there's a treat to look forward to,' Lily replied as she kissed him again. 'I'll bring a wheelchair with me,' she said as she walked away to make her telephone call.

Chapter 28

Later Monday afternoon, whilst Lily was still there, Beverley, the nurse, wheeled a portable ECG machine to Duncan's bedside. She subsequently spent what felt to Duncan a long time asking him questions, explaining the procedure and just generally being pleasant and reassuring.

Duncan had to sit up while she stuck small, round rubber pads onto his chest near his heart, and a little higher. A couple more were placed on the back of his shoulders, and finally some on his wrists and ankles. These were connected to the machine which obligingly bleeped as an electronic line wiggled pinnacles and troughs across a monitor.

Lily asked the pertinent questions. What was the test for? What would it show? And, as Beverley saved the results electronically to Duncan's medical file, what happens now?

Duncan was too tired to remember much of the information and Lily had been rather quiet after the nurse finished. When Duncan enquired if she was okay, she said she was hungry. She had been staring longingly at the uneaten cheese and tomato sandwiches and carton of red jelly that had been brought for Duncan's tea. As he still couldn't eat, he told her to help herself. But she said no, explaining that her Mum would have a cooked meal waiting for her when she arrived home. Lily left at eight o'clock telling Duncan she would ring first thing in the morning to see if the results from the tests were back.

When Duncan was wheeled back to his bed after a late evening visit to the bathroom, he found Dr Kittson waiting. He looked up from the notes he had been reading.

'Hi, how are you feeling?' he asked.

Duncan stood very unsteadily as the nurse drew the wheelchair away from him. She removed Duncan's dressing gown and helped him back into bed, allowing him to lie down flat and not even attempting to pile extra pillows under his head.

'Dizzy,' Duncan replied. 'My head just goes round and round every time I try to move. I daren't stand up on my own. I feel so stupid and pathetic.' He had to stop speaking in order to swallow against the nausea. He hadn't actually eaten since breakfast time and had only drunk about a glassful of water during the afternoon, despite Lily's encouragement. 'Have you got the results from earlier?' he asked to distract himself.

'Yes,' Dr Kittson replied. 'I came to tell you that I would like a few more tests to be carried out. There is a definite irregularity in your heartbeat, so I think it wise to investigate further. As you know, your blood pressure is low and this is obviously a symptom, not the root of the problem. There are several possible causes and I would like to eliminate these before we look elsewhere. Tomorrow, I want you to have what is commonly known as a bubble test.'

Duncan's forehead creased and he nodded slightly, hoping Dr Kittson would clarify.

'The correct term is a transthoracic echocardiogram. It is a thorough test on your heart. We inject a saline solution into your bloodstream and use a scanner – like your wife would've had when she was expecting your son – to watch as this passes through your heart. The bubbles make it easier to trace the passage of blood.'

'Why would you be doing that?' Duncan asked,

bewildered.

'We think you might have what is known as a "patent foraemen ovale" – better known as a hole in the heart.'

Duncan was shocked. He knew all babies were born with an opening in the dividing wall of their hearts. It had something to do with the fact that, while the foetus is in the womb, their blood is oxygenated from the mother's body, so there is no need for it to flow either to or from their lungs. Jack had been checked when he was born, and again at about three months. The paediatrician had assured them that all was well so they'd had no cause to think about it since.

'This evening might not be the right time for a full explanation but, to set your mind at rest, put simply the "foramen ovale" part of the term refers to the actual opening between the top two atria – sorry, chambers of your heart. This should have closed naturally soon after birth. But, for some reason, it didn't. It isn't unusual for it not to close completely. About five percent of the population has a hole in the heart – well, somewhere between three and eight per cent, depending on which literature you read. The condition doesn't seem to unduly affect most of these people, but it can leave some vulnerable to certain types of stroke later in life.

'The word "patent" in this context means to allow a free passage. In effect, the term "patent foramen ovale" means that there is a significant opening between the two upper chambers in a heart that allows the unoxygenated blood coming into the first chamber to flow straight through to the second without going to the lungs to be relieved of the carbon dioxide, or to be re-oxygenated.'

'I see,' said Duncan. But Dr Kittson knew he did not.

He stretched his arm forward and placed his hand reassuringly on his patient's shoulder.

'Don't worry about it tonight,' he stated. 'I'll come and see you tomorrow and we'll go through the whole thing again.' The doctor stood up and started to walk away when Duncan spoke.

'I should be in court the day after tomorrow. I received a magistrates' summons for an accident my Mum and Dad had with my tractors and slurry tanker. I entered a guilty plea, but I'm not sure what else I should be doing.'

Dr Kittson returned to Duncan's side. 'Your mother contacted me earlier about that and I've already written a letter to the court stating you are too ill to attend. She said she would deliver it straight to them. You mustn't worry about that, or about the tests. You are my patient and, while you're under my care, you will rest and forget about the outside world and all its problems. Is that understood?'

Dr Kittson's voice suddenly sounded rather harsh, even to his own ears. He was extremely tired after working a very long shift, but he knew this should not affect his professionalism. He smiled at the young man in the bed before him.

'We'll sort you out first. And then, when you're better, you can sort them out! Is that a deal?'

'Yes,' Duncan replied rather weakly. 'Okay. Thank you.'

'Fine, I'll leave you to sleep now.'

Chapter 29

Monday evening, Rosalie went to bed after watching the local news on television. Ben had improved during the day and was snoring in his basket.

Rosalie settled herself in bed and picked up her book. She read a couple of sentences before hearing Ben's basket creak, followed by his paws padding across the vinyl. She sighed, got up, pulled on her dressing gown and went downstairs. She switched on the kitchen light and found Ben at the back door. His head was drooping. The original smattering of grey around his mouth had over the years, silently and insidiously, crept along his nose; it now haloed each eye and the skin beyond his lashes was red and loose; his pupils were cloudy and distant. He looked every one of his eleven years.

'What's up, Ben? Do you want to go outside?' she asked softly, unnecessarily, as she stroked his head with one hand whilst unlocking and opening the door with the other. Ben's tail twitched in response.

She trailed her hand along his back bone as he walked unsteadily past. It felt sharp and prominent. She had to admit to herself, he was an old dog.

Ben stood a few yards from the door and sniffed the night air. Rosalie busied herself tidying the kitchen cupboard tops whilst waiting for him to return. After a few minutes, by which time he would usually have been back, she opened the door and went outside.

The garden was dark compared with the kitchen and her eyes took a few moments to adjust. There was a summer-warmth in the night air and the lawn was fresh from a shower earlier in the evening. She heard a rustling near the apple tree, just beyond the reach of light from the kitchen window. As she walked towards the sound, she heard Ben vomiting.

'Oh, Ben. What have you been eating?' she asked quietly, calmly. 'Something that you shouldn't, no doubt, eh?' He side-stepped stiffly away from her then promptly nibbled the grass. 'Come on, don't do that! Let's get you back indoors.'

Ben slowly followed her into the kitchen and walked straight to his basket. This was unusual because he normally had a drink of water after going outside. He settled down with a dejected huff, licked his lips and swallowed several times.

Back in bed, Rosalie had just retrieved her book when she heard Ben moving again. She got up and went back downstairs.

After five minutes of following Ben around the wet lawn in her slippers as he sniffed and investigated each clump of grass and plant, Rosalie called him indoors with an unnecessarily harsh edge to her voice. His head hung low as he trailed behind her.

When Rosalie heard Ben walk to the back door a third time, she sighed heavily and laid her book down on top of the duvet. But, instead of getting up immediately, she waited and listened.

Silence.

Then she heard a thud, a scuffling and an unearthly keening sound.

Rosalie ran down the stairs. She found Ben collapsed at the back door. He was panting hard and trembling violently. He seemed unable to make his hind legs work properly, although his forepaws were scrabbing at the doormat in an effort to stand up. His head was hanging slightly to one side and the skin on that side of his face drooped loosely down.

'Oh, my goodness. Ben! What's the matter?' Rosalie whispered in panic. Touching Ben's coat, she could feel he was very hot. His tongue, although still its usual pink colour, was dry and his breath rasped.

'It's okay, Ben. Come on, boy,' she said quietly, trying to calm him. Although he seemed to be looking directly at her, the pupils of his eyes were opaque and unseeing. She knelt down and held him, but this only unsettled him. He tried to pull away.

Rosalie fetched the blanket from his basket. He gave a slight wag of his tail when she helped him crawl onto it. He was still distressed and panting so violently that it was shaking his whole body.

In desperation, Rosalie telephoned the vet, Bladestraw's in Cliffend. The on-call answer service person advised that a vet would contact her within fifteen minutes.

She carried the telephone handset upstairs with her as she quickly dressed. She was back in the kitchen, slipping her feet into her shoes, when the vet rang. It was the head vet's son, Matthew Bladestraw. She gave her details as well as Ben's, and described his symptoms.

'I think he's had a stroke,' she concluded.

'Okay,' the voice on the other end of the telephone said. 'Are you able to bring him to the surgery?'

'I, er, I don't know. I'll have to lift him into the car and I'm on my own. Can't you come here?'

'I could,' he replied hesitantly. 'But, if Ben hasn't had a stroke and just needs treatment, I may not have the necessary medication or equipment with me.'

'Right,' she said. 'I'll see what I can do.'

'Okay. How long will it take you to get to the

surgery?'

'About half an hour, I suppose. Maybe a little longer – it's a good twenty minute drive.' Rosalie was shivering and felt annoyed as she anticipated the vet's one-word answer to be 'okay' again.

Instead this time he said, 'I'll meet you there in half an hour. Has Ben deteriorated while we've been speaking?'

Surprised at the question, Rosalie glanced down. Ben's eyes were still unseeing, he was panting harder, trembling more and he appeared to be reaching forward on his belly towards her.

'Yes, I think he has,' she admitted.

'Okay.' (*I'll scream if he says that once more!* thought Rosalie.) 'I'll see you soon.'

Rosalie returned the handset to the holder, took her jacket off the hook on the back door, shrugged into it and picked up her keys. Edging around Ben, who was still lying on the blanket, she managed to open the back door. She went to the car, opened the rear hatch and arranged an old rug on the floor. She returned to the kitchen and crouched down beside Ben.

'It's okay.' (*That word again*) 'Come on, old boy. We've got to get you up and into the car.'

She put one hand through under his elbows to take some of his weight then slipped her other hand and arm round his rump end. Gradually, keeping her knees bent and back relatively straight, she lifted too many kilos of unyielding canine bulk off the floor, feeling the pull on her shoulders, her back muscles and her legs. Ben's trembling momentarily ceased and his panting turned to a soft groaning. Then he shuddered and gasped as she started to move.

'Come on, Ben.' Rosalie tried to sound cheerful, but

the pressure on her chest was too much for her to speak and walk. The soles of her feet were being pushed down far into the ground and her teeth were grinding with the strain. By the time she reached the car, she was only just able to lower Ben gently without dropping him.

'I hope Mr Bladestraw is feeling strong,' she muttered breathlessly.

Chapter 30

Rosalie drove towards Cliffend, praying there wouldn't be any police cars about – or, if there were, they would at least have the decency to escort her to the vet's before setting in motion speeding or dangerous driving charges. Even the seriousness of her present predicament couldn't stop her thinking that, as she was in court on Wednesday anyway, they could deal with any additional infringements at the same time.

Rosalie heard Ben give a slight yelp as the car jolted over a nasty ridge in the road. He soon started panting again. She called his name tenderly, knowing that this would probably be his last journey. She slowed for the double bends then sped dangerously through Ashfield and along the road to Cliffend town.

Soon the surgery was in sight. She drove too quickly through the opened gates, the wheels skidding on the gravelled car park surface. She headed straight to the front door of the low, modern building. The vet appeared from inside the only other car there.

'Hello, Mrs Stickleback? I'm Matthew Bladestraw,' he said, holding out his hand for her to shake.

He was quite a short, slight man (*not very helpful for lifting heavy, sick animals*, Rosalie thought somewhere inside her distraught mind) and about thirty years old, if that. Without being asked, he helped Rosalie carry Ben into a consulting room, where they laid him on the black-topped examination table. The vet switched on the computer and brought Ben's details up on the screen whilst Rosalie explained again what had happened. Her mind tried to distract her from the present horror by noticing the veins in Matthew

Bladestraw's forearms standing proud of his skin in the same manner as she remembered his father's did.

Mr Bladestraw listened to Ben's heart and looked into his glazed eyes. All the time Ben was panting faster and faster, his trembling was swaying the table on which he had been placed. When the vet eased a thermometer into the appropriate orifice, Ben registered a flicker of indignation. The vet assured Rosalie that that was a normal reaction, and a good sign in the present circumstances. He then carried out a thorough examination of Ben's body, feeling his ears, legs and paws, his neck, back, flanks, chest, stomach, rump and finally his tail, which was curled up tightly under his tummy by then, despite the thermometer.

After a few minutes, the vet retrieved the instrument and looked at it.

'Yes, his temperature is up a little, but that's not surprising considering the state he's got himself into.' He listened to Ben's chest again, trying to close the dog's mouth in order to hear his heart more clearly above the laboured breathing.

'Okay, let's get him on the floor and see if he can stand,' he then said.

They lifted Ben down but, as soon as they tried to stand him up, his back legs collapsed. Eventually, with their help, Ben stood. But he was panting and shaking, with his head hanging down and his back arched, forcing his hind legs far apart. Then he slowly slid to the floor.

Rosalie's heart was breaking as she watched.

'Shhhh … Ben, my love,' she murmured. 'Everything will be all right.'

But she knew no medical intervention could save him. There was only one thing that would stop his suffering. The tears fell unashamedly from her eyes, down her cheeks and onto Ben's chocolate coat.

The vet reached over, opened a cupboard door and took out a small box of tissues. He silently handed it to Rosalie. She extracted several sheets and dabbed at her eyes and nose.

'Okay, Mrs Stickleback,' Mr Bladestraw eventually addressed her as he crouched down beside them. He gently placed his hand on Ben's head. 'I think you were right, Ben has probably had a stroke.' He let Rosalie digest this for a few moments before continuing. 'You have two options. I could sedate Ben, settle him here for the night and carry out some tests on him in the morning. Then I'll let you know where we go from there. Or ...' He paused and ruffled the fur on Ben's neck. 'I could put him to sleep now.'

Rosalie bent her head over Ben's coat, absorbing his scent and the feel of his hair as she tried to control the absolute terror inside her. She wouldn't allow Ben to suffer like this. And she couldn't leave him here overnight, even if he was sedated: he would think she had deserted him.

'I'll give you a few minutes with Ben while I just go and check on our overnight patients.'

And he left.

Rosalie hugged Ben tight, but he was not comfortable with this. She loosened her embrace.

She looked at him and whispered, 'I've always said I wouldn't let you suffer, haven't I, Ben?' He responded slightly when she said his name. 'I love you. You've been such a faithful friend, and I can't bear to see you struggle.' She was crying now.

Rosalie was coaxing Ben's head with one hand and holding him as closely as he would allow with the other when Mr Bladestraw returned. Ben's trembling had lessened a little, but the awful panting continued. A cloud of fur was gathering on the floor around them, his coat being in a permanent state of moult.

'I can't leave him like this. I've always said I wouldn't let him suffer,' she stated. 'I think I have to let him go.' Tears streamed unstemmed down her cheeks.

'Okay, Mrs Stickleback. I understand. There's a form you need to sign. I'll bring it through then I'll go and get the treatment.'

'Will I be able to take him home afterwards? I would like to bury him in our garden.' She felt pathetic asking this, clutching at something to deflect the full force of this devastating blow – a glimmer of light beyond that dreadful, dreadful darkness. 'He loves the garden,' she mumbled, to herself more than to the vet. 'He was trying to get out there when he collapsed.'

'Of course, Mrs Stickleback.'

Rosalie clung to Ben, telling him that soon it would be all right. She had to let him go.

She wanted to tell the vet about all the things they had done together throughout his life. How, at first, when the twins had asked for a puppy, she had said no. Then, after she had denied them a pet for so long, she didn't know how to say yes, until Henry suggested the twins give her a puppy for her birthday. She had grown to love him. He was such good company, especially after first Sarah then Duncan left home. But this story would probably just sound ridiculous.

'Oh, Ben!' she cried.

Chapter 31

The vet returned within a few minutes, placed the form on the black-topped table and bent down to stroke Ben's head before disappearing again.

Rosalie stood up to retrieve the paper. The sudden movement made her head sway; her side where she had been holding Ben felt very cold. He looked towards her as she moved away and attempted to pull himself forward, still panting – trying to convey something to her. His trembling was not so violent now and Rosalie could see that he was weakening.

'It's okay, Ben,' the vet said when he came back again. He'd brought in various pieces of equipment but Rosalie did not want to look at them. Instead, she studied the photocopied A5 form. The printing was lightly blurred. She read it as carefully as the smudges and her tears would allow. The vet had already filled in her name and address, together with Ben's details.

'You just need to sign the bottom.' Above the dotted line for her signature was the instruction that the body would be taken home, with the alternative for incineration crossed out. The vet handed her a pen.

Rosalie told herself that it was not like a death warrant because Ben could not live as he was and he would not recover. There was no choice. Her hand shook as she signed; she hardly recognised her own writing. She hesitated at the next line where the date was to be written.

'What's the time?' she asked. Seeing the young man frown in response, she continued, 'I mean, I need to put the date in, but I haven't got my watch on. I don't know if it's past midnight or not.'

Mr Bladestraw glanced at his watch. 'It's ten past twelve.' And he told her the date.

Rosalie thanked him and wrote it down. She was still trembling as she handed back the form.

He looked at it.

'Yes, that's all okay,' he said. 'And you're sure this is what you want?'

Rosalie nodded and repeated, 'I can't let him go on like this. And I couldn't leave him here.'

'Okay,' said the vet. 'Let me explain what will happen.' He knelt down beside Ben. Rosalie did the same.

'I will give Ben an injection – it's like an overdose of sedative. He won't know anything about it. He will just go to sleep, then his heart will stop and he will slip away. He won't feel any pain. It's quite quick. But I must tell you that you may see small movements afterwards, like a muscle twitch or air escaping from his lungs. These might look as if he's still alive, but he isn't, it's just his body settling.'

Rosalie nodded. She understood. She didn't want to, but she did. Although she was trying desperately not to cry, tears cascaded down her cheeks. She tore more tissues from the box and held them against her face.

The vet tactfully did not notice this. He picked up the pair of electric clippers.

'I just need to shave a tiny area on his front leg in order to find a vein for the injection,' he explained in a low, even voice.

He took one of Ben's paws, held it as steady as he could through Ben's shaking and quickly, gently removed a small patch of hair.

Ben tried to pull back when he felt the strangeness of what was happening.

'It's okay, Ben,' Rosalie whispered. 'It'll soon be over now. You'll soon be all right.' Inside, she was screaming, *No! No! Don't do this! Don't let him go.* But on the outside she had to be strong. She found her fingers surreptitiously gathering the shaven tufts and secreting them in her jacket pocket.

'Okay,' the vet said. 'Now I have to ask you to help me. Usually I have a nurse to do this, but I need you to place your thumb here.' He pressed his own thumb into Ben's shaven skin. 'You need to exert enough pressure to raise the vein in front so I can inject him.'

Rosalie looked at Ben's face. She could see he was worsening; he was losing his battle. She whispered, 'Ben, I have to say goodbye now. I love you. Please, please understand.' She kissed him one last time, hugged his neck and held his head close to her for a moment before taking his paw and pressing as the vet had instructed.

'That's fine. Okay, it'll soon be over, Ben.' He inserted the needle. 'You can let go now.' The vet slowly pressed the plunger.

Rosalie cradled Ben's head again.

Suddenly, that dreadful panting stopped.

The vet continued to empty the syringe. Ben no longer trembled.

Then there was nothing.

Ben's head flopped back. His red-rimmed eyes were only half closed and his mouth was slightly open.

And that is how he would remain. There were no other movements. No muscle twitches. No exhalations.

The vet withdrew the needle and placed the stethoscope onto Ben's chest.

'He's gone,' he confirmed softly. 'You might see or feel air being pushed out as his lungs empty, but he's free of his distress now.'

'Oh, Ben!' Rosalie cried quietly.

'I'll leave you for a few minutes now.' He closed the door gently behind him.

Rosalie gathered Ben's empty, unresponsive but still warm body into her arms. She rocked him back and forth, not able to do anything against the cold, hard hurt inside.

In the silent, clinically lit, pristine consulting room, Rosalie was taken back to those desperate days after her parents' sudden deaths.

She recalled sobbing in her brother's embrace when they were told about the accident – she couldn't remember by whom, although she had a vague memory of Nora Stickleback being present.

She had learnt that nothing and no one could assuage the agony. Her grief was a burden only she would endure, until time taught her how to cope with her losses.

Back then, her solution had been to fall in love and marry. And that proved a disaster. Except that it produced the twins. But they, too, had left her – not gone completely, but they were not hers anymore. And now Ben was dead.

He was at peace.

Rosalie silently thanked God.

Chapter 32

Matthew Bladestraw returned a while later. Rosalie had lost track of time. Ben was drifting further away. She eventually relinquished her hold and gently settled him back onto the floor. Still crying inside, she stood up.

'I'm sorry, I expect you need to lock up and get home.'

'It's okay. Take as much time as you need, Mrs Stickleback,' he said reassuringly. 'When you're ready, I'll help you carry Ben out to your car.'

A familiar, sour smell reached Rosalie's nose.

'Oh, I think gas is escaping from the back end,' she said apologetically.

'I'm afraid his muscles have relaxed and his bowels have opened,' the vet explained. 'His bladder is emptying too.' He quickly, quietly mopped up the messes, then went to a cupboard on the other side of the consulting room and produced a large white incontinence pad which he placed under Ben's rump.

'You'll need this in the car – to protect the interior,' he stated. Rosalie nodded.

'I'll just go and open the car door,' she said.

The air outside was sweeter and the silence struck her.

'Oh, Ben,' she sighed as she stared up to the black-domed sky.

Reluctantly, she returned to the consulting room a few minutes later. 'The car's ready,' she told the vet and waited for his usual one-word reply.

'Okay,' he stated, almost as if not to disappoint.

Rosalie automatically went to Ben's soiled rear end and wrapped the pad around. She wanted to protect his dignity; it was her job to look after him, even in death. The vet took hold of his front, carefully keeping his head level. This time it was Rosalie who said, 'okay.' Then they slowly lifted him up.

Ben's body already seemed much heavier than when they carried him in. It was a slow and awkward walk to the car. The darkness of the outside seemed to offer deference and discretion to their task. They managed to lay him down gently. Rosalie arranged the pad properly under then tenderly tucked the rug around him.

Now, his stillness seemed unnatural – he was not quite at rest. He needed to be at home, in his garden. She closed the door quietly, so as not to disturb him.

'Okay,' the vet said. 'I'll let you get off now.'

Rosalie looked at him, trying to retain her self-control.

'I just want you to know that you did the right thing,' he added quietly.

'Thank you,' Rosalie replied. She held out her hand which he shook again.

'Thank you,' she repeated. It sounded inadequate, but she was so grateful that he had stopped Ben's suffering.

She turned to go, but then swung back again.

'The bill ...?' she asked.

'Don't worry about that now,' he said, patting her arm quietly.

Rosalie tried to smile but she doubted he saw.

'Thank you,' she said again. She walked around to the driver's door and climbed into her car. As she drove hesitantly out of the entrance, she gave a slight wave to the vet who was standing by the open door.

Chapter 33

'Here we are, Ben. Home again,' Rosalie said quietly as she switched off the engine, leaving the driver's window partly open. She stepped out of the car and walked around to the rear. She lifted the hatch door and turned back the corner of the rug she had folded over Ben. He looked the same as when they had placed him in. Motionless. He would never move again.

'Oh, Ben,' she cried. She carefully re-arranged the cover, softly closed the hatch and locked the car.

The house was silent. And it felt so hollow and cold. She sat at the kitchen table, staring at nothing. Eventually, she looked up at the clock. It showed the time was five past one. Then she glanced over to Ben's basket. It was empty. His lead hung on the hook by the door and his water bowl was half-full on the floor by his bed. Ben's food dish, which had been washed after he finished his tea, now stood on the cupboard top ready for breakfast time.

She leant forward and rested her arms on the table, buried her face and sobbed, covering the silence of the house for a while.

When the tears had extinguished themselves, she took a sheet of kitchen tissue off the roll and blew her nose. She switched off the kitchen light and walked along the hall then upstairs and into her bedroom. She slowly undressed. Once in bed, she pulled the duvet up close under her chin and closed her eyes.

But she could not sleep. Every time she felt herself drifting, she thought she heard Ben downstairs. For the remainder of the night she moved restlessly around her bed. She tossed off the cover then pulled it back. She arranged, rearranged and plumped her pillows, then shuffled them around again. Several times she suddenly sat up and listened. Then she remembered and threw herself back down and buried her face.

As soon as she could see daylight through the curtains, she got up, dressed and went downstairs. It was quarter to five. She felt so tired, miserable and lonely. And her back was beginning to stiffen from lifting Ben.

She took a glass from one of the cupboards, ran the cold tap, filled it with water and drank half. After slipping on her wellies, she unlocked the back door and went outside. She collected her spade, which was hanging in the shed, plus a large sheet of plastic. She walked down the garden to where the lawn met the flowerbed at the furthest end of the linen line. It was one of Ben's favourite places.

She started by cutting out a square of turf, which she moved on the plastic sheet. A robin came to watch and soon began to dive onto the disturbed soil for insects. Working steadily, it took Rosalie about forty minutes to dig a grave large and deep enough for Ben. She stood back and studied the empty hole. She was warm from her exertions and her back really ached now. Despite it being June, she could feel the chill coming out of the deep earth pit. *Well, that's the easy part done,* she told herself. *The next job will be a lot more difficult.*

She walked to her car, unlocked it and opened the rear hatch door. Her hand shook as she lifted the rug and touched Ben. His silky brown coat felt as soft as it always had, but now he was completely cold and his limbs were rigid. His body was just an empty shell, his eyes were still half closed and his stiff tongue partly protruded from his mouth.

Rosalie removed the slightly yellowed incontinence pad from beneath his rump and disposed of it in the wheelie bin. She also unclipped his collar, slid it away from under his neck and took it into the kitchen. She returned to the car and, bracing herself, she heaved his front end up enough to push her hand underneath him. Slowly and gradually she managed to haul him out. He felt heavier than in life and his limbs were unremitting. She thought her heart would burst with the effort as she staggered around the corner and over the lawn to the grave. Once there, she sank to her knees. She was at the limit of her strength now; every muscle hurt.

'Oh, Ben!' Rosalie murmured. After a few moments, she backed herself around on her knees and slowly edged her feet and legs down into the grave. She pulled Ben towards her and somehow managed to drag him to the lip. A shower of soil rained down, some finding its way into her wellies. She then used her body and legs to support him as he slowly slid to a rest on top of her feet. Gently pulling these from under him, she crawled up and out then onto the lawn. She was exhausted.

She leant back down inside the grave and stroked Ben's flank. She gently manoeuvred his head into a position she thought might be comfortable, rearranged his paws and finally lowered the flap over his ear to protect the delicate insides. Then she savoured her last glimpse of her beloved pet.

She retrieved the rug from her car and covered his body before carefully shovelling the soil on top of him. She pressed it down gently while she worked, not wanting to stamp on Ben deep underneath. However, there was a considerable amount of earth left after the hole was filled. She decided to leave it and deal with it later.

Her last job was to replace the turf. Having completed this, she stood back and watched as the robin fluttered around, still snapping up insects from the leftover earth, flying off and returning a few seconds later.

'Goodbye, Ben,' Rosalie said quietly. She walked to the shed, found an old stick and cleaned the blade of the spade before returning it to its hook. She closed the door and went indoors.

Before Rosalie could finish taking off her boots and jacket, the telephone rang. She was so tired, both mentally and physically, that she would have preferred to leave it. But she was concerned in case someone was trying to contact her with news of Duncan.

'Hello, Rosalie speaking' she said into the mouthpiece.

'Oh, you are there, then?' Henry's exasperated tones sounded harsh in her ear. 'I've been calling you for the last half an hour – I thought you were always up and about early.'

Rosalie really did not wish to bandy insults with Henry this morning. 'I was out in the garden. Was there something you wanted?' she snapped.

'No need to be so touchy,' Henry retorted. 'I just wondered what had happened about Duncan's summons. What's wrong with you anyway?'

'Ben died last night. He had a stroke. I've just buried him in the garden.'

'Oh, is that all?' Henry said insensitively.

Rosalie began to feel the fury rising.

'WHAT D'YOU MEAN, IS THAT ALL? He's been with me far longer than you ever were!' Rosalie shouted into the phone.

Henry then said the worse thing he possibly could

have.

'Well, I don't know why you're making such a fuss. After all, he was only a dog. And to begin with, you didn't even want a pet anyway!'

Rosalie slammed down the telephone receiver, leaving a sharp *shhhhup* resounding in Henry's ear. Unlike when Lily finished her call a couple of days ago, he could hear this was definitely a bad-tempered termination.

Chapter 34

Tina had not expected to sleep well on Monday night, but she did, although at one point she thought she heard car doors banging outside somewhere close by, followed by the sound of the vehicle speeding away. She also vaguely registered another – maybe the same one returning – in the early hours.

When she awoke at around six o'clock Tuesday morning, she realised the workmen had not said what time they would be starting; she definitely did not want them to find her in bed. She dressed and made breakfast out of the remaining confiscated provisions. She was about to plunder more when she heard a vehicle slowing down outside. Reversing warnings sounded and eventually it parked, but the engine was not switched off. Instead, after a few minutes, a metallic whining filled the air, followed by clunking noises.

Tina dashed outside to find a large skip being unloaded into the lay-by in front of the post office and shop. She disappeared back into her quarters. She heard a persistent knocking on the shop front and hoped the driver would think there was no one there. A short silence brought a sigh of relief and she relaxed, only to be startled by work-boots on the path outside, followed by tapping on the back door.

'I'll be out through the shop in a minute,' Tina called, hoping the man would heed her hint that he was not welcome near her private living area.

'Oh, Bertha, how come I ended up with all this hassle?' she asked, opening the door through to the shop. *I'm still talking to a stuffed teddy bear*, she then told herself in disbelief, followed by more disbelief that she was also still talking to herself.

'You all right, love?' the skip man asked loudly as Tina opened the front door. 'Only I thought I heard an argument going on?' He had to shout because he'd left the lorry engine running.

Tina blinked, undecided as to whether he was joking, or she really had been talking to herself and Bertha loudly enough for him to hear.

'The radio's on,' she blagged. The man clearly did not believe her. 'Anyway, er, what can I do for you?' she asked, as if the large, overbearing rubbish skip now firmly installed three yards from the shop doorway, next to all the discarded fittings, was not a good clue.

'Sign here,' he said, handing Tina a form attached to an old-fashioned clip board – like the one holding the grid of possible names for the teddy bear at Cordnell's fête. He indicated where her signature was required. 'And print your name underneath, please.'

Tina obliged and returned the document to him.

'I'll be back on Friday to collect it,' he informed her. 'And I'll try not to wake you up next time!'

'Charming!' Tina responded sarcastically.

'No problem,' he assured her before turning and walking back to his lorry.

Bernie, Fred and Fido, the At Hand clearance men, arrived soon afterwards. They greeted Tina, indicated their desire for tea and biscuits then carried on with their work when this was fulfilled.

The food – contents of freezers (Tina tried to remember the condition of the frozen ready meal she'd prepared yesterday, but decided it must have been okay because she didn't feel ill), the chillers, and the fresh fruit and vegetable section, plus anything else deemed perishable – was placed in a designated container they brought with them. This was to be removed and disposed of by the local authority's environmental health department.

Postman Jim stopped on his way from Cliffend to the villages beyond Pepper Hill and finalised the arrangements to take Tina to lunch at the pub. At around 11.30, an hour before their assignation, and having washed up a round of mugs from yet another tea break, Tina selected a comfortable summer dress and a pair of not-so-practical sandals.

Bathing during the day gave Tina a holiday feeling and, as she washed her hair, she recognised that she was looking forward to her outing. The weather was warm and kind, drying her hair before she had time to look for her hairdryer.

Chapter 35

Unlike the previous nights, Duncan did not sleep well on Monday. Dr Kittson's words had unsettled him; anything to do with the heart sounded serious. It worried him. Several of the beds around him were empty and, although the lighting was dimmed, it remained distractingly bright. He could not shut it out.

But the worst disturbance of all was caused by Mr Millston in the bed next to him: he snored so loudly at times that Duncan thought it equalled the volume from Cliffend's harbour foghorn. He tried to think of this as amusing as he endured the pattern it followed; for a few minutes it grew louder and louder, and then culminated in a closed-throat, choking noise and a surprised snort which, luckily, was crude enough to rouse the perpetrator. Mr Millston muttered, swallowed a few times then returned to sleep. For a while he appeared to breathe normally, until the whole process was repeated. He was totally oblivious to the disruption he was causing.

Duncan did not like to complain; unless he pressed the button for a nurse, there was no one to say anything to anyway. He finally slept, but it was a restive, tense, semi-conscious sleep that left him exhausted. His dreams were lively and vivid, some involving the pipe from his sludge tanker being fed into the cannula penetrating the vein in his hand.

He was desperately screaming 'No!' in that ineffectual, nightmarish manner, when he heard clanking next to him.

A nursing assistant placed a breakfast tray on the bed-table before drawing it up towards him and encouraging him to sit up to eat.

He propped himself up on one elbow, ignoring the swimming sensation in his head and the pressure on his bladder. He managed a little porridge and drank half the portion of orange juice.

Mr Millston was now wide awake and refreshed from his good night's sleep. As soon as he finished his meal, he went off for a shower, greeting Duncan as he left with, 'morning, son. Grand day, isn't it?'

Duncan did not reply, but raised his plastic glass containing the orange juice in a 'cheers' gesture.

Beverley, the senior nurse, arrived just after the breakfast trays were removed.

'How're you this morning?' she asked whilst checking the chart at the end of Duncan's bed.

'Tired, I didn't sleep very well,' Duncan replied, rubbing his hand over his face, his fingers exploring the wound on his head. He wanted to clean his teeth, have a shower, shave and make himself more wholesome and presentable, but he wasn't even certain if Lily had brought in anything clean for him to wear.

'Oh, I'm sorry to hear that. Was anything wrong?' Beverley asked as she came to the side of his bed.

'No, not really, just strange surroundings, I think,' he replied, deciding not to grumble. 'But I do need the toilet,' he added.

'Right, okay. Shall I ask Dr Kittson to write up on your chart for a sleeping tablet tonight? Hopefully that might help. Meanwhile, you have some tests this morning. But, first things first, I'll get someone to take you to the bathroom.'

A few minutes later, a young nursing assistant, not the same one who delivered and removed the breakfast trays, brought a wheelchair over to his bed.

Duncan saw that her name was Jenny as she helped him into the chair. He felt uncomfortable and insecure; the material of the seat and back yielded too easily with his weight and creaked with every movement.

The girl pushed him along the ward to a recess with several doors leading into the washing and toilet facilities. She applied the brake to the chair, opened one of the doors and helped Duncan to his feet.

'You'll find everything you need in there,' she said, obviously expecting Duncan to walk in and attend to his ablutions unaided.

He smiled thinly and thanked her.

Duncan was suddenly depressed and emotional. Yesterday, Lily had helped him. Today, he was expected to do this himself. He took a very tentative step, reached for the door-post and clung onto it. He was shaking badly and felt his legs would collapse beneath him.

As a distraction, he said to the young nurse, 'I'm sorry to be a nuisance, but I've left my wash kit in my cabinet. Could you bring it for me? And a pair of pyjama shorts? I think my wife left clean ones yesterday.'

'Oh, you won't need pyjamas,' she responded cheerfully. 'There's a theatre gown on the stool in there for you. Just put that on when you've had your shower. It fastens at the back, so if you can't manage to tie it up, call when you're ready and I'll do it.'

The young nurse left and, with all the noises and smells and bustle of a busy hospital around him, Duncan slowly made his way into the wash room. He was leaning over the sink, clutching onto it with both hands, trembling uncontrollably and scared he would faint, when a male nurse came in with his wash kit.

'Jenny didn't realise you needed some help, so I'll give you a hand,' he said, smiling, not noticing the flush of embarrassment that had chased the paleness out of Duncan's face. 'I'm Luke, by the way.'

Luke eventually wheeled the refreshed patient back. Duncan noticed the time was nearly nine o'clock. His neighbour, Mr Millston, was sitting in the chair reading a newspaper.

Duncan's bed was unmade, but Luke helped him back in anyway. 'They'll tidy up when you've gone for your tests,' he explained. 'Shouldn't be long now.'

When he was lying down again, Duncan rested his head thankfully on his single pillow. He closed his eyes, feeling totally weak and humiliated.

'An angel, that one!' Mr Millston called over. 'Even if he is a chap! They're all angels. Don't you agree, son?'

'Yes, seems like it,' Duncan replied brusquely, hoping not to get involved in a conversation.

'Yes – angels, all of them. They treat me better than my wife ever did!'

Duncan smiled, unsure of how to respond. Mr Millston returned to his newspaper. The vision of the clock face returned to Duncan's mind as he felt himself drifting away. Then he suddenly remembered the magistrates' court hearing the following day. His heart began to pound and he started to panic, which brought on the nausea again. He tried to stay calm by telling himself that his parents would let him know what happened.

Duncan was expecting a fine for allowing an unroadworthy vehicle to be taken onto the highway – that was all he was guilty of. But that hadn't really been his fault. His father didn't allow him time to think when he said he would drive the tractor over to the Old Police

House. His mother's actions caused the tractor to be taken. His father's obstructiveness forced his mother to behave as she did. And Duncan was in the middle.

At some point, his mind must have surrendered and taken his thoughts into sleep again.

Half an hour or so later, Luke reappeared with the wheelchair. This time he was also carrying an electronic tablet.

'Mr Stickleback?' he asked with a smile. 'Although I told you my name, we weren't formally introduced before, were we?'

'Duncan,' he replied. 'Duncan Stickleback, but don't blame me for that.'

'Duncan's all right,' Luke said as he positioned the wheelchair and set the brake. 'I've never heard of Stickleback as a surname before, though. Anyway, I've just got to check your details.' He consulted both the electronic gadget and the label bracelet on Duncan's wrist. 'Right, that's all in order. I have to take you down to the medical physiology department for some tests. Did Dr Kittson explain the procedure to you?'

'Well, no, not really. Last night he said I ought to have, I think he called it, a *bubble test*. Is that right?'

'Yes. The posh name is *transthoracic echocardiogram with the use of agitated saline solution.*'

'Yes, I vaguely remember he said something like that!' Duncan's smile was ironic.

Mr Millston looked up from his paper.

'Sounds painful to me,' he warned. 'You want to watch that you come back here with everything intact, if you're off to some "ology" department!' The advice was humorous, but Luke turned to Mr Millston.

'And you're down for tests this afternoon, I believe,' the nurse said. 'Not looking for a heart though, something lower on the anatomy, I was told. Any ideas?'

'You keep your looking to yourself, thank you!' retorted an unamused Mr Millston. He seemed to suddenly change his opinion of Luke. 'And you, son,' to Duncan, 'keep a close eye on them.'

Luke ignored Mr Millston and helped Duncan into the wheelchair. As they started to move, Duncan closed his eyes and concentrated on not allowing his breakfast to reappear. He felt a chill as they left the ward. He held the blanket close to him; his view of the world was much lower than he was familiar or comfortable with.

Luke sensed his anxiety and started to chatter.

'There's nothing to worry about in the test this morning, Mr Stickleback,' Luke said as they reached the end of the corridor and waited at the lift. Duncan did not reply. 'Yes, Stickleback is an unusual surname, isn't it?' Luke commented when they entered.

'I think so. Dad didn't have any aunts or uncles, or brothers or sisters, so there's just us now. Three of my grandparents passed away – on the same day, actually – but that was a long time ago. Grandma Nora went on a cruise holiday and never came home; I don't really know how she died.' Duncan sighed sadly, but then cheered. 'But I've got a little boy, Jack,' he continued. 'When he was a baby, my Dad used to sort of sing his name like a nursery rhyme. "Jack Stickleback, Jack, Jack Stickleback." It annoyed my wife and eventually he stopped. She doesn't get on with my parents. I don't blame her really.'

There was a silence between them as the lift whispered away on its descent. 'Does it worry you?' Luke asked.

'Not really.' Duncan shrugged. 'Well, maybe. But

Jack'll have to toughen himself against worse things than name chanting. And Lily stays away from Mum and Dad if she can.'

Duncan was deep in thought when they arrived outside the medical physiology clinic. Luke pushed him through the double doors and past the waiting area. Half a dozen people sitting on the seats looked up.

Luke bent over Duncan.

'You've been given priority over the other patients today,' he whispered. 'So no gloating as you think of them having to hang around here for an extra twenty minutes or so while you're seen first.'

Chapter 36

Duncan waited in a small, square, white-painted, windowless treatment room whilst Luke went to tell someone he was there. Sitting in the wheelchair, he still felt cold and eventually realised he was shivering. His mouth was dry, but he did not think he would be able to drink anything.

The room contained a black examination couch, with the surface protected by a continuous sheet of off-white paper towelling. This was pulled along the length, supplied from a wide roll attached to the wall behind the raised head. Next to this was a stand holding a machine about the size and shape of a small microwave oven. There was a screen where the window of the door would have been, along with banks of buttons not dissimilar to an oven's controls.

Duncan was thinking of Jack and Lily, wondering what they were doing, rather than imagining what the other curiously shaped implements on the nearby trolley were for. He was startled when another nurse, an older woman, opened the door and came in.

'Good morning, I'm Gwendolen,' she said, smiling at the nervous young man in the wheelchair before her. She had a different air of authority to Beverley and Luke, but was nonetheless pleasant and reassuring. She wore a darker uniform and her name badge gave other details, but Duncan could not decipher them.

'Hello,' Duncan replied quietly.

The nurse reached for his hand and checked the name tag fastened around his wrist.

'Gosh, you feel cold,' she exclaimed. 'I'll find you an extra blanket.' She went out again and returned very quickly with a clean, white cellular hospital blanket. She partly unfolded it and wrapped it around his shoulders. He leant forward in the chair.

'I think your gown has parted company with itself at the back,' Gwendolen said. 'That's probably what's letting in the chill. Don't worry, I'll sort you out in a minute when we settle you onto the couch. But first, before Mr Stott arrives – he's the one who will be carrying out the tests – I need some vital statistics.' She turned to the trolley of implements and selected the thermometer, which looked like a chunky door handle.

When Duncan first arrived at hospital, he'd expected a stick thermometer to be placed in his mouth; he was surprised by this new style. Gwendolen took off the cap and held it to his right ear. Checking the reading, she tapped something into the electronic tablet containing his file. 'Next, your blood pressure, which I think has been causing concern.'

Duncan sat passively as this test was completed, not understanding the figures that were quoted.

'Is that okay?' he enquired.

'Not really,' the nurse admitted. 'It's a bit low. How do you feel at this moment?'

'Cold, my head is spinning and I feel as if I want to lie down, preferably before I fall out of this chair,' Duncan stated. He sounded pathetic, even to his own ears.

'Oh. Right. Well, hold on tight for a few more minutes because I need to check your weight next.' She folded the blood pressure equipment away. 'Any idea how much you usually weigh?'

'About twelve stone, I think. Its ages since I last hopped on the bathroom scales – and they're set to kilograms, so I'm not really sure. Might be a bit less than normal at the moment 'cause I haven't really eaten much since I've been here – in hospital, I mean.'

'Okay, well, I'll have to take you back into the waiting area. We have a special cubicle there with a set of scales that you sit on,' Gwendolen explained. 'Don't worry about feeling dizzy because you'll only have to stand while we transfer you.'

This task was soon completed. Duncan weighed in at just under twelve stone, which Gwendolen told him was about right for his height, age and occupation.

Mr Stott was in the consulting room when they returned.

'Ah, good morning there, young man,' he greeted Duncan and introduced himself. 'I see you've been put through the wringer already by our extremely efficient nurse Gwendolen.'

The nurse smiled indulgently and handed Mr Stott the electronic tablet on which she had recorded the various information. He seated a pair of flimsy, half-rimmed spectacles on his nose and read the details. He then removed his glasses and looked directly at Duncan.

'Right,' he said. 'Well, this morning we are to perform a transthoracic echocardiogram with the use of agitated saline solution. Otherwise known as a bubble study. Don't look so worried, young man,' he joked as he tapped Duncan's shoulder with his glasses. 'Gwendolen here will look after you. And there's nothing awful about the test. We'll let you climb onto the couch. I see you already have a cannula. Right, I'll be back in a few minutes then we can begin.'

Mr Stott left the room. Nurse Gwendolen wheeled Duncan to the side of the couch and applied the brake. She asked him to try to stand up again, which he did.

Before he knew anything, he was skilfully conveyed to the couch where he heard the paper towel sheeting crinkle beneath him.

'Now for the bad news,' the nurse informed him. 'I need to remove the top part of your gown.' She helped Duncan to lean forward and untied the loosely knotted lower tapes, the top ones still being undone from earlier. She then drew the garment forward over his shoulders to his waist and covered him with the two blankets from the wheelchair, one folded around his lower trunk and legs, the other placed over his chest and shoulders. Duncan registered their soft texture: although they smelt unfamiliar, they reminded him of Lily and Jack. He was suddenly overwhelmed with homesickness.

'There, we can find you a bit easier now,' Gwendolen said, smiling.

Duncan tried to return the gesture, but he was feeling too emotional to look at the older woman's face. He laid his head back and closed his eyes but, when Gwendolen picked up his left hand and adjusted the cannula, he immediately tensed.

'It's okay, just relax now,' she reassured him.

At that moment Mr Stott returned.

'Ah, good,' he pronounced with satisfaction. 'We're ready to proceed.'

Chapter 37

Postman Jim the Second arrived on time to collect Tina from the shop and post office. He was driving a red car.

'My predecessor's vehicle was an ex-Royal Mail van,' Jim explained as they settled in. 'The stickers were all removed from the outside, but you could still see where the insignia had been. When I took over his rounds and people found out that my own car was red, it reinforced my nickname. I only live up the road on the outskirts of the village and I use the shop here. The Fighting Cock's my local, so I'm often seen around. Plus Jim the First used to, er, *unofficially* give people lifts from one end of the village to the other. It started off in his own vehicle, but he soon started using the post office van as well, so I was expected to carry on.'

'That sounds like a sackable offence,' Tina stated dubiously. 'I used to work at the post office in Cliffend – I lived there for a while as well.'

'Oh, I see,' Jim said, nodding doubtfully.

'I was – am – married to George Tillinger – Rosalie Stickleback's brother, so I know the family. We've been away for six or seven years now, but George and I are no longer together. We didn't ever actually live in PepperAsh, but I have been told some of the history. I can't recall much about the postman giving lifts, though, but I thought there was quite a good bus service running from Mattingburgh to Cliffend that passed through the village on the way.'

'Yeah, well, the main offender wanting lifts seems to be the rector – Quinny. So perhaps they just didn't run when he wanted them to. And it would be a hard-nosed bureaucrat who enforced the *no passenger* rule for him,'

Jim mused.

'Doesn't he have a car of his own?' Tina asked. Although she vaguely remembered Quinny, she had never met him.

'No, no. He said he failed his driving test several times when he was younger and gave up in the end. Now he just relies on other people; if there's no one around, he walks. I have seen him on a bike, but he's probably more dangerous on that than he would be in a car. He's quite a character. You'll love him when you meet him.'

'I don't think I'm up to bantering with God-botherers,' Tina said with feeling, remembering Mrs Moddson and the kindly vicar at Cordnell.

'Oh, I don't really think he believes much in *God*,' Jim laughed. 'He should probably be retired, anyway'.

'How old is he?' Tina enquired, visualising a hippy-styled, sandal-wearing chap with a long cloak, beard and a balding head of straggly hair.

'Well over seventy, I would think. We'll pass the church and rectory on the way to the pub. Talking of which, we'd better go.' Jim started the car and set off in the direction of Ashfield.

The route had not changed much since Tina last drove between Pepper Hill and Ashfield. The road was wide enough for two large vehicles to pass, but the verges were badly maintained with grass, cow parsley and, in places, brambles hanging over. The greenery was lush from the recent rain, although the high colours of the early summer flowers were beginning to fade. Above them, the sky was a deep, calm blue with a few pure white clouds floating by.

'How's the refit coming along?' Jim asked, breaking the short but companionable silence.

'Fine, I think. But I still haven't been able to contact Mr Dentforth about the post office. Maybe he's treating me like the church bosses treat Quinny – just hoping I'll get on with the job so he can forget me!' They both laughed at this.

'I've completed a stocktake of the dry or sealed goods: non-perishables, tins and things. I ignored all biscuits and the like because those three ...' she momentarily struggled to describe the eating machines undertaking the work. '... Bernie, Fred and Fido. Yes, *Fido*, I daren't ask why he's called Fido. Anyway, they don't seem to understand the concept that goods should be paid for. But I can't really complain. From reading their work schedule, they've cleared and cleaned up far more than they need've done, including setting traps for the mice. But I did see a few cardboard boxes filled with something or the other coming out of their van and going into the skip earlier, which definitely wasn't rubbish from the shop. I overheard one of them – Bernie, the really tall one – saying that his wife had told him to declutter his garage and workshop ready for when they move in a couple of weeks' time.'

Jim was laughing at this. 'Yes, that sounds about right.'

'But, won't the skip man check to see what's in there before he takes it away? Or the disposal company? They'll need to know in case something's been dumped that's toxic.'

'It won't be your problem, will it?'

'Well, I signed for the skip. Doesn't that make me responsible for its contents when it's taken away?'

'I shouldn't think so. It would be the company who hired it – At Hand, I presume,' Jim explained.

Still smiling to himself, he slowed his car as they

approached the rectory and church on their left.

'Just checking to see if the old boy is around and needing a lift.'

Satisfied that Quinny was not waiting, Jim gently increased his speed and continued the journey.

'Does Duncan still run the slurry business at Tidal Reach?' Tina asked as they approached Ashfield.

'Yeah, has done for years. He's married now with a son, but I expect you know that.'

'Yes, George did say something. We didn't go to the wedding – can't remember why now. We sent something for the baby when he was born, though – Jack, he's called.' Tina did not want to recount details to a stranger of how her marriage had crumbled.

'So, you know old Henry Stickleback, then?' Jim asked lightly. He now questioned the wisdom of taking Tina to lunch at The Fighting Cock.

'Yes, although we didn't used to spend much time in the pub.' She paused, looked down at her hands and fiddled with her fingers. 'Actually, I didn't get on too well with George's family, especially Rosalie and Henry,' she explained. 'And I doubt if the twins even remember me now. I always seemed to say the wrong thing, so I kept out of everybody's way. George and I were living in Cliffend but George was away a lot of the time – he's an engineer of some sort, works for the MaCold company, on the oil and gas rigs.'

'Oh,' was Jim's only response.

The sun felt extremely warm on Tina's face as she climbed out of the car and followed Jim across the car park to the entrance of The Fighting Cock public house.

She felt very self-conscious walking into the bar. Although the place had obviously been redecorated during the intervening years, it looked much the same and had retained its previous style. The bar ran along the wall opposite the door, with the fire-place fitted into one corner. It was a large room where the tables were well spaced, allowing customers to walk by without having to weave around those seated.

Jim steered Tina to the bar, with its warm brown polished surface, the usual display of glass bottle optics, wooden and porcelain-handled pumps and gold-coloured drip trays. Henry was giving change to a customer. He turned to greet them.

'Hi, Jim,' he said. 'Who's your friend?' Then he raised his eyebrows in recognition. 'Oh, it's you. Hello, Tina.' His voice contained an unanswered question as he returned his eyes to Jim.

Tina had a very different memory of Henry to the man she saw in front of her. He now mesmerised her, with his dark, almost black hair, slightly flecked with grey, and his reddish beard. His still raised brows were black, but Tina had no idea what colour his eyes were.

'Hello, Henry. You obviously know Tina. She's the temporary post-mistress at Pepper Hill,' Jim feigned introduction. He turned to Tina and continued, 'Henry Stickleback, still landlord of this esteemed establishment.'

'Pleased to see you again, Tina,' Henry said as he held out his hand. Tina took it; her fingers barely visible, enfolded as they were in his bear-like paw.

'And you,' she reciprocated.

'Taken over from old Poskett at the post office, have you?' he asked whilst stirring a dark and rich-looking liquid with a long-handled spoon inside a tall ceramic pint pot depicting a proud cockerel, presumably representative of the pub's name. Tina could not decide if it was tea or coffee inside the mug, then she remembered that Henry's speciality was a mixture of the two.

'I'm only standing in until those in charge decide what to do. The business is a bit complicated with both the At Hand shop and post office being managed together,' Tina stated.

'I see,' Henry said as he looked around as if searching for someone.

'George isn't here with me, if that's what you're wondering,' Tina said. 'We've split up, but we're still in touch. In fact,' Tina removed her mobile phone from her bag, 'I'll send him a text, if there's a signal here. I haven't been able to contact him from Pepper Hill and I'd better just let him know where I am.'

'I expect he'll be surprised that you're here of all places!' Henry commented with heavy emphasis.

'Good,' Tina retorted. 'I hope he is! And, while I have a signal, I'll try my manager again, too. Excuse me a moment.'

After texting George, Tina left a message for Dentforth, updating him on the refurbishment work and asking him to please respond to her calls, as she really did need to know what was happening with regard to reopening the post office. She returned to the bar and chatted companionably with Jim.

Tina began to relax. Henry's (questionably *home-made*) beef stew was very tasty. As she sipped her second glass of wine, she began to take an interest in the conversations around her. She tried to pick up on the subtleties of the gossip and tittle-tattle, as well as the asides, undertones and innuendos that one had to be alert to. 'Forewarned is forearmed' as the proverb says, and a good post mistress needed to be aware of everything around her.

Chapter 38

'So what exactly did they do?' Lily asked later on Tuesday afternoon as she sat beside Duncan's bed. She arrived shortly after two o'clock; Duncan had eaten most of his lunch and so far had kept it down. He was drinking slowly from a glass of water as they talked. He told her that he felt a lot better, although the wound on his head was itching. Jack was with his *sensible grandparents* and Duncan had momentarily forgotten about the court case the following day involving his own parents.

'They had a scan machine, like they used on you when you were pregnant with Jack,' Duncan explained. He was confident the doctors now knew why he'd been ill and was hopeful something could be done about it. 'And, when they injected this liquid in through the cannula ...'

'The saline ...?'

'Agitated saline solution,' Duncan recited. 'It's like salt-water with bubbles in it. It travels to the heart in the bloodstream – feels cold when it first goes in, though. They move the scan thing across your chest – they rub that jelly stuff over your skin first, makes a right mess!'

'Yes, I remember,' Lily said.

'And, as the blood passes through the heart, it's shown on the screen. They can take pictures, just like when you had your scan. But the ones they took today, they fed straight into their computer so they would have a record of what was going on. Anyway, the second time they injected this liquid in, Mr Stott told me to squeeze. I didn't really know what he meant so tried to squeeze my hands – you know, like *make a fist*.' He demonstrated to Lily. 'But nurse Gwendolen whispered, "Pretend you need a poo, only don't do one!"'

'That sounds awful!' Lily exclaimed, remembering the pelvic floor muscle exercises recommended to her after Jack's birth. Realising her voice might have been a little loud, she looked apologetically over at Mr Millston in the next bed. He was asleep, but thankfully not snoring.

'No, it was okay. I didn't feel anything. Well, perhaps a peculiar sensation at times. But it didn't hurt.'

Lily smiled as he talked; she thought he looked so much brighter this afternoon.

'Mr Stott did the tests four times with the bubble liquid and said that I'd got quite a nasty hole in my heart. He said he couldn't say for definite that *that* is what's making me ill, but he thought it really ought to be closed now while I'm still fairly young, because these types of holes can cause strokes when you get older. Apparently, one of the Osmond Brothers had a stroke because of a hole in his heart.'

'Really? I didn't know that. Which one was it? Oh, it doesn't matter. But this operation thing, is it dangerous?'

Questions poured out of Lily. She was suddenly horrified as she imagined a long incision being made down the middle of Duncan's chest to give access to his heart, leaving a zip-like scar.

'No, it's quite simple according to Mr Stott. It isn't even a proper operation – a *procedure*, they call it. They feed a metal thing in a tube through an artery in your groin, push it right up and position it in your heart.'

As Lily's face creased with anxiety, Duncan was pleased when Dr Kittson arrived, saving him from further explanation.

'Good afternoon, Duncan. How are you feeling?' the doctor enquired.

'A bit better now I think I know what's wrong.'

'Ah, yes. I've come to talk to you about that. And good afternoon to you too, Mrs Stickleback,' he addressed Lily.

'It sounds dreadful, this hole in the heart. Will he be all right?' she asked.

'Yes, yes, of course he will. Well, there's an element of risk in any surgical procedure, but he'll be fine. Let me explain it all to you both.' He drew the curtains around Duncan's bed and perched on the edge at the side where Lily was sitting.

Lily thought curtains would not prevent the doctor's explanation being overheard in the ward, but she soon forgot about this as she listened.

'Right, well, Mr Stott carried out the bubble study this morning and he has passed the results to me. Duncan, you have in fact got a patent foramen ovale ...'

'I thought he said he had a hole in his heart?' Lily interrupted.

'Yes, that's what it's called. There's more than one kind of hole in the heart, but yours is in the wall between the two upper chambers, the atria. Let me explain. Blood flows around your body, carrying oxygen to your muscles and organs. It also takes away the carbon dioxide, amongst other things. The large vein, called the vena cava, brings deoxygenated blood to the heart from your body, entering into the right upper chamber, called the right atrium. The blood needs to be cleaned of impurities, and then it collects oxygen. To do this, it travels down into the right ventricle – a ventricle is a lower chamber; there are two, of course, corresponding with the two upper atria. From the right ventricle, the blood is pumped to the lungs along the pulmonary artery. It passes into the veins and travels down the capillaries in the lungs. Here, the carbon dioxide is removed when you breathe out. The oxygen that is absorbed when you breathe in is taken back into the left ventricle via the pulmonary veins. From here, it is pumped to the left atrium or upper chamber and then out around the body.'

He paused for a moment, hoping this explanation was detailed enough for all relevant information to be conveyed, but not too confusing with all the many technical terms. The young couple's expressions were of worry and concern but their calmness reassured him that he had found the right balance.

He cleared his throat before continuing.

'However, in your case, Duncan, the opening between the two upper chambers was allowing blood still carrying the waste products to flow across into the other upper chamber and be pumped straight out around the body without being cleansed or oxygenated. I expect you remember from my previous explanation, that this hole or opening is present in all babies before they're born. Their blood is cleansed and re-oxygenated by their mother's bodies. Plus, of course, whilst babies are in the womb, their lungs don't work anyway.'

Both Lily and Duncan were silent. They had been watching Dr Kittson as he spoke. Now they looked at each other. Duncan suddenly reached for Lily's hands.

'It's okay. I know it sounds frightening, but we can put things right. Don't worry, Duncan,' he said reassuringly. 'I'll arrange for you to be transferred to Mattingburgh hospital where they can affect a closure. I think I half overheard you telling your wife what that involves. But I'll go through it again with you anyway, just in case anything was left out.' He was smiling as he glanced at Lily.

Dr Kittson felt sorry for them. He'd had to check the details of recent events in order to draft the letter to court for his head of department to sign which stated Duncan was not fit to attend the hearing. The information he discovered whilst doing this confirmed there were grave problems within the family.

Chapter 39

The atmosphere was convivial in the bar of The Fighting Cock. When Henry was close enough to hear and join in the conversation, those present discussed Poskett's recent death and the search for relatives. They touched on the unfortunate demise of Rosalie's pet Labrador, Ben; Tina spoke of hearing vehicle movements during the night in question. At this, however, Henry harrumphed loudly then busied himself elsewhere.

As soon as he was out of earshot, the topic moved to the Sticklebacks' sludge tanker prang. Tina asked if this was the cause of the awful smell around the Old Police House. The explanation of this naturally progressed onto Duncan's unfortunate sudden illness, which most people attributed to the stress caused to him by his parents. By the time Henry returned, they were innocently relating tales of Quinny's strange behaviour and lack of transport.

'Would you like another?' Henry asked Tina, with the wine bottle poised over her glass. She had finished her second a while ago but was too engrossed in the gossip to think about a refill.

'No, thank you,' Tina replied. 'I've still got a lot of work to do when I get back.' She felt unable to refer to her temporary billet as home, so basic were the facilities and restricted the space. Plus, it was not exactly private, if she needed to rest after an over-indulgence. 'But I would really like a cup of coffee,' she added as an afterthought.

'Don't go getting Henry to make it for you,' Jim quipped, 'or you'll end up with something like that concoction!' He indicated to the ceramic pint pot. Others around the bar murmured and chuckled their agreement, but the man himself was not amused.

'If you think you're so clever, young Jim,' he countered without smiling, 'then you'd better come around here and make it yourself!' He pointed in the direction of the half open door which led through to the kitchen area.

'And I'll have one as well,' another customer added.

Five minutes later, Jim returned carrying a tray with five ordinary mugs of straightforward instant coffee. Tina smiled at the irony: she felt as if she'd been making drinks for the refit team for days when, in fact, it was barely twenty-four hours since they'd first appeared.

'If you ever get bored sorting and delivering letters,' Henry said appreciatively. 'You can always come and work for me.'

'No thanks, mate. You've already got help here.' Jim nodded towards Polly, who was charming a pair of gentlemen close by with her low-cut blouse and elegant, sensuous hand gestures. 'Anyway, I'd better be going after this.' He lifted his mug. 'Cheers!'

Everyone raised their coffee in salute.

'Would you like a lift back?' Jim asked Tina.

Before climbing into the postman's car, Tina took out her mobile phone to check for calls, texts, emails – anything – from either Dentforth or George. There was nothing.

When Tina arrived back at the shop and post office in Pepper Hill, the van was not there, which told Tina that the three workmen were still at lunch. She took advantage of their absence to have a look around the premises. The paint drying on the walls caused a strong smell and new units were in the process of being assembled, with tools, lengths of wire and other fitters' paraphernalia strewn across the floor. The place was a mess.

But Tina refused to feel despair: she had just enjoyed a nice lunch, convivial company and had not disgraced herself by accepting a third glass of wine. But, despite the coffee, she was still thirsty. Whilst leaving the shop, she heard the refit team returning. She thought it was probably time to make another round of drinks for them anyway.

From the back room, she heard the banging and singing commence. Just as she finished placing their mugs on a tray to be carried through, there was a knock on her door.

'Nice timing,' the really tall chap, Bernie, said. 'By the way,' he added as he held out a flattened black box with two cables leading off, one length terminating in a mains power plug and the other being a computer connection. 'Fred kicked into this when he was in the store room earlier. Think it has something to do with your internet.' He handed it to Tina then picked up the tray from the draining board. 'Cheers for these,' he called as he receded.

'Thanks,' she said quietly. She plugged in the device, rebooted her laptop and sighed victoriously before settling down with her coffee to work through the surprising number of emails that were suddenly appearing.

Amongst the communications was the awaited message from Mr Dentforth, to which he had attached the contract for her temporary posting. She read it through. Then she read it again. Something about it perturbed her, but she could not pin-point exactly what. The main agreement appeared to be quite straight forward. But ...

'What d'you reckon, then, Bertha?' she asked the teddy bear. Ms Bunfighter sat passively on top of the armchair back, resting against the wall behind. She offered no opinion on the matter. 'You're really not much help, you know!'

As Tina stared at the screen, the internet connection was interrupted. It reconnected a few minutes later but quickly died again. After struggling for another quarter of an hour, she decided to leave it until later, hopefully by which time it would have settled.

However, just as she was about to log out, she spied the icon advising her that a new email had arrived. Again, it was from Mr Dentforth. He informed her that, as the At Hand shop refit was almost complete, he would recommission the post office the following Monday morning. He finished by enquiring if she had printed out and signed her new contract yet.

Chapter 40

Sarah Stickleback had worked for the Perrona Dawn leisure company since leaving school at sixteen. But now, they insisted on implementing their policy with regard to employees in her situation – as they perceived it. She was ordered to commence her leave as from Tuesday afternoon.

In addition to her own problems, for nearly a week now, Sarah'd had a feeling that there was something wrong with Duncan. They had spoken on the telephone about a fortnight ago; although he said everything was fine, he'd seemed reticent. She did not like to ring again so soon: it might be seen as interfering, especially now he was married and settled with Lily and little Jack. There were times when she felt, or imagined, Lily was jealous of her and her twin brother's relationship. And she knew Lily barely tolerated their parents; she felt the same way about her mother.

Sarah set off from Fenstone, hoping her Dad would be at The Fighting Cock. Even she'd noticed Henry had become more and more reluctant to leave his premises over recent years. He always stated it was best to be on-site, even if he was only relaxing in his own rooms rather than actually working in the pub, in case something went wrong or needed his attention.

There were only a handful of other vehicles in the car park. A red car with two people inside was leaving as she arrived.

She climbed clumsily out of her own car, thinking her poor old Dad was now in for a shock! Hoisting her bag strap onto her shoulder until it was comfortable, she decided to ask Henry in a little while if he would carry her case in from the boot. She then slowly and carefully crossed the gravel surface to the open front door.

Sarah found the pub quite dark after the bright sunshine outside. A faint smell of stale cigarettes still lingered, even though the smoking ban had been in force for several years and the interior had since been refurbished.

Henry was at the bar serving a customer with a pint of bitter and a glass of white wine – dry, Sarah guessed as she looked over to the table where a lady sat waiting.

'Be with you in a minute,' he said, instinctively sensing someone's arrival but not glancing away from the till.

The man pocketed his change, picked up the two glasses and returned to his companion.

'Yes, and what can I get you?' Henry asked before he looked up. Then he saw Sarah. 'Oh!' He just managed to mouth the word.

'Today, I'm so thirsty that I would even try one of your own special brews, Dad,' she said brightly.

'Sarah!' Henry cried as he opened the heavy wooden bar flap. 'Ah,' he then added, stopping short to take a good look at her.

Sarah was considerably shorter than her twin brother and father, and probably not even as tall as her mother. She wore her shoulder-length blonde hair loose; it was as wild and straw-like as Rosalie's. Her face was blessed with a broad smile which emphasised her rosy cheeks, smooth complexion and blue eyes. She had a pleasing, rounded figure – not fat, not thin. Today she was dressed smartly in a navy suit, but the jacket buttons were pulled tightly across her front and the waistband of her skirt hung beneath her bulge.

'Er, is there something you need to tell me?' Henry asked cautiously. 'Does your mother know?'

'No. And no. Don't worry, it isn't what you think,' Sarah said casually. 'Oh, come here, Dad. I haven't seen you for ages, don't I deserve a hug?' She opened her arms wide and stepped forward.

Henry had to stoop to embrace his daughter.

'Last time I saw you,' he said softly into her lemon-scented hair, 'you had young what's-his-name in tow – and, as I remember, he was none too pleased when he met your old Dad. What had you been telling him? Where is he now?'

'Too many questions,' Sarah stated as she stepped back. 'I wasn't kidding when I said I was thirsty. And I'm hungry. You know what they say about eating for two? I actually think I've got two in here – after all, I am a twin myself, aren't I?' She laughed as she rubbed her stomach. 'So I feel like I'm eating for three. Could be four. Could be just me, and I'm greedy.' Seeing Henry's baffled expression, she took pity on him. 'Make me a drink and I'll tell all,' she enticed mischievously.

'Maybe you should call your mother and invite her here too, because there are things we really ought to let you know as well.'

'Oh, what have you two been up to now?' Sarah asked, her tone sounding exasperated. 'When I spoke to Duncan …'

'When did you speak to Duncan?' Henry interrupted sharply.

'A couple of weeks ago. He said things were quiet, but that you two were both keeping him busy. He seemed a bit down, though. Is everything all right?'

'Come through to the kitchen and I'll explain,' Henry urged. Polly's shift was not due to start for another hour, so Henry cast an eye over to the corner where one of his regular customers, Max, was sitting.

Max had become almost a permanent fixture now he was retired following an accident with a combine harvester. He lived in one of a row of small cottages not far along the road from The Fighting Cock.

'I'll just be through the back, Max. Call if anyone wants a refill,' Henry said.

'Right,' Max replied before turning back to his companion. They were leaning over a mobile phone listening intently to a horse race, Max have laid an extravagant bet on an outsider.

Once in the kitchen, Henry filled the kettle then cleared a pile of paperwork off the table.

Sarah sat down, groaning slightly as she relaxed into the shape of the wooden chair.

'So, which shall I do first, ring your mother or listen to your explanation?'

'There's nothing to explain.' Sarah followed her father's glance to her stomach. 'Oh, you mean this? Well, I wouldn't worry about it. The short version is, well – you know.' Sarah's face suddenly glowed crimson. 'Anyway, it isn't anything to do with young what's-his-name – as you so delightfully called him!'

Sarah suddenly made herself cough, which forced her to clear her throat. She hoped her father wouldn't notice the false cheerfulness in her voice. 'Well, a few months ago – Easter time roughly – I thought I might be pregnant. So I did a test, one of those home predictor things – you know, the *pee on a stick* variety?'

Henry flinched. She didn't mean to embarrass him, but she was trying not to remember the terror forced upon her. In her flippancy, though, she knew she was lying to maybe the only person who could really help her.

'It was positive,' she continued. 'So I went to the doctor. But ... it turns out it's a phantom pregnancy – some hormonal problem or the other. Anyway, she – the doctor – contacted the hospital. I went for more tests and they confirmed that, no, I wasn't pregnant. They gave me leaflets to read and suggested I make an appointment to discuss my problem with a counsellor. I ignored it – and them. I put my head down and got stuck into work, until they told me to take maternity leave. I couldn't persuade them that I wasn't actually having a baby; they said they had their insurances and things to think about. So, here I am! Do you need an extra barmaid for a while? Does Polly still work here?'

'Whoa,' Henry exclaimed. 'My turn to say *too many questions.*' He was shaking his head, hoping to free it of confusion as he started to make the tea/coffees. 'Just changing the subject, are you sure about this?' he asked, holding up his pint mug.

'Ah,' Sarah replied hesitantly, remembering Duncan's face when he'd once tried it. 'Maybe not. Just a glass of water will do for now, please, Dad.' Then, with a satisfied sigh, she leant back and massaged her rounded belly.

Chapter 41

On Wednesday morning, Henry arrived early at Cliffend magistrates' court. He was familiar with the square and angular building from his regular attendances for renewals of and extensions to his publican's licence.

Henry waited outside for his solicitor, young Mr Andrew Brideman. The legal advice he received over the telephone was to plead guilty to the two charges being brought against him.

Henry couldn't explain why he had not braked in time to prevent the collision. And, if the magistrates focussed on that particular point, Mr Brideman foresaw a problem.

But Henry had not really taken in all that was said: at the time, his mind was preoccupied with his daughter's surprise visit and his son's illness. Now he was regretting his lack of attention.

It was a warm day with a gathering sea breeze. Henry appreciated the coolness; he felt uncomfortably hot in his suit. His shirt collar was too restricting and he'd knotted his tie inexpertly. Also, the waistband on his trousers was tight and, worst horror of all, when he looked down earlier as he climbed out of his car to check he hadn't scuffed his shoes, he noticed he was wearing odd socks – one dark green and one dark grey. It was an easy mistake to make; he had dressed in a hurry, distracted by Sarah waddling about downstairs. He was not used to company in the mornings. Sarah had fussed her way through breakfast, reassuringly promising to help Polly look after the pub if he were locked up today.

Henry sighed; he did not like being away from the pub. He looked at his watch; there were still a few minutes to go before he expected Mr Brideman. He began to pace the walkway from the marked parking bays to the steps and back again. Eventually, his solicitor arrived in a brand-new, shiny black car. Henry guessed it cost at least double his own annual earnings.

Andrew Brideman was not looking forward to this case. He'd inherited the Stickleback portfolio from his Uncle Ambrose a while ago. Andrew had always wanted to be a lawyer. His ambition was to be a barrister of great notoriety, working in a big city, winning popular cases and commanding huge fees. After gaining a slightly disappointing law degree, he started his career in the family practice at Cliffend. Now at thirty-one years of age, he recognised he'd become lazy and content.

Right now, he pinned on his professional smile as he walked towards his client, thinking, *oh God, how bloody provincial – his trousers are too short and he's wearing odd socks!*

Chapter 42

Rosalie had called into Cliffend magistrates' court the previous day to deliver her and Duncan's acknowledgements of the summons, together with the letter from the hospital confirming that her son was too ill to attend court. Today she drove into the car park in time to see Henry and his solicitor climb the steps to the entrance.

She chose a space next to a rather posh, shiny black vehicle; her own car cried out in sharp contrast to its immaculate neighbour. Ben's chocolate-coloured hairs were still everywhere; she felt a heavy sadness when she thought about him. Her muscles remained stiff from lifting Ben, then digging his grave and burying him.

Rosalie had managed to rest for a while the previous afternoon. However, her sleep was interrupted when her daughter, Sarah, telephoned to say that she was at her father's and would be over to see her soon.

How was Rosalie? Oh, fine, except for the rather messy 'prang', as everyone was calling the accident last week, and the court case today. How was Sarah? She was sorry to learn that Ben had passed away. And, well, yes, she did have some news, but she would have to tell her face-to-face, after court today. No, it wasn't worse than Rosalie stealing Duncan's tractor and tanker. No, it wasn't as bad as Duncan being in hospital. No, she hadn't had a premonition that her twin brother was ill. Yes, she may have shared a very confined space with him for the first nine months of their existence (eight and half, actually – hadn't Rosalie been the one to tell them they'd arrived in a hurry, two weeks early?). But

Sarah had stated many times over the years that, no, she couldn't read Duncan's mind and, even if she could, she didn't particularly want to. After all, he was a boy and she was a girl!

Rosalie stood up and smoothed down her skirt, worrying what on earth Sarah meant by saying she had some news. She picked up her bag and jacket from the passenger seat, the latter still containing Ben's odour.

As she reached the steps up to the courthouse entrance, she suddenly wondered whether she had brought along the summons. She stopped and opened the zip on her bag to look inside. Although concentrating on her search, she caught sight of a man standing just inside the glass door. Before she completely recognised him, he pulled open the door for her.

'Hello, Rosie. What on earth have you done this time?'

Rosalie looked up, forgetting all about the paperwork. There was only one person in the whole world who dared to call her *Rosie*, a name he used to tease her with throughout their childhood and teenage years.

'George! What are you doing here?' Rosalie exclaimed as she allowed him to hug her.

George Tillinger was a lot taller than his sister. He made her feel safe. Although he was the younger of the two, he had always been dependable. And sensible. Without him, she was sure she would not have survived their parents' deaths.

George suddenly found that he could not speak. He had been feeling guilty for a long, long time that he hadn't contacted his sister – but not quite so bad as he felt about neglecting his wife. But George could only deal with the situation in front of him at any one time, and he rarely factored in wider elements. Even now, Tina was for later; Rosie's problems were sufficient for the moment.

George had always been uncomfortable with the continuing war between Rosie and Henry. He wasn't even sure if they were aware that he knew about the gift that caused the ructions. The longer he spent in their company, either individually or both together, the more likely he felt he would reveal his knowledge. Then he would be expected to take sides and become just as embroiled in the animosity as they were.

Tina hated the atmosphere in the Stickleback/Tillinger family; she had been glad to move away to Treemoore. But then George deserted her, citing work commitments. He recognised he really was the worst kind of coward.

'Well?' Rosalie demanded as she pulled away, sensing her brother's deliberate hesitation.

'I originally intended to come down to PepperAsh to see Tina, I've been back at Treemoore. Tina and I are, er, not together at the moment – trial separation, you might call it. I haven't spoken to her for a while, but she emailed me yesterday lunch time to say she was at Pepper Hill. She's been filling in at various post offices since we split up, covering temporary vacancies or leave. But before I could start my journey, Sarah rang yesterday afternoon from Henry's pub. She said Duncan was ill and you two were in court today. So I drove over from Treemoore last night and booked into the Thrimbale Hotel.'

Rosalie was very surprised to hear this. 'The Thrimbale, eh? You are going up in the world, little brother!' This was, at one time, the most prestigious –

and expensive – hotel in Cliffend. It was also the establishment where Rosalie and Henry spent their one and only night together as Mr and Mrs Stickleback. Swallowing down this uncomfortable fact, she continued, 'What's happened to you and Tina, then? Huh! You're just as bad as Henry and me! Is she our new post mistress? How long are you staying?'

'One question at a time please, Rosie. I'm more interested in trying to help you two out of this mess!'

'Yes, but you can't just turn up and not let me know what's going on. Which is precisely what Sarah's just done!' Rosalie exclaimed.

'Okay.' George sounded exasperated as he faced Rosie. 'Firstly, Tina and I are just having some time apart. Secondly, we won't end up in court for fighting each other in the street – hopefully, anyway. And thirdly, Tina will be here for a while, probably until the rightful owners of the shop and post office premises are traced. I think Henry's lawyer, Brideman, is dealing with the matter.'

Rosalie shook her head at the news, glad for the distraction from her own misdemeanours.

'I knew someone had moved into Poskett's place, but I didn't realise it was Tina. Why on earth hasn't she come over to see me? And I still don't see why you're here, at court,' Rosalie stated.

'I haven't really got time to explain everything now. Let's just get this hearing over with, then we can talk properly.' George was anxious to steer Rosie inside because proceedings were due to start in fifteen minutes.

Chapter 43

Henry and Mr Brideman were standing inside the foyer. As George and Rosalie joined them, the two brothers-in-law acknowledged each other with a nod. If Henry was surprised to see George, he didn't show it.

Immediately in front of them, a short counter-type barrier impeded their way. Fixed at a break in the middle were two structures resembling door-frames, standing side by side. They were, in fact, walk-through metal detectors. Two court security officers stood next to these devices.

'Would you like to come this way, please?' one of them called out to the group.

'Which court are you attending?' the older of the two officers asked.

'Court three,' Mr Brideman answered for the group.

'Okay. Could you empty your pockets of everything metal and place the items in the trays,' the guard instructed as he pointed to the receptacles in question.

Henry and Mr Brideman each went to one of the officers. As bidden, they took out keys, coins, mobile phones and other requisite objects from about their persons and placed them in the trays.

'Thank you. Now please walk through the metal detectors.'

Predictably, as they did, both detectors were activated. The noise was not too loud, but it niggled Rosalie. The security officers then asked their respective clients to stand away from the frames and raise their arms out straight to the side so their hands were at waist level. They ran hand-held detectors over the two men and concluded by indicating they wait on the other side of the barrier.

Next it was Rosalie and George's turn. Rosalie took her keys out of her jacket pocket.

'What about my bag?' she asked.

One of the security officers took it from her.

'I'll have to search it by hand, if that's okay with you, madam?' he stated.

Rosalie nodded and walked through the doorframe. No alarm sounded, for which she was grateful. Nothing happened when George walked through the other one either. She watched with gathering embarrassment as the officer rummaged inside her bag.

'Don't worry, madam,' he commented with a grin. 'I do this all the time. I won't give away any secrets.' She actually managed to return the smile as he handed it back to her. 'Don't forget, everyone, make sure your mobiles are switched off in court. Thank you.'

Rosalie collected her keys. She heard one of the officers giving directions up to court three, telling them to check in as soon as they arrived.

When they reached the top of the stairs, George urged Rosalie to take a seat while he went to the desk to join Henry and Mr Brideman. Having stated their names, including Rosalie's, and confirmed the hearing they were attending, George returned to his sister. He asked if she had engaged a solicitor.

'No. I'm pleading guilty, so I didn't think there was any need. When I called in here yesterday, they said I would be assigned a duty solicitor if necessary. I thought *he* ...' she indicated towards Henry standing with Mr Brideman some distance away, '...was pleading the same, so I'm not sure why he's forking out for legal representation.'

'Perhaps he's claiming mitigating circumstances,'

George said flippantly.

'I'm the one with *mitigating circumstances*,' Rosalie retorted, causing everyone waiting outside the courtrooms to turn around. She immediately regretted drawing attention to herself.

'Shh, Rosie,' her brother warned. 'There's no need to be like that. It isn't going to help.' George sounded annoyed, but he reached his arm around his older, not so big, sister to try to convince her of his support.

Rosalie opened her mouth to speak again and George took a deep breath and cut her off.

'Now, don't start! I've only been talking to you for a few minutes and you've already snapped at me twice.'

'Well ...'

'Shut up and listen for a minute,' George said firmly as he pulled his arm away and turned to face her. 'Let me explain. I'm here to try to help you, but I've also got my own problems to sort out. Sarah rang me yesterday to ask if I could do anything for you two because she couldn't stand the idea of you and Henry arguing again. And she said she wouldn't be surprised if your bickering was the cause of Duncan's illness.'

He paused for Rosie to digest this. 'By the way, Sarah doesn't know about Tina and me yet. She said she's spoken to you, but you were already upset.'

'I was asleep when she rang.'

'Asleep in the afternoon! That's unlike you. What's the matter?'

'Nothing. Well, you'll probably think it's nothing.'

George raised his eyebrows at her as if to say he would be the judge of that.

She continued, 'Ben, my old dog – you remember him? Big, fat chocolate Labrador?' George nodded. 'He was taken ill Monday night. I had to rush him over to the vet here in Cliffend. He'd had a stroke, but Mr Bladestraw couldn't do anything for him. He had to be put down. I didn't get much sleep after that, so yesterday I was resting on the sofa when Sarah rang. I'd buried him earlier in the morning. He was very heavy. I had to carry him on my own. I hurt my back a bit.' Rosalie finished her explanation by rubbing the offending vertebrae.

'Oh,' George replied. Sarah hadn't mentioned Ben. But then, she did have an enormous problem of her own that she hadn't yet shared with her mother.

George was very confused at all the half-truths, resentments and anger. He placed his arm gently around Rosie's shoulder again and drew her to him. 'I am sorry to hear about Ben,' he said quietly. 'I remember him when he was a puppy. He'd been with you a long time, hadn't he? You must miss him.'

'Yes. At least you understand,' Rosalie said. 'Not like *him*.' She nodded over to Henry again. 'He just said he couldn't understand what all the fuss was about, after all, Ben was only a dog – which surprised me because it was him who bought Ben for me in the first place!'

'Ah,' George replied. A moment's silence passed. 'Well, let's forget about that now. You'd better tell me exactly what happened with this *prang* of yours. Plus I need to know how Duncan is. And, what on earth do I have to do to stop you and Henry trying to kill each other?'

'Yes, well, we'd better hurry. We've only got four minutes before we're due in.' Rosalie pointed to the clock over the double doors leading into court three. 'Why d'you want to know anyway?'

'Because if you and Henry start shouting at each other when you get in there,' he explained patiently as he nodded towards the courtroom, 'you're both likely to be done for contempt.'

'But …'

'And, no, I don't trust either of you to behave like adults.'

The usher, a tall, elderly man in a long black gown over a grey suit, came out of one of the courtroom doors. George thought it was now too late for Rosie's explanation.

The usher cleared his throat to make an announcement.

'Ladies and gentlemen, the case concerning …' He looked down at the paper in his hand. '… Stickleback and er, Stickleback. And Stickleback …' He raised his head to resume in a more positive voice, '… has been postponed for a short while. One of the magistrate's cars has broken down and he's just called a taxi. So, perhaps you would like to take refreshment in the cafeteria. He should be here within the hour. I will call you back in good time.'

Rosalie looked anxiously at George but felt relieved.

'Come on, Rosie,' George said. 'If we get a move on we can be served first, then we'll have time to go through things.' He looked around. 'Which way is the café?'

'I don't know, I've never been here before,' Rosalie replied. She then added in a raised, angry whisper, '*And don't call me Rosie!*'

Chapter 44

The cafeteria was a little way along the corridor from the waiting area, just beyond the doors leading to the Ladies' and Gents', the location of which Rosalie noted for later. There was only a short queue at the counter when George and Rosalie arrived, although the place itself was quite full. They bought a pot of tea for two, a scone and a teacake then walked towards the only vacant table which was in the far corner. Rosalie was explaining to George that she didn't really feel like eating when Henry arrived at their table.

'Do you mind if I join you?' Henry asked, looking ill at ease in his suit and tie; his hair was neatly combed and his red and grey beard inexpertly trimmed.

Rosalie actually felt a moment's sympathy for him, but the old resentments soon surfaced.

'I don't think we should ...'

'Of course it's all right, Henry,' George stated. 'Please sit down. It's good to see you again, although, as the cliché goes, I wish the circumstances were happier.'

'Anyone would think we're heading for the guillotine, George.' Rosalie's voice was spiteful, which earned her a tap on her ankle. 'Oi, don't kick me. We're not kids now, you know.'

'Then stop acting like one,' George replied sharply, suddenly losing patience and realising he longed to talk to Tina. He hoped at least *they* would be able to carry on a polite conversation – if she was sober, of course. And that was another problem.

A longing came over him to be offshore again; dealing with strong winds, lashing rainstorms, heavy sea swells, petulant bosses and belligerent rig workers suddenly seemed easier than coping with irrational and emotional family members.

Rosalie realised she was indeed being childish, but seemed unable to help herself; she was mortified at having to appear before the magistrates.

George calmly took the teapot, cups and saucers, milk jug and sugar bowl off the tray and placed them on the table.

Undeterred by the siblings' squabbling, Henry sat down opposite and proceeded to unload his purchases onto the remaining space: a pot of tea, a cup of coffee and an empty cup, plus, of course, milk and sugar.

'Is your solicitor joining us?' George asked Henry as he poured tea for himself and Rosalie.

'No, he's gone back to his car to make a couple of calls.'

'Oh, I thought perhaps - with the tea and the coffee.'

'No, no. Don't you remember? I like a mixture of the two, although I doubt I'll be able to make it strong enough with these.' Henry was smiling. He felt surprisingly comfortable in his brother-in-law's company, having forgotten the reason they were all here.

'I didn't expect to see you today, George,' he added as he topped half of the coffee from the cup into the empty one without spilling any. He then filled them both up with tea from the pot. He was heaping sugar into each when George replied.

'No, I expect not. I don't know if you've heard but Tina is your new temporary post mistress at Pepper Hill. I've finished working for MaCold on the rigs for a while, and we – Tina and I – have got a few things to sort out.'

'Yes, I spoke to Tina yesterday. She came into the

pub.' Henry was careful not to reveal that she was in company. 'She didn't say much, just that you hadn't been together for a while.'

'No, well, things have been difficult ...' George stalled with his reply. He couldn't really explain the reasons why they were apart, and he didn't want to reveal too much. 'Tina left Treemoore while I was still based out of Aberdeen. She was fed up with working on temporary assignments with the post office, but somehow ended up in Pepper Hill to fill in after Poskett died. I don't know if she asked to come here, or whether the position was foisted on her. She'll no doubt tell me in time.'

George hoped this was detailed enough to satisfy Rosalie and Henry: he did not wish to reveal any more until he had spoken to Tina. He vowed to ring her this evening, when the hearing was over. He missed her. Then he realised Henry and Rosalie were waiting for him to carry on.

'We're selling the house at Treemoore, so we'll just have to see what happens next. We've got a lot to discuss. Anyway, before I could do anything else, Sarah rang to say Duncan was in hospital and that you two were in trouble again. So, if you don't mind, since we're here, let's talk about you. We've got about forty-five minutes before the hearing begins.'

Chapter 45

As they waited, Rosalie realised her muscles were becoming stiffer and stiffer – both from the lifting and digging yesterday, plus all the tension she felt building up inside her now. She was worried about Duncan and the tests he was having on his heart this morning. She also wanted to see Sarah. She wished the missing magistrate would hurry up and arrive so they could proceed. Without finishing her coffee, she excused herself and went to the ladies' toilets.

As she washed her hands, there was a knock on the outer door.

'Rosie, are you all right?' George called from the corridor. 'The usher has just called us back. They're ready to start now.'

'Okay. I'll be out in a minute.'

She finished drying her hands then checked her face in the mirror. No make-up, no pretence, just her. They would judge her on whom and what she was, not a smart, clever impersonation she'd donned for the occasion. She quickly combed her hair, straightened her collar, picked up her bag and left the cloakroom.

'Come on Rosie,' George urged as she re-joined him. 'The usher's just called you and Henry into the courtroom to have a word with the court clerk and, in your case, the duty solicitor.'

Rosalie realised she was shaking.

Sensing this, George squeezed her hand then pointed to where the usher was holding open the door to the court. Henry was waiting for her.

'I'll be in the public gallery, not far away,' George assured her.

'This way, Rosalie,' Henry said, holding out his arm. Surprisingly, he suddenly felt quite protective of her. 'Come on through. The sooner we get this mess sorted out, the quicker we can all be back home.'

Rosalie did not really want to accept either his kindness or help – after all, it was his fault they were here. But she smiled faintly at him.

Henry and Rosalie entered the courtroom together. It was large and square with a high ceiling. There were two rows of public seating to the left behind a barrier, solid to waist height with a sheet of protective Perspex reaching up level with the top of people's heads. To the right were four rows of seats and, at the back, furthest from the door, sat a reporter from the *Cliffend Herald*.

Rosalie suddenly froze. Attending court was a completely new experience for her; she felt intimidated by the formality. There was no window, which perhaps explained the dry and dusty atmosphere.

She saw the bench, a raised dais on which were placed the enclosed desks and seats for the three magistrates. High on the wall behind these hung the golden royal crest. A man in a smart suit sat at a smaller desk on the floor level; in front of him were three files together with an open laptop. The usher indicated that Rosalie and Henry move forward for him to introduce them.

'Mr Henry Thomas Stickleback and Mrs Rosalie Andrea Stickleback. ' He turned to them. 'Mr Smith, the court clerk.'

'Ah, yes. Mr and Mrs Stickleback.' Mr Smith spoke quietly as he removed the folder closest to him. Inside was a summary of the case. He quickly read the page. 'This is all somewhat unusual, I think. Of course, the charges themselves are quite common, but the circumstances from which they arise are – well, shall we say – unique. At least, I've never come across anything like it before.' He looked up at Rosalie and Henry then removed his glasses. 'Who are your representatives?'

'Mr Andrew Brideman,' Henry replied, looking across to the door then back at the court clerk. 'But I'm not sure where he is. When we were told the hearing was delayed, he said he was going back to his car to make a couple of calls.'

The usher was still standing behind them. 'I'll just see if I can find him,' he offered.

The court clerk turned to Rosalie. 'Who is your representative?'

'I was told I would be assigned a duty solicitor,' she replied, her voice barely audible.

'Okay, well he's not here either.' The clerk was beginning to sound annoyed. 'Perhaps you two could just wait in the witness area.' He pointed to an enclosed section opposite the rows of seats containing the journalist. 'We're not using the box for the accused.' He pointed with his pen to a construction typical of how Rosalie imagined the dock to be. 'It's been closed for health and safety reasons; one of the floorboards has worked loose.'

Rosalie and Henry sat in the witness area, both feeling like naughty school children.

'A right muddle up this is turning out to be,' Henry whispered. 'And a complete waste of time!'

'Why, have you got more important things to do?' she hissed in reply.

'Of course I have!' Henry snapped. 'And so have you! Have you forgotten Duncan is having tests on his heart this morning?'

'Well, at least they'll find one. Which is more than

could be said if they were testing you!'

This angry exchange was interrupted by the door opening to admit two suited gentlemen, each carrying a wallet file. One was Mr Brideman. He acknowledged the court clerk before approaching Henry and indicating that they should speak at the further end of the seats. The other gentlemen also greeted the clerk. He then smiled at Rosalie. She stood up, unsure of what was expected of her.

'Good morning, Mrs Stickleback. I'm Mr Leadermann, the duty solicitor.' He entered the witness area and they shook hands. 'Please, sit down. We just need to go through everything. You're pleading guilty to taking a vehicle without the owner's consent and driving said vehicle without insurance. Is that correct?'

Rosalie's voice was subdued as she confirmed this, choking a little as she spoke. 'It was my son's tractor and slurry tanker. I didn't think he would mind. You see, I'd asked him three days before to empty my septic tank, but his father ...'

'The ownership of the vehicle isn't in question, Mrs Stickleback; neither is the purpose for which you appropriated it,' Mr Leadermann interrupted. 'What is important here is that, although you took it without asking permission, you did not intend to permanently deprive the owner – your son, that is, Duncan Thomas Stickleback – of his property.'

Mr Leadermann paused for a moment. He could see his client was confused and wondered if this had been explained to her. As far as he was concerned, this was a domestic dispute – and he was actually finding it hard to take the matter seriously. He smiled again, reminding himself to be professional. 'You were going to return the vehicle in the same state in which you found it, weren't you?'

'Yes,' Rosalie replied. 'As soon as I'd emptied my septic tank. Only then, the tanker would've been full. It was empty when I took it.'

'Okay, all that matters is that you intended to take it back, undamaged.' He made a note on his papers. 'Are you qualified to drive tractors? I mean, what does it state on your driver's licence?' Rosalie searched in her bag and found the document. Mr Leadermann checked it. 'Yes, that's fine,' he confirmed. 'But you didn't have insurance?'

'I can drive any vehicle quoted on my licence with my own insurance policy, but I'm only covered for third party damages. I, er, didn't think to bring the certificate with me, though.'

'Mmm, the trouble is, your insurance will only cover you if you obtained prior permission from the vehicle's owner. Okay, we can't help that now. Just plead guilty and hope it will lessen the penalty. Oh, and if you're given the opportunity, say how sorry you are and that it won't happen again. I will, of course, state this for you, but it wouldn't do any harm for you to repeat it.'

'Yes,' Rosalie replied, swallowing hard as she spoke. She just wanted this ordeal to be finished with.

Mr Leadermann then excused himself. He stood up and walked out of the witness area. He approached the court clerk still sitting behind his desk, bent forward and began to speak with him.

As Henry waited for Mr Brideman to finish writing notes, he scanned the interior of the court and nearly missed his solicitor talking to him.

'Well, Mr Stickleback, we have a problem. And that is, why didn't you brake as soon as you saw the tanker was parked on your side of the road? In his statement,

PC Yates said there was adequate distance for you to stop.'

'The loading arm was dropping in front of me, and I just ...' Henry struggled to explain, wondering why Brideman had not dealt with this earlier.

Their conversation was then interrupted by the court clerk. 'Are we all ready to proceed?' he asked.

Henry was disconcerted.

'Leave it to me,' said Mr Brideman. 'And just answer the questions truthfully.'

'All rise, please,' stated the usher in a sonorous voice to the assembly.

The two solicitors retreated to the desks set at a ninety-degree angle on the right-hand side of the clerk, near the witness area.

A well-dressed, middle-aged lady with stiffly coiffured hair entered the courtroom and stood at the desk opposite them, on the left-hand side of the court clerk. She carried a slim brief case bearing the insignia of the Crown Prosecution Service.

At the same time, George Tillinger walked quietly over to the public gallery. He nodded discreetly to his sister, who looked self-conscious standing next to her adversary; her estranged husband.

The thought struck him that, if he did not try to make amends with Tina, he could also soon be described as an *estranged husband*.

Chapter 46

The three magistrates, two gentlemen and a lady, all dressed formally in smart suits, entered their area from a door at the back. The chairman of the bench took the slightly raised central chair whilst the other man and woman seated themselves either side.

The usher then indicated for everyone else to sit down.

The court clerk remained standing and introduced the cases.

'With your leave, these three cases will be dealt with consecutively,' he concluded.

The chairman looked down at the papers on the desk in front of him before nodding his agreement.

At that moment the main courtroom door opened. Four members of the public walked in and quietly seated themselves in the row behind George. Henry recognised two of them as drivers of the cars that had stopped near his tractor, who were subsequently sprayed with effluent.

The court clerk resumed.

'With your leave, Sir, the first of the three cases is brought by the Crown Prosecution Service, represented today by Mrs Pringle, against Mr Duncan Thomas Stickleback, the owner of the vehicles involved, and the son of Mr Henry Thomas Stickleback and his estranged wife, Mrs Rosalie Andrea Stickleback, the latter two defendants being present here today.

'Unfortunately, Mr Duncan Stickleback is ill in Cliffend hospital. He was taken there by ambulance early in the morning following the incident that gave rise to today's proceedings. You have a copy of the letter from his consultant explaining why he is unable to attend. There is also a copy of his statement taken on the day of the incident, together with a copy of his guilty plea to the charge of allowing a vehicle with a known mechanical fault to be driven on a public highway.'

There was a pause as the three magistrates read the appropriate documents.

Mrs Pringle also turned and studied these.

'I see that Mr Duncan Stickleback, in his defence, states that events happened very quickly and his father suggested that he, that is Mr Henry Stickleback, drove the faulty tractor,' the lady magistrate stated.

'I believe that is so,' replied the court clerk.

During the few moments of conferring between the three magistrates, both Rosalie and Henry sat with their heads bowed.

'Well, this all appears to be straightforward,' the chairman said. 'We pronounce the charge be upheld and Mr Duncan Thomas Stickleback be fined.' He stated the sum then turned to Rosalie and Henry. 'We wish your son a speedy recovery from his illness.'

'Thank you,' Rosalie and Henry acknowledged in unison.

The court clerk wrote notes and discarded those case papers to one side before picking up the next file.

'We now have the case of Mrs Rosalie Andrea Stickleback.' He paused, looked at Rosalie and said, 'Mrs Stickleback, please stand.'

Rosalie stood up and took a small step forward.

'Rosalie Andrea Stickleback, you are charged with taking a vehicle without the owner's consent and driving said vehicle on a public highway without insurance, the vehicle in question being a tractor towing a domestic waste slurry tanker, both owned by your son. How do you plead?'

'Guilty,' Rosalie replied. She could hardly say the word, her mouth was so dry. Her legs were trembling and her face blushed red hot.

'Sirs, Madam,' the court clerk addressed the bench. 'Taking the defendant's plea into account, the appropriate penalties amount to a fine, a community service order, or a combination of both, or possibly a short custodial sentence. The last would probably be suspended, as this is the defendant's first offence to be brought before the court.' The clerk looked up from his papers. 'I would ask the defendant's solicitor, Mr Leadermann, to speak.'

The chairman of the bench nodded towards the duty solicitor.

Mr Leadermann stood up, addressed the bench and explained the circumstances that led to Rosalie taking Duncan's tractor and tanker.

'Thank you Mr Leadermann,' said the chairman. He then conferred again with his two fellow magistrates. He turned to Rosalie. 'I just wish to clarify that the sole reason for taking the vehicle was to empty your septic tank, a job which you had requested your son to do, but he had not done so?'

'Yes.' Rosalie thought she would like to have explained more – that her tank was full and was beginning to smell in the hot weather. But she couldn't find the words. Having heard the whole event recited in public by strangers, she could understand why other people might see her actions as ridiculous. She also realised she had not had the chance to apologise. It was too late now.

She began to feel dizzy and reached out to hold onto

the ledge in front of her. Her heart was hammering hard. This caused her to wonder what was happening to Duncan. Her thoughts had drifted when she heard her name spoken again. She looked up quickly, realising the chairman was addressing her.

'Mrs Stickleback, the bench finds you guilty of the charges brought against you. We have looked at the circumstances, and you will be fined.' He consulted the papers in his hand before quoting the amount. 'We would state that, although guilty of this, we find you were in no way responsible for the consequent collision. The police report is clear that you parked in a legal, sensible manner for the task to be undertaken.'

'Thank you,' Rosalie whispered. She was still trembling, but felt immense relief. When she looked over to George in the public gallery, he smiled at her.

'You may leave the witness area, Mrs Stickleback,' the court clerk stated. 'Mr Leadermann will explain everything to you.'

'Thank you,' Rosalie said quietly. She repeated this to the three magistrates.

As Rosalie stepped down, Mr Leadermann indicated for her to follow him. The court clerk then turned to the bench and suggested that, as the time was nearly noon, they should break for lunch before hearing the final case. The chairman agreed to this and stated the court would reconvene at one o'clock.

'All rise,' the usher instructed. Everyone stood and the three magistrates left the courtroom via the door behind them.

Chapter 47

Immediately after speaking with Mr Leadermann, Rosalie told her brother that she wanted to go home. George walked with her out of the courthouse and over to her car. The sunshine was extremely bright compared with the artificial lighting inside the building.

George offered to drive Rosie back as he noticed she was looking very pale, but she insisted she would be all right. She promised that, as soon as she arrived home, she would prepare and eat lunch.

'I also need to contact the hospital to see how Duncan is as soon as I can,' she explained. 'I want to visit him this evening, tell him what happened in court and find out if they have the results of his tests yet.'

'Okay, Rosie. Now, you're sure you are clear about the fine, how to pay it and what else you need to do?'

'Yes, Mr Leadermann explained it all to me. I have to pay within a month, but arrangements can be made for instalments if I can't afford the lump sum.' Rosalie sighed heavily and looked into the distance. 'I can manage it, that's no problem. It's just that I'm so angry about the whole thing – if Henry hadn't ...'

'Now calm down,' George said firmly as he placed his hands on her shoulders and forced her to look directly into his eyes. 'Henry didn't make you take Duncan's tractor. You did that of your own volition.'

'Okay,' Rosalie agreed, shrugging herself free. 'But I want to go home.' She unlocked her driver's door. George then opened it and she climbed in. 'Are you leaving now?' she asked.

'No, I'll stay and see how Henry gets on. You know, the drivers of the other cars were there this morning. I think they'll want to see if Henry is found guilty before deciding whether to make a civil claim against him for damages.'

'Oh,' Rosalie sighed as she fastened her seat belt. The inside of the car was hot and she could smell Ben. Placing the key in the ignition, she turned it far enough to activate the electrics. She pressed the button on the inside handle to lower the window. As George gently closed the door for her, she asked, 'am I liable too?'

'No, I don't think so. It was Henry who crashed into you. The magistrate said you were parked legally, so I can't see how they can say you caused their cars to be covered in sludge.'

'That's good,' Rosalie said with relief. 'I don't want any more hassle. I'd better get back …' She was going to say she needed to check that Ben was okay after being left on his own for the entire morning. Then she realised. She lowered her head for a moment. When she looked back up at George, her eyes were sparkling with unshed tears. She smiled faintly.

'Wish Henry good luck from me, will you? I know we don't get on, but I didn't want to see him end up in court. I don't think business is that good at the pub, so he really won't want a heavy fine.'

'Okay, I'll tell him,' George said. He stepped back from the car and raised his hand to wave.

Rosalie attempted to start the engine, but it waited until the second try before firing.

'Bye,' she called as she reversed out of her parking space and drove towards the exit.

Chapter 48

Henry Stickleback sat awkwardly in the cafeteria at the courthouse. Andrew Brideman approached his table and was taking the seat opposite when George entered. George saw Henry was busy and purchased his own lunch then sat at another table. As he ate, he had time to think about his own situation.

Things might have been so different for both him and Rosie if they had not suddenly lost their parents. But then, thousands of people could possibly say the same. His sister hadn't coped well with the trauma. Sometimes George wondered if he'd buried some of his own grief in deference to hers.

The accident happened during Rosie's last year at school and, consequently, she failed all her exams. She was encouraged to enrol on a course at Cliffend College – Clifftech. But she didn't finish the year; instead she became involved with Henry. They married the summer George finished taking his GCSE exams, two years after the accident.

George started working for MaCold in their Cliffend base before even leaving school and he continued to work locally until just after marrying Tina.

He and Tina were settling in Treemoore when Tina started hinting that she would like a baby. Instead of discussing this properly, George bought his dream car; a yellow sports model he named *Hercules.* MaCold offered him the project manager's job in Aberdeen and, despite Tina's wishes to remain, he moved up there.

The project finished three months ahead of schedule and there were substantial bonuses as a reward. George saw this as a favourable time to try to sort out his marriage. But before he came ashore, Tina reminded him that they were supposed to be attending her friend's wedding. In the end, though, he'd had to let her down. Later that same evening, she informed him of *Hercules'* little accident. Whilst admitting she was unsettled and discontented, she omitted to tell him about her drinking. But he already knew. Instead, she said she'd had the opportunity to fill in for a while at another post office.

A few weeks after this, George packed his belongings and left Aberdeen with the intention of returning to Treemoore. By chance before he left, he mentioned to a colleague that he owned a sports car he no longer wanted. The man was interested and bought it, unseen, asking George to arrange delivery and to charge the extra cost to him. George mentioned the windscreen had been smashed; although intrigued by the story behind this, the buyer didn't think it would be a problem.

When George moved back to Treemoore, he quickly found a job in the town's employment agency, overseeing the creation of apprenticeships within local industry. He and Tina had been in contact; he wanted to suggest selling the house, but this seemed too final. He procrastinated. He was pondering the irony of Tina's email when he received Sarah's telephone call in which she sketched over her own problem but detailed her parents' accident and her brother's illness. He packed immediately and drove to Cliffend.

George booked a room for a couple of nights in the Thrimbale Hotel. He did not wish to impose upon his sister by staying at the Old Police House, the home of their childhood, although he knew he would be welcome to do so, even at short notice. Besides which, if he moved in there, he would be too near the post office and shop, and he was not yet ready to confront Tina.

George was jolted back to the present when Mr Brideman left Henry's table. George stood up and walked over.

'Where's Rosalie?' Henry asked.

'Gone home. I walked her out to her car about half an hour ago. She was feeling a bit overwhelmed.'

'Oh. Anything in particular wrong? Apart from the obvious, of course.'

'I think she's just tired. And stressed. She hasn't caught up on her sleep since losing Ben. She was worried about the outcome today. And about Duncan, and Sarah.'

Henry did not reply. He too was concerned about both Sarah and Duncan. And about this case. And the fact that trade at the pub was not too good: it should have picked up at the beginning of the summer but it was still relatively slack.

'Anyway, Rosie asked me to wish you luck,' said George.

'Thanks.' Henry then added, 'I don't know how you get away with calling her *Rosie*; I'd be slaughtered if I tried!'

'Brother's prerogative, mate. Anyway, all the best from me, too.' George patted Henry's shoulder then drifted away.

The usher called them back into court. George was in the gallery when the drivers of the cars caught up in the mayhem re-appeared; the other two members of the public were absent. Then the newspaper reporter returned with a clatter at the last minute.

Chapter 49

Rosalie's journey from Cliffend to Pepper Hill took her through Ashfield. For a moment or two, she wondered whether to stop at The Fighting Cock to see Sarah. But she decided against the idea: she did not know how long Henry's case would take, and she definitely didn't want to see him again today.

Rosalie had never quite managed to resolve the way she and Sarah parted all those years ago. Although Sarah had apologised – after Rosalie had also said 'sorry' – Sarah was distant and never really wanted to be alone with her mother for long. And she definitely did not discuss her private life with her.

Rosalie arrived at the Old Police House and her first task was to telephone the hospital to ask after Duncan. She filled a glass of water before dialling.

When she told him the outcome of the court case, the relief made her feel even more tired. She finished the water, locked the back door and walked through the hall and up the stairs. She showered and, leaving the tiles around the unit to dry themselves instead of wiping them down, walked barefoot back to her bedroom, shut the door, closed the curtains and went to bed.

Here, she wept tears of anger, relief and grief, until she finally fell asleep.

Chapter 50

Henry arrived back at The Fighting Cock in time to see the coach that ferried the local children to and from Cliffend High School pull up at the bus stop near his car park. Several youngsters, in their light green summer uniforms, disembarked.

Henry occasionally had problems from the older students. With their newly-acquired driver's licences as ID, some tried to purchase alcohol from his premises. Did they really think he didn't know their ages? And, even if they were eighteen, he had a personal rule not to sell intoxicating liquor to anyone he knew to still be in full-time education.

As Henry closed the driver's door, he heard a girl's voice from the group call out.

'Hi-ya, Mr Stickleback. Not been locked up for poking your missus, then!'

This was followed by raucous giggling from the senior students. The younger ones were keeping themselves apart; most had already drifted away from the bus stop.

Henry ignored them. He hooked his finger through the loop of his suit jacket and swung it over his shoulder. As he crossed the sunny car park towards the open pub door, he felt an immense relief to be home again.

When Henry walked in, Sarah was behind the bar serving Max, who was muttering surprise that the pint consisted of the correct head-to-beer ratio.

Sarah caught him eyeing the glass with suspicion.

'I was pulling pints as soon as I could reach the taps, Max, as well you know!' Henry heard her say as she whisked away the proffered fiver and headed to the till.

'Afternoon, Henry,' Max turned and greeted him. 'I approve of the new barmaid!'

Henry glared at him. 'Have some respect,' he growled. But he'd turned away before he could see the satisfied smile spread across the old man's face.

Of course Max realised it was young Sarah Stickleback. It was the bump he was more interested in – he noted she wasn't wearing either an engagement or wedding ring.

Gossip had been a bit short in PepperAsh since the Stickleback prang and Poskett's untimely demise. Quinny wasn't in, so Max was hoping to learn something of interest elsewhere. He supped his beer slowly.

'Hi, Dad,' Sarah said brightly as she handed Max his change.

Henry leant forward and kissed her lightly on the cheek.

'Hi, love. How's it going?'

'Not too bad. Max here has been telling me some of the village news.' Her penetratingly blue eyes returned to Max, who lifted his pint to her. 'Anyway, I'm more interested in how you got on at court? How was Mum?'

'She's a bit down at the moment, I think – and not just about the court case. She's worried about Duncan, of course. And that dog of hers ...'

'Old Ben, you mean?'

'Yes, well, she's missing him.'

Henry realised Max was listening, but was then distracted when he saw the rector enter.

'Well, hello there, Henry,' Quinny called across the bar. 'How'd it go?' he asked. 'And I'll have a pint – it's hot out there.'

Sarah reached for a glass.

'I've only just got in. I want to get changed and have something to drink myself before I'm ready to tell you both ...' Henry glared first at Max then Quinny, '... what happened so you can then broadcast my news to the village.'

Although the words were spiked, Henry's voice was playful. He knew it was better to laugh at himself with them, rather than wait until he was out of earshot before they made fun of him.

'Short of a sermon for Sunday, are you Quinny?' he continued. 'Or for Poskett's funeral? When is that, by the way?'

'Not sure what's happening about old Poskett. Can't get hold of any relatives. The solicitor is dealing with everything,' Quinny replied vaguely.

Henry didn't wait for further information. Still thirsty, he turned from his customers to make his way through to the kitchen. He draped his jacket over the back of the nearest chair, picked up the kettle and filled it.

Sarah followed him through when she finished serving Quinny.

'Did he pay?' Henry asked as he started to prepare his own tea/coffee concoction. 'Want anything to drink?'

'No, thanks.' Sarah shook her head. 'And, of course, Quinny didn't pay. Max did!'

'He nicked a packet of crisps the other day,' Henry said without malice. 'Quinny, that is.'

The kettle began to boil as Sarah sat down at the kitchen table. Henry filled his ceramic pot and, as he continued to stir all the taste out of the tea bag into the coffee, he sat down opposite his daughter.

'You look well,' he said.

'You look tired,' she responded. 'Come on, tell me what happened. How did Mum get on?'

Henry took a long swig then repeated most of the court's proceedings. He finished by explaining the penalties they all received.

'They fined me for driving a vehicle that was unroadworthy. And for dangerous driving. Plus I got given six points on my driver's licence – oh, I've got to surrender that at some point. And pay Brideman's bill, when it comes in. Luckily I pleaded guilty, or I think I would've got a lot more.'

'Dad, I'm so sorry,' Sarah sympathised.

'It isn't your fault, love,' he said. 'The magistrates wished Duncan a speedy recovery!' He paused for a few moments, wiped his hand across his face and scratched his beard. 'What a mess, eh? My licence for this place is due for renewal soon. And I now have a criminal record and that could affect my application.'

Unbeknown to either Sarah or Henry, Quinny had crept towards the door that opened into the kitchen. He smiled when he overheard this news: grinning because it was good news, not laughing at Henry's expense – although he did think that *expense* was the operative word.

Quinny sidled back along the bar's edge to his former place next to Max.

'What's the news?' Max asked.

'Can't hear anything when they're right through there – my old ears aren't as good as they used to be!' Quinny supped up and replaced his glass on the bar top. 'Right, I'm off,' he said. 'Got to get home and make some telephone calls. I really do need to sort out Poskett's funeral.' He leant towards the door and shouted to Henry and Sarah, 'I'm off now.'

'Okay. Bye. Thanks,' Sarah raised her voice to answer.

Henry also finished his drink. He stood up and said, 'I'd better change out of this suit. Can you carry on in the bar for a while?'

'Of course,' Sarah replied. 'Take your time. Are you going to see Duncan this evening?'

'I'm not sure. I'll have to speak to Rosalie to find out who else is going. I don't think there's a restriction on the number of visitors he can have now, but it's probably best if your mother and I aren't there at the same time.'

'I really ought to speak to Mum again. But I don't quite know how I'm going to explain this,' she said drawing her hand gently across her stomach. 'She'll probably think it's real.'

'Isn't it?' Henry asked. He was no psychologist, but a phantom pregnancy? Yes, he knew they existed but, to him, this looked real.

No one offered to give Quinny a lift to Pepper Hill. It was late afternoon but the sun was still hot. Shielded from the wind by the hedge along the side of the road, he felt sticky and irritable. He needed to rest by the time St Jude's and the rectory came into view. Yes, he was getting old. And he still had to find Poskett's next of kin.

'Damn it!' he shouted heavenward. 'I could do with a little help down here!'

Chapter 51

George Tillinger waited until Henry drove away from the courthouse car park before also leaving. He walked the few streets back to the Thrimbale Hotel.

George intended to go to the hospital later to see his nephew, Duncan, but was unsure of the visiting times. He asked the hotel's concierge – a dapper man in a smart maroon uniform.

'Six thirty 'til eight, sir,' he informed George. 'Would you like a light meal before you go?'

'If that's possible, yes please.'

Whilst he sat in the restaurant waiting to be served, George wondered if he ought to ring Rosalie to check who else would be visiting; he didn't want to overcrowd Duncan's bed. But he knew she had gone straight home from court to rest and decided to risk going anyway. He could always leave if there were too many.

George was looking forward to catching up with Duncan, and Lily whom he presumed would be there. George and Tina had not attended their wedding – he could not even recall why now. He realised he'd never seen his great-nephew, Jack, who must be nearly three by now.

After George finished his meal, he looked at his watch and saw he still had an hour to spare before he could visit Duncan. Feeling the need for some fresh air and exercise, he decided to walk to the hospital. As he set off through the town of his formative years, it became a journey of nostalgia.

He passed the pub where he'd had his first beer (no, it had not been in The Fighting Cock!). And there was the bank with whom he'd opened his initial account after starting work. Next he encountered Cliffend High School where he and Rosie both attended; the facade still looked the same. His memories of their earlier years there were good, but not the latter ones. George turned away and continued his meander.

Not far from the school was the bus station and, further along, the town hall and a small, open grassed area. He lingered for a while; leaning his hands on the back of a park seat, he glanced slowly around at the colourful shrubs, lush green lawns and smart pathways. But the effect was somewhat spoilt by the profusion of discarded blobs of chewing gum on the pavement slabs.

George had not been here for several years and, as the evening was warm and bright, he was tempted to take a wander along the gravel walkway that led down to the River Potch. As he approached the river bank, he saw a houseboat moving slowly through the water. It was painted blue, the shade of a summer's sky. The name *Germander Speedwell* decorated on the side. Small, bright blue coloured flowers with green stems were intertwined with the lettering.

On this warm, sunny evening, George's thoughts returned to that blissful bank holiday weekend he'd spent cruising the river with Tina. He guessed they had fallen in love then, but George did not like to analyse situations. It had been peaceful but passionate, relaxing but exhausting – the sort of holiday whose memories remain for ever. Even at that time, he could understand why his parents had wanted a few days' break all those years ago. He imagined his mother relaxing on board, just like the lady he spied sitting on the rear deck of the *Germander Speedwell*. She was wearing a cool summer dress, the skin on her arms and shoulders bore the pink of recent sunburn. She rested her bare feet on the lower railing and drank a sip of white wine from a long-stemmed glass. Her companion wore a straw sunhat and his light-coloured shorts were stained with engine oil.

George pondered how carefree and at ease the couple looked. As the houseboat chugged away upriver, he realised the lady at the back was not as young as he'd first thought. Maybe they had their problems, the same as everyone. Other people's lives often seemed idyllic, at least from the outside. He presumed they would moor at Ashfield Staithe for the night. He prayed their fate would be kinder than that of his parents. Then he felt the merest tickle on his arm. He looked down and saw a gnat had landed on him. He swiped at it viciously.

The town hall clock chimed six fifteen. George continued his walk to the hospital.

Upon entering, George asked the young man at the desk for Duncan's whereabouts and was directed to the correct ward. When he arrived at Duncan's bed, his nephew smiled and reached out his hand.

'Hi, hello,' Duncan said as they shook. 'Long time, no see – as they say. How are you?'

'Yeah, I'm very well, thank you – compared with you, anyway. What's with the cut and bruising?' George asked, indicating to Duncan's temple.

'Oh, it isn't as bad as it looks,' Duncan said, self-conscious that it seemed to draw everyone's attention.

'Looks like you've been in a boxing ring,' George told him, as he sat down in the armchair beside the bed.

Duncan was keen to leave the subject.

'Mum rang earlier,' he explained, nodding towards the portable telephone now standing by the window at the end of the bay. 'I haven't got my mobile. She isn't coming in this evening, thought she'd give everyone else a chance. She said you'd been in court with her. She also told me the verdicts – no more than we deserve, really.' Duncan's smile fell away.

'Well, no more than those two deserve,' George stated sternly. 'But it's still all very unfair on you.'

'Maybe you're right. I don't know. But I'm not sure how much more I can stand. I mean, I don't suppose either of them realise, but I'm going to be seriously out of pocket over this. I know I would've had to fix the loader anyway, but now I'll have to get the tanker mended as well. And I don't think just welding a piece of metal over the hole will be enough. If the force of the spike going into the tank didn't buckle the frame, then I'm sure I damaged it when I pulled it out.'

George frowned as he listened. 'Why don't you let me take a look at it? I mean, I am an engineer, after all – and a practical one, not just someone who plays with computers and rulers, flow charts and numbers – look, I've still got oil under my fingernails!' He raised his hands and they both laughed at the black smudges.

'Would you?' Duncan replied with relief. 'That would take a load off my mind. Thank you.'

'What would take a load off your mind?' Lily asked. She had arrived in time to catch Duncan's last words.

Chapter 52

'Hello, love,' Duncan said to Lily. 'You remember my Uncle George?'

George stood up and again extended his hand. 'Hello, Lily.' He noticed a change – a new lightness – in Duncan's spirits as she bent over to him and kissed his lips.

'Where's Jack?' Duncan asked Lily.

'He was tired, so Dad offered to put him to bed.'

'That's a shame,' George said. 'I was looking forward to seeing my great-nephew.' He indicated for Lily to sit in the comfortable chair whilst he fetched a flimsy, moulded plastic one from the stack near the telephone machine by the window.

'Have you heard what happened in court?' Duncan asked as Lily sat down.

'Yes, Henry rang Dad to explain,' she answered wearily. 'Let's hope that's the end of the matter.' She paused and looked intently at her husband. 'I forgot to tell you, I called into the pub to see him on Monday. We ended up having quite a chat.'

'See, I told you he wasn't all bad.'

'No, well, I'm not sure I'd go as far as to say that. Anyway, how are you?'

'Uncle George has offered to have a look at the tanker, to see if it can be mended. That's what we were talking about when you came in,' Duncan replied. 'Anyway, just changing the subject, I have some news. The nurse told me, just before you arrived, Uncle George, that they're transferring me to Mattingburgh hospital tomorrow. And they can do the closure procedure on Friday. They'll still have to do a final test first – like a scan, but they need to look at my heart from inside the gullet so they'll put a camera down my throat. I'll be sedated, they said, but not completely out. Apparently, you know what's happening at the time because they need you to swallow a tube with the camera in it, but you don't remember anything about it afterwards. They also said the closure can be carried out straight away, if it really does need doing. They'll put me under a general anaesthetic for that though – at least, I hope they will.' Duncan was suddenly subdued; he found the prospect quite daunting.

'It all seems a bit quick, doesn't it?' Lily said, somewhat alarmed.

'They've had a cancellation for a cardiac procedure on Friday, apparently,' Duncan responded. 'Dr Kittson isn't on duty until tomorrow morning, but the nurse who told me – Luke, you remember? He usually helps me wash and all that. He said I'll be taken there in a community ambulance – like a bus.'

'Good job I brought clean clothes in for you the other day, then,' Lily said.

'I bet your Mum and Dad will be pleased that something's happening at last,' George added.

'Mum seemed to be, I told her on the phone earlier. I said I'd ring her tomorrow, if I can, just to let her know how I get on. Dad doesn't know yet. I'll tell him if he comes in later.'

'Yes, well, if it hadn't been for all the trouble your mother caused in the first place …'

'It's okay, Lily,' Duncan said, stemming his wife's diatribe. 'I'm supposed to be keeping myself calm, you know.'

'Sorry, love. It's just that …'

This time it was George who interrupted. 'If it helps

at all, she is feeling very guilty, even if she hasn't admitted as much.'

'I don't want her to feel bad, not really.' Duncan spoke quietly, looking first at his Uncle George then at his beautiful young wife. 'I just want all the arguing and the problems it causes to stop.' He shrugged.

George noticed he looked tired.

'Right, well, I'll do what I can to sort out that big sister of mine,' he said tactfully, rising from his chair. 'I'll leave you two alone now. You look as if you need to rest, Duncan. Good to catch up with you, Lily.' He felt able to give her a swift farewell kiss on her cheek. 'I look forward to seeing young Jack soon.' He touched Duncan's shoulder briefly. 'And I'll have a look at your vehicle as soon as I can.'

'Thanks, Uncle ...'

'George will be fine,' he said with a smile. 'None of that *uncle* business now you've got a family of your own – makes me feel too old. We'll save that for Jack, shall we?'

'Fine by me.'

'Bye,' Lily said as George left.

They listened to his footsteps receding on the polished floor.

'He's nice,' Lily remarked.

'Yes, he's always been good to Sarah and me, but he hasn't been around much,' Duncan confirmed. 'Mum's okay, too, really.' Lily made a *huh* sound. Duncan continued. 'She's been on her own for a long time now, you know. Her Mum and Dad, my grandparents, were killed when she was only sixteen.'

'I know that,' Lily snapped. 'But it doesn't excuse her behaviour.'

'No, maybe not. But think how you love your

parents, and how they love you. Remember how much you rely on them for help and support, especially with Jack. Look at the wedding they gave us, for a start. My Mum didn't have any of that. Yes, hers was paid for by an insurance her father took out when she was born, but she didn't have her Dad to give her away. Her mother wasn't there to help organise it, or go with her to choose the wedding dress and make sure she looked okay on the big day, was she? What would you do if your parents suddenly weren't there?'

Lily was frowning. She wasn't ungrateful for everything she had; she just didn't like being reminded of it.

Duncan's tone was more considerate when he spoke again.

'Remember that Mum was eight years younger than you are now when her parents died. She got married not long afterwards, probably in an effort to find some kind of security. We all know that didn't work out, and then she had to bring Sarah and me up more or less on her own, didn't she? And when she can't cope with things, she gets angry – especially if she asks for help and is ignored.' This reminded Duncan of the chip pan fire again; absentmindedly, he scratched the scar on his wrist.

Lily was quiet for a while. He reached for her hand and held it until she looked up at him.

'I'm sorry. I didn't mean to criticise,' she said. 'It's just that their fighting has made you ill.'

'Well, maybe it just brought it to a head. The doctor said I've always had this hole in my heart, but I obviously haven't had any bother with it until now. It wasn't anybody's fault that it didn't close up as it should have done after I was born. At least it's been found now, and they're going to do something about it. Yes, Mum and Dad's prang might have been the catalyst that made us realise something was wrong. Anyway, this time last week, I didn't know there was anything the matter, did I? None of us did. And if I'd really exerted myself at any time in the future, who knows what might've happened.'

Duncan could see Lily was still upset, so he didn't say any more.

Lily did not want to tell Duncan her good news like this – that she thought she might be expecting again. If her dates were right, it might be an Easter baby. On the other hand, it could just be the worry that was making her period late.

At that moment, she heard footsteps approaching Duncan's bed. She glanced around and she saw her father-in-law walking towards them with Duncan's twin sister, Sarah, following.

And suddenly it looked as if there would be another baby Stickleback in the family soon anyway.

Chapter 53

Bernie, Fred and Fido, the At Hand refitting team, finished their work late on Wednesday afternoon. They then celebrated with a final mug of tea before leaving. The skip was still firmly planted in the lay-by. The discarded fittings, shelving and spoilt non-food stock filled it level; Tina wondered if any extra waste would appear before it was removed on Friday.

Tina was pleased with the refurbishment. Outside, a new frontage had been attached – arriving almost as a complete unit, requiring minimal fixing and a single electrical connection.

A faint odour from the sewage spill across the road still pervaded the area, but it had not entered the shop and post office – the interior of which smelt of fresh paint and brand-new electrical appliances.

The new displays and fixtures were sparkling; the sun shining through the windows gleamed off the surfaces. Everything seemed bright and clean and hopeful.

Tina finished stocking the shelves during the evening. It was hard and lonely work. Bertha Bunfighter was perched to the side of the shop counter near the till to oversee the proceedings. Tina wondered if that might be a good place for the enormous teddy bear when the new facility opened; it – she – would provide a topic of conversation to break the ice with her customers. Looking at Bertha now, Tina decided this position warranted a new ribbon, the existing one being brown and orange, it barely (huh, *bearly*, maybe!) contrasted with her brown colouring. A bright yellow or light green silk would be better.

Just after eight o'clock, the telephone rang – the line having now been mended. Tina answered the extension in the store room office. It was Mr Dentforth. He confirmed that he would be arriving in Pepper Hill on Friday morning to finalise the reopening of the post office, set up the computerised systems and alarm, and authorise everything for Tina's use. After this, he informed her, she would be online, therefore on call, 24/7.

Tina hated that expression: it meant she would never have a moment's peace. As she listened to her manager's detached voice, she retrieved her mobile phone from her pocket and found there was still no signal available – not even for emergency calls.

'While I'm there, I'll also check on the refurbishment of the shop – make sure it isn't just a cheap and tatty botched job that will reflect badly on the integrity of the post office,' he stated with proprietorial bluster.

Tina was about to ask if the leasing procedure had been completed, or even if the proper owner had been found yet, but Mr Dentforth was still talking. 'I'm not really happy to share the premises with a franchise,' he mooted. 'Especially under the present circumstance, but I suppose there's no feasible alternative.'

You're not happy, Tina thought. *You should try being here, then!*

When the telephone call was over, Tina picked Bertha up by her shoulder and carried her through to the back room: she thought it would be better not to leave the bear in the post office for Mr Dentforth to see. When she felt a slight ripping, she instinctively clutched Bertha's fat body to her, her wrist resting against something small and hard. But, as she'd already concluded this was possibly some kind of voice mechanism, she dismissed it immediately.

She walked through to the back room and plonked Bertha down on the table. She made herself a cup of tea and slumped into a chair opposite. Holding her face in her hands whilst her drink cooled, she wished with all her heart that she was somewhere – anywhere – else other than here.

Pleasant solitude had plummeted to pure loneliness. And it was overwhelming. Nothing could block out the empty, aching blankness.

Tina pressed her eyes with her finger tips, causing a kaleidoscope of colours to stream onto her retina. It took a few moments for her to focus after releasing them and, when she could see properly again, she was looking directly into the face of her giant teddy bear.

Bertha looked just as unhappy and dejected as Tina felt. She still missed George and she knew her present circumstances – the fact that she was, in effect, camping in a stranger's back room – was her own fault.

After a few moments of self-indulgent misery, Tina remembered she had happened across a bottle of sherry whilst investigating the contents of the kitchen cupboards a couple of days ago. She was tempted.

Tina didn't drink because she liked the taste – she had tested a wide variety of alcoholic beverages just to make sure: she drank to make herself feel better. And she needed that right now. Fully aware that any pleasure would be ephemeral, she pictured her discovery, hiding from view. It would not take much energy to retrieve it.

The sherry was in a blue bottle. Tina knew from experience that blue glass was the most difficult of all colours to dispose of at recycling centres. The majority of actual bottle banks tended to provide receptacles for green, brown and clear glass. Sometimes, though, there would only be two containers: one for clear glass and the other simply labelled coloured glass. Tina would have to investigate the local facilities – probably on the supermarket car park at Cliffend, which would prove problematic if anyone from At Hand saw her. She argued that this was extremely unlikely. Anyway, that was a puzzle for tomorrow.

Today's dilemma revolved around how much sherry she should drink in order to lift her mood from its present doldrums, but not become incapacitated. Maybe just one glass would be okay; then, because the bottle would not be empty, she need not worry about having to dispose of it. She could still picture the bottles she'd left in Cordnell.

Eventually, and despite Bertha's obvious but unspoken disapproval, Tina rose hesitantly from the table and crossed the room to the cupboard. She opened the door. There it was; the blue sherry bottle, two-thirds full. Tina reiterated the thought that she could have just a single glass.

It was good sherry. Not cooking sherry. On one occasion, Tina had drunk quite a lot of cooking sherry. She could not remember how many times she had refilled the glass, or how big the glass itself had been: she didn't measure her intake; she was in control. Hadn't she stopped at two glasses of wine at lunch yesterday in the pub with the postman?

But this evening, before she actually drank any, Tina thought of George. He hadn't replied to any of her texts or emails. He obviously didn't want anything to do with her anymore. She found a small glass and returned with this and the bottle to the table. She sat down again.

Whilst they were together, George had spoken very

little about his and Rosalie's family. There were rumours that Henry's father, Woody, was an alcoholic, but he'd died long before she and George met.

Mona's wedding invitation came into Tina's mind. She had just wanted to attend a social event with her husband, for them to be seen by the world as a normal couple. She needed the security of knowing that they *were* a normal married couple; that they enjoyed being together, with each other, feeling warmth by a casual touch, standing side by side. She imagined them, George and Tina Tillinger, in their smartest finery; Tina smoothing George's tie and smiling back at him as he tucked a strand of stray hair behind her ear. She longed for intimate, shared moments.

Their own wedding had taken place in a register office, with two friends as witnesses and only a few others plus her grandmother, Hilda, joining them for a drink afterwards. Tina felt cheated at the time, but George insisted that big weddings did not make for happy marriages. He cited Henry and Rosalie's as an example. And, although it was obvious to her George knew why the Sticklebacks split up, he would not tell Tina. This made her feel second best: although couples are supposed to tell each other everything, George would not break Rosalie and Henry's confidence.

Tina found her mind wandering to George's car *Hercules*. She was shamed of damaging the windscreen. She should have baulked now at the idea of drinking, of losing both control and dignity. But she didn't.

She poured a measure of the dark amber liquid and sipped, appreciating its texture, aroma and taste.

She felt the tears. George would start divorce proceedings soon. His lack of contact made this obvious. Waiting for that final cut was intolerable.

Chapter 54

Tina suddenly drank all the sherry she had poured. It was sweet and thick – the label described it as 'rich and full-bodied'. It burned its way down. She hoped that, because of its supposed good quality, her hangover tomorrow would not be too severe.

Soon the alcohol entered her bloodstream and glowed its warmth through her body. Her extremities began to tingle and a silly smile planted itself on her lips. Finally, her brain was flooded and her thoughts became fuddled. Never mind. She could try not to drink again tomorrow.

Tomorrow. She would be okay. Tomorrow was Thursday. Friday, she would have to be sober. Christ! She had to see the slimy Dentforth at nine o'clock on Friday morning. The day after tomorrow. But Thursday was okay. It could serve as a buffer, to absorb the aftermath of this evening. She poured another glass – generous would be a modest description. Turning to the teddy bear, she saluted and drank. Bertha Bunfighter scowled.

The grin on Tina's lips broadened. Her hands shook as she tried to fill the glass, chinking the bottle top on the rim. She took a long sip this time, satisfied that she could distinguish the taste of oak casket from the sun-ripened grape.

Tina sighed as her mind grew further detached from her surroundings. This was the escape she wished for. She stared at the window. Surprisingly, the daylight was still strong outside, albeit low on the horizon. She had no idea of the actual time; she could not focus on the wall clock or on her wrist watch. The feeling of missing George hit her again. And that cold, hard lump of hurt and loneliness was expanding from her diaphragm, pushing up into her throat, burning with the acid that was returning the alcohol.

She sighed, realising that inebriation was not the best state in which to dissect and examine her and George's relationship. But her limbs were relaxing nicely and, although her thinking still came from behind her eyes, her mind was distanced from her head.

George.

She thought her husband must be having an affair. She wouldn't have been surprised if there had been the odd one-night stands, or even a couple of short flings – after all, he was away from home for long periods of time. Also, she knew he was not always offshore; he did shifts onshore as well, both in the company's office and fabrication yards. A dark part inside was jealous and she momentarily wished she'd had the courage to seek comfort elsewhere. But that was not in her character. Tina was faithful – foolish, but faithful. Then she thought of Jim and shame crashed down onto her.

She took another mouthful of sherry and noticed the dark amber colour appeared lighter when there was less left in the glass. Maybe she should top it up again. But she didn't want any more to drink either. She screwed the top back on the bottle.

Now she needed a glass of water. And a visit to the toilet. Steadying herself, and still holding her half-full glass, she tentatively stood up and started to walk slowly across the kitchen towards the sink.

By the time she reached her destination, her legs were wobbling. She held onto the sides of the sink whilst the scene in the garage at Treemoore came to her mind again. She giggled at the memory of *Hercules'* broken windscreen. How she hated that stupid car!

Suddenly, she was too angry to finish the sherry. In a swift fling – which made her lurch to one side – it was disappearing down the plug hole.

Tina wondered what damage neat sherry would do to the waste water pipework, especially as, yes, she thought she could now detect the odour from the sludge spillage outside the Old Police House coming up.

She was beyond appreciating the irony of worrying about the drains whilst merrily consuming vast quantities of alcohol and not thinking of the harm it was causing her own systems.

She turned on the tap and rinsed the glass, and then ran cold water until it was full to the rim. She slowly drank this, letting the chilled purity settle the furnace inside her gut. She was sorry. So sorry. Sorry for everything.

Eventually, Tina placed the empty glass upside down on the draining board and returned unsteadily to her chair at the kitchen table.

Bertha was watching.

Tina wanted to berate the bear for disapproving so visibly. But, instead, she leant her elbows on the table top, crossed her arms and laid her head on them, face down.

She could hear her heart beat now. Her bladder was still full, but she would have to hold it. She could sleep, if she wanted. If only her heart didn't thud so loudly. Must be something about the room, Tina mused; persistent and indomitable banging. She was surprised that she could still use – and use correctly – such long and complicated words, although she was not sure she was capable of spelling that second one.

Tina felt she must be dreaming. The workmen told her the story of Phil the newspaper delivery man peering into the kitchen window and seeing Poskett in the chair, the very same chair that was opposite the table.

Poskett was dead. Tina could picture the scene.

She presumed the banging, thumping sound from Phil probably did not stop immediately. Just like it would not stop now.

Tina was beginning to question whether or not she believed in ghosts. She always disputed their existence. Maybe a re-enactment was taking place, because she thought she heard a voice. It sounded muffled. Like it was outside. Somebody was calling. Calling her name.

'Tina?' someone – a man – roared. 'Are you all right in there? Tina? Open this bloody door!'

He sounded angry. Tina thought, *perhaps it's Phil with tomorrow's newspaper delivery. No, that can't be right; the shop isn't opening tomorrow. Tomorrow, Mr Dentforth is coming. No, he isn't. Tomorrow is Thursday. He's coming on Friday. I'll be sober by then.*

The thumping started again. *Oh God, it is Dentforth! It must be him.* But she did not stir to let him in.

Then the voice yelled at the window, 'Tina? Get up and open the door.'

She recognised him. It was definitely not Arthur Dentforth – or Phil, whom she'd never met.

Tina raised her head and glanced reproachfully at Bertha Bunfighter, who was scolding her for ignoring whoever was hammering at the door.

Tina finally rose and crossed the room. She turned the key, unlocked the door and stood aside to avoid being hit when it was forced inwards.

George was very angry.

Chapter 55

George patted his hand down the inside wall for the light switch. In the sudden brightness, Tina stood squinting at him, as if she didn't know who he was.

'Tina!' Although he was livid with rage, he was not angry with her. She had changed so much. He felt remorse that he couldn't even remember when he'd last seen her – seven months ago, maybe more. They had communicated, talked on the phone, emailed, texted – but her recent messages had gone unanswered. And he hadn't come home to her probably since Christmas.

She had lost weight and her clothes were grimy, but that was possibly because she had been working to get the shop ready rather than the result of self-neglect. She was, however, blatantly drunk.

Tina did not respond to George. But she did look frightened.

George would never physically hurt anyone. He had seen both fist and cat-fights at work; he'd even stepped in to break some up. He reached forward, intending to place his hand on Tina's shoulder and encourage her towards a chair at the table where, through the window, he'd seen her sitting. But she flinched before he touched her, stepping back and nearly stumbling. He reached out and caught her, but she was not comfortable with his support.

The realisation that Tina was defensive and wary injured George more than if she had thrown scalding water over him.

'It's okay. I just want us to sit down,' he explained, trying not to patronise. He hoped his tone was firm but gentle.

Tina did not respond but he felt she was trembling. She smelt of sherry and he could see the blue bottle behind her.

'This way,' he coaxed, guiding her.

As they approached the table, George looked around. There was a duvet and pillow stashed on the sofa and he was astonished to realise that this single room must be where Tina was living and sleeping.

'I'll make some coffee,' George said quietly, walking towards the work-top. He was furious with himself; he had not bothered to check that she was adequately housed, here or at her previous assignments. Even though they were not together, he recognised he had a moral responsibility towards her welfare: he was the one who left. Even if he no longer loved her, he would always care about her.

As George made black coffee (there was no milk in her fridge, nor much of anything else); he wondered how long she had been sitting in the dark, by herself, drinking. *For about four years,* he answered himself reproachfully.

When he placed the cup on the table in front of Tina, she moaned that she did not want coffee – black or otherwise.

'Just drink it,' he advised, hearing in his tone the reluctant authority he'd employed with Rosie in the courthouse cafeteria. 'It will help you to sober up.'

She did not reach for it.

'Please,' he added quietly, trying not to plead.

She remained motionless, her eyes glistening and hands shaking.

George sat down at the table next to her; the space opposite was occupied by a big, ugly, brown teddy bear.

'Who's your friend?' he asked in a light, amused tone as he thrust his thumb in the bear's direction. When he looked again, however, there was something oddly familiar about it: something unsettling.

Tina glanced at the stuffed toy, paused for a few moments then cleared her throat.

'Bertha,' she announced proudly.

'Bertha?' George repeated.

Tina nodded and redirected her gaze from the bear in order to study the coffee in front of her.

'I won her, at the fête in Cordnell just before I left. Had to guess her name. I called her Bertha. Bertha Bunfighter. She looked miserable.'

'So do you.' George tried not to smile at the name, and wondered how Tina had thought that up.

'I feel miserable ...' Tina started to say.

George's temper suddenly snapped.

'I'm not surprised. Is this where you've been living? I know old Poskett died, but they could've sorted you out somewhere more suitable to stay! Why didn't you contact Rosalie?'

Tina was startled at his harsh tone. She pulled her hands away and tried to stand up.

George reached out for her, but she recoiled again. He drew back and left his arms slightly raised, his palms submissively facing her.

'Sorry, I didn't mean anything. I wouldn't hurt you, Tina. You know that.'

A long silence ensued. After a while, George sensed she was relaxing a little: the hunch in her shoulders had fallen slightly and her jaw slackened. She looked exhausted. He gestured for her to sit down again and, to his surprise, she did. He ventured to ask again who was in charge of her assignment.

'Mr Dentforth,' Tina volunteered. 'Arthur Dentforth. My area manager. You met him once, years ago when we first moved to Treemoore,' she explained guardedly.

'Dentforth – yes, you told me. Fat chap, sweaty. He's got a red face, and bad breath.'

'Yes.' Tina leant forward, rested her arms on the table top and wrapped her hands around the coffee cup. The coffee now felt cool enough to drink. But she did not have the confidence or strength to lift it to her lips.

She looked up at her husband. The room was swaying in waves. George watched her. In his face she read his guilt; he could not berate her for being inebriated because his absences had made her so unhappy. But her own bitterness had contributed to his betrayal. And now, here they were sitting at a kitchen table in a room where neither of them belonged.

'What's the time?' Tina asked. Her thoughts were lucid and she did not slur her words, although she could not quite fathom why the hour was important.

George consulted his watch. It was an expensive, all-purpose, air-tight, water-resistant model that someone special who was not Tina had bought for his birthday before last. He unclipped it from his wrist and slipped it into his inside jacket pocket.

'I think it's broken,' he said to explain the removal. 'The time doesn't matter. I'll stay with you here tonight and we'll try to sort things out in the morning. If you can't manage the coffee, I'll get you a glass of water – it'll probably do you more good than caffeine, otherwise you won't sleep.'

George stood up, lifting his chair to avoid scraping the feet on the hard floor, and removed Tina's cup from her hands. A few moments later, he replaced it with a clean, water-filled glass.

'I've just drunk some water,' she said, but sipped a little anyway before carefully rising to her feet. 'I need the loo.'

When Tina returned, she side-stepped around George and collected Bertha. The bear stared at him as the pair receded to the sofa. Tina did not bother to make up the bed but settled down along the seat. She dragged the duvet over and arranged the pillow under her head. Clutching the stuffed toy to her like a shield, she quickly fell asleep.

Chapter 56

Duncan had spoken to Rosalie on the telephone. On the one hand, she was apprehensive about his tests and possible procedures but, on the other, extremely relieved that he would not be waiting months for his treatment.

Later during the evening, Rosalie looked out of the front window of the Old Police House and spied a familiar car parked in the lay-by near the post office and shop, next to the rubbish skip. She surmised George was visiting Tina.

Rosalie had hoped George would ask to stay at the Old Police House with her rather than pay for an expensive hotel room. But he hadn't. So she reasoned that, if George and Tina were to be reconciled, they would not want Rosalie in the adjacent bedroom.

On Thursday morning, Rosalie resolved to ring Henry's pub and speak with Sarah. But before then she needed to tidy Ben's things away. He was gone. She had shed tears and would probably cry for him again at some point. But he had died, and that was that.

She shook the dog hairs from his blankets and towels before putting them through the washing machine. She cleaned his food and water bowls, but left the bag and a half of Ben's food in the cupboard, thinking she would take them to her neighbour who owned three Spaniels. Next, she took Ben's basket out onto the lawn and scrubbed it thoroughly.

Maybe she would have another dog at some time in the future – perhaps buy a puppy, or find an older dog that needed a new home. Either way, the basket needed to be clean, although she knew, to a dog's nose, she could never entirely erase the scent of a predecessor.

She left the basket in the sunshine to dry before tackling other housework.

Two hours later, just as she completed the last of the dusting and vacuuming, the telephone rang. She hoped it would be George saying he would take up her offer. She now realised that, sub-consciously, she had been tidying the house in preparation.

'Hello. Rosalie here,' she said into the receiver.

'Hi, it's Sarah.'

'Oh, hello, love.' Disappointment and excitement were both evident in Rosalie's voice.

'You sound as if you were expecting someone else, Mum.'

'No, no, love. It's so good to hear from you. I was going to ring you later, for a chat. I'd love to see you.'

'That's what I was ringing for. But firstly, are you okay? Dad said you, er ...'

'I'm fine, thank you,' Rosalie interrupted. 'I think everything just got a bit on top of me, especially with Duncan being taken ill and Ben dying. And it was a surprise to see your uncle again. But I must admit I feel relieved now that the court case is over with.' She paused before adding, 'and the outcome could have been worse. I mean, could you imagine your father and me having to do some kind of community service?' Rosalie laughed.

'Well, not together, no. Anyway, I wondered if you could come over here for lunch?'

'What, to the pub? Today?' Suspicion suddenly replaced the cheerfulness in Rosalie's voice.

'Yes, I want to talk to you – to you all, actually. I've invited Uncle George as well, so he can act as referee, in case we need one – which I hope we won't!'

Rosalie was silent for a moment before agreeing.

'What time do you want me there?'

'About one o'clock. Polly will be in to look after the bar so we won't be disturbed.'

'Okay, that sounds fine. Would you like me to bring anything?'

'Just a sunny disposition,' Sarah joked. 'Seriously, though, Mum, please be in a good mood. And don't argue with Dad. I want to talk to you both, but I don't want to have to worry that either of you will pick a row just for the sake of it.'

Again, Rosalie was silent. *Are Henry and I really that bad?* she asked herself.

'Okay, I promise I'll behave if he behaves.'

'MUM!' Sarah shouted. 'You're at it already. You just can't help yourself, can you? Just remember that Duncan might ring while you're here – to let us know how things are going. So at least keep calm for that.'

Their conversation concluded with Rosalie undertaking to remain civil throughout the discussions, no matter what – which sounded rather ominous.

Sarah thought this pledge was possibly a good sign. Rubbing the sore underside of her bump where her skin was being stretched by the weight above it, she hoped her mother would remember the promise when she actually saw her.

Chapter 57

Nurse Luke arrived on Duncan's ward after breakfast on Thursday morning. Duncan had managed to shower, shave and dress himself – but, as a consequence, the dizziness returned with a vengeance. He was sitting by the bed staring at the floor when Luke brought the wheelchair for him.

'Not feeling so great this morning?' Luke asked.

Duncan glanced up and carefully shook his head, just once.

'Okay, mate, we'll soon have you on your way. Just think ahead, it won't be long before you can lie down again. Have you got everything?'

'Yes, my bag is all packed – Dad and my sister helped me last night, and I've just shoved the things I used this morning in the top. Lily will sort it out later when she visits.'

Luke helped Duncan transfer from the comfy chair to the wheelchair. Although it was summer, he placed a blanket around Duncan's legs. He suddenly became aware that his patient was in distress. Deftly, he retrieved a grey cardboard dish from behind the bedside locker and placed it on Duncan's lap – just in time for breakfast to return.

'I'm so sorry,' said Duncan as Luke discreetly held the box of tissues towards him. He took one and another, then a third to wipe his mouth and chin. His clothes were okay, but the blanket was now soiled. The smell made him want to retch again, which further humiliated him.

'Don't worry about it. I've cleaned up worse!' Luke joked as he drew the curtains around Duncan's bed area. But this made Duncan feel even more disconsolate. If Lily had been there, he was sure he would have wept.

Luke replaced the cardboard bowl with a fresh one, explained that he would be back in a minute or two and went to dispose of the waste.

He returned with a face cloth and plastic wash-bowl containing warm water.

'We'll soon have you spruced up and ready,' he said as he produced a fresh face cloth and towel.

A little while later, Luke wheeled Duncan out to the community ambulance. The driver, who was as bright and cheerful as Luke, operated the lift mechanism. Duncan plus wheelchair were soon winched into the back and clamped into place, with restraining belts drawn around the patient.

'You're lucky,' Luke explained. 'We've got the whole bus to ourselves this morning!' And he settled himself into an ordinary seat opposite.

Chapter 58

On Thursday morning, George woke to find himself still sitting in the chair in the back room of the post office and shop in Pepper Hill. His spine was aching and his legs and shoulders were stiff. It was daylight; bright sunshine streamed through the window. He glanced at his wrist, but then remembered he'd removed his watch last night and stowed it in his jacket pocket, which was hanging behind the door.

He quietly stood up and stretched. He felt grimy and tousled, his chin irritated with the overnight growth of bristles. He hated stubble. He scratched, first his face, then anywhere else that itched. He finally glanced at the wall clock which showed it was half past seven.

George expected to see Tina still asleep on the sofa, but she was not there. He walked over and picked up the large teddy bear, now discarded on the floor. *Bertha Bunfighter, eh?* Smiling, he examined it, thinking how scruffy and dejected it looked.

Shops and market stalls were full of such toys, but he kept feeling this one was somehow familiar, especially with its untidy repair to the stitching on one shoulder and the lumpy stuffing around it. Even the faded and fraying orangey-brown ribbon bit into his memory. Mainly, though, he was piqued by its sad expression. It needed cheering up, he deduced. Just like poor Tina.

A few minutes later, Tina returned. She was wearing her dressing gown and sported a towel turban around her head, having obviously showered and washed her hair.

'Morning,' she said quite cheerfully.

George guessed she must have a supply of aspirin or

paracetamol in the bathroom cabinet and had taken a couple some while ago; there was no way that she would not have a hangover this morning. But then he realised, he really didn't know Tina any more.

'How are you feeling?' he asked as he moved towards the sink area, intending to fill the kettle and prepare coffee for them.

'Oh, you know. Not too bad,' Tina replied blithely as she unfurled the turban, bent forward and began to rub her scalp rigorously with the towel. She stopped and added, 'I didn't want to disturb you earlier or I'd've made us some tea. Or coffee. Not sure which you prefer nowadays.'

George ignored the snipe as he opened the fridge. It had not magically filled itself over night and there was still an absence of milk.

'Whichever of the two, it'll have to be black. Why haven't you got any groceries?'

Tina ceased drying her hair, sat down at the kitchen table and explained that, with the post office and shop refurbishment work being carried out, she hadn't had a chance to go to the supermarket.

'The stock now in place doesn't include perishables – you know, processed meats, dairy products, fruit and vegetables. That's still all got to be sorted out. By yours truly, by the way, in case you're thinking I've got help stashed away somewhere.'

The kettle boiled. Feeling a little chastised, George made black coffee. Tina combed out her damp hair; it was long, brown and shiny, and hung in relatively thin strands which George knew would burgeon as they dried. The silence was thick between them. But the coffee smelt enticing; it made Tina's stomach rumble.

'Can we call a truce?' she asked. 'I'm starving.'

'I can hear,' George replied. 'I thought you'd at least have the decency to have a hangover this morning.'

'I didn't drink that much,' Tina said quietly. 'I was just surprised to see you. I thought you were still in Treemoore, teaching youngsters to be engineers. I texted. You could've replied, not just shown up on the door step.'

George sat down, bowed his head and carefully considered his response.

'The lecturer's post was only temporary. MaCold said I could have a break then start on another project in a few months' time, if I wanted to carry on working for them. But I don't think I do.'

Tina did not answer. She scrutinised her hair for split ends and let the silence grow.

George looked around the room. In daylight it looked even shabbier than it had last night. It was depressingly old-fashioned with furnishings from a previous generation. Tina deserved better than this.

'I could come and help you here for a while,' he offered in a conciliatory voice. 'If you want me to.'

Tina stopped her inspection. This suggestion was unexpected. As much as she thought no one could surprise her anymore – either with kindness or cruelty – she was astounded.

'That would be, er … I would like that very much,' she finally managed to say. 'But where would we …' She looked around the room. 'This, and the bathroom and cupboard upstairs, is all I have access to. The rest of the house is locked off. Mr Dentforth is supposed to be sorting it out with a solicitor or somebody. A chap called Brideman, I think. But no one has come to see me about it. I'm not even sure if I should really be starting up the shop again. The At Hand franchise people are keen for it to reopen; apparently, it's quite *a good little earner*, as the saying goes. But, I mean, I don't know who's legally responsible for the premises.'

During this speech, George had been scrutinising her. He'd forgotten how animated her face became when she was excited or anxious. He allowed a smile to spread.

She saw this and frowned.

'I knew you would laugh at me. Everything I try to do is inconsequential to you, isn't it?'

'No, no. I wasn't laughing *at* you,' George stated quickly. 'I'm just so pleased to see you.' He waited a few moments. 'I got rid of *Hercules*. Sold him to a collector, smashed windscreen and all.'

'I fell,' Tina snapped. 'I accidentally smashed the glass,' she repeated the pathetic explanation she had offered at the time.

'Yeah, I know. I watched the footage of you trying to find your front door key when you came back from the chip shop, remember? Anyway, it doesn't matter,' George stated. 'I'm glad you're okay – in general and especially after last night.'

'Oh, yes. That's right. Go and throw that at me!' Tina shouted at him. 'So I had a little drink. Wouldn't you if you were stuck here – or anywhere – on your own all the time?'

'Yes, I think I would,' George agreed quietly. He sipped at his coffee as he thought back to yesterday and all that happened: the courtroom, Rosie, Duncan. 'Yes,' he said again.

Tina, faced with George not responding to her anger, picked up her coffee cup and drank some.

'I hate black coffee,' she declared after the first mouthful.

'So do I,' George affirmed. 'Get dressed and I'll take you out to breakfast.'

'That sounds nice,' Tina said, a wide smile appearing. 'Where were you thinking of going?'

'I'm booked into the Thrimbale Hotel in Cliffend, we could go there. And I can have a shower and shave.'

'You can shower here, at least I've got that facility,' Tina countered.

'It'll be easier with my own gear,' George stated, rubbing his bristly chin.

Tina hesitated for a moment. 'Your offer of a hotel breakfast is very tempting. I thought for a moment there you were going to suggest The Fighting Cock in Ashfield.'

'No, not this morning. I don't think Henry does breakfasts, although he could probably rustle up something for us. But I've been invited there for lunch.'

Tina looked askance at George.

'Sarah has invited Rosie and me – Henry will be there, of course. But yes, I think it might be a bit of a battle. Sarah's expecting but is telling everyone it's a phantom pregnancy, which no one believes – not even her, I'm sure.'

Tina did not know how she was expected to respond to this news, so she ignored it. 'What did you tell them about us?' she asked as she resumed combing her hair.

'Nothing. But I mentioned that your job now involved filling in for post office employees who were either away training, on maternity leave and the like, or who just wanted some time off, for whatever reason.'

'A *peripatetic manager* Mr Dentforth called me the other day,' Tina interjected.

'And what did you call him in return?' George asked as he finished his coffee.

'Not repeatable, well what I thought wasn't. Tell me more about breakfast.'

'Are you up for it?'

'I would like to, I must admit. But I'm supposed to be here in case … Oh, sod it. I've only been away from the place a couple of times since I arrived on Monday. The first time I just drove up the road 'til I could get a phone signal, and the second time I went to lunch in Ashfield. I think I deserve a few hours out.' But then she reconsidered. 'What if the At Hand people come to deliver any more stock?'

'They'll have to leave it, wait for you or go away and come back again later when you're here,' George said decisively. 'Right, I'll just …' He pointed to the door to the hall.

'Oh, yes. Okay. The bathroom's up the stairs, second door along. I'll be getting ready.' Tina turned towards a cupboard where her suitcases were stored to retrieve some clothes.

Chapter 59

Tina dressed quickly whilst George was in the bathroom. She put on a soft pink T-shirt, a pair of light denim jeans and flat white sandals. The waistband was loose and, when she glanced at her reflection in the window above the sink, she saw her cheeks were drawn and her shoulders looked bony. She felt self-conscious when George returned and asked if she was ready. She smiled at him and nodded before retrieving her bag from near the sofa. She patted good old Bertha Bunfighter's head and joined George at the back door.

When they stepped outside to walk to the car, the sunlight was so bright it hurt Tina's eyes. She realised that, despite the recent lovely summer weather, she'd spent most of her time indoors since arriving in Pepper Hill. The feel of a fresh breeze on her face was pleasant and uplifting.

George clicked his key towards a large, dark blue vehicle parked in the lay-by behind the full waste skip. Tina wanted to compare this with the sporty yellow *Hercules*, but the words would not form into an acceptable comment. George opened the passenger door for her and she stepped daintily in.

The Old Police House was visible as they turned left out onto the road, but Tina was unable to see Rosalie as they passed. George drove eastwards, over the culvert, through 'The Tunnel' – a stretch of road shaded by trees whose branches met over the top of the vehicles. They soon left its cool darkness and started to ascend the hill.

When the rectory and St Jude's Church came into sight on Tina's left, she smiled.

'Better slow down and check to see if that rector chap

– Quinny – wants a lift,' she advised.

'I beg your pardon?' George asked quizzically, secretly enjoying being with Tina. She seemed fresh and light and uncomplicated today, compared with the last time they spent time together. Since they'd been apart, he hadn't thought much about her. And that was his greatest fault, he had often been told: *out of sight out of mind*. George concentrated only on the matters and persons with him at a particular moment and forgot about everything else.

'Quinny,' Tina was explaining. 'The Reverend Quintin Boyce. Apparently, it's traditional around here to give him a lift if he's waiting, or walking along the road, or just hanging around. I don't think he can drive; he relies on everyone else's transport. He's quite a character – they were talking about him when I went to the pub yesterday with ...'

'It's okay, you know. You are allowed friends, male as well as female,' George stated. He didn't mean to sound condescending but was afraid that was how his remark would seem.

'And what about you?' Tina snapped back, suddenly annoyed at being patronised. 'Have you got any *friends*, anyone special you spend time with?'

George concentrated on his driving for a moment before saying quietly. 'No one else except you.'

'But you have had?' she fired aggressively.

George did not reply. The silence extended. As they approached Ashfield, The Fighting Cock came into view.

'I don't expect you'll want a big breakfast if you're off for lunch with your family later,' Tina said, deciding the previous matter was not worth pursuing.

'They're your family as well,' George stated.

'Not really. I don't know the Sticklebacks that well, do I? But, I suppose you're going to say that's *my* fault!'

George tried to ignore this. Eventually, he decided to be honest. 'You asked a little while ago if there was anyone special I'd been spending time with.'

'Well?' Tina suddenly did not really wish to know the truth. 'Is there?'

'No, not now.' George then inhaled deeply and explained, 'But I was seeing someone in Aberdeen. A woman called Lorna. In fact, for a long time we lived together.'

'Stop the car,' Tina screeched. When George did not react, she yelled louder, 'STOP THE CAR!'

George braked hard, causing them both to jerk violently against their seat belts. Tina undid hers, snatched at her bag, opened the car door and was gone before George could say or do anything further.

Chapter 60

Without switching off the engine, George opened his door and called Tina's name. But she was marching away from him.

He rubbed his hand over his face and scratched his still unshaven chin before swivelling back into the car seat properly. He stared ahead, trying to decide the best course of action. In the end, he slammed his fist against the steering wheel and swore.

His feet found the pedals; he depressed the clutch and selected first gear. Checking his interior mirror, he saw Tina disappearing from view. He pressed down the accelerator, released the handbrake and set off.

Tina's energy quickly began to dissipate; she had not eaten breakfast and her meals yesterday were scant. Her only drink so far this morning had been a glass of water before her shower and a cup of black coffee with George afterwards. She felt both hungry and thirsty. The sun was hot and her thin-soled sandals were not designed for walking great distances.

And, in her head, the conversation between her conscience and her mind ran unchecked:

If you hadn't found fault with George every time he came home on leave, he wouldn't have stayed away for so long.

If he hadn't stayed away so long, I may have been less resentful!

Maybe a bit more understanding, more loving?

I couldn't bear to let him touch me when I knew he'd been with someone else.

You didn't know he had someone else.

I knew he had someone else!

You did not know he had someone else.

I KNEW HE HAD SOMEONE ELSE!
The final voice shouted at her as if she were stupid. Tears were smarting her eyes and soon she could not tell if the runnels of moisture on her cheeks were sweat from exertion or tears from her misery. A car was driving towards her; she hid her face in the crook of her arm so the driver could not see.

Unfortunately, the vehicle slowed down and stopped. Tina hurriedly attempted to dry her eyes.

Poskett's body was still in the mortuary in Cliffend hospital. The coroner had been informed of the gentleman's unexplained death and a post-mortem examination was ordered. The pathologist could not report any specific symptoms or diseases being attributable to the cause of death, other than old age. An inquest was due to open early the following week; it was expected to be adjourned until more details were available.

Mr Ambrose Brideman was the solicitor dealing with the will and legal side of the matter. PC Yates found the delays in sorting things out frustrating and needless. Apparently, there was a problem contacting the next of kin, though in this day and age of modern technology and communications (it was 2016 after all, with computers, iPhones and tablets), Yates thought it couldn't be *that* hard for people to be traced. The police officer needed to search the premises again – the business and the home – to see if there were any clues about his family. Yates' pet hate was rummaging through other people's possessions.

He had called at the post office in Pepper Hill a few minutes earlier. There was no reply, despite the new post mistress's (or whatever she was called) car being parked in the driveway. He was on his way back to Cliffend station when he saw a woman hurrying erratically towards him, obviously in distress.

Best stop, he thought. 'Can I help you?' he asked as he climbed out of the patrol car.

'No, thank you, officer,' she blurted, sniffing as she searched her bag for a tissue.

'Maybe I could give you a lift somewhere?' he offered. 'Where do you live?'

'Pepper Hill,' Tina advised him. 'The post office – temporarily, anyway.'

'I've actually just been over there to see you. You're Mrs Tillinger, aren't you? Mrs Tina Tillinger?'

Tina nodded.

'Good, glad to meet you,' he said, extending his hand. 'I'm PC Owen Yates. I need to have a look through Mr Poskett's belongings to see if there is anything there to indicate next of kin or any other family. Shall I give you a lift back and perhaps you could let me in?'

The officer's look told Tina this was not a suggestion. She didn't particularly want to return but she had nowhere else to go.

'Are you any relation to George Tillinger and his sister, Rosalie, and all the other Sticklebacks around here?' he asked as she settled into the patrol car's passenger seat.

''Fraid so,' Tina confirmed. 'You make me sound like I should be swimming around in an aquarium.'

'No offence meant, Mrs Tillinger, I can assure you.'

'Please, call me Tina.'

'Tina, then.'

When they arrived at the shop, PC Yates politely refused Tina's offer of a cup of black tea or coffee. She invited him to look around the shop and the rooms she had access to. They searched through the paperwork in the office area of the stock room before PC Yates wearily climbed the stairs.

He scrutinised the bathroom. (Tina had already checked the cabinet and found only the usual toiletries and a packet of ubiquitous pain killers; Poskett had not kept his prescribed medicines – if indeed he had any – in there.) Next, Yates opened the airing cupboard door, hauled out the contents: blankets, sheets, towels and all the usual cloths and rags, but no clues or secret boxes of papers were hidden there. After helping Tina to return the cupboard contents, he walked along the landing towards the door leading to the bedrooms. He tried the handle. It was locked.

'I would need to obtain a warrant to break in,' he told Tina. 'Maybe we could have another look around downstairs, specifically for a key that might fit?'

Half an hour later and still no further forward, PC Yates said he had to return to Cliffend. He handed Tina his card with his contact details.

'Can't always guarantee answering the mobile though,' he said. 'Either because I'm busy, driving or there's no signal. But just leave a message if by any miracle something useful turns up. Or ring Cliffend police station.'

Tina agreed to do so. She walked outside with him to the lay-by, shielding her eyes from the blazing sunshine. The police car was neatly parked in front of the full waste skip. This reminded Tina that the lorry driver said it would be removed Friday – tomorrow, the same day Mr Dentforth was due to visit. PC Yates climbed into his car, turned it around and waved as he drove away.

Chapter 61

George continued his journey from Ashfield to Cliffend. When he arrived back in his room at the Thrimbale Hotel, he plugged his mobile phone into the charger. He showered, shaved then changed into clean clothes and went down to the restaurant for a leisurely breakfast. On returning to his room, George rang Rosalie to ask if she would like company at the Old Police House.

'Half of it belongs to you,' his sister reminded him. 'You can stay here any time you want.'

George ended the call, packed and paid his bill before driving back to Pepper Hill. It was late morning when he arrived at the Old Police House and parked in the driveway. He glanced over towards the post office and At Hand shop and wondered if he ought to call in on Tina again. He wanted to make amends for their disagreement earlier but, in the end, he decided to wait a little longer before speaking with her.

George smelt the sewage effluent, which was still staining the road surface, as soon as he stepped out of his car. The stench chased away all other thoughts.

Rosalie opened the front door before he had taken his suitcases out of his car.

'Hi, Rosie,' he greeted, receiving a mock cuff around the ear for his audacity.

The Old Police House had four bedrooms and a bathroom upstairs. The ground floor included the original office area, which was now a study; a lounge, and a kitchen-diner which looked out on to the rear garden.

The main bedroom, Rosalie and George's parents' room, had been left empty since their death. It was redecorated after the chip-pan fire, but now Rosalie stored everything in there that she didn't use but wanted to keep, the latest additions being Ben's basket, bowls and other things.

George carried his cases up to the room of his childhood, which had later become Duncan's before he married Lily. Sarah's room, slightly smaller than her brother's, was the one Rosalie had grown up sleeping in. The other, the smallest bedroom, was the one she utilised now, keeping Sarah's ready if she ever decided to return.

George and Rosalie still jointly owned the Old Police House, although over the years, Rosalie ran and maintained it. Henry had paid more than his share towards the twins' upbringing, being quite generous in the circumstances, George sometimes thought. But he, George, had looked after Rosie, in a financial sense if not by actually being there: he'd always felt that she was his responsibility despite him being the younger of the siblings.

George unpacked his few items of clothing and personal things before making his way downstairs. He found his sister in the kitchen brewing a pot of tea.

'Cheers,' George said as he accepted his mug. He wandered over to the back door, opened it and looked out at the garden. The area was not large – certainly not as big as it had seemed when they were children. He scanned the lawn and saw the raised mound at the far end. He guessed this was old Ben's grave. A peace settled on him which he simply breathed in for a few moments.

'I'd forgotten how nice it is here,' he said quietly.

'I wouldn't want to live anywhere else – proved that, didn't I? Couldn't stay away for more than a day!' Rosalie stated.

George turned and looked at her. She had not changed much over the years.

'Anyway, what are your plans now?' she asked, not appreciating his scrutiny.

'I'm not sure. Maybe I'll stay here and help Tina over the road in the shop and post office – if she'll let me, of course.'

He recounted the events of last night and this morning, to which Rosie responded,

'Oh!'

Chapter 62

Late on Thursday morning, Andrew Brideman consulted his watch; another hour or so of solid work, then he hoped to take a long lunch and possibly not return this afternoon. The weather was gloriously hot outside and he was in need of a few hours away from the office. His eyes ached from staring at the computer monitor.

However, just as he stretched to re-awaken his circulation, the telephone rang. Without thinking his reaction could disrupt his plans, he reached out and picked up the receiver.

'Andrew Brideman, how can I help you?' A scowl drew across his face as he listened.

It was Mr Griffin from Maude and Griffin, Funeral Directors, who explained that they were unable to contact the only known relative of Mr Poskett – an estranged daughter. They were informed that Mr Poskett had lodged his will with Mr Ambrose Brideman and wondered if the solicitors knew how to contact the lady in question.

'I'll have to check my files and get back to you. I know my Uncle Ambrose dealt with the will. If you could just hold on for a moment, I'll see what I can find out.'

'I was just speaking to Mr Ambrose Brideman. *He* said *you* had all the details and he put me through.'

The old bastard, thought Andrew. But to the gentleman on the telephone, he was more polite.

'Right, well, could you leave it with me and I'll call you back?'

'Thank you. I don't suppose you could possibly

make this a matter of priority, could you, Mr Brideman? You see the deceased is still in the hospital mortuary and, well, arrangements need to be made.'

'Very well, I'll see what I can do.'

Whilst thinking to himself that his long lunch and afternoon off would not now happen, he made a note of the caller's company telephone number.

Andrew consulted the firm's files on his computer, but he found no record of Poskett's will. He went through to the main office, which included the reception area, but neither the secretaries nor the receptionist were at their desks. He cursed.

The solicitors' confidential papers regarding their clients were held in an old-fashioned bank of grey metal filing cabinets located in the strong room downstairs. Andrew descended the steps, unlocked the door with his key and, against the opposite wall, found the drawer marked 'P – Q'. He opened it, retrieved the relevant file, pushed the drawer back with his knee and returned to his office.

Moving his laptop aside, he opened out the file and began to read through the contents. He quickly located the deeds to Pepper Hill's post office and shop. Flicking through the various documents, he also discovered the contract for the At Hand shop franchise before finally locating a copy of the deceased's will.

This stated that Mr Heston Poskett of sound mind (*which is more than could be said of some PepperAsh residents,* Andrew thought) wished to be buried in St Jude's churchyard.

The usual and expected information appeared. Poskett had bequeathed a generous sum to the local air ambulance, a charity he had supported for many years. There was also a small legacy for St Jude's Church.

Andrew was not surprised by any of this. He continued reading. Eventually, he found mention of a child. A daughter.

So Poskett did have a daughter! She would be, Andrew made a quick calculation, about thirty-five years old now. He must have been in his late forties when he'd had some kind of affair.

Andrew read on. The will detailed that the mother, Maris, had abandoned the baby, leaving it to be brought up by the grandmother, Hilda. But, before leaving, she named her Bettina. The child had taken her mother's family name, Guthrie, as Poskett had not officially acknowledged the child by claiming paternity on the birth certificate, and it was likely the daughter was not aware of her father's identity. A trust fund had been set up for her. It had never been touched; Andrew was staggered at the amount accrued.

He reached for his telephone handset and dialled Maude and Griffin's number.

Chapter 63

The telephone in the rectory study rang in the late afternoon on Thursday. It was Cliffend's funeral directors, Maude and Griffin, wanting to speak to the Reverend Quintin Boyce regarding Mr Poskett's funeral.

'Mr Brideman has just contacted us with the news that we can go ahead with the funeral, once all the paperwork has been complete,' the detached voice of Mr Maude – or was it Mr Griffin, Quinny had already forgotten – was explaining. 'They just needed to contact the daughter …'

This statement jolted the reverend's attention.

'A daughter? I didn't know he had a daughter. Who …? Where …?' Quinny questioned, incredulity sounding in his voice. The fingers of one hand were desperately searching for the elastic band on the other wrist. He paused before asking, 'Who is this daughter?' He was thinking if it happened to be someone local, the scandal would keep the gossips busy for months – nay, years.

'Her name is Bettina, maiden name of Guthrie, but you might know her as Tina Tillinger. She's married to George Tillinger. She works for the post office and has just moved into Pepper Hill, ironically to take over following Poskett's death.'

Quinny swallowed whilst pinging the band several times in succession until his skin was sore and his eyes watered. He tried to clear his throat before attempting a reply. Eventually, he stuttered, 'I, er, well, I see. I … Gosh, this is a shock. And such a coincidence. Does anyone else know?'

'Not according to Mr Brideman. I'm only informing your good self so you'll understand the delays involved. For instance, as you know, the grave site hasn't yet been chosen; therefore, we can't issue instructions for the excavators to dig.'

The funeral director and the rector talked for a few more minutes but nothing new was disclosed, other than Quinny being assured that, as far as he was aware, Mr Brideman had not yet spoken with Tina. Quinny was left in a quandary as to whether he should approach her.

After much deliberation, Quinny decided to walk to Pepper Hill to see if he could talk to Tina – not to discuss Poskett, but just to offer pastoral reassurance. But, before he could do anything else, he needed some lunch: Quinny was never at his best when he was hungry.

He wandered through to the kitchen, but nothing in the fridge looked appetising. No one had left a casserole for him recently (he thought he could include a few words about *charity beginning at home* – preferably his home, the rectory – in his sermon on Sunday). The only remaining slices of bread in the pantry were beginning to grow green mould.

He gave the rubber band on his wrist a good ping. It snapped. So did Quinny's patience. He returned to his study to collect another from the hoard in his desk drawer.

With his new talisman secured, he returned to the kitchen where he eventually found a nearly empty packet of plain biscuits. But the survivors were soft. He sat at the table and ate them anyway, straight out of the packet, leaving the crumbs for whichever good lady cleaned that week.

He thought, if he was forced to go to Pepper Hill, and if by any miracle (he raised his eyes to the ceiling in supplication) the shop was open, he could stock up on food. But then he would have the problem of carrying his groceries back. Life was full of puzzles.

At that moment, the letterbox rattled, followed by the doorbell ringing. Wondering if this could be the answer to the prayer he had not quite formulated, he stood up as quickly as his arthritis would allow and walked down the hall to the front door.

'Ah, just the gentleman I was in need of,' Quinny advised the young postman, who was holding out a parcel. 'Thank you,' he said, peering beyond the postman to the welcome sight of the bright red van. But it was facing towards Ashfield. 'Er, which way are you going, son?'

'Why?' Jim asked. He was wearing khaki uniform shorts, which looked incongruous with bright green hiking socks and scuffed trainers sporting ripped fluorescent flashes. His red T-shirt showed his right arm to be tanned from driving with his window open to the sunshine, his left being several shades paler.

'Just wondered,' Quinny replied nonchalantly, shaking away his thoughts. 'I, er, need to go and see your new friend at the post office, er, to stock up on supplies – if the shop is open yet.' Quinny was hoping the more details he volunteered, the greater the likelihood of obtaining a lift, especially if he mentioned the post office.

'No, it isn't open yet – next week, I think,' Jim replied. 'I should officially be going to Ashfield,' he said with fake exasperation. 'But I'm sure I could turn round and run you over to Pepper Hill first.'

'Not too sure about the "run you over" bit, son. But

I'll take you up on your offer anyway. Thanks. Give me two minutes.' Quinny took his parcel without interest, walked back to the study and left it on his desk. He picked up the papers concerning Poskett's funeral and returned to the hall where he collected his jacket from the hook rack before stepping out of the front door. 'Right, lad, I'm ready.'

During the journey, although still hungry, the rector acknowledged that he was generally at peace with the world and its inhabitants. Just to confirm this, he pinged his new elastic band.

It broke.

'Bugger!' he muttered.

'D'you need another?' Jim asked, trying not to smirk. He'd noticed the rector kept post office-issue faded red rubber bands on his wrist. He'd heard of this particular kind of therapy, but he could not imagine which obsession Quinny was trying to break. He presumed he was not an alcoholic because he'd seen him drinking beer in the pub. Jim didn't wish to delve into other people's private problems, so he simply extended the offer, 'I've got plenty. They're in the glove box.' He pointed to the flap on the passenger's side of the dash board.

'Thanks,' Quinny said as he replaced his second lost band with three new ones that were all slightly less faded. He told himself, as he clicked shut the flap, that he would take two off when he returned home and add them to his collection for future needs. 'I don't see so many left lying on the road now. Didn't they start a campaign, especially against postmen dropping their rubber bands, them *Keep Britain Tidy* lot, or *Don't Be A Tosser*, or whatever the anti-litter louts call themselves nowadays?'

'Yeah, that's right,' Jim agreed with a laugh. 'You'd think they'd do something about all the fast-food boxes, beer cans and juice cartons that are thrown out of car windows – not to mention the bottles filled with lorry drivers' pee that end up in their rest areas! It was all on the news again last week. Did you hear? They could sort that lot out instead of persecuting us poor, hard-working mail delivery operatives. By the way, you can't call us postmen now, you know.'

'Oh, is that right?' Quinny replied. He received a nod of affirmation before he continued. 'Well, what do you call women postmen, then? Femail – spelt F E M A I L of course – delivery operatives?'

'No, wrong type of male. They're mail delivery operatives as well.'

'Gosh, it's all too complicated for me!' Quinny was silent for the remainder of the journey.

'There you are,' Jim declared as he parked outside the post office in the designated lay-by, just in front of the level-filled rubbish skip. Tina's car was standing in the driveway to the side of the building, the windscreen reflecting the bright June sunshine.

The shop and post office looked light and clean – fresh with new hope. The woodwork around the door and large window at the front was repainted. New double doors had been fitted, obviously to accommodate up-to-date security measures as well as facilitate a disabled person's entrance – there was now a low-rise ramp with a grasp handle clamped to the door frame.

A long pearl-coloured sign had been fixed above the window, with the words 'At Hand' in bright green lettering. A small sign, still hanging at a right angle to the wall, announced in red text to travellers from both directions that here also was the post office.

'It's still closed up,' Jim observed. 'But the renovations look as if they might be finished.' The doors were firmly shut but, from the vehicle, they could see an official notice stuck to one of them.

'I'll go and find out what it says,' Quinny said. He struggled out of the van.

'D'you want me to wait? For you to see if she's in, like? You might need a lift back if no one's home.'

'Haven't you got letters and things to deliver?' Quinny asked, slightly suspicious that this young lad might be lusting after the new lady. He was particularly cautious, especially in view of the information the solicitor had recently imparted. He did not think now was the time for further complications.

As Quinny stood up and straightened his aching knees, he thought he could still smell the sewage stench from the spillage at Rosalie's just across the road. He coughed, missing young Jim's reply and had to ask him to repeat it.

'Just over in Ashfield. I'll pass the rectory on the way back, won't I?'

'Yes, that you will, lad,' Quinny agreed, suddenly cheerful again. 'Well, if you don't mind hanging on a few minutes.'

Chapter 64

Quinny walked up to the main entrance and peered at the ridiculously small print on the notice. It informed him that both establishments – the At Hand shop and post office – would reopen on Monday morning.

He stepped back to survey the frontage. *Bright to the point of garish,* he concluded to himself. *But at least passing traffic would see it.* He returned to the doors and knocked. Unsurprisingly, there was no reply. He knocked again, louder this time. Again nothing.

'I'll just try round the back,' Quinny called to his self-appointed taxi driver who nodded in reply. As he walked to the rear, Quinny remembered the last time he visited, just after Poskett's death. The place had felt the particular cold that is the grip of the recently departed. Now, he peered in through the new window but could not see any movement. He knocked on the door anyway. No answer. He waited, tapped again. Still no response.

'Oh well, I tried,' Quinny muttered to himself as he returned to the front. As he rounded the corner, he heard and saw Rosalie Stickleback talking to his young friend in the van.

Rosalie looked up as he approached.

'Isn't Tina there?' she asked.

'Well, she isn't answering if she is,' Quinny stated. 'This is *Tina,* as in your sister-in-law, your brother's wife, isn't it?'

'Yes,' Rosalie replied defensively. 'Yes, but I haven't seen her for years. They moved away, over to Treemoore. I didn't know she'd moved back here. We didn't keep in regular touch. George worked for that big company, MaCold. He was offshore most of the time.' Rosalie hesitated for a moment, reflecting on her words and regretting her lack of sisterly care. Then she shrugged and blithely resumed. 'George has just moved back into the Old Police House. I expect he'll be across to see her later.'

George was, at that moment in time, driving to Cliffend. The manager from the Thrimbale Hotel had rung, George having given the number of the Old Police House as a contact. Apparently, he'd left behind his mobile phone and charger. He told Rosie he would meet her at the pub after he'd retrieved them.

Rosalie shuffled her feet uncomfortably and squinted against the bright sunshine.

'Going back to the subject of the post office,' she said, 'I was wondering what's happening about Poskett's funeral? Someone said they thought it was next Wednesday but I haven't seen any announcements yet.'

'No, it hasn't been confirmed,' Quinny replied sharply. 'The funeral directors said they'd put a notice in the newspaper.'

The rector's somewhat snapped response surprised Rosalie. The benefit from Qunny's soft biscuits earlier had now left him. He was hungry and grumpy. Again.

'Anyway, we can't stop all day, Mrs Stickleback. I need my lunch, and my young friend has just offered to drive me back home. So I'll say good day to you.'

'Right, well. Sorry, I didn't mean to delay you.' Rosalie shook her head in confusion, turned away and walked up to the post box. She drew an envelope out of her pocket and was about to push it into the box when the postman called to her.

'Would you like me to take that, Mrs Stickleback? Otherwise, it won't be collected until tomorrow.'

'Oh, thank you,' Rosalie answered. 'That would be very helpful.' She walked back to the post van and handed it through the driver's open window.

Quinny fastened his seat belt as Jim started the engine. Jim reversed the van into the post office driveway, carefully minding not to touch Tina's car, and drove away in the direction of Ashfield.

Rosalie waved thanks to him as he left. She received a couple of flashes of his hazard warning lights in return. She smiled, realising she felt a lot better – not just free of the worry and aching from the past couple of days, but less weighed down, less guilty somehow. And now, with George moving in, she could await the outcome of Duncan's tests with company, instead of imagining all kinds of horrors on her own.

She consulted her wristwatch; it was time for her to get ready and go to The Fighting Cock for lunch.

Tina listened to most of this conversation as she sat on the floor in the corner of the shop. She was looking at the screen of her mobile phone, watching the signal icon fade in and out. Dentforth had ironically used the land-line.

She could not yet face telling the residents of PepperAsh that they had lost their post office. Dentforth's voice still echoed in her ear, his tone jubilantly stating that, as she had not acknowledged the contract, yet alone signed it, within the given time, the facility was being withdrawn. *Oh, hadn't she seen there was a deadline?* he'd gloated. *Well, she really should read things through thoroughly, then, shouldn't she?* He cited the cutting of costs, small outlets not being viable, etc., etc. Dentforth was triumphant: he had won a battle Tina was only partly aware they were engaged in.

She held her face in her hands as the engine sound faded. The quiet inside the shop was broken only by a faint squeak then a scuffle which brought into view a mouse. Tina wondered if it was the one she had seen when Postman Jim the Second first unlocked the place for her. Maybe it was a different one.

Could be worse, she thought to herself. *It could be a rat.*

As the Royal Mail van approached the rectory, Quinny's stomach gave a loud rumble. He rubbed it dolefully, remembering that he did not have any groceries in the house.

'You sound as if you haven't had any grub for a while,' Jim commented.

'Er, no – well, just a couple of soggy leftover biscuits earlier. Food was my next priority,' Quinny replied, suddenly jovial and expectant.

'Well, I'm due my break now anyway. We could stop at the pub in Ashfield.'

'I, er, I don't have any money on me, young man.'

'That's okay, I can shout you a pint and a sandwich.'

Quinny frowned. This chap was being very kind and helpful, almost too much so. What was it he had thought about charity earlier?

'That's very good of you,' he replied. 'But I can't guarantee you entry into the friendly hereafter just for buying a cantankerous old rector a meal, you know.'

'Oh, I don't believe in all that life-after-death rubbish. Do you?'

'Well, I ought to, don't I?' Quinny chortled; he was enjoying himself again. 'After all, I am the rector.'

Chapter 65

When Sarah finished speaking with her mother that morning, she'd called her uncle's mobile to remind him about lunch. He didn't reply so she left a message.

Sarah had not seen George very often since her spectacular exit from family life at sixteen to start work with the company her mother believed was responsible for George and Rosalie's parents' deaths. But he always remembered her and Duncan's birthday.

Sarah rang him Tuesday when she first arrived back at Ashfield. She thought someone ought to let him know about her parents' most recent mishap, the impending court case and, of course, about Duncan. She also wanted him present today when her mother learnt of her situation.

Sarah drove to the supermarket in Cliffend's retail park to purchase all the items necessary for lunch. She decided they would have baked potatoes, salad and a choice of boiled eggs, ham-off-the-bone, grated cheese and tinned salmon. Or all of them, if they so wished. Pudding could just be something simple: ice cream, maybe a choice of two flavours – vanilla and chocolate.

Strawberries were in season; maybe she should buy a couple of punnets as well. And cream. She had not had any cravings with her phantom pregnancy; that was one of the reasons she knew it wasn't real.

The only items she was not sure about in the meal were the baked potatoes. She remembered a particularly nasty incident with a flying spud many years ago at a Guy Fawkes' Night celebration. This had ended with the whole family being the disgrace of the village.

Later, as Sarah pottered in the kitchen of The Fighting Cock, Henry watched for a while as he leant against the door frame. She was wearing a pair of white knee-length shorts under a garment that resembled a man's large, light-blue cotton shirt. Although the front was buttoned and the sleeves rolled up, it was far too big for her. The more Henry looked at it, the more it reminded him of one he owned. It disguised her bump better than the suit she had been wearing when she'd arrived on Tuesday afternoon. But the swelling was still visible. He wondered what Rosalie's reaction would be.

Henry walked back into the bar before Sarah realised he was spying on her. He'd nearly finished setting up, but he needed to shower and change his clothes before the other guests arrived. Knowing the occasion was important to his daughter, he did not want to be the cause of any conflict by wearing jeans and a beer-splattered T-shirt.

Two minutes later, Sarah called through to the bar.

'Dad, don't forget to get ready for lunch. Mum and Uncle George will be here soon.' She didn't hear his reply because the rector came in through the open pub door, closely followed by a rather good-looking young postman.

Chapter 66

Rosalie arrived at The Fighting Cock's car park just before one o'clock. She was wearing a pale pink, sleeveless, light cotton summer dress plus white sandals. She carried a small white shoulder bag with limited holding capacity. She was trying to tuck her keys in it as she approached the pub's open front door.

There was a private side entrance to the living quarters at The Fighting Cock, but this was very rarely used. Henry was standing behind the bar when Rosalie walked in. He looked up.

The sunshine from outside cast Rosalie's figure into silhouette. She crossed the room towards him and, as her features took form, he suddenly saw the bride he married all those years ago. Rosalie looked so refreshed and beautiful that she made Henry, who was still waiting for Polly to arrive before he could shower and change, feel dishevelled and grubby.

'Hello,' he said. 'You look nice.' His voice sounded feeble but his sentiment was honest. He hoped she would recognise this. Needless to say, the comment had the opposite effect; Henry witnessed her shoulders stiffen defensively. 'As you can see,' he added quickly, 'I'm not ready yet. I've been waiting for ...'

'Sorry I'm late,' Polly burst in, interrupting Henry's explanation. She was also wearing cool cotton, but her dress managed to display her curvaceous figure and cleavage.

'Right, I'll go and get changed,' Henry announced. 'Sarah's in the kitchen, Rosalie, if you want to go through.'

'Thanks,' Rosalie muttered to Henry as she also

acknowledged Polly.

Sarah was facing away from the door as Rosalie walked in.

'Hi, Mum,' she said brightly, only half turning her head. 'I've nearly finished preparing lunch. Come and have a cuppa while we wait for Uncle George to arrive – oh, and for Dad to get ready. You know the men in this family, always late.'

'Right,' Rosalie told her daughter's back. She was tempted to rush over and capture Sarah in a warm hug but she didn't think this would be welcome. Although the years since Sarah left home had lengthened, the antagonism – and the slap – would always be there between them. Rosalie sat down on the only easy chair in the kitchen and admired the lunch spread out on the table.

Henry suddenly appeared.

'Sarah,' he asked. 'Is that shirt you're wearing one of mine? Or am I imagining things?'

'Yes, you're right, it is,' Sarah replied with the smile that was kept especially for her Dad. 'No, you're not imagining things.'

Then, she turned to Rosalie. 'And you're not imagining things either, Mum,' she added defiantly. 'I have got a bump, but I'm not pregnant.' She carried the two mugs of tea (mugs of ordinary tea; not her father's appalling concoction), handed one to Rosalie and gave her the briefest of kisses on her cheek.

Not wishing to witness the inevitable inquest, Henry took the opportunity to disappear; he was sure he could find another shirt from somewhere, even if it hadn't been ironed.

With her free hand, Sarah dragged a chair noisily from the kitchen table to sit next to her mother. 'But I do feel rather tired in all this heat. And, as you can see, I have the obligatory swollen ankles.'

Rosalie was shocked. Her daughter certainly looked pregnant – not only was there a visible bulge and distended ankles, she had also gained weight around her hips and bust, and her face seemed fuller. But then, Rosalie thought, she had not seen Sarah for many months. Before further comment could be made, George clattered into the room carrying two bottles.

'Don't quite know what I was thinking of, bringing wine to a pub, but there!' He placed them on the worktop near the sink, stepped towards his niece and kissed her cheek. 'Hard luck, Sarah,' he told her. 'Phantom pregnancy or not, you're banned from alcohol. Hi, Rosie. I said I'd be here in good time, didn't I? I got my phone and charger from the hotel okay, but had to stop off and buy these.'

George's cheerfulness suddenly annoyed his sister. But then, as Rosalie silently admitted to herself, she was easily irritated at the best of times.

'Has anyone heard from Duncan?' George asked.

'Not since we visited him yesterday,' Sarah answered. 'Just after you left,' Sarah nodded towards her uncle, 'his transport was confirmed. He said he would ring when he was settled at Mattingburgh and tell us the visiting times for this evening.' She turned to her mother. 'He'll probably come through Ashfield and Pepper Hill on his way from Cliffend to the city. He's got to go in an ambulance. Lily wanted to drive him, but he has to be under medical supervision. That male nurse, Luke, is going with him.'

'What exactly are they going to do?' Rosalie asked as she sipped her tea. She was only just keeping up with all the news her family were inflicting upon her. She wasn't sure if she believed that Sarah's pregnancy wasn't real. Nor did she dare ask George about Tina. 'He didn't say too much about it to me.'

'More tests first, I believe,' George replied as he looked around for glasses. 'Then if they still think it's necessary, they'll go ahead and do the closure. But I don't really know what either involves.'

After a while, Henry returned to the kitchen, freshly showered, his hair and beard were still damp and his shirt creased. His belt buckle was hanging a little below his waist to allow for his expanding stomach and his feet were bare inside flip-flops.

Rosalie noticed his toe nails needed cutting. She raised her eyes back up to his face and found him smiling down at her.

'Sorry for the wait, folks,' Henry announced.

The sound of voices laughing and bandying comments travelled through the open door from the public bar. He turned around to look in that direction.

'I'd better just go and check that Polly's managing okay.' Henry sauntered proprietorially through, only to return a few moments later. 'Yeah, everything's under control. She says she'll call if she needs a hand.'

'Right, let's get started with lunch, shall we?' Sarah said as she suddenly stood up.

'Hang on a moment,' Rosalie interjected, also rising to her feet. 'You haven't really explained the bump.'

'It's a phantom pregnancy, Mum.' Sarah sighed as she sat down again, her face glowing red with exertion and embarrassment. 'There's some hormone treatment I can be given if it hasn't sorted itself out soon.'

Rosalie recognised the stubborn expression on her daughter's face and knew there was no point in arguing, especially with an audience who had obviously known about this before her.

'It looks pretty real to me. Have you seen a doctor, or a midwife?' she enquired aggressively.

'Well, it isn't real and no I haven't *seen* anyone!' Sarah snapped as she raised herself up awkwardly again. 'So, finish your tea, or bring it to the table with you. George, you can uncork the wine. Dad, get that tray of baked potatoes out of the oven – and switch it off as well while you're there.' Suddenly realising she was being rather dictatorial, she softened her tone and added with a smile, 'Oh and Mum, Dad, no throwing things at each other, please. Especially not the spuds!'

Chapter 67

Duncan was asked if he wanted something to help him sleep on Thursday night. He said 'yes,' because, although he had been quite cheerful when Lily, Jack and the *sensible grandparents* visited earlier, he was actually quite nervous about the following day.

When Luke settled him in on the ward at Mattingburgh hospital that morning, he assured him he would be back tomorrow to accompany him during the tests and, if necessary, for the closure procedure. He told Duncan he wanted as much experience in every field of medicine as possible, because he was considering applying to join the Army when he was twenty-five, in a couple of years' time.

'Don't know why I want to wait till then,' he confided to Duncan. 'It just seems like a good age for a change; you know – a quarter of a century, a third of three score years and ten, or thereabouts.'

'Yes, I do know,' Duncan responded. 'I'm twenty-five. I feel I should be getting somewhere in life. But I just seem to be dragged into siding with one parent then defending the other.'

Luke smiled. 'Yeah, I know. There's a report of the court case in the *Cliffend Herald* today.'

'Oh, God!' Duncan exclaimed as he clasped his hand over his eyes. 'Whatever do people think?' It was not really a question, but Luke answered anyway.

'Don't worry about them. Just get yourself right. Then you can sort your parents out. Make it your quarter-century milestone ambition in life.'

'Great. Thanks. Maybe I should join the Army, too – just let them get on with it.'

'What? And leave that lovely wife and son of yours? And the new nipper! Don't be daft, mate!'

As the sedative took effect, Duncan was thinking about being back at home in Tidal Reach Cottage with Lily and Jack. And a new baby.

Chapter 68

Duncan woke early on Friday morning. He felt tired and confused but attributed this to the sleeping pill he'd taken the previous evening. The skin on his hand irritated where the cannula was attached; he had absentmindedly scratched it during the night.

He tried to distract himself by looking around the ward. However, the beds were arranged in such a way that neighbours were not visible to each other. Privacy may have been the idea behind the design, but it made him feel isolated. He closed his eyes and waited.

Duncan's tests and procedure were scheduled to start at ten o'clock. There was a notice above the head of his bed stating *Nil By Mouth*. Other instructions given to him last night were to eat nothing after six o'clock in the evening and not to drink anything, not even water, after eleven o'clock. His mouth now felt dry but he could not tell whether that was through thirst or trepidation.

He tried to relax. In turn, this made him aware of his heartbeat. He began to imagine he could feel the blood rushing into his heart and being pumped straight out again, uncleansed and unfortified – dirty and toxic.

A clock somewhere in the ward slowly ticked time away. Although Duncan could hear it, he couldn't see it. He remembered that only a week ago nobody knew anything about his heart defect. He felt so weak and tired at the moment that he could not understand how he'd ever had the energy to work at the pub, run his own business and help Lily look after Jack.

Through the haze of his thoughts, Duncan heard footsteps. But they were in another part of the ward – somewhere near the clock, he reckoned. He kept his eyes closed, wishing the time would quickly arrive when things could start to happen. He'd never had an anaesthetic and, although Luke said he would be there, his fears were not completely allayed.

During Sarah's visit on Wednesday evening, she'd told him not to worry about his operation – it was a *procedure*, he reminded them. She assured him that he would not know anything about it. Naturally, this made him even more anxious, especially when their Dad pointed out that Sarah was in so much pain when admitted for an emergency appendectomy that she was probably too drugged to recall anything anyway.

Although he would never admit it, this meaningless one-upmanship upset him. His family always seemed to be too busy scoring points off each other to realise they were actually worsening the situation they were supposed to be helping.

After Henry and Sarah left, Lily was scathing about Sarah's *phantom* pregnancy. As he replayed his wife's words, Duncan slipped into a state between wake and sleep. He saw himself holding his sister's baby. He was not sure if it was a boy or a girl, but Lily was saying it was hers. Duncan tried to explain that it wasn't important whose it was; the only thing that mattered was that it was a Stickleback. And, when he looked down at the baby's face, it turned into a fish with enormous lips and unblinking eyes.

'Morning, Duncan,' Luke said.

Duncan was startled awake. He tried to raise his head but immediately felt dizzy, even though he was still lying down.

'No need to rush, you've got plenty of time. I'll bring you a wheelchair and take you over to have a shower.'

A while later, with Luke's help, Duncan's ablutions

were complete. He was back on the ward lying on his bed already in a theatre gown. Luke left him to rest. He returned carrying a grey cardboard dish containing two disposable plastic razors. He drew the curtains around.

'I've had a shave,' Duncan said in a puzzled tone as Luke placed the dish on the bed.

'Oh, these aren't for your face,' Luke responded.

Duncan did not understand for a few seconds but, when he realised what Luke meant, he flushed with embarrassment.

'You mean …?'

'Yes. They use a tube to deliver the *amplatzer* – that's the plug. It's like a tiny scouring pad, but try not to think about it like that,' Luke chuckled. 'Anyway, it'll be fed to your heart through a vein which is accessed in your groin. So the skin will have to be naked. Er, can you manage, or would you like me to do it?'

'I'll do it myself,' Duncan replied indignantly. He sat upright but the movement was too quick.

'Listen, mate. It'll take me five minutes. It's no big deal,' Luke said in what he hoped was a reassuring voice. 'I'm asked to do this sort of thing for blokes all the time in preparation for hernia repairs, prostate operations and vasectomies.'

Duncan tensed and held his breath as the nurse began. 'You're allowed to breathe, you know,' Luke eventually said. 'It'll make my job easier if you relax.'

Duncan reluctantly smiled at this, causing his shoulders to loosen their tension and his fists to unclench.

True to his word, Luke was quickly finished.

'Not long to wait now,' he commented. 'Just lie back and let it all happen!'

Luke soon returned with a porter. They wheeled

Duncan's bed through a labyrinth of corridors and into a lift; the motion made Duncan feel queasy. They emerged and travelled a short distance before waiting outside a pair of double doors that the porter opened with a plastic swipe card.

'How on earth do you find your way round this place?' Duncan asked.

'Satnav, mate!' Luke replied brightly. 'They're a marvellous invention, you know. Last week, we were supposed to be taking an elderly lady to have a hearing aid fitted, but she ended up in the delivery suite giving birth to triplets.'

'Don't listen to him,' the porter interceded. 'Without me, he'd be lost.'

Duncan was smiling when he arrived in the cardiac suite.

'That's a good sign,' Mr Stott, the cardiologist, greeted him. 'I like cheerful patients. Has Luke been telling his awful jokes? He's only been here a few hours and already he's a legend.'

'I can believe that,' Duncan replied, squinting; the lights in the room seemed very bright and the glare cut into his eyes.

'Good, right. I'll be back in a minute,' said Mr Stott. 'I'll leave you in Julie's very capable hands.' He indicated to a nurse wearing a light blue theatre suit complete with hat that covered her hair. She said hello to Duncan whilst Mr Stott left the room.

'First of all,' Julie said, her voice giving no indication of her age. 'I need to check your wrist band.' She lifted his hand and twisted it round to read the details 'Good,' she murmured. 'Let's get you onto the stretcher. Then we can lift you over to the treatment area.'

With help from the porter, Luke and Julie, Duncan

hoisted himself up, bottom half first then the top, to allow the fabric of the stretcher to be fed underneath him. The poles were then inserted along the sides and he was swiftly, expertly, lifted onto the other bed. He heard the porter remove his bed, leaving just Julie, Luke and himself. Julie asked him if he knew what was about to happen. He said he thought so.

'Well, I'll remind you anyway. First, we are going to carry out a transoesophageal echocardiogram. You've had a test where the flow of agitated saline liquid through the heart was recorded by a scan across your chest?' Duncan nodded. 'Well, for the test today, a camera will be guided down your oesophagus into the chest cavity and positioned behind your heart. This will give us a clearer picture than the scan did because your ribs won't be in the way. Are you okay with all this so far?'

Duncan nodded again. He actually felt quite sick and didn't really want to know the details.

'When the camera is in place,' Julie continued. 'We'll pump in the solution – just like last time. The monitor will follow its progress. While the camera is there, if the results are the same as before, we'll go ahead and affect a percutaneous closure – that just means we'll deliver the "plug", if you like to call it that, through a tube fed into a vein in your groin. Do you understand?'

Again, Duncan nodded. He was blinking his eyes quickly and swallowing hard.

Nurse Julie pressed her hand onto his shoulder.

'Don't worry about it, you'll be fine,' she said reassuringly. 'Right, well, first things first. I'll need you to sign a consent form.' She handed him a pen and a clipboard with a sheet of paper attached.

'Take a couple of minutes to read it. If there's

anything you're not sure of, just ask.'

Julie moved away and began preparing instruments on the other side of the room.

Duncan's eyes would not focus properly, so he held the board and sheet up in front of his face and tried to read the print.

Someone stepped forward. Duncan didn't immediately recognise him until he offered to help. It was Luke. He was now wearing a suit similar to Julie's.

Duncan eventually managed a very shaky signature. Luke then returned the form to the nurse who glanced at it.

'Right, let's get you ready. First, I need to check your cannula.' She took his left hand and quickly, skilfully examined the tube's insertion, soothing her thumb over his reddened skin.

'Yes, that all seems okay. Now, could you try to sit up for me?'

'Here, mate. I'll give you a hand,' Luke offered.

'I need you to open your mouth,' Julie stated when Duncan was propped up.

Duncan obeyed. He felt helpless and couldn't control his shaking. He knew he had to trust the skills of others but it was a very hard thing to do.

He remember Lily telling him that, during the worst parts of giving birth, she got through by telling herself it was all happening to someone else.

'I have to spray a local anaesthetic onto the back of your throat. It'll taste bitter,' Julie explained. She sprayed once, waited a moment and sprayed again.

Duncan tried to swallow but immediately felt numbness spreading around the back of his mouth and down his throat. And, yes, she was right; the liquid was indeed very bitter. He was concerned now in case he wanted to be sick. However, he didn't have time to say anything.

'Just once more,' Julie said. Duncan obligingly opened his mouth again. 'Right, now, lie down on your left side if you could, please.'

Whilst he was making himself comfortable, Mr Stott returned to the room.

'How are we getting on?' he asked.

'We're nearly ready,' Julie replied before moving around to the left side of the bed. She then gathered Duncan's head into her arms. 'I have to hold you still while the tube with the camera is inserted.'

Another figure appeared and prepared a syringe. 'Right, I'm now giving you a sedative,' he said. 'You won't be unconscious during this test, because we need you to swallow the tube. You might find that part of the process uncomfortable, but you won't remember anything about it afterwards. So just relax and don't worry. You're in good hands.'

As the contents of the syringe were emptied into the cannula in Duncan's hand, Julie placed a plastic shield in the shape of a short piece of pipe into his mouth and over his teeth.

'This will stop you biting the tube,' she explained.

'Soon be over now, mate,' Duncan heard Luke say. 'And I'll be here all the time, to observe – make sure you're okay.'

Duncan thought Luke must be somewhere near his head. But he couldn't actually see him. Things were becoming hazy and his thoughts were muddled. He felt a misty panic rising and surround him. He could feel a cold flow in his arm. Someone asked him to imagine counting backwards. Ten. Nine. Eight. Nothing was happening. Se ...

Chapter 69

Rosalie was eating lunch with her brother, George, at the Old Police House on Friday when her telephone rang. It was Lily.

'Luke rang from Mattingburgh hospital to say that Duncan was out of surgery.' Lily sounded so relieved; Rosalie smiled thankfully. 'The closure was successful and he is recovering well. Dad said he'll drive me over to see him this evening.' Lily sensed Rosalie was also going to ask about visiting. 'He isn't allowed anyone else tonight,' she added quickly. 'If everything's okay tomorrow, they'll transfer him back to Cliffend to recuperate over the weekend then he can probably be discharged on Monday.'

'Oh, that is a relief,' Rosalie said.

'May I have a quick word with Lily?' George asked when he thought the conversation between his sister and her daughter-in-law was drawing to a close.

'Lily, just before you go, George would like to speak to you.' She handed the telephone to her brother.

'Hello, Lily. It's good news, I gather.' George listened as Lily happily repeated the information. 'I am pleased,' he stated. 'Now, if you remember, I offered to go over to Tidal Reach and have a look at Duncan's tractor and tanker for him. I'm free tomorrow.'

'Okay. But I'll probably be at the hospital. Actually, I'm at home now. I came to collect some things to take in to Duncan this evening. Could I ask you another favour?'

'If I can help, I will,' George responded.

'Thank you. There are three phone messages on our machine from people wanting their septic tanks emptying. Could you deal with them, please? I don't know what to tell them as I have no idea when Duncan will be able to start work again.'

'Yes, of course. I'll take our previous conversation as Duncan's permission. I'm sure I can operate the equipment ...'

'Well, if you're in any doubt, just ask Rosalie – she knows!' Lily's voice was harsh, but George shrugged.

'Yes, that's as maybe. But we really don't want any more hassle,' he replied.

'No, of course not. I'm sorry,' Lily said quietly. 'Hopefully, Duncan will be home soon. I don't know what he'll do about the business until he's fully recovered, though.'

'Well, at least I can make a start tomorrow. Just give him my best regards when you see him this evening. Tell him not to worry. It'll be a while before I need to find myself a proper job again, so until then I can help him out.'

'That was very good of you,' Rosalie said when George returned the telephone to its cradle.

'Well, other than possibly giving Tina a hand when the shop and post office reopens, I don't have any plans at the moment, Rosie.' He saw his sister frown. 'I'll be quite happy just to stay around here. You lot certainly seem to have got yourselves into a fix. There's Henry with the pub – his licence is due for renewal and now he has a criminal record. Sarah and her *phantom pregnancy*. Duncan's illness. Not to mention, of course, Tina and me. And then there's you ...'

'There's nothing wrong with me!' Rosalie exclaimed defensively.

'No, of course there isn't.' He paused before quietly adding, '*Rosie*.'

Chapter 70

The same afternoon, Tina was outside depositing a bag of waste into her wheelie bin. She heard a vehicle travelling from the Mattingburgh direction. It began to slow down as it approached the lay-by.

The car came into view and Tina saw Arthur Dentforth, her area manager, in the driver's seat. Her heart thudded. The original appointment had been for Friday morning and, as he had already told her that the post office facility would not now be reopening, she was not expecting to see him.

She retreated along the side path to the back room. Bertha Bunfighter, Tina's prize big, brown teddy bear, sat on the chair at the table, watching uncomfortably.

Dentforth saw Tina hurry away. He parked untidily in front of the skip, quickly climbed out and followed.

Tina turned the key in the back door before he tried the handle. He hammered to be let in.

She would not open the door.

'What are you doing here?' she shouted.

'I just need to sort out a couple of things,' he called back. 'It'll only take a few minutes.'

'I'll open the shop door,' she replied, reasoning it would be safer to talk to him by the front entrance where there was a possibility of passers-by seeing them.

She sprinted from the back room through the hall and into the shop, hoping to meet him outside. But, for a man with such a portly figure who was at least two decades older than her and showed no outward sign of athleticism, Dentforth surprised her by arriving first. As soon as he heard the hasp release, he blocked her exit and pushed his way into the shop. The lowered blinds rendered the interior in shadow.

'Mr Dentforth, good afternoon,' Tina greeted him politely, if not a little breathless.

But he was not interested in social niceties. Tina shivered. Dentforth was angry, his breathing was heavy. She felt she was in danger, but stared boldly, defiantly at her adversary.

Dentforth was a large man, not particularly tall, but his protruding stomach gave him considerable bulk and weight. Standing between her and the doors, he prevented most of the daylight from entering.

His face was flushed and glistening with sweat; his chin sported grey, uneven bristles. He was not wearing the jacket of his suit and his tie had also been discarded. He smelt as if he had not showered recently. She turned her head away to avoid breathing in his fetid breath – but as she did, he stepped closer.

She realised that, unless she could run to the hall and lock that door before he caught her, she was trapped. She forced herself to turn her head back and look at him. He snorted into her face and she could not stop herself wincing against his disgusting halitosis.

'Are you here to tell me the post office has changed its mind and we can reopen soon?' she asked with a slight tremble in her voice. It was a pathetic attempt to distract him.

'You would like that, wouldn't you? Eh?' he snarled, injecting more foul air into the confined space between them. Tina frowned. 'I'd been trying to get this crappy hole closed for years, but that wanker Poskett wouldn't let go. The *powers that be* told me to get it shut, get rid of it. But no, that bastard kept showing a profit – guess he knew how to keep the At Hand people sweet, and they brought the customers in. Well, now it's all gone!

Finished!'

Tina smarted at the news that the post office would have closed anyway. She wondered why she had been sent here at all. Dentforth noticed her concentration momentarily slacken and pounced forward. He clasped one hand on each of her shoulders, digging his fingers and thumbs viciously into the joints.

'Gotcha,' he growled.

Tina screamed. No one but Dentforth heard her.

He began to shake her. As her body was forced forward and back, forward and back, again and again, her head jerked violently to keep up, hurting her neck and throat muscles. His fat hand suddenly clenched into a fist and he punched, his knuckles connecting with her left jaw.

She received the crunching blow with a yelp of pain. The volition of his delivery released her from the grip of his other hand and propelled her sideways.

She fell and was stunned for a second. Quickly regaining her senses and despite her injuries, she managed to scramble to the hall door.

Fortunately, Dentforth's earlier burst of speed had deserted him; he was now clumsy and slow. She slammed the door shut before he lunged at it. She was shaking so badly that, at first, her fingers would not obey when she tried to push home the bolt. Eventually, she succeeded. She leant against the wall then slid to the floor and stared at the door to the under-the-stairs toilet.

Dentforth rattled the knob beside her. He swore with such ferocity that fear robbed her of the ability to react.

As Tina forced herself to think, her breath choked her. Her eyes were watering and the entire left side of her face felt enormous with the pain centring around the point his fist had made contact. Two of her bottom teeth were loose. She felt her cheek on the outside, then probed with her tongue around her gums. She tasted an iron-rich, metallic substance which, when she prodded with her fingers, she discovered was blood.

Panic forced her to gather herself sufficiently to stumble along the hall and into the back room. She also locked that door behind her. Her feelings of relief were short-lived as, within minutes, Dentforth was outside the rear door again – hammering, shouting and kicking. *So many times recently,* a hysterical voice inside told her, *has that door been attacked!*

She still trembled as she searched her pockets, but her mobile phone was not there; not that it would probably have worked anyway, the signal being so inconsistent. The landline extension was two paces from her, but such was the savagery and vitriol of Dentforth's abuse, she was too petrified to reach for it.

Tina looked around the room, searching for a means of defence. The only thing she saw was the teddy bear. Her terrified mind could even find humour in the fact that she had named the stupid thing *Bunfighter.* BUNFIGHTER?

Tina was not laughing, though. She was crying as she pressed herself into the farthest corner of the room. Gone was the fool-hardy drunkard who had carelessly tossed an engineering brick through the windscreen of her absent husband's sports car in Treemoore all those months ago. Neither was she now the stroppy wife who stomped away from said husband, having just had news of his affair confirmed.

Instead, she was crouching in a corner, whimpering with fear at the thought of Dentforth breaking in.

Through the furore, Tina suddenly heard the

screeching of brakes belonging to a heavy, diesel-engine vehicle on the road at the front of the building. Dentforth's assault on the door suddenly ceased. The sound of thick chains clanking became audible, followed by a juddering that could be felt through the ground.

"Ere, mate,' a man called above the noise. He must have walked along the path to the rear of the premises and was now addressing Dentforth. 'That your motor?' Tina recognised the gruff voice from earlier in the week. 'Can you shift it? I need to pick up that skip.' There was a pause. 'Cheers!'

All further communication, if any, was muffled by the lorry manoeuvring into place. There came a thud as the stabilisers took purchase on the ground then the lifting gear was engaged. Machinery clunked and spluttered, chains clanked and hydraulics groaned as the container, now heavy and cumbersome with detritus from the At Hand refurbishment, was hoisted on board and clanged into place.

The stabilisers were retracted, the brakes released and the lorry finally retreated. Silence followed, broken only by the occasional vehicle travelling along the road.

A jubilant blackbird then began to sing. But Tina did not move. Instead, she quietly wept.

Chapter 71

Duncan was still dazed and weak from undergoing his procedure when Lily visited on Friday evening. He'd been instructed to lie completely flat and motionless until told otherwise.

However, he managed to describe to Lily a little of what he could remember, finishing with, 'I was back on the ward when I came round. They'd strapped what felt like a block of plastic into my groin to stop the vein opening up. They took it off about an hour ago.'

'Does it hurt?' Lily asked anxiously.

'Not really – might do more when the painkillers wear off, but it's okay at the moment.' Then he added with a smile, 'I daren't move, though, in case it starts to bleed.'

Lily smiled back. She suddenly felt so tired that she could easily just lie unmoving on a bed for a few hours. She had not slept very well for over a week now; all the worry about Duncan was keeping her awake.

'Oh, by the way, I spoke to your Uncle George,' Lily stated, suddenly remembering. 'He said he'll help you out with the business until you're back on your feet. But he's a bit worried about using your equipment – you know, after ...'

She repeated a little of the conversation and Duncan agreed that of course it was okay for George to drive whatever machinery he needed to. They remained silent for a while, listening to the gentle murmur of the hospital.

Lily suddenly seemed startled.

'What about your heart, how does that feel?' she asked.

'Okay. No different, really,' Duncan replied. 'They said the plug-thing was embedded okay and that the flesh would grow in through the mesh, which will hopefully seal the hole completely ... Lily, are you all right?'

'No,' Lily answered. 'Where's the nearest toilet, I think I'm going to be ...'

'NURSE!' Duncan yelled as he pressed the button on the call device. He was helpless, not even able to sit up.

Lily scuttled, with her hand over her mouth, to where she thought the nearest Ladies' toilet was located. A nurse hurried around the corner from their station in the opposite direction.

'My wife isn't well,' Duncan quickly explained as he pointed.

The nurse just stared at Duncan. 'Can you check she's okay, please? She thinks she might be pregnant again.' Finally, the nurse darted away towards the toilet.

Ten minutes or so later, she brought Lily back and helped her to sit down on the bedside chair.

'I've just rung Dad, he's on his way in,' Lily explained quietly. 'He gave me a lift here and he's been waiting in the car park. I'm sorry, Duncan, I think your description was just a little too graphic.' Her face was extremely pale and she looked exhausted.

'You just rest, my dear,' said the nurse. 'Would you like a cup of tea or anything?'

'No, thank you,' Lily replied. 'I'm okay, really.'

'Right, well, you have to take care of yourself so that you can look after your family, and the new little one. Congratulations, by the way,' she said. 'When is it due?'

'End of January, beginning of February next year. I'm not sure yet, it's still very early days.'

Vince appeared after a few minutes. He said a quick hello to Duncan before helping Lily out to the car.

After they had gone, Duncan felt very restless and emotional. He pretended to be asleep when the nurses carried out their evening checks. He just wanted to get better and be back at home with his family.

Chapter 72

After breakfast on Saturday morning, George left the Old Police House in Pepper Hill to meet Duncan's father-in-law at Tidal Reach in Ashfield.

Vince Hallett, dressed in his gardening clothes, introduced himself to George. He had brought Jack along with him. This was the first time George had seen his great-nephew; he was fascinated by the little lad, in whom he could see a likeness to both Duncan and Lily.

Vince led George into the cottage in order for him to collect Duncan's business messages from the answerphone.

'I'll have to make sure the remaining machinery is still okay before I get in touch with these people,' George told Vince as he indicated to the notes he was writing. 'I don't want to make arrangements if the equipment doesn't work.'

With that, he went back outside to his car and changed into a boiler suit, which was far from new and bore the MaCold company logo on the back. He also swapped his shoes for his steel-toe-capped safety boots.

George started by checking the engine and mechanisms on Duncan's good tractor, the one Rosalie had borrowed. Everything seemed to be fine. Although it had not been sprayed too badly with slurry, he stretched the hose over from the standpipe in the corner of the yard and gave it a quick wash down, brushing the residue into a drain in the middle of the concrete area installed for that purpose. When it was clean, the bright yellow paintwork shone in the sunshine; the purple lettering invited the eyes to read *Duncan Stickleback, Septic Tank Services.*

George drove this tractor down to the pasture land where the two tankers – the undamaged one and the ruptured one – were both standing side by side. He ensured the good tanker was empty before coiling up the pipe work and towing it back. He parked in the yard again, hosed out the inside of the tanker, cleaned the pipes and allowed the residue to flow straight into the central drain. Then he tackled the outside.

When this was finished, he returned indoors to contact the three people who needed their septic tanks emptying. Two calls went through to their respective answer machines, where he duly left messages. A woman replied to his third; she was very insistent that her tank be emptied immediately because it was almost overflowing and smelt very badly. George smiled at the similarity of this situation to that in which Rosalie recently found herself.

'Right, if you could just confirm your address, I'll be there as soon as I can,' he said as he checked his note. The premises were only a short distance down the road – one of the cottages in the same row as Max's home.

An hour or so later, with the first job completed and the sludge emptying out in the bottom pasture, George towed home the damaged tanker. But before starting work he thought he'd check on Vince and Jack.

Vince was busy in the front garden, weeding the flowerbeds and generally tidying up. Jack, much to George's surprise, was sitting in the middle of the slightly overgrown lawn where a crop of molehills seemed to have broken out. The soil in the mounds was a rich, shiny brown, in stark contrast to the succulent green of the fertilised and irrigated grass. Jack was excavating one of the molehills with his toy digger and loading the earth onto the back of a matching lorry.

'Will you be in much trouble with Lily if Jack gets himself too dirty?' George joked.

'Probably,' Vince replied. 'But he's enjoying himself, isn't he? I think it's the first time his toy digger and lorry have been played with outside – it's about time they got a bit of muck on them!'

They both stood watching Jack as he went about the serious business of removing one of the molehills. When he'd finished loading the lorry, he trundled it over to another of the miniature heaps, his lips vibrating and spraying spittle as he imitated the *brrmmm, brrmmm* engine noises. He brought the toy to a halt, reversed it into place then scampered back across the lawn to retrieve the digger. He roared this over to join the lorry and proceeded to unload the soil to create one enormous mound. Having patted the sides smooth, wiped his hands down his T-shirt and shorts, he looked around for another molehill. He spied one over the far side of the lawn, pushed his two toys towards it and began the process all over again.

'I promised the girls I'd mow the grass here this morning, but I'm a bit stuck now – I don't want to disturb Jack,' Vince said.

'I'll go make us a brew and we can take a break for a while,' George suggested, smiling at Vince's description of his wife and daughter. 'What about Jack, would he like a drink?'

'Oh, I expect so. I think there are some small cartons of orange juice in the fridge, just bring one of those out for him.'

Chapter 73

A little while later, George left Jack and Vince on the lawn and returned to the yard area. First, he inspected the tanker; it had been spiked at the end, slightly off centre. Three of the purple figures just after the beginning of Duncan's telephone number were indecipherable. A trail of dried sludge clung under the hole and down onto the frame. The smell pinched at George's nostrils. He decided to give it a through clean and let the sun dry the outside before attempting any repairs.

With this complete, he turned his attention to the tractor with the faulty front loader. This had been reversed into the barn with the arm down and the prong resting on the ground. Before he could attempt any work, he needed to move it out into the yard. He started it up and tried to raise the loader arm, but it would not lift. In the end he was forced to push the base with the spike along the ground in front of him.

The noise brought Vince round, carrying his grandson, to see what was happening. He stood to one side of the big barn doors as, accompanied by sharp scraping, grinding sounds and disguised by clouds of dust and jets of black exhaust smoke, George drove the tractor out. He tied not to notice the groove he'd worn into the surface of the concrete and parked with the loader resting on a patch of grass just off the main yard area. He switched off the engine and waited for the juddering to stop before he climbed down. The air was filled with a mixture of dust, oil and diesel, which was replaced with the stench of slurry when the exhaust fumes floated away.

'We wondered what on earth was going on,' Vince said. He set Jack on the ground but held tightly onto his hand, telling him not to go near either the tractor or tanker.

'I think you can safely say we've got quite a job on our hands,' George stated. 'Best thing to do is to get the front loader off so that the tractor is useable. I'll take a look at the mechanism when I've sorted the tanker.' As he was explaining, he and Vince plus young Jack still clutching his grandfather's hand, walked back to inspect the punctured tank.

'Wow, that's quite a gash Henry managed to make,' Vince said with a wry smile, recoiling a little at the stench.

'Poooo!' Jack agreed, elongating the word until he ran out of breath.

'Reckon it could've been worse,' George said. 'The hole was probably made bigger when Duncan pulled the spike out, but it's patchable. He was worried that the frame had buckled – either when Henry forced the spike in or when he drew it out. But I think it's okay. Do you happen to know if Duncan has a welding kit?'

'Yes, at the back of the barn,' said Vince as he pointed. 'There's two, gas and MIG. I guess gas would be better for this job. The rods, gloves and visor should all be there as well. You can probably find some metal somewhere around here to use for the repair.' He looked at his watch. 'Look, it's nearly lunchtime and I'm supposed to take this young man …..' he looked down at Jack, 'back soon for something to eat. Maybe you'd like to join us. I'll ring Irene.'

'That would be great. Thanks,' George replied as he wiped the sweat and grime off his face with his hand, leaving a black smear across his cheek.

Jack grinned at him and bounced excitedly on his toes. He almost extricated himself from his grandfather's grip until Vince bent down and whisked him up.

Vince carried Jack with one arm and held his mobile in the other as he walked around the side of the cottage. He eventually persuaded his phone to find a signal and rang Irene to advise her that they had a guest for lunch.

George checked Duncan's welding equipment; he was impressed with the condition of everything. His nephew was obviously a neat, tidy and diligent young man. George was not sure who he'd inherited this trait from, unless it was his grandfather Derek.

George removed his boiler suit and work boots and locked them in his car before going into the cottage and wash his hands and face. He then collected Jack's toys from the front lawn and gave them a good shake to rid them of as much the soil from the molehills as he could before carrying them to Vince's car.

As Vince strapped Jack into his seat, he told George that he had spoken to Irene.

'She'll have lunch ready by the time we get there. Oh, and she said that Duncan was transferred to Cliffend hospital from Mattingburgh this morning – possibly came past here while we were busy. Irene and Lily will take Jack to see him later, so we'll have the whole afternoon to concentrate on the work.'

Chapter 74

On Saturday night, Henry checked that the doors and downstairs windows were all locked before he went upstairs to bed. The light was still on in Sarah's room. He knocked on the door.

'Come in,' she called. She was sitting in the easy chair by her bed, wearing a light dressing gown over a loose, long T-shirt-style night dress. The bump protruded aggressively. She was resting her swollen ankles on a suitcase lying flat on the floor in front of her. She looked very tired and uncomfortable; her face was flushed and she was fanning herself with a thin paperback book.

'Wouldn't you be better in bed?' Henry asked.

'Probably, but …' Her voice was quiet, barely recognisable as belonging to the confident young lady downstairs in the bar a couple of hours ago.

Henry edged past her and sat on the side of her bed. He removed the book she was flapping, took her hand and held it to his chest.

'If there's anything wrong, you can tell me. Can't promise I can put it all right, but I'll do my best to help. You know that, don't you?' He paused while she lowered her head and covered her eyes with her other hand.

'Oh, Dad. I don't think there's anything that can be done.'

'Well, tell me anyway.'

'I can't,' she cried.

Henry held her close as she leant into him and sobbed.

Chapter 75

Penelope Stickleback was born at two forty-six on Sunday morning at The Fighting Cock in Ashfield, PepperAsh. She was delivered by her grandfather after a very short labour. The ambulance arrived in time for the professionals to deal with the placenta and cord. Henry then accompanied his daughter and grand-daughter to Cliffend hospital.

He was left in the waiting area while mother and baby were taken into the maternity unit. The doors were locked behind them and access could only be gained by entering a code on the key pad. There was no one anywhere for him to ask if everything was all right.

Henry missed Sarah and Duncan being born; many times over the years he wondered if Rosalie would've allowed him to be with her anyway. If he had, he thought perhaps having to act as midwife to his daughter might not have been such a shock. Trying not to remember the details, nor to think about the mess he would have to clear up when he returned home, he paced the confined area, growing more and more anxious as time passed.

Finally, in an effort to occupy himself, Henry convinced himself he was thirsty. He wandered down to the ground floor and made his way to the café area by the entrance, his footsteps echoing on the empty corridor floors. The serving counters were shuttered and closed; the entire place was deserted.

Henry looked around for a clock. It read 4.06 a.m. Three vending machines stood at the far end of the seating area. Henry didn't have any money with him so he strolled over to the water fountain near the counter, picked up a disposable plastic cup, filled it and drank. He then returned to the maternity wing.

There was still no one to ask if he could see Sarah and his grand-daughter. After a long wait, he began to wander restlessly back along the corridor. Eventually he found his feet were taking him towards the cardiac department.

Duncan was drifting in and out of sleep when he suddenly became aware someone was standing by his bed. The figure was in shadow, but he could make out the person to be tall and large, with dishevelled, greying dark hair and a beard.

'Dad?' he asked anxiously, struggling to wake.

'Hello, son. Don't worry, nothing's wrong – just thought I'd pop along and tell you that you're an uncle.' Henry could not restrain the pride in his voice, although he kept his tone hushed in deference to his son's condition. Duncan's unshaven face looked extremely pale, the only colour being the livid wound at his temple.

'What?' Duncan asked incredulously. Although still drowsy and weak from the procedure and yesterday's transfer to Cliffend hospital from Mattingburgh, he quickly realised the implications of his Dad's news. 'So, it was a real pregnancy?'

'Oh yes, it was real all right – as I discovered in the early hours of this morning!' Henry was smiling broadly. 'The baby was born just before three – not sure of all the vital statistics, but I'm sure the women-folk will soon find out and let you know. Her name is Penelope, which Sarah is already shortening to Penny.'

Duncan seemed a little overwhelmed. 'But she insisted it was a phantom pregnancy,' he said, frowning.

'Yes, but I think she was probably the only person who believed that.' Henry yawned, then continued, 'I haven't spoken to a doctor or nurse or midwife, or whoever sees to them. But I expect they'll both have to stay in until someone gives them the all clear. Penny's tiny, but not quite small enough to cause concern – the paramedics said they didn't think she was premature and there's no problem with her breathing or anything, so she should be okay to come home later today. The last thing Sarah said as she and the baby disappeared to be examined was that she didn't have anything ready.'

'We'll lend her some things if she's desperate.' Duncan then raised himself up and smiled at his father, unable to contain himself any longer. 'I've got some news as well,' he said. 'It's not general knowledge, but Lily thinks she might be expecting. It's very early days as yet, so don't say anything, especially not at the moment – I don't want to spoil Sarah's surprise!'

'That is good news! Well done, son.' Henry patted Duncan's shoulder proudly. 'Gosh, the Stickleback family really is expanding.'

'Thanks, Dad. But remember, keep it to yourself. Although I suppose, if you think anyone needs to know, you'd better tell them.' Then Duncan asked, 'What's the time?'

Henry looked around again for a clock. 'It's quarter to six. I'll ask at maternity if I can ring your mother from there – I didn't bring my phone or anything with me. I came in the ambulance with Sarah and the baby, and I've been hanging around ever since.'

'And what's going on here?' nurse Luke asked, suddenly appearing beside Henry. 'Bit early for visitors. Mind you, mate,' he said, giving Henry a good look up and down. 'You look as if you've been up all night anyway!'

'Actually, I have,' Henry replied. 'Well, nearly all night. I think I did get a couple of hours' sleep before I was rudely awoken. I'm not used to someone screaming "Dad!" at me in the middle of the night anymore.'

'Why, what happened?' asked Luke.

'My sister's had her baby,' Duncan answered.

'Wow! That was quick. I thought you said it was a phantom pregnancy.'

'That's what she told us …' Duncan said.

'… But none of us really believed it,' Henry finished for him.

'Well, congratulations all round,' Luke said with a grin. 'I'll see if we can celebrate with a cup of special hospital tea – can't run to champagne.'

'Er, before you go, could I borrow your phone, please?' Henry asked.

Chapter 76

At around six o'clock on Sunday morning, George answered Rosalie's telephone with caution.

'Old Police House?'

'Morning, George. It's Henry,' he said cheerfully into Luke's mobile phone as he stood outside the front of Cliffend hospital, breathing in the fresh air and feeling as if he were the happiest man alive.

'Oh, hello, Henry. You sound very pleased with yourself,' George replied suspiciously.

'I am!' Henry stated emphatically. 'Well, not with me, but with Sarah.' He paused for a moment, feeling tears gathering and his throat thickening. He pressed the thumb and forefinger of his free hand into the inside corners of his eyes and swallowed several times before he was able to speak again. 'I'm just ringing to let you know that Sarah had a little baby girl last night – well, in the early hours of this morning, to be exact.'

'What?' George almost shouted. 'Did I just hear you right? Did you say that ...'

'Yes, you're a great-uncle again! Rosalie and I are grandparents for the second time round.'

'Oh! Well, er. I don't quite know what to say.'

Rosalie appeared at the kitchen door and overheard George's last comment. She saw her brother's broad smile. 'Who's that? What's going on?' she demanded urgently.

George moved the mouthpiece aside and lowered his voice. 'It's Henry. I'll explain in a minute.' He then gleaned as much information as he thought would satisfy Rosalie.

'Are they going back to yours this morning?' he

finished by asking.

'I'm not sure when they'll be discharged. I haven't seen anyone to speak to yet. I was just left waiting, so in the end I wandered over to see Duncan. That nurse, Luke, lent me his phone – I came out without mine. He's going to chase them up in maternity when I get back. Sarah will obviously have to wait for the all clear, but yes, I expect they will. Thing is, I, er, haven't got my car here; I came with Sarah and the baby in the ambulance.'

'That's no problem,' George said. 'I'll finish getting ready and drive over to the pub and pick it up. Where will the keys be?'

'Thanks. I'll ring Polly, she can get them for you. I was going to say, bet you can't get away without that big sister of yours. But, of course, she'll have to drive you over to the pub, follow you here then take you back, won't she?'

'Yup. And we'll all be glad of Rosie's help, I expect!'

'Yes. Listen, George, I've been thinking a bit about all the stuff that Sarah and little Penny will need. We've got nothing at the moment.' Henry hesitated before adding, 'Actually, there is another favour I wanted to ask you.'

'Oh yes, and what's that?'

'Could you call in at that new baby shop on the retail park in Cliffend? It's near the big supermarket – Rosalie will show you. Or, if that isn't open, maybe the catalogue shop in town will be. I need a baby carrier, you know, a cross between a child's car seat and a carry cot. You can get them for a new-born, or one that a new-born can fit into; I'm not too sure of the details, but I expect the assistants will be able to help. You see, we can't bring the baby home without her being strapped into a proper seat, apparently.'

'No, I guess not. Couldn't you borrow some of Jack's stuff? It would see Sarah through for a while, wouldn't it?' George enquired.

'I'd rather not worry Duncan or Lily at the moment,' Henry explained carefully. 'Anyway, keep this between ourselves. And definitely *do not tell Rosalie*, but Lily thinks she's pregnant again, so they'll need to hang on to Jack's baby things.'

'Oh, right. Well, okay.' George was lost for words. 'Anyway, I'll do what I can. I'll see you later.'

'Thanks, George,' Henry said. 'And I'll pay you of course ...'

'No, no.' George interrupted. 'Have this on me.'

'You know, George, I'm too tired to argue. So, thanks.'

George was smiling as he finished the call. Rosalie, in contrast, was scowling as she stood, hands on hips, waiting for an explanation.

Chapter 77

On Sunday morning, Reverend Quintin Boyce was ravenous. All he could find for breakfast was a tin of rice pudding that he remembered rescuing from the harvest festival donations last autumn: it was three months out of date then, and his conscience wouldn't allow it to be given to the poor. He heated the creamy mixture in a saucepan on his cooker, stirring it whilst pinging the elastic band on his wrist. The band broke. He cursed. Sighing, he carried the wooden spoon as he walked through to his study and rummaged on the untidy desk to find a replacement. The absence of his talisman left an emptiness which the cross under his shirt could not quite fill.

As he searched, he noticed the spoon was dripping dollops of rice onto his correspondence. Eventually, he found a new rubber band and slopped more rice around as he slipped it on to his other wrist. By the time he reached the door leading back to the kitchen, the rice in the saucepan was spluttering; he could smell it burning on the bottom.

He quickly stirred the rice and tipped it into a dish – the last remaining clean one – and placed it on the table. He collected a dessert-spoon from the cutlery drawer.

He sank down into the chair with his head low as if in prayer. But a crushing misery was the true cause of his shoulders slumping. Even the rubber bands remained idle.

After several minutes indulging in self-pity, Quinny managed to locate his inner piety. He ate the burnt rice, which had cooled nicely by then. After this he made a pot of tea, but was then further dismayed to find that he had no milk or sugar.

The At Hand shop in Pepper Hill still had not reopened: if he wanted – no, needed – provisions, he was going to have to ask someone for a lift into Cliffend. Preferably before lunchtime, as he'd heard that the supermarket did a very good Sunday roast in their cafeteria.

Quinny closed his eyes and saw slices of succulent roast beef, pink in the middle and grey/brown towards a dark and appetising edge. His stomach rumbled painfully. Crisp and golden Yorkshire puddings sat beside bright orange baby carrots and vivid green peas. There might even be runner beans, cabbage or swede, but not spinach, or turnip, please, although a floret or two of broccoli would be acceptable – even cauliflower, maybe. His mind moved around the plate to the roast potatoes – almost brittle on the outside and creamy, soft and fluffy on the inside. There would be boiled potatoes, too; new ones, small, with the skins still on. A rich brown gravy– holding a tang of meat juices, herbs and a hint of onion – would give off the most glorious aroma, taunting his taste buds. In his imagination, it smothered the plate, with just enough fat floating on top to make the vegetables glisten.

Quinny hurriedly sipped his black, unsweetened tea and twanged the elastic band on his wrist to remind himself to be practical and think logically.

Of course, there was the problem of justifying the Church's official stance regarding Sunday trading. On the one hand, he needed food urgently. On the other, most people working today would probably not have gone to church even if they had the time free.

He thought on. Maybe he just didn't have the answers. He usually tried to understand everyone's point of view and not express his own too bluntly. Shops opening on the Sabbath had given rise to as many heated discussions in the bar at The Fighting Cock as the banning of smoking in public places. Even his use of the word *Sabbath* had caused controversy during one such debate: that was Saturday, anyway, wasn't it? Only transferred to Sunday by Easter. Then the word "only" hung in his mind in big, big letters.

He finished the last of his tea, stood up and transferred the crockery and cutlery into the sink. He rinsed his hands and wiped them down the front of his trousers, gathered his prayer book and Bible off the table and finally left the house.

He was still hungry. He was in a bad mood as well. The glorious sunshine did not help to soothe him. He quickly reached the pathway to St Jude's Church and was scrunching along the gravel when he suddenly realised he had forgotten to lock the rectory door.

'Bugger,' he muttered to himself as he continued towards the already open church. Inside the air was pleasantly cool; the white walls reflected the morning sunshine and made everywhere bright and light and clean. He breathed in deeply, pinged his elastic band again and tried to tell himself that the world was good. Really, it *was* good.

As if to emphasise the sentiment, he heard someone say, 'Good morning, Reverend Boyce.' It was Mrs Ervsgreaves, the organist and good lady of the parish. Her voice rang out and echoed against the whitened walls. 'What did you just say? I couldn't quite hear.'

Mrs Ervsgreaves' presence demanded absolute attention. This began with the pronunciation of her name, which required concentration and accuracy so as to avoid being corrected by the lady herself. Her first name, Quinny discovered many years ago, was Delilah. But no one ever called her that, not even her husband – well, not in public anyway. Quinny thought his mischievous inner demon had finished tormenting him for today, but it was now daring him to call Mrs Ervsgreaves *Delilah*.

Delilah Ervsgreaves was always cheerful on a Sunday morning – annoyingly so, despite the weather, world affairs, the state of the economy and the increasing price of beer down at the pub. Not that she ever drank beer in the pub. *That could be the problem*, Quinny deduced. She had no perspective. Not even with the name Delilah.

Mrs Ervsgreaves had taken on the role of organist many years ago. Her husband was one of the churchwardens. She was not a natural musician, but she soldiered on with fortitude whilst constantly complaining that she never complained. She was substantially built, with dewlaps wobbling between her chin and neck. She was a very good cook and she dressed immaculately for a lady of her respectably retired age.

'Morning, Mrs Ervsgreaves,' Quinny replied, fixing a grin to his face. It was then he realised he'd forgotten to shave.

'Reverend, there's something I've been meaning to ask you.' Her smile suddenly vanished and she became serious.

'Oh? And what is that?' Quinny asked in his best rector's voice, aiming for a tone of magnanimous concern, but actually achieving suppressed irritation.

'Has there been any news of Mr Poskett's funeral? It's been a while now, and I'm a little concerned that … Well, that there may be no one to make the arrangements.'

'I haven't heard anything yet,' Quinny answered, allowing the pique he'd been controlling to surface. Suddenly he did not particularly want to be interrogated by a busybody old biddy parishioner, even if her steak and kidney pies were delicious.

'Oh.' She looked away before persisting; 'And what has happened with the shop and post office? I believe they've brought someone in to open it up again. But when?' She gently patted Quinny's arm, which irked him even more. Her hand was liver-spotted, wrinkled and she wore numerous and heavily jewelled rings, which were the only items about her entire person that spoilt her air of good taste.

She looked down at her hand and blushed before quickly withdrawing it and stepping back.

'I understand your concern, Mrs Ervsgreaves,' Quinny said kindly, ignoring her discomfort. 'Now, I have a favour to ask you, would you be so kind as to give me a lift into Cliffend after this morning's service?'

'Of course, Reverend,' she replied, glad to be of help. 'Please come and have lunch with Mr Ervsgreaves and myself first. Then we'll drive you into town this afternoon.'

Quinny thought *perfect!* Mr and Mrs Ervsgreaves lived in a large, comfortably provided house, the first dwelling in the hamlet of Ashfield as one approached from the Cliffend direction. Mr Ervsgreaves was a retired accountant; he was also church warden, treasurer of the Parochial Church Council and one of the army of gentlemen who kept the churchyard and rectory garden in good order. A stalwart of the parish in every sense! Good man – deserved a medal, in Quinny's estimations, especially being married to Mrs

Ervsgreaves. He pinged his rubber band again and asked himself whether he'd ever heard Mrs Ervsgreaves use her husband's Christian name either. *No,* he thought; *don't tell me! It can't be Samson!*

However, with slow deliberation and not wishing to appear devious or manipulative, Quinny sighed.

'Yes,' he replied. 'That sounds splendid. Thank you. But now, I really must get ready for this morning's service.'

Chapter 78

George's explanation to his sister was as brief as he could get away with. She agreed to drive them both in her car to The Fighting Cock, which luckily was on the way to Cliffend, in order for George to collect Henry's car. Henry asked Luke if he could use his phone a make a second call. He rang Polly and persuaded her to go into the pub early to give George the spare car key which was kept by the till.

Rosalie and George would drive in convoy into town, purchase the baby carrier and then go over to the hospital. All the shuffling and swapping reminded Rosalie of the fiasco after the tanker prang outside her house when the various vehicles had to be sorted, recovered and returned. Today, however, her mind was too full of thoughts about her new grand-daughter and Duncan's condition to worry over that unfortunate incident.

George checked online to see if the Baby World store had a suitable carrier. They were out of stock. Then, whilst researching other outlets in Cliffend, the internet connection disappeared. He consulted Rosie and they decided to take a chance in town.

Having collected Henry's car, they eventually reached the catalogue shop and managed to park both vehicles outside. Luckily, waiting restrictions were not enforceable on Sundays because, not only did the shop have a suitable model, but the young man serving them – a new father himself – demonstrated how the carrier, which also folded out to become a stroller, clipped onto the seat belt fitting.

They finally arrived separately at the hospital.

Rosalie secretly hoped to see Sarah and Penny, as well as sneak in a visit to Duncan. But George guessed her plan; he asked, then ordered, her to stay in her car.

Henry was in the corridor by the maternity unit waiting area. George congratulated him again, handed over the car keys and explained that they would probably be quite a while in the Baby World shop.

He returned to the car park and climbed into Rosalie's car. She treated him to a sullen silence. George ignored her. The windows were open, which made Ben's moulted hair swirl around in the breeze as they drove along.

The recently opened Baby World shop was adjacent the big supermarket. They parked easily.

'Have you got that list?' George asked Rosalie as they climbed out of the car.

'It's right here,' she replied cheerfully, now being too happy to sulk. She waved the piece of paper containing a vertical column of scribbled writing. 'I keep thinking of extra things baby Penny will need.' The excitement in her voice made George smile.

As they walked the short distance to the main entrance, Rosalie shaded her eyes from the hot sun. The wind ruffled her untidy hair.

'Right, then,' George exclaimed. 'We'd better go and get everything for this new little Stickleback – I presume she'll be a Stickleback. Has Sarah said anything about the father?'

'No, and I didn't ask before because she was adamant that she was having a phantom pregnancy. I don't know if Henry's managed to get any more out of her.'

'Well, perhaps it's best not to bombard her with too many questions at the moment. We'll just have to wait until she's ready to tell us.'

The entrance doors slid silently open and they walked in. The interior was quite cool compared with outside: an air conditioning unit throbbed above them.

On a banner curved above the inside of Baby World's entrance was a slogan stating they stocked everything from before conception, for the mum-to-be, the birth and through to infancy. *Shame they're out of baby carriers, then,* George thought.

True to the banner's statement, the entire shop was filled with stacks and plinths and shelves of everything one could possibly imagine that would be needed, plus a lot more besides. A bright green vinyl pathway swirled around the displays of pretty pastel-coloured baby suits, cardigans, booties, socks, rugs and blankets. The delicately coloured items were interspersed with stronger shades for the fashion conscious.

Further along were stands of easy to clean plastic bibs; bottles of various sizes, some with bizarre shaped teats; trays and training cups and spoons, the latter having curiously curved handles. George picked up a box containing a kit for expressing milk, held it up and gave a bewildered look to Rosalie. She took the box from him and replaced it on the shelf.

'Don't ask!' she advised.

In the centre of the shop was a range of tough, rigid trolleys, pushchairs, highchairs, cots, and car seats for toddlers, but apparently no carriers for babies! This merchandise stood on its own island of the green vinyl, above which hung a placard with bold letters, reading *Home Delivery Available.*

When Rosalie saw this, she pointed it out to George.

'Someone should've told Henry,' she said. 'He could've given them a ring last night instead of struggling on his own!'

George chuckled. He then followed Rosie as she looked around. Near the prams and pushchairs were shoulder bags in matching fabrics, fitted out with disposable nappies and changing trays, bottles, towels, creams and wipes. Off to one side was a display of fluffy bears and rabbits, along with every other imaginable animal made into a cuddly toy. She picked up a small, soft brown dog and stroked it. Despite all the excitement, Rosalie suddenly missed Ben.

George blinked his eyes and scratched his head. He could feel his credit card over-heating, even secreted away as it was in his wallet.

'Right, where do we start, then Rosie?' he asked. 'You have experience at this.'

'Not sure I'm any more qualified than you, really.'

'At least you're a parent, which is more than I am. Or ever will be!'

Rosalie decided to ignore any self-pity that might be in her brother's voice.

'The twins were born a long time ago, you know,' she replied. 'And I didn't have to shop for everything all at once. Back then, the colours seemed to be limited to pale pink, pastel blue, white, lemon, light green or tangerine orange. Now, well ...' She picked up a teddy bear the same size as the toy dog and waved her empty hand in an ark to take in the vast choice.

The teddy bear, George realised. *Bertha Bunfighter*. Could there be something hidden inside? And the idea of a baby's nimble fingers being able to prise it out caused him alarm. But, feeling this was ridiculous, he pushed the thought aside and concentrated on the task in front of him, compartmentalising his life again: not thinking of the toy bear, or of Tina alone at the shop.

'What about when Jack was a baby?' he asked.

'Er, I just gave Lily and Duncan money for a nice pram, plus some other bits and pieces. I wasn't allowed to get involved much,' Rosalie confessed, dreading the next question, which inevitably came.

'Why?'

'Well, I overhead Lily telling Duncan that she didn't mind the *sensible grandparents* helping – meaning her own parents, Vince and Irene. But she didn't particularly want the *idiot grandparents* interfering – meaning Henry and myself, of course. Apparently, we *just cause problems.*'

When George heard this, he turned his face away, trying but failing to conceal the smile he felt his sister would not appreciate.

'I know,' Rosalie reproached. 'You agree with them. And, I must admit, I do too – to a degree, that is.'

'Yes, well,' George stalled. He then changed the subject. 'Come on, Rosie, let's get a move on or baby Penny will be a terrible teenager before we're out of this shop. So? Where to?'

'Nappies!' Rosalie squirmed at her nickname. But she refused to be baited. 'I guess they're first. I remember I was always terrified of running out. But then I did have twins to deal with. And wipes, Sarah'll need wipes, and tissues … And we want something to carry it all in.'

George obediently walked back to the store's entrance where the trolleys were lined up outside.

As he pulled one free, he thought he saw a rector, climbing out of a very posh car over on the supermarket car park, accompanied by an elderly couple. He frowned. *Surely, a man of the cloth would not be shopping on a Sunday, would he?*

Chapter 79

As a result of the unorthodox delivery, Sarah and Penny had to wait to be seen by the doctor before she could be formally discharged. He was delayed because of an emergency admission: a young mum required a caesarean section.

Eventually, mother and baby were seen and, apart from a little attention to a small tear in the birth canal, both Sarah and Penny were pronounced in good health. Fortunately, after the birth, Henry's common sense told him to make sure the baby was breathing (she had screamed even before her feet were free); he'd also saved the placenta for examination.

Henry reluctantly left Sarah cradling Penny late in the morning. He wondered whether to try to catch up with Rosalie and George at the Baby World shop but he was still feeling bewildered and tired. He decided to have something to eat and drink before doing anything else.

When he arrived back at the pub, the bar seemed dark and gloomy against the bright sunshine outside. A group of regulars was just finishing a round. Polly collected the glasses from the front of the bar. When she bent forward, the men imbibed the full benefit of her tight top – the fabric's strident pink colour helping to force their eyes onto the more comforting pale flesh shades looming from the low V-neck.

'Hello, Grandad,' she greeted Henry.

He smiled. His customers raised their nearly empty glasses in a toast and expressed their expectations of a free celebratory drink, or two.

'One,' he instructed Polly amidst the camaraderie

and well-wishes.

His exit into the kitchen was accompanied by the echoes of 'skinflint' and 'miser'. If he'd seen Quinny in the bar, he would have attributed the final call of 'mean old bugger' to him.

Polly followed Henry through. She gently laid her hand on his forearm, her red nails in contrast to his relatively pale skin.

'Seriously, though, well done,' she said. 'It couldn't have been easy.' Her eyes, although shadowed and highlighted, reflected her genuine concern. Her layered made-up face showed honesty and empathy.

Henry thought back to the sounds and the smells and the sheer hard work of the birth: the unknown, the panic and the pain; so much blood and liquid. He shuddered before raising his eyes to the ceiling and commenting that Sarah's room was in quite a mess.

'Don't worry, I'll sort it all out,' Polly reassured.

'I can't ask you to do that!'

'You're not asking, I'm volunteering.'

'Well, there's an awful lot to clean up. You'll have to order a new mattress – neither of us exactly knew what we were doing.'

'Right,' Polly said eager for the challenge, and the opportunity to spend someone else's money. 'The Home Warehouse Store in Cliffend has got a sale on. You go and rest. I'll deal with it. I'll check on the damage in a minute – when I've served this lot.' She nodded through the open door. 'Here, give us your credit card, then I won't have to bother you again.'

'Thanks, Polly. I don't know …'

'… what you would do without me,' Polly finished for him. 'I know! Go on with you. Don't go getting all soppy on me just because you're a grandad again.'

She held out her hand for the card, which she grasped between her fingers, again displaying her long, scarlet-painted nails. She then strolled back into the bar.

Henry smiled. Friend. If only she wasn't gay. He sighed as he turned away. But then, she wouldn't have been available for the likes of him, anyway. Besides which, he thought he would only ever be in love with one person – Rosalie.

In the kitchen, Henry found peace in the ritual of making his tea/coffee concoction. He sank into one of the chairs at the table, surprised that he felt extremely weary. He took a sip of his drink.

'Just the job!' he exclaimed quietly to himself.

With a deep breath inwards, Henry was energised towards the fridge. Blessing his daughter's generous grocery shop earlier in the week, he thought of his wallet. Then he remembered he'd given Polly his credit card. But, before he had time to question his wisdom, he heard the lady's high heels clipping their way up the stairs and along the landing to Sarah's bedroom.

Polly had worked at The Fighting Cock for so long, she knew the house and business almost as well as he did himself; they respected and trusted each other. Henry had been aware of her sexuality from their first meeting, but neither of them ever mentioned it. He could see that she was attractive. He was often amused by her antics with the punters. And she had proved herself to be a good friend many times. Today, for example.

Henry gathered together the ingredients for his late breakfast; sausages, eggs, mushrooms and bacon. Finally, he pulled open the salad drawer and took out two rounded, plump, red-ripe tomatoes. Elbowing shut the fridge door he carefully made his way to the cooker and tipped the contents of his cupped hands onto the adjacent work top.

At first, Henry could not find his frying pan. It usually resided on the hob, with the fat in place protected by the lid of a large saucepan.

Sarah had obviously been tidying up! Henry began to pull open the cupboard doors. He eventually found the pan in the unit between the fridge and the cooker, thoroughly washed and, in his mind, ruined.

His good mood was evaporating. Taking a spatula from the drawer, he spitefully sliced a generous corner off the block of lard from the fridge, flicked it into the frying pan and switched on the heat.

As Henry sat down to eat, he felt he was consuming his last peaceful, cholesterol-laden meal. From henceforth he was condemned to noise, confusion, vitamins and nutrition, untidiness and penury. He would finally be amidst a family again. He anticipated it with relish as he squeezed the contents from a near-empty bottle of tomato ketchup onto his plate.

Chapter 80

Sarah and Penny were both kept in hospital overnight because the baby had developed a temperature. But they were due home today and, naturally, Rosalie was looking forward to seeing them. She thought she might buy a card for Sarah to congratulate her on Penny's birth. It was something she hadn't thought of yesterday whilst shopping with George. She could also slip a cheque inside; maybe Sarah would use it to open a bank account for her.

Poskett's shop sold cards but it was still closed; Rosalie concluded that she would have to drive all the way to Cliffend. It was time-consuming and inconvenient. *The sooner Tina got her act together and opened up, the better,* she thought impatiently.

Rosalie didn't mean to be unkind towards her sister-in-law: really, she was frustrated with Sarah. She wished her daughter would contact her. But she knew, after the way she had treated her when she was sixteen, it was obvious Sarah would go to her father for help rather than to her. This made the need to send a card seem disproportionately important.

Rosalie was not short of company, however, with George having moved back into the Old Police House. At that very moment, he and Vince were tinkering with Duncan's machinery at Tidal Reach. And Lily was at Cliffend hospital, waiting to bring Duncan home. Rosalie smiled at the irony of both her twins leaving the same hospital on the same day.

The sound of the front door bell broke her reverie. When she opened the door, PC Owen Yates, in uniform, was standing back from the step looking upwards at the façade of the Old Police House.

'There used to be a blue lamp above the door when the village bobby lived here,' Rosalie informed him, wondering what on earth she was in trouble for now.

'Right,' PC Yates replied hesitantly.

'Well, can I help you?' she asked irritably.

'Er, possibly,' he said as he studied the woman in front of him.

Rosalie was wearing a light green dress. Her wiry, blonde hair was neatly tied back and the slightest touch of make-up gave Owen the impression that she may be on her way out. But the overall effect was spoilt by the fact that she was frowning.

'Can I come in, please? I need a word.'

'I'm now leaving for Cliffend,' Rosalie answered, immediately defensive.

'I won't keep you long, I just want to run an idea past you,' he stated firmly.

Rosalie led them to the kitchen at the back of the house.

'Would you like a cup of coffee or tea?' she asked in a discouraging voice.

'Yes, please. Tea would be nice, thank you,' PC Yates replied smiling, ignoring the nuance. He looked around the kitchen. It was a spacious room with a large cream-coloured cooking range at one end which gave the place a true feeling of a home.

He sat down at the table whilst Rosalie busied herself making a drink and tipping biscuits on a plate which she then placed near her guest. She set tea in a china cup and saucer in front of the policeman and drank hers from an ordinary mug.

'I seem to remember someone saying that you've recently lost your dog,' PC Yates said as he reached out for a custard cream.

'Yes,' Rosalie answered. 'He had a stroke and I had to have him put to sleep. It was last Monday night, early Tuesday morning – nearly a week ago now. Why?'

'What sort?' he asked.

'Labrador, chocolate.'

'Have you thought of getting another dog?'

'Well, maybe. Not yet, though. Eventually, I might. A lot has happened recently. I need time to sort a few things out.' She concluded her explanation abruptly.

PC Yates drank more of his tea. 'If you did decide to have another, would that be a puppy?'

'Possibly. Probably. Why?'

'How would you feel about re-homing an older dog?'

'I don't know, I hadn't really thought about it. Why?' Rosalie's voice was rising and she became agitated. He was deliberately evading her questions but expected her to answer his – typical policemen, she thought.

'It's a very long explanation, so please bear with me.' PC Yates ignored Rosalie's surreptitious glance at her watch. He inhaled deeply and began.

'When I have time, I help out at the police dog unit near Mattingburgh – you know, the national centre. There were complaints about some of their training methods a couple of years ago. As a result, they did a television documentary to show the kind of work the dogs really do. That was when I got involved. Although I don't really want to go into that side of policing myself, I do like dogs and the unit needs volunteers to help with training – to act as stooges, provide numbers for crowds, that sort of thing.

'To cut a long story short, one of our local dog

handlers has, er, resigned. Obviously, I can't give you any details, but his two dogs now need a home, preferably together. They're in the training centre at the moment, they've been there for about three weeks and their kennel space is needed.'

'Can't another officer take them on?' Rosalie enquired. She could guess what PC Yates was going to ask.

'Er, unfortunately, no. They're both getting on a bit, although we're not exactly sure how old either of them is. They're being retired.'

'Oh?'

'They weren't bred specifically for the job. Dill came from a dogs' home. We think he has been mistreated at some point: he doesn't like raised voices and sometimes cringes away if he thinks he's done something wrong. And the other one, Docker – well, he's a right character.'

PC Yates smiled as he made the last comment. He reached for a second biscuit, a digestive this time. He sprayed crumbs as he spoke.

'Poor old boy. He was possibly the runt of his litter, but you'll love him when you see him. He is, unfortunately, somewhat deaf, although that can be selective. The two dogs are used to being with each other so it would be best if they're kept together.'

'What breed are they?'

'Labradors. Both sets of paperwork say Labrador-cross, but what the *cross* is, is anyone's guess, especially Docker.'

'Oh,' Rosalie said again, thoughtfully this time. Despite everything going on with her family at the moment, she did miss Ben – not that any other dog could replace him.

'Do you have a photo of them?' she asked involuntarily.

'No, but I could bring them over this afternoon for you to meet.'

'This afternoon? That's a bit quick. I've got a lot to do,' Rosalie said, abruptly standing up. Still holding her mug, she took PC Yates's cup and saucer away, although it was obvious he had not quite finished.

He quickly reached out for the last biscuit before the plate vanished as well.

Rosalie rinsed the crockery, dried them and replaced them in their cupboards.

'Well, they need a home now,' Yates carried on explaining. 'There's no one to look after them properly long-term and, like I say, the training centre needs the space. They could come to you for a couple of weeks' trial, just to see how you get on.'

He stood up and walked to the kitchen window, looked out onto the back garden and saw a gate leading out to a well-worn path around the field beyond.

'Right, I'd better be off.' He then thanked her for the refreshments and her time.

'Well, thank you for …' Rosalie started to say, then stopped when she realised that, actually, she had nothing to thank him for. But good manners were instilled in her as a child and she felt obliged to finish the sentence. '… er, for thinking of me. But I'm not sure I can help you.'

Chapter 81

Rosalie did not mention PC Owen Yates's visit to anyone, especially George. He had enjoyed Ben when he was at the Old Police House, but did not feel strongly about dogs in general. Despite Rosalie's initial reluctance to have Ben as a puppy, he had proved to be an invaluable companion to her over the years. She really missed him now.

After lunch, she signed the card she'd bought for Sarah and Penny – *Congratulations On The Birth Of Your Daughter* was emblazoned on the front in pink stylised text over a sentimental crib. She looked over to the telephone, longing for it to ring and for Sarah to say she and the baby were home. Instead, the front door bell rang.

PC Yates was not in uniform this time. Rosalie thought he looked very different in casual clothes – a purple T-shirt, jeans and trainers.

'Hello, Mrs Stickleback,' he said enthusiastically. 'Right. Well, the dogs are in the back of the car.'

Rosalie looked beyond PC Yates to a dark-coloured estate vehicle. She then glanced both ways along the road, expecting to see a proper police car.

PC Yates guessed what she was thinking.

'I'm off-duty. My work with the dogs is voluntary,' he explained.

'Oh, yes, I remember you saying.' Rosalie was suddenly embarrassed. 'I'd better come and see these two dogs, then.' PC Yates's face brightened immediately so Rosalie thought she ought to caution his eagerness. 'I'm not making any promises.'

'Okay, I understand. I tell you what, I'll bring them

round to the back garden where they can have a little run about.'

'Oh, well, right. I'll go and open the side gate.'

Rosalie walked back through the house, went out into the garden and unbolted the gate. She was in the kitchen again before realising the dogs were likely to be thirsty after a car journey. Ben's food and water bowls were upstairs, together with the rest of his things, safely stored away after his sudden death.

Rosalie took a chance that PC Yates would be a few minutes and dashed up to her parents' bedroom where she stored everything she didn't want to throw away. She quickly found the two earthenware, biscuit-coloured dog dishes; one bore the word 'Food' on the outside, and the other 'Water'.

Before descending the stairs, Rosalie paused at the front landing window and looked down. She saw one dog jump carefully down out of the back of the police officer's car. He was black, the usual Labrador shape, although his tail was quite low and still. As he gave himself a good shake, Rosalie could see loose hair flying off him. He looked up at PC Yates, his ears to attention. When the police officer clipped on his lead and spoke to him, his tail flickered a little in response.

A few moments passed and Rosalie could see that a lot of encouragement was needed for the second dog to leave the car. She thought she had better go downstairs and fill both bowls with water.

She was thoughtful as she returned to the kitchen. There were many questions she had to ask, such as whether she would be entitled to any financial help with their food and care – after all, they were both elderly dogs and vet's consultations and medical treatments were not cheap. She had not received the invoice for Ben's final visit yet, and that would be on top of the court fine.

She heard a tentative knock, the back door opened and suddenly the kitchen was full of fur and flurry as two dogs, now off their leads, filled the room with their noise and energy. Their claws made clipping sounds on the vinyl as they explored. They panted with excitement, not knowing whether to greet the stranger or investigate her home first. They bashed their poor tails against every side surface and corner possible.

'Come here, you two,' PC Yates called.

Both dogs ignored him for a moment then the larger of the two bounced cautiously up to Rosalie and sniffed at her hands before turning his attention to her heels, her legs and all around her. When he had finished his investigation, he stood in front of her looking up with his slightly out of focus brown eyes.

He started to pant and his pink tongue hung over to one side of his open mouth, revealing a row of crooked and yellowing bottom front teeth. She noticed with dismay that his ribs were visible, his coat was dull and he had an out-door dog smell about him. He was starting to grey around his nose and lips, and his ears seemed long and floppy.

'This is Dill,' PC Yates told Rosalie.

She bent down and reached out both hands slowly towards him. She saw a flicker of uncertainty, but, as soon as she gently touched his head and calmly stroked him, he relaxed. She was rewarded when his tail started to wag.

'Hello Dill,' she said quietly. He looked up at her.

PC Yates watched intently, noticing that all looked well between them. Unfortunately, they had momentarily forgotten Dill's partner, Docker. They quickly remembered him on hearing a crash from the hallway.

'Docker!' PC Yates yelled towards the open door. 'My fault,' he explained to Rosalie. 'I shouldn't have let go of him.' Another clatter caused Yates to hurry to the hall. 'I'd better go and find him. He's probably gone off to search the place!'

'What d'you mean?' Rosalie asked as she followed.

'I took their leads off, so Docker possibly thought they were working and needed to give the place the once-over.'

Rosalie's eyebrows rose and her eyes widened in question.

'Docker is an extremely active sniffer dog – drugs, firearms, lost property and people. He can't understand that he's retired now; he still thinks everywhere has to be investigated. That's one of the problems we've had with finding them a suitable home.' The policeman shrugged.

Docker suddenly reappeared; he was panting with his slobbery pink tongue hanging over his lips, which made him look as if he was smiling. He was stocky, but not fat: a solid and proud little dog. He had very short legs, with enormous paws. His head, although Labrador-shaped, was quite large, and his disproportionately long tail continually lashed from side to side, whipping Rosalie's calves as he strutted by.

Suddenly, he pushed his wet nose towards her and lifted the hem of her skirt to have a good sniff.

'Pack it in, Docker!' PC Yates snapped.

Rosalie grabbed his collar and hauled him away.

'Don't know why I bother shouting – he's choosing not to hear me.'

'I can see that!' Rosalie said as she bent down and

stroked him, hoping to calm him.

They started to walk back to the kitchen and, more through curiosity than obedience, Docker followed. Dill quietly stood guard at the door, but Docker trotted straight under his tummy through the gap between his back and front legs, swiping everything in sight with his totally out of control tail as he went.

'Er, is it all right if they go out in the garden? I did shut the side gate behind us.'

'Yes, I think so,' Rosalie replied.

'Go on, you pair. Outside,' PC Yates ordered as he pointed.

Docker sniffed cautiously then strutted out, claiming his place as leader. Dill followed.

'It's easy to see who's the dominant one,' Rosalie commented.

'Yes. Docker may be the smaller of the two, but he's definitely the boss. Dill has been neutered but Docker hasn't, so you'll have to watch him if there are any bitches on heat within a radius of about five miles,' PC Yates concluded with a laugh. However, seeing the look of almost horror on Rosalie's face, he hastily backtracked. 'He can be a bit – how shall we say – passionate. I hope you're not easily embarrassed.'

Through the open back door, Dill could be seen cautiously sniffing the grass, wandering slowly around and finding his bearings; whereas Docker suddenly charged towards where Ben had recently been buried.

'What's that?' PC Yates asked.

'My old dog Ben's grave,' Rosalie answered. 'He won't dig …?' The remainder of the question was lost as PC Yates sprinted out into the garden.

At this point, Rosalie was deciding that, whilst she might have been able to manage one, she couldn't see herself coping with both dogs. Dill suddenly appeared quietly by her side

'You come here, my man,' Rosalie whispered. Dill sniffed quietly around the kitchen, paying particular attention to the area around the stove where Ben's basket had been. She admitted to herself again that, yes, she really did miss Ben.

But Dill isn't Ben, Rosalie reminded herself. As a distraction, she made coffee, this time using mugs for both her and her guest. She sat down at the kitchen table and, when she opened another packet of biscuits, Dill was instantly at her side. She held out a piece for him.

Dill flicked the tip of his tail as his crossed eyes watched Rosalie. He was still standing up and she gave him the command to sit. As he looked at her, she could see his eyes were struggling to focus.

'Sit,' she told him again. Eventually he obeyed. Rosalie rewarded him with another fragment of biscuit. Dill gently took it from Rosalie and nestled against her leg. As she stroked him, he slid slowly to the floor. Then, with a groan, he rolled over onto his back, holding his legs in the air for her to tickle his tummy, which she obligingly did.

Chapter 82

A sound from outside made Dill quickly stand back up. PC Yates was walking across the garden, bending sideways holding onto Docker's collar.

Docker saw Dill standing patiently beside Rosalie. He pushed his way in between them and looked up expectantly at her. Poor displaced Dill simply went to the other side and nuzzled his nose into Rosalie's spare hand.

'You'd better tell me a bit more about these two - but it's only fair to warn you that I don't think I'd be able to manage the two of them,' she said whilst fussing both dogs.

Docker suddenly landed his two slightly earthy front paws on Rosalie's lap. He grunted as if the effort hurt him. He pushed his nose under her elbow, demanding she look at him, wagging his tail until the tip was alternately beating the table leg on one side of him and the chair leg on the other.

'And it's no good you trying that on me, Docker, not if you're going to try to dig up poor old Ben,' she mock-scolded him.

PC Yates sat down in one of the chairs opposite Rosalie. He picked up his mug of coffee and watched her interacting with the two dogs. Rosalie gently lifted Docker's front feet off her lap and replaced them onto the floor so that getting back down did not jolt him. She then played equally with each, not letting Docker dominate.

'I really don't think they can be separated. May I call you Rosalie?'

'Yes, just so long as you don't shorten it to Rosie.

And what do I call you?'

'Owen. Except if I'm on an official visit, then it's PC Yates.' He was grinning when he said this.

Eventually, Rosalie smiled as well.

'I'm sure we can persuade him to behave,' he said, indicating to Docker. 'They'll love your garden.'

Rosalie looked down, first at Docker because he expected to be top priority, then at Dill, the bigger, quieter dog. Rosalie sighed. Feeling sorry for them, she asked Owen to tell her a little more about their backgrounds.

Owen drew a breath. 'Well, Dill there ...' and he pointed to the bigger of the two dogs, '... is what is known as a passive sniffer dog. For example, he's trained to search people for drugs, say, at train stations, queues waiting to go into night clubs and that sort of thing. If he smells an illegal substance – cannabis, heroin, cocaine, ecstasy, all the usual – he will just sit down in front of the person, or their bag or whatever. His handler then detains the suspects and calls for someone else to search them.

'Sometimes, though, he'll just howl when he has a find, which can be a bit disconcerting – and not strictly in the training manuals either.' He paused and took a sip of his drink. 'The dogs are rewarded for their finds with a time of play with a tennis ball.'

'Oh,' Rosalie said. 'I was wondering what the inducement was for them to work. You hear a lot of rumours about how trainers punish the dogs when they don't do as they're told.'

'Yes, well, as I said this morning, there was a lot of bad press a while ago. But all the training centres are subject to spot checks by animal welfare inspectors now, any time of the day or night.' He sipped again from his mug. 'Have you thought where they could sleep?'

Rosalie was shocked at Owen's audacity. Docker sat up. He'd been lying down on his tummy with his large head resting on his front paws. He was suddenly alert and difficult to ignore, as Rosalie discovered when he tried to jump up on her lap again.

She looked down. Neither dog could be called handsome, but they both had their own endearing qualities. Both were black but, when the sun shone into the kitchen from the open door, a light brown tinge – almost ginger in places – could been seen in Docker's fir. His coat was softer to the touch than Dill's, which was wiry and as black as anthracite, this only being broken in places by the odd tuft of grey, especially on his face. Both dogs wore thick dark brown leather half-choker style collars. They continued to push their noses into Rosalie.

'Are they hungry?' she asked.

'They're Labradors! Well, Labrador types, anyway. They'll always be hungry. I didn't know if you'd still have any dog food, so I brought a couple of bags with me.' He didn't tell Rosalie that he had, in fact, purchased these himself in the hope to sway her decision.

'I've got a bag and a half left over from Ben,' Rosalie stated. 'I meant to take it to my neighbour, but never got round to it. It's for *senior* dogs, so I suppose it will suit these two okay. Anyway, you told me a bit about Dill, what about Docker?'

Owen finished his coffee and swallowed hard.

'Docker is classed as an active sniffer dog. He searches places rather than people – cars, houses, rooms, alleyways, fields, ditches, hide-outs, premises of any sort. He will also hunt for missing persons but that's not his main work.'

Rosalie smiled and Owen Yates suddenly realised how attractive she was. He calculated that she must be seven or eight years younger than himself. The idea of asking her to look after these two redundant dogs might be the best he'd had for a long time – both for professional and personal reasons. He would have to check on the dogs regularly, at least for the first couple of weeks, and then – providing Rosalie kept them – she may need help looking after them, especially Docker, who had suddenly become rather over-excited and seemed as if he was about to mount Rosalie's shin.

Luckily, something outside suddenly caught his attention and he looked towards the garden.

'Have a biscuit instead,' Rosalie bribed as he was about to launch himself towards the open door.

Despite his previous deafness, he heard this. As did Dill. She broke one in half and fed them both whilst Owen quietly got up and closed the kitchen door.

'You've got a way with them,' he commented. He sat down again, looking straight at her, noting that her eyes were light blue. 'Well, can they stay?' he asked hopefully.

'I'm not sure yet. What else should I know about them?'

'They were both highly regarded as sniffer dogs, especially Docker. He's won awards for his finds. They used to work as a team if, say, a raid was taking place on a pub or such like. Dill would check the people and Docker would search the premises.'

Rosalie laughed as she imagined Dill and Docker investigating Henry's regulars at The Fighting Cock.

'What's so funny?' Owen Yates asked.

Rosalie shook her head, declining to share her thoughts.

'Nothing, honestly. Please, carry on.'

'Not much more to tell.'

'So, if I do have them, even just for a trial, what do I do if they find something?'

'They probably won't. But, on the off chance, just ring me. Here …' he said as he took a card out of his pocket and handed to her. 'Both my mobile number and the one for the police station at Cliffend are on there. The best advice I can give you, even for a temporary period, is to keep the dogs away from crowds or strangers – or people you do know if you think they may be into something dodgy!'

He looked at his watch. 'Anyway, I'd better go. I'm back on duty early tomorrow morning. I've got their food in the back of the car, as well as other bits and pieces. I'd better just unload them and be on my way.'

'But I haven't agreed to have the dogs yet,' Rosalie protested.

Chapter 83

Lost in a form of suspension, like a twig trapped inside a jar of treacle, Tina moved between the back room, the shop and the bathroom, with only that stupid teddy bear for company, which she held close to her as she tried to sleep on the sofa bed at night.

Whilst forcing herself to shower every morning, she inspected the injuries Dentforth had inflicted. The bruises were lessening and the pain was fading, although two of her teeth were still tender. It was the humiliation that crippled her: the loss of her pride, dignity and safety, her independence and security.

No one came near the shop and post office. Tina did not even hear the postman. George was obviously too busy doing whatever George did when he forgot about her. Rosalie – well, she didn't really know her sister-in-law, so there was no reason for her to pop in. The rector hadn't called, either in person or by phone. In fact, no one had rung. Not being a regular church-goer, she wouldn't have expected a pastoral visit anyway.

But it would have been nice if someone cared.

She felt as though she might as well not exist.

Dentforth had won. It was an age-old theory believed by some men that being in a position of power, however tenuous, is attractive to women; they just feel they are entitled to take whatever they want.

Tina was now taking what she wanted, too: she collected tins, packets and cartons of food from the stock. Occasionally she prepared herself a meal, but invariably ate very little; her teeth and jaw reminding her of the attack each time she chewed. She borrowed paperbacks from the display near the At Hand counter to read, but then couldn't remember the characters or stories afterwards. Listening to the radio, she didn't hear a word that was spoken or enjoy any of the music. Nothing served as a distraction from the horrors of recent events.

The atmosphere indoors was hot and claustrophobic. The curtains were drawn, the shutters closed and the doors locked. She did not dare venture outside, although she was desperately lonely and hurt and miserable; reminders of Dentforth's visit surrounded her.

There was a heavy shower during Monday evening, but the thirsty ground quickly soaked up the water, leaving no trace other than dew by morning. Tuesday promised to be another hot, sticky day.

In the afternoon, the restless silence was broken by a large vehicle arriving in the lay-by outside the shop and post office. Tina felt so desperate for human contact that she wanted to go and see what was happening. But even the thought of stepping outside made her tremble.

Eventually, however, she opened the back door. Then she found it difficult to actually walk over the threshold, so frightened was she that Dentforth was lingering somewhere close by, waiting to pounce at the first opportunity.

After several minutes, and feeling a warm breeze enticing her, she eventually released herself from her self-imposed imprisonment. She felt disorientated and dizzy as she looked over to the source of the noise. The sun, still hot and strong, reflected brightly off a lorry cab. Across the bonnet were painted the words 'Experienced Secure Removals'.

The vehicle had parked in the space vacated on Friday by the rubbish skip. A man in overalls climbed out and walked towards her. She felt his eyes studying the red mark on her jaw where Dentforth had punched her. At least it was fading. She was surprised he noticed at all, so invisible she now felt. He passed no comment as he asked her to sign at the bottom of a sheet of paper, agreeing to the removal of post office property from her premises – namely the self-contained kiosk.

Tina hesitated, wondering whether or not she was actually authorised to do this. But the man gave an impatient tut, so she acquiesced and scribbled her name. He whisked away the clipboard, tore off the top of the triple-layered document and handed it to her, asking as he did so to be shown the item in question.

Tina led the way into the shop and was about to offer him a cup of tea when he complained, but not necessarily to her, 'well, they got it in 'ere, so it must come out. Dunno 'ow, though!'

He turned back and inspected the newly installed double entrance doors. He looked around again and muttered before striding back to his vehicle.

Tina decided she would like a cup of tea anyway. She retreated from the shop to the back room, thinking that she did not need to be present for the actual dismantling of such an important part of her livelihood. Even now, after four days on her own – and sober, she would like George to know! – she could not fathom why Dentforth had unleashed such spite on her.

Tina tried to tell herself that the closing of the facility was not personal; it was a rational, professional decision made by the organisation: fewer and fewer transactions were now taking place within the post office environment. She had seen the footfall decline herself in recent years. The only saving grace seemed to be the increase in online sales, auction sites and other internet commerce, and the subsequent need to send goods through the post to customers. Although even here there was competition with all the new parcel delivery services who seemed to operate at a cheaper, quicker and more efficient rate.

She made a cup of tea but had to drink it black because so far she had not dared to drive to the supermarket for milk. She stood at the window watching as the lorry driver opened up the container on the back of his trailer. A few minutes later, on an integral elevator, a purpose-built forklift-style mini vehicle was lowered to the ground, its prongs facing forward. Attached at various points to the uprights, safety fasteners glistened in the bright sunshine.

Fascinated, Tina observed this disappearing towards the shop entrance doors. Despite her rationality of a few moments earlier, a feeling of loss, disappointment and almost bereavement suddenly overwhelmed her.

She sat down at the kitchen table opposite Bertha's chair. She stared at the big brown teddy bear as she held her cup close to her chest. She became aware of a slight rumbling through the ground and presumed it was the fork-lift returning to the mother vehicle with its bounty.

After a few minutes, the man shouted through the open doors. 'Right. All loaded. I'll be off now.' He didn't wait for a reply. Perhaps he misinterpreted the dejection on Tina's face as lack of interest, or maybe he only saw the result of Dentforth's violence and didn't want to be involved. He was, after all, only doing his job.

Tina listened to the lorry start. The engine revved, the brakes were released and it slowly pulled out of the lay-by.

'Bastard,' Tina muttered. 'Dentforth, you bastard,' she said a little louder. 'You know, Bertha, old girl, I think we had a lucky escape.' She took a sip of the tea and shuddered, not for the first time, at the realisation of what could have happened. She repeated, 'bastard!' She then drank a little more. 'Well, we'll make this business work, with or without him!'

Tina was seething by the time she finished her tea and realised anger was a more productive emotion than defeat. She suddenly sprang up, snatched poor Bertha and clutched the bear to her side before marching through to the shop.

The double entrance doors had been left open. There were scuff marks on the frame where the forklift had miscalculated the gap.

The recess where the post office kiosk previously stood was now stark, reminding Tina of a burglary scene from a film. The bare wall was dark grey, whereas all the others were gleaming white: the At Hand refit team were unable to paint behind because it had been clamped down. The floor tiles were grubby and a rectangle of grooves marked where the kiosk once stood. Cobwebs, fluff and dirt, scraps of paper, a coin, a blue biro pen top, a hair-grip, an old key and a few spilt sweets had accumulated.

Tina bent down to pick up the key, wiped it on her jeans then studied it. She was sure it was the wrong sort to fit the landing door upstairs. She placed it on the counter near the cash register, thinking she would check later. She propped Bertha beside it to supervise the forthcoming operations before closing the double entrance doors.

First things first, she told herself as she systematically opened all the window shutters and blinds. The light streamed in, illuminating the ghosts that Tina now needed to exorcise.

However, despite the rallying and motivational phrases she was running through her mind, Tina fought hard not to be demoralised. She took cloths and scourers from the stock, found a mop and broom and filled a bucket with hot water then added a squirt of liquid soap. She carried these through to the shop where she started to clean. And, as she worked, she planned.

Many things needed to be sorted out if she intended to stay. The shop would have to reopen as soon as possible; therefore she needed to ratify an agreement with the franchise. She would contact the solicitor tomorrow morning to clarify leasing the premises.

The only good thing to come out of losing the post office facility was that Tina would never have to confront Arthur Dentforth again. But it was too late for that to be of comfort. She was already contaminated. She formulated several versions of the story to tell George – each ending with the question of why hadn't he called to see her?

Two hours later, Tina was ready to action her newly devised scheme to re-arrange the shop.

One set of shelves, which held family-sized packs of King's Krisps, was quite shallow in comparison to its neighbours. The display was topped with a plywood caricature of a crown painted a gaudy gold, the capitals decorated with large, brightly coloured plastic gems. To complete the regal theme, the side edges of the unit were purple, but the outer left was scratched and marked. Tina thought a move to the recess would hide this.

Despite the crisp packaging being of vibrant primary

colours, the display had been squeezed in between the greetings' card stand on one side and the chiller cabinet on the other. Located there, the products did not have that eye-catching 'buy me' element they should. She also felt that, if she moved the unit, the adjacent chiller would benefit from the extra ventilation, as if she needed to justify her decision.

Tina could feel her enthusiasm wane and her limbs weakening as she unloaded the crisp bags into half a dozen wire shopping baskets from the stack near the entrance. She was tired, having not eaten properly over the past few days. Although anger may have provided her initial energy, it did not give sustained strength.

From her vantage point, Bertha, if she could have spoken, would no doubt have advised caution as Tina began to pull at the shelving. It was unstable and top-heavy.

Although she heard and felt the structure start to fall, Tina could not move away quickly enough to avoid it, nor was she strong enough to hold it back.

The sound felt like thunder as the unit crashed down onto her. As it fell, the edge of the plastic crown on the top caught Bertha's left shoulder. Impaled on one of the taller coronet columns, the bear was yanked to the floor. The sudden jerk caused the thread on the repair seam to rip and split the fabric apart. A gold locket complete with matching chain bounced on the tiles, the clasp failing upon impact and forcing the front to open.

The bright sunshine of the summer afternoon poured in through the shop window, lighting up a perfect diamond glittering from its hiding place inside a golden heart lined with red.

Chapter 84

The number of minutes and hours that passed before a cold, wet nose and a slobbering, rasping canine tongue tried to arouse Tina did not matter. She would not wake.

Tina Tillinger would never open the At Hand shop; she wouldn't contact Mr Brideman to sort out the lease on the premises, nor speak with her in-laws, or make friends in her new home.

Bertha Bunfighter would not be presented with a brand new, bright green silk ribbon.

George would not receive her apology for their most recent argument, nor could she ever heal the heartbreak caused by all those who betrayed her throughout her life.

She was destined never to know the whereabouts or circumstances of her mother, nor learn the identity of her father.

Tina died alone.

She died in pain.

She believed herself unwanted, and unloved.

And those who should have cared were so close by.

But she felt they just couldn't be bothered with her.

Chapter 85

Paul James, Postman Jim the Second, had not seen Tina for a few days. When he stopped in Pepper Hill to empty the post-box on Tuesday, he noticed the shutters had been raised and presumed progress was being made towards reopening both the At Hand shop and post office. He did not know about the closure of the facility.

Suddenly, there was a commotion from the Old Police House across the road. Jim heard Rosalie Stickleback calling something that sounded like,

'Docker!'

Then, a small black dog with an enormous head and disproportionately large paws raced across the road. There was a wild and determined look in his eyes; his pink tongue lolled over yellowing fangs. His ears flapped behind him and his long tail propelled his aged body forward. He was closely followed by another – larger, also black – dog, with the same intense concentration on its face.

Jim swore at them, then at Rosalie for letting them loose on the road. He thought she would've realised how dangerous this was, how fast the traffic travelled through, despite the thirty miles per hour speed limit.

The dogs ran directly to the shop's entrance and thudded into it. One door gave way against their force, having probably not been properly closed.

Jim followed them inside. His stomach heaved when he saw Tina's body crushed underneath a set of King's Krisps shelving that appeared to have fallen on top of her. A bloody gash had opened the top of her skull, her shoulders were contorted and one arm was stretched forward, as if she had tried to wriggle free. And a large, brown teddy bear was caught on a fake crown above the shelves as it lay on the floor. Wire baskets of crisps had been splattered around; some of the packets were split and their contents spilled. Tina's fingers almost touched one.

Jim crouched down to her.

'Tina?' he called. 'Oh God, Tina!'

She did not move.

The smaller of the two dogs was sniffing and licking Tina's hand. But to no avail. The second dog snuffled in Jim's ear before sitting down. He leant against Jim, threw back his head and took in an incredibly deep breath.

Then he howled. The sound would haunt Jim, and everyone else who heard it, for ever.

By some fluke of luck, or chance of miracles, PC Owen Yates arrived in the shop.

The last time Yates had seen Tina was Thursday when he'd given her a lift back from Ashfield. He intended calling on her again to see if she was settling in okay, but he'd been ordered to take three days' leave to even out his shift duties. He spent most of the weekend at the dog unit. Yesterday, he'd managed to sort out a new home with Rosalie Stickleback for Dill and Docker, about which he was feeling extremely pleased.

Even the previous day when Yates was in such close proximity to the post office and shop, he had totally forgotten about Tina. Today, when he set off from the police station in Cliffend to patrol his patch, he was called to the airfield at the top end of Pepper Hill where the owner, a Mr Vince Hallett, had reported damage to the grass runway. He said vandals had dug holes along the take-off and landing strip. Yates asked his superior why anyone would use up time and energy to do that. He was ordered to go and find out.

However, he did not reach the airfield, having been distracted by Rosalie running across the road at Pepper Hill in front of him. He stopped to reprimand her, but she disappeared into the front doors of the newly refitted shop. (Some days later, PC Yates was advised that the holes in the runway were caused by the local mole catcher who had been directed to the wrong field.)

Inside the shop, Yates knew it was fruitless to call Docker, the smaller of the two dogs: he was almost deaf wouldn't hear above Dill's howling anyway. Yates tried to haul him back, but he was very strong. He suddenly squirmed on his belly under the shelving, his paws swimming to gain purchase against the floor. He then disappeared.

Rosalie was standing in the corner, shocked at the scene and noise before her – the postman was calling Tina's name, Dill was howling and Yates swore as he attempted to move debris out of the way.

Yates peered under the shelving then turned to Dill.

'Will you shut the fuck up!' he suddenly yelled.

The silence that followed was broken only when he and Jim lifted the shelving unit off Tina. They found Docker snuggling into her side, keening and dribbling and nudging her cold, lifeless body, trying to rouse her.

But Rosalie could see that it was too late to save Tina. Far too late. Her skin held a vague bluish tinge. She was already dead.

PC Owen Yates retrieved his mobile phone from his pocket, stabbed at the numbers, then cursed that he should at least be able to make emergency calls from the shop, even if there was no signal for anything else.

Rosalie then saw the big teddy bear, impaled on the King's Krisps gaudy display crown.

A wave of shame and incredulity washed over her when she thought she recognised the bear: it was the one Henry had given to her the morning after their first night as a married couple, over a quarter of a century ago. Then, it was wearing around its neck a gold locket which had been a gift from her parents. But, instead of the precious photos of Annie and Derek she'd had developed to fit, it held the diamond from Nora's engagement ring.

She had left the hotel, still wearing her nightdress and clutching this bear. A taxi drove her back to the Old Police House where she had lived ever since. She could not remember seeing the teddy bear since Quinny asked for donations for a fête, several years ago now. She had no idea what had happened to it since then. She hadn't even thought about the locket.

Until now.

It was lying on the floor, concealed by a torn green crisp packet that had been kicked out of the way in the kerfuffle to reach her sister-in-law.

Whilst Yates re-dialled, the postman knelt next to Tina, even though there was obviously nothing he could do for her. He didn't even attempt to move Docker.

Rosalie thought she would not interfere. She stealthily bent down and picked up the golden heart and chain from under the crisp packet. She snapped it shut, deliberately not wanting the see the treacherous diamond. She slipped it into her pocket. As she fingered its shape, she found the forgotten tufts of Ben's fur she'd retrieved secreted there from that terrible night he was euthanised.

Swallowing hard, she moved forward quietly and attached Dill's lead to his collar, hoping he would not start his infernal howling again. Dill looked up; there was confusion in his eyes. His pink tongue bounced in time with his open-mouthed panting and his tail brushed an arc on the ground behind him.

Rosalie stared at him, not quite understanding why he looked so pleased with himself. But, from Dill's point of view, he and his partner had found the body and told everyone where it was, even if no one else was aware it was missing.

'He wants his reward for doing his job,' PC Yates shouted to Rosalie as he waited for someone to answer his emergency call. 'A game with his tennis ball! Go and play with him, preferably in your garden. Take him away from here. I'll deal with ... Hello?' He'd turned his attention back to his mobile phone. 'Yes, ambulance. The post office in Pepper Hill, near Cliffend. Yes, I'm PC Owen Yates, number – FUCK!' he bawled as the signal cut out. 'For Christ's sake, does nothing ever work properly in this God forsaken shit-hole?'

Rosalie remembered thinking a while later, as she heard a siren approaching whilst playing ball with Dill in her back garden, that Pepper Hill was not a shit hole, although there was definitely still a faint smell of sewage from her recent tanker spillage.

Chapter 86

It could have been the community's collective dream, if one believed in such things. In reality, it was more like their nightmare.

The wickerwork coffin containing the last mortal remains of thirty-five-year-old Tina Tillinger stood on the catafalque at the top of the nave aisle in St Jude's Church, PepperAsh. The warm summer sun shining in through the gleaming windows dispersed colours from the glass onto the white-washed walls and stone floor. But the chill in the air remained.

The inquest into Tina's death had been opened and adjourned, the post mortem examination completed, and the coroner had agreed to release the body. Provisionally, the cause of death was stated as the result of a blow to the head. But there were other, older injuries – bruises deep into her shoulders, loose teeth and a fractured jaw – that needed investigating.

Tina's widower, George, several years her senior, gazed at the single wreath – his – placed on top of the coffin. It was heart-shaped, made up of red roses with four white blooms arranged to form a diamond just off centre. George did not understand the design, but Rosie suggested it and it felt right. Henry looked at it with faint recognition but said nothing.

George knew he should have gone to see Tina after their most recent falling out. He could have helped with the preparations to reopen the shop, then she might not have tried to move the display shelving on her own. Somehow, though, he'd had something more important to do.

He always seemed to have something more

important to do than care about his wife. This time it had been legitimate; he was helping Duncan. But that would not assuage his guilt.

George knew Tina was due to meet her area manager the day after their argument because details of the post office reopening needed to be finalised. He was not aware at that time the facilities had been withdrawn.

Tina hinted many times over the years that she did not trust Arthur Dentforth, laughing that his halitosis made her eyes water if he stood too close. In truth, she was hiding behind a joke: she had actually feared for her safety in his company.

At George's feet was a very large, plain linen tote bag containing that enormous, ridiculous teddy bear, Bertha Bunfighter which Tina had won at a fête just prior to her move to PepperAsh.

At first, he did not realise Bertha was the same bear Henry had given to his sister, although it felt familiar. He remembered properly when Rosie explained. He did not, however, know the locket had been hidden inside: he thought Rosalie had kept it.

Rosalie sat next to George in church; her back was straight and her face defiant. Her confusion at finding the locket again sent a shiver through her. George sensed this, but he could not reach out to her because he was sinking too deeply into his own misery.

Rosalie still found it difficult to believe that the teddy bear was the same one she had disposed of all those years ago. As time passed, somewhere in her mind she must have realised the locket had disappeared with the bear. But she'd never deliberately sought it out because just to look at the diamond clasped where her parents' photographs should have been was still too painful.

She suddenly heard Tina's name spoken. She drew

in a deep breath and released it slowly, determined to make herself believe it was not her fault that her sister-in-law hadn't walked the short distance across the road to ask for help. After all, she had recently been in a similar position with her full septic tank. But no one had come to her aid, even when she asked.

Besides which, Rosalie's thoughts were filled with baby Penny and her own twin grown-up children, plus the two dogs she had recently been persuaded to rehome. The locket could wait. Maybe she would eventually explain everything to Henry; maybe they could start again.

Absent-mindedly, she reached out her hand to Henry, sitting on her other side. He quietly accepted it, wrapping his fingers around hers.

Henry was wearing the suit and tie in which he had attended court following the prang with the tractor outside Rosalie's home. Whilst dressing this morning, he paid absolute attention to ensuring his socks were a matching pair and that his shoes were clean. He had gone into Cliffend on Friday for an appointment with the barber to have his hair cut and beard trimmed. Looking in the mirror earlier, he acknowledged that the latter was now more grey than red.

As he stared at the woven coffin, Henry regretted that he hadn't been more welcoming to Tina. In his defence, when she was in the bar with the postman the other day, he recognised the fascination in her eyes as he poured the wine. But, in all fairness, she resolutely refused a third glass.

Henry found himself lowering his head to disperse the memories of his father, Woody, his degeneration into alcoholism and his ultimate death. Henry had been amazed to learn that Tina possessed the big teddy bear.

He had no idea how it came to be the prize in a 'Guess the Name' fête competition in a town many miles away from PepperAsh.

It did not matter: nothing would bring Tina back. Still, he was sparing no expense for the wake after the service. He'd left Sarah and Polly in charge of the caterers whom he'd hired to provide and set up the buffet at his pub. But even he recognised this was a poor substitute for the hand of friendship.

Duncan Stickleback sat with his wife in the second pew back. Duncan was not really paying attention to the proceedings; he was not a 'church person'. He was engrossed in his plans to expand his business. His Uncle George had agreed to invest and Duncan had a new slurry tanker on order. Duncan was trawling through the details (or he would've been if he didn't have to attend his Aunt Tina's funeral) of impending local farm auctions for a decent second hand tractor to augment his existing plant.

Duncan acknowledged a discomfort, however, when he studied the single wreath on the coffin. It was a heart of red roses with a few white flowers near the middle to indicate a diamond. His father told him the story. The gem would be approximately where the plug in his own heart had been inserted. For a reason he did not understand, this made him feel guilty. People had been so kind to him, but he had not even enquired at the time how Tina was managing with the arrangements to reopen the post office and shop. Although quite ill himself, he could at least have asked.

Lily's thoughts, however, were with her unborn baby. After all, as far as she could remember, she had never met Duncan's aunt. Tina hadn't even bothered to come and see Duncan in hospital when he was ill, nor had she attended their wedding.

In the five or so years Lily had lived at Tidal Reach and driven through Pepper Hill on her way to either her father's airfield or to Mattingburgh, she hadn't used the shop – old Poskett's prices were much higher than the supermarket at Cliffend.

Lily felt a twinge from inside and rubbed her swelling stomach. As soon as they were able to tell her the sex of this little one, she could start choosing possible names. She hoped it would be a girl. It would be nice to have a son and a daughter, but another son would be okay. Maybe it was twins. Two boys or two girls. Or a boy and a girl, like Duncan and Sarah. She wondered what Jack was doing at this moment; her parents had taken him to the beach at Cliffend.

Lily smiled at the thought of her son paddling in the sea, holding tightly onto Irene and Vince's hands. But the cameo quickly faded as her attention was pulled sharply back to the coffin. Apparently, the solitary wreath on top was supposed to symbolise something lost.

But Lily had not lost anything. And, no, she would not feel guilty about Tina either.

Sarah Stickleback was sitting in the kitchen of The Fighting Cock. She finished folding napkins for the buffet and looked over to the cot where baby Penny was asleep. She had decided to give Penny a middle name – Bettina. Penelope Bettina Stickleback. It was rather long-winded and Penny would probably complain at some point, but she felt she would at least be doing something to carry on her aunt's memory. After all, as far as she knew, Tina had no family of her own, only George, Sarah's mum Rosalie, and all the Ashfield Sticklebacks.

Just at that moment, Polly came into the kitchen to speak to Sarah.

'Right, we're ready out there now. There's a few customers already in, but I reckon they'll just join the wake when everyone else gets here.'

Inside St Jude's Church, the Reverend Quinny announced the Twenty-third Psalm, *The Lord's My Shepherd*. Mrs Delilah Ervsgreaves played the introduction to the tune *Crimond* with more gusto than skill.

Everybody stood up, but no one sang particularly well.

Paul James had torn up his home-made nick-name badge and vowed he would never answer to 'Postman Jim the Second' again. When he first arrived at the church, the pew he'd sat down on emitted an odious noise. He stood up again and moved to the row behind. At any other time, he might have found this sound funny. Today, it was anything but.

Today, he was here to be angry, not amused. Because he was the person who found Tina.

He could not rid himself of the image: her head caked with dried blood; her cold, white – almost blue – hand reaching out from under the shelving that crushed her. He choked as the congregation half-heartedly sang the words 'goodness and mercy'. He forced himself to look around. The church was clinical and clean. The colours from the stained glass reflected on the white walls and cold, hard surfaces. The vases of flowers made a valiant attempt, but failed to cheer the mood.

People were wearing their best attire – smart black to crisp denim, with many plain colours and floral patterns in between. Paul's eyes traversed the outfits rather than the people, until they rested on Tillinger and the Sticklebacks.

George was not singing. At least he had the decency to bow his head in shame. His face looked red and unhealthy. The postman prayed that it was not the widower's suit making him feel sticky, hot and uncomfortable, but remorse.

Paul James lowered his head as well. He thought Tina was incredibly pretty, with a bright and lively personality. He would have liked to know her better. He felt a rush of hatred towards George – in fact, towards everyone – for ignoring her. But he was, in a way, just as bad – he had not called in to see her either. Still, she should never have tried to move the shelving herself. She could have asked him to help. He remembered the panic he'd felt as he crouched down and called her name.

He now whispered 'Tina,' unable to prevent his eyes moistening.

The thin and self-conscious voices in St Jude's conjured their own images of 'death's dark vale', and were now singing about dwelling in God's house for evermore. Then the last chord of the organ died; Mrs Ervsgreaves noisily pushed in the stops. When silence finally descended, the rector climbed into the pulpit and invited the congregation to sit.

'Bettina Tillinger, or Tina as she was known,' he began the eulogy, 'had only just moved to Pepper Hill.' The fingers on one of the rector's hands were trembling as they desperately clung to a faded red rubber band around his wrist. He hadn't known Tina that well, only meeting her once recently at The Fighting Cock when she accompanied the postman for lunch.

'Tina wasn't new to the area. She grew up in nearby Fenstone with her grandmother. She left school at sixteen and started working with the post office. It was whilst working in the Cliffend branch that she met George Tillinger. They married and, shortly afterwards, moved to Treemoore where they made their home until recently ...'

George could not listen. The irony that *they made their home* in Treemoore, was unbearable. It had not been a home in the true sense. Tina worked and resided there, mostly on her own, whilst George disappeared to Aberdeen. And, yes, he *had* had a relationship with another woman. But he quickly shut out those thoughts.

The rector cleared his throat before continuing.

'Tina arrived, not quite a stranger, but someone with few friends. However ...' Quinny's voice suddenly grew deep and sonorous, echoing off the cold white walls. 'We have to ask ourselves, did we welcome her as kindly as we should have done? Maybe, in future, this can be a reminder ...'

He realised nobody was taking any notice. So he changed his tone.

'Tina did not die immediately in that shop. She must have struggled to free herself from under those heavy shelves. She obviously suffered a time of pain – we cannot know how long, of course, nor the torment that passed through her mind as she hoped, prayed, that someone would find and help her. No one did, of course. And she died alone. She was probably very frightened, very scared indeed ...'

Peoples' heads shot up. Their eyes were now watching him; their ears listening and their minds imagining the horror. *There*, he thought with malicious satisfaction; *that got your attention.*

There were tears in some eyes when he finished his rant. He was unapologetic for his cruelty, but recognised that he was as much to blame as everyone else. It had been the Monday before he even thought about Tina, what with hospitality from the Ervsgreaves on the Sunday, together with all the excitement of baby Penny Stickleback's arrival, plus old Poskett's corpse somewhere in the background quietly awaiting burial. Someone had cheerfully reminded him that it would eventually be the council's job to dispose of the body as environmental waste. He'd felt sick at that but still couldn't summon the energy to pursue the matter.

He told himself that the problem with Poskett was the real reason he had not visited Tina. He had hoped Brideman would explain her paternity and the legacy, but Quinny since discovered the solicitor had taken a sudden holiday. And now it looked as if everything would be left for George to deal with.

The funeral service dragged on. Mrs Ervsgreaves played the last hymn and Quinny gave the final commendation. Maude and Griffin's pall bearers whisked the wreath off the top before manhandling the flexing wicker coffin onto their shoulders. Tina did not weigh much, for which they were grateful. They carried it soberly outside into the brilliant sunshine whilst the usher directed people to leave their pews in turn and follow on.

Led by the rector, the mourners processed to the open grave dug in the Pepper Hill portion of the churchyard. Everyone then shuffled into position to view the final rituals. A few more tears were shed. Ladies worried about their expensive shoes being spoilt by the damp grass and soil; men, through embarrassment, yearned to be away from here to imbibe in either alcohol or nicotine – or both.

The coffin creaked when lowered on its ropes into

the cold open maw of the grave. When Quinny finished speaking, the undertakers produced a box of earth. The usher held it forward for George to take a handful of soil to throw onto the wicker coffin. He shook his head. Instead, he removed the enormous toy teddy bear from the tote bag and tossed it in.

One person gasped, but the remaining mourners were silent.

George walked away. As he always did.

Chapter 87

The Monday morning following Tina's funeral found Arthur Dentforth waiting in the lobby at Mattingburgh head office to see his own superior. He was informed that an inquest had been opened into the death of Mrs Bettina Tillinger at Pepper Hill's former post office and At Hand shop. Mr Dentforth was advised to attend the coroner's court as a witness.

However, before that, head office were to look into Arthur Dentforth's handling of Mrs Tillinger's temporary assignment to Pepper Hill, including why no formal employment agreement had been prepared and why proper accommodation was not provided for her.

There was also the question of his visit on Friday afternoon. Initially he denied he had been to Pepper Hill, but the skip man verified his presence. A police investigation revealed his fingerprints on the rear door, the front entrance and various surfaces in the shop. None, however, were found on the actual King's Krisps shelving unit. But the historical injuries to Tina's jaw and each of her shoulders were, at that time, still unexplained.

When news spread that Dentforth was to be questioned, a young woman whom he had considered nothing more than a silly flibbertigibbet from the post office in Cliffend made a complaint about him behaving in an inappropriate manner towards her. A specific incident was cited. It could easily have been explained as a mistake, a prank, an accidental reach of his hand.

As soon as the enquiries started, however, several other young women came forward with similar tales of sexual harassment. Most of the activity had taken place nearly twelve months ago. He seemed to remember this being a particularly uncomfortable interlude for him, but couldn't really explain why. Only that he had got away with it.

If only these empty-headed, vain little teasers could take a joke, Dentforth thought. *Anyway, didn't they invite advances? Dressing the way they did, with their buttocks showing above the waistbands of their jeans at the back, and their boobs hanging out of the fronts of frilly, insignificant tops, showing off their underwear to all and sundry?* In his younger days, outfits of this kind would only be seen on harlots and strumpets, whores and prostitutes. They begged for attention, didn't they? And then, when a man takes notice, they cry *rape.*

One girl was different, however. That was the one he thought would've complained at the time. But she hadn't. So, because she remained silent, he thought his behaviour was acceptable. It had been pensioners' fortnight at the Perrona Dawn leisure complex in Fenstone, but the basement ballroom was hired out for a single day's communications training course.

The access area curved around the seating that surrounded the empty dance floor, and the corridors leading to the cloakrooms were nicely secluded. Approaching the young blonde woman, in her smart suit, modest heels and confident air, Arthur Dentforth thought she was one of his employees. Instead, it transpired that she worked for the complex.

She stopped when he asked her the time. They spoke, pleasantly. Then his hands betrayed him. Before he could prevent himself, she was struggling to stop him. He was a large, heavy man. She was short. Nevertheless, she screamed and fought. But no one else was likely to come down there. Her calls for help went unanswered, as is so often the way. And there was no harm done after all, was there? She hadn't said anything at the time. She wouldn't now, would she? Not months afterwards. Yes, he thought he was invincible.

The door in front of him opened and a woman's voice enquired, 'Mr Dentforth?'

He nodded and boldly said, 'yes.'

'Would you come this way?'

He followed, confident he could explain.

Chapter 88

Sarah had tried to tell her Dad the truth only hours before Penny was born. She admitted the pregnancy was real and not a phantom one, but she could not say any more. Henry knew as soon as she had returned to Ashfield that something was dreadfully wrong, but he sensibly waited until Sarah was ready to clarify.

He urged Sarah to go to the police, offering to accompany her wherever and whenever she wished. He assured her that, despite not knowing the attacker's name or being able to give a proper description, if she could state the time, date and whereabouts the incident took place, Perrona Dawn would hopefully have records of all the people on the premises that day.

Then Penny arrived so unexpectedly. Sarah was engrossed in motherhood, but it was the news that Tina may have been attacked during the week before her death that broke her silence.

Two days after Tina's funeral, a detective inspector from Mattingburgh Police Headquarters arrived at The Fighting Cock, together with a specialist female officer trained to deal with victims of serious sexual assault and rape. They took a statement from Sarah and a swab from both Sarah and Penny for DNA purposes.

'I was told to check one of the fire doors in the hall downstairs where the communications convention was taking place,' Sarah explained.

'Where was this?' she was asked.

'In Perrona Dawn's leisure complex in Fenstone, I was working there. The alarm had gone off twice and security said the door was being tampered with. The manager suspected one of their delegates was trying to open it. There were plenty of notices stating they were to remain closed. But people at these functions get silly sometimes, or they just want to go outside for a cigarette.'

Sarah stopped speaking for a moment. She swallowed several times and wiped her eyes. 'The corridor leading down to the hall entrance kind of sweeps around in a curve.' She moved her arm in a semi-circle. 'There was a man hurrying towards me. He put his hand out to stop me, like that.' And she gestured. 'He asked me the time.'

'Did you notice anything about him? Would you be able to describe him?'

'He wasn't tall – not like my Dad,' she said pointing to Henry who was standing near the door with baby Penny in his arms. Sarah needed to be able to see her but didn't want to hold her whilst relating this. 'Big, very hot.' Suddenly she recalled, 'he had really bad breath.'

These details were written down before the next question.

'Can you describe what happened? Take your time.'

Sarah's eyes filled with tears and her whole body began to shake as the words fell reluctantly from her lips.

Henry turned away. His fury was mounting. But Penny, the result of the attack, murmured as she slept. He forced himself to remain calm.

The officer paused, allowing Sarah to blow her nose, wipe her eyes and have a sip or two of water. Then Sarah completely surprised everyone by saying, 'I've got the clothes I was wearing. The suit. It hasn't been washed or anything.'

The detective inspector glanced over to the woman

officer. Neither spoke for a moment. They seemed to be holding a silent conversation; its tone was of suspicion and disbelief.

Sarah saw this.

'After he left me, I ran back to my room,' she clarified. 'I didn't know what to do. I felt ...' Sarah's strained face turned away. She was silent for a few minutes. The officer had to prompt her. 'I had a bath. Several. In fact, I sat in there for the rest of the day. Kept refilling it with hot water. I wanted to wash away his touch, his ...' She shuddered violently.

Sarah had not even considered at the time the possibility that she could be pregnant. She just hoped and prayed that the awful man had not transferred any infectious diseases to her.

'Someone knocked on my door a couple of times, but I didn't get out,' she concluded.

'Why did you keep the clothes?'

'The company had sent round an email a few days before, saying that a new style of uniform would soon be issued to all employees as part of an autumn rebranding exercise. It'll probably still be on my laptop, you can read it if you can find it.'

'Thank you, yes, we'll do that later. Please, carry on.'

'Perrona Dawn's company policy on uniforms states something along the lines of, "If a garment is soiled or damaged beyond reasonable cleaning or repair, the employee is required to surrender it at the time of obtaining a replacement." I think I thought the same applied when new uniforms are issued. I don't really know what I believed. But I put the skirt and blouse in the company bags we were all issued with. My knickers were ripped, I ...'

Sarah faltered. She shook her head and blew her nose

again before continuing, 'I ... tore them into tiny pieces and flushed them bit by bit down the loo. I was scared they'd jam up the system, but they didn't. At least I don't think they did. I hated touching them, but I had to get rid of them.'

Sarah was wringing her hands one around the other, shredding the damp tissue, trembling and crying openly. Henry placed Penny back in her cot and went to his daughter.

'I think that might be enough now,' he told the police officers.

'Is there any chance you could just fetch your clothes for us?' the woman officer enquired, ignoring Henry's scowling, reddening face. Sarah sniffed violently.

'Come with me, Dad,' Sarah said as she stood up. 'Just keep an eye on the baby for a moment,' she told the officers.

Henry followed Sarah upstairs to her room. She asked Henry to take her suitcase down from the top of her wardrobe. It was the one she had been using as a footstool only a few hours before Penny was born. Someone had tidied it away when the mattress on her bed was replaced and the crib brought in.

Sarah was more composed when they returned to the kitchen. She handed the bag containing the clothes to the woman officer and finished her explanation.

'When the new uniforms were issued, they told us to bin the old ones. I didn't – don't really know why. I'd tucked the bag in the lid pocket of my case. When I packed to leave, I just brought it with me.'

'Why did you leave?' Sarah couldn't remember which officer asked this question.

'I received a warning. I said I'd suddenly been taken ill that day, but the manager didn't believe me. I'd also applied for a team leader's position, with more responsibility and a bigger salary. By the time they looked at the applications, there was a note on my file stating that I'd disappeared off-duty without explanation. When I didn't get the job, I guess I was upset. I couldn't seem to do anything right after that and made loads of mistakes, silly ones. I was sick a lot and began to put on weight. Luckily, the new uniform was looser than the old one. But finally, someone guessed. I denied it, told them it was a phantom pregnancy. No one believed me, of course. So they forced me to go, citing maternity leave. You can read that in the emails as well.'

'Where's your computer?' they asked.

'It's upstairs,' Henry stated. 'I saw it a few moments ago. I'll go and get it, shall I?'

'Yes please, sir,' the police officer said whilst Sarah nodded.

A few more formalities were completed, the officers left after reassuring Sarah that they would be in contact again soon.

Sarah leant against her father; he wrapped her in an embrace. Henry looked down at baby Penny asleep in her cot. He found he was clenching and unclenching his jaw and gritting his teeth with fury and helplessness.

'Oh God, Dad' she cried into his chest. 'Whatever's Mum going to say?'

'Don't worry about Rosalie,' Henry assured her, pleased to be able to focus on something he could influence. 'I'll deal with her.' To lighten his promise, he added, 'If she causes any trouble, I'll set George on her. And if that doesn't work, Polly, Quinny and Max can all have a go too!'

Sarah laughed.

Dear Reader

If you have enjoyed reading my book then please tell your friends and relatives and leave a review on Amazon.
Thank you.
Franky

More **PepperAsh** stories coming soon.

Have you read the first two in the series?
Both are also available on Amazon

The PepperAsh Clinch
and
The PepperAsh Redoubt

Acknowledgements

I have scribbled stories for years, but it was not until I joined the Waveney Author Group that I achieved my ambition to be published. I would like to say an enormous thank you to Suzan Collins for all her kindness, support, and practical help. Thank you, also to the other members of WAG. I would also like to thank Pat for proof-reading my novel, and Alex for her encouragement.

And finally, the biggest thanks of all goes to my dear husband, John, for all his hard work and support, especially on the technical side.

Cover: John Sayer

Editor: Alex Matthews
www.bookeditingservices.co.uk

Reader: Pat Vellacott

The places featured in the PepperAsh stories are all fictional, although there may be a passing resemblance to towns and villages around the coastal area of the Suffolk/Norfolk border. The characters, personalities and their predicaments are also completely fictional.

About the Author

Born in Felixstowe, Franky moved to North Suffolk as a small child. She still lives close to the Norfolk/Suffolk border, with her husband, John, and their yellow Labrador, Boris.
Franky trained as a shorthand/typist/secretary and worked as such in a variety of industries, including a rock and sweet making factory, an offshore oil and gas platform construction company, and as a local government officer. Other employments include music engraving, and over two decades as a parish council clerk.
Her hobbies include music - she plays tenor recorder, guitar, piano and church organ, and the last of these led to her becoming the chapel organist for twenty years in a local prison.

Her other interests are dressmaking, artistic roller skating, walking her dog in the countryside and reading.

This is Franky's third novel, and also the third in The PepperAsh series comprising,

The PepperAsh Clinch – Book one
and
The PepperAsh Redoubt – Book two

If you would like to know more about Franky and to follow her on Facebook please go to Franky Sayer Author.